The Spanish Brothers.

A TALE OF THE SIXTEENTH CENTURY.

1898

Lamplighter Publishing
Waverly, Pennsylvania

The Spanish Brothers.

First Printing, November 2006
Second Printing, September 2007

Published by Lamplighter Publishing; a division of Cornerstone Family Ministries, Inc.

The Lamplighter Rare Collector Series is a collection of Christian family literature from the 17th, 18th and 19th centuries. Each edition is printed in an attractive hard-bound collector's format. For more information, call us at 1-888-246-7735, visit us at www.lamplighterpublishing.com or write:

Lamplighter Publishing
P.O. Box 777
Waverly, PA 18471

Author: Deborah Alcock

Chief Editor: Mark Hamby
Copy Editors: Debra L. Nichols, Deborah Hamby
Layout and Design: Kenn Anderson, Jr.
Cover Design: Jennifer L. Hamby

ISBN: 1-58474-134-1

PREFACE.

"Persecution bursts suddenly upon the secret converts in Seville. Carlos was imprisoned and put to the Question, but no tortures could induce him to deny his Lord, or betray his friends."[1] The Inquisition. The Question. The horrors of the Auto-da-fé. Through the courageous fortitude of great heroes and heroines of faith, *The Spanish Brothers* lifts the soul clear above the anguish to the glory that we know and believe in, strengthening our faith and inspiring us to press on.

This dramatic account of the Spanish Inquisition will leave you speechless. The conviction and courage demonstrated by sixteenth century believers puts our present-day calamities in perspective, sharply, yet gently reminding us of the truth of the Word and the power of our Savior's love. All else pales in comparison.

This is a passionate book, a riveting work. It is historical, bringing us into the very presence of the individuals—ordinary yet extraordinary—who faltered neither in their faith nor their love for the One who is Truth. This book gives great power to those whose faith is faltering in prolonged anguish and suffering. It transcends this finite world and takes us to higher ground, upon which we can—and will—rejoice forever.

May we uphold each other in prayer as we endeavor to be forever faithful,

Mark Hamby
Romans 8:17-18

Publisher's note: The content of this book contains phraseology indicative of the time, culture, and belief system portrayed in the story. In order to accurately depict that period in history, we have chosen to leave these portions of the text as they were originally written. However, vain references to God have been omitted. The rules of punctuation, spelling, and even sentence structure of the 1800s were different than our present-day standards. We have chosen to keep the original format as much as possible, editing only when deemed necessary.

[1] From "The Author of the Spanish Brothers (Deborah Alcock) Her Life and Works" by Elisabeth Boyd Bayly.

CONTENTS.

THE
SPANISH BROTHERS.

I.

Boyhood.

"A boy's will is the wind's will,
And the thoughts of youth are long, long thoughts."
LONGFELLOW.

N one of the green slopes of the Sierra Morena, shaded by a few cork-trees, and with wild craggy heights and bare brown wastes stretching far above, there stood, about the middle of the sixteenth century, a castle, even then old and rather dilapidated. It had once been a strong place, but was not very spacious; and certainly, according to our modern ideas of comfort, the interior could not have been a particularly comfortable dwelling-place. A large proportion of it was occupied by the great hall, which was hung with faded, well-repaired tapestry, and furnished with oaken tables, settles, and benches, very elaborately carved, but bearing evident marks of age. Narrow unglazed slits in the thick wall admitted the light and air; and beside one of these, on a gloomy autumn morning, two boys stood together, watching the rain that poured down without intermission.

They were dressed exactly alike, in loose jackets of blue cloth, homespun, indeed, but so fresh and neatly fashioned as to look more becoming than many a costlier dress. Their long stockings were of silk, and their cuffs and wide shirt-frills of fine Holland, carefully starched and plaited. The elder—a very handsome lad, who looked fourteen at least, but was really a year younger—had raven hair, black sparkling eager eyes, good but strongly marked features, and a complexion originally dark, and well-tanned by exposure to sun and wind. A broader forehead, wider nostrils, and a weaker mouth, distinguished the more delicate-looking younger brother, whose hair was also less dark, and his complexion fairer.

"Rain—rain! Will it rain for ever?" cried the elder, whose name was Juan, in a tone of impatience; or rather, his proper style and title (and very angry would he have felt, had any part been curtailed or omitted) was Don Juan Rodrigo Alvarez de Santillanos y Meñaya. He was of the purest blood in Spain; by the father's side, of noblest Castilian lineage; by the mother's, of an ancient Asturian family. Well he knew it, and proudly he held up his young head in consequence, in spite of poverty, and, of what was still worse, the mysterious blight that had fallen on the name and fortunes of his house, bringing poverty in its train, as the least of its attendant evils.

"'Rising early will not make the daylight come sooner,' nor watching bring the sunshine," said the quick-witted Carlos, who, apt in learning whatever he heard, was already an adept in the proverbial philosophy which was then, and is now, the inheritance of his race.

"True enough. So let us fetch the canes, and have a merry play. Or, better still, the foils for a fencing match."

Carlos acquiesced readily, though apparently without pleasure. In all outward things, such as the choice of pursuits and games, Juan was the unquestioned leader; Carlos never dreamed of disputing his fiat.[1] Yet in other, and really more important matters, it was Carlos who, quite unconsciously to himself, performed the part of guide to his stronger-willed but less thoughtful brother.

[1] An authoritative and often arbitrary command.

Juan now fetched the carefully guarded foils with which the boys were accustomed to practise fencing; either simply for their own amusement, as now, or under the instructions of the grey-haired Diego, who had served with their father in the Emperor's wars, and was now mayor-domo, butler, and seneschal,[2] all in one. He it was, moreover, from whom Carlos had learned his store of proverbs.

"Now stand up. Oh, you are too low; wait a moment." Juan left the hall again, but quickly returned with a large heavy volume, which he threw on the floor, directing his brother to take his stand upon it.

Carlos hesitated. "But what if the Fray should catch us using our great Horace after such a fashion?"

"I just wish he might," answered Juan, with a mischievous sparkle in his black eyes.

The matter of height being thus satisfactorily adjusted, the game began, and for some time went merrily forward. To do the elder brother justice, he gave every advantage to his less active and less skilful companion; often shouting (with very unnecessary exertion of his lungs) words of direction or warning about fore-thrust, side-thrust, back-hand strokes, hitting, and parrying. At last, however, in an unlucky moment, Carlos, through some awkward movement of his own in violation of the rules of the game, received a blow on the cheek from his brother's foil, severe enough to make the blood flow. Juan instantly sprang forward, full of vexation, with an "Ay de mi"[3] on his lips. But Carlos turned away from him, covering his face with both hands; and Juan, much to his disgust, soon heard the sound of a heavy sob.

"You little coward!" he exclaimed, "to weep for a blow. Shame—shame upon you."

"Coward yourself, to call me ill names when I cannot fight you," retorted Carlos, as soon as he could speak for weeping.

---

[2] A steward in medieval times who managed the retainers of a noble house, supervised feasts and domestic ceremonies. Sometimes seneschals were given additional responsibilities, including the dispensing of justice and high military command.

[3] "Oh, poor me."

"That is ever your way, little tearful. *You* to talk of going to find our father! A brave man you would make to sail to the Indies and fight the savages. Better sit at home and spin, with Mother Dolores."

Far too deeply stung to find a proverb suited to the occasion, or indeed to make any answer whatever, Carlos, still in tears, left the hall with hasty footsteps, and took refuge in a smaller apartment that opened into it.

The hangings of this room were comparatively new and very beautiful, being tastefully wrought with the needle; and the furniture was much more costly than that in the hall. There was also a glazed window, and near this Carlos took his stand, looking moodily out on the falling rain, and thinking hard thoughts of his brother, who had first hurt him so sorely, then called him coward, and last, and far worst of all, had taunted him with his unfitness for the task which, child as he was, his whole heart and soul were bent on attempting.

But he could not quarrel very seriously with Juan, nor indeed could he for any considerable time do without him. Before long his anger began to give way to utter loneliness and discomfort, and a great longing to "be friends" again.

Nor was Juan much more comfortable, though he told himself he was quite right to reprove his brother sharply for his lack of manliness; and that he would be ready to die for shame if Carlos, when he went to Seville, should disgrace himself before his cousins by crying when he was hurt, like a baby or a girl. It is true that in his heart he rather wished he had held his peace, or at least had spoken more gently; but he braved it out, and stamped up and down the hall, singing, in as cheery a voice as he could command,—

"The Cid rode through the horse-shoe gate, Omega like it stood,
A symbol of the moon that waned before the Christian rood.[4]
He was all sheathed in golden mail, his cloak was white as shroud;
His vizor down, his sword unsheathed, corpse still he rode, and proud."

[4] A crucifix.

"Ruy!" Carlos called at last, just a little timidly, from the next room—"Ruy!"

Ruy is the Spanish diminutive of Rodrigo, Juan's second name, and the one by which, for reasons of his own, it pleased him best to be called; so the very use of it by Carlos was a kind of overture for peace. Juan came right gladly at the call; and having convinced himself, by a moment's inspection, that his brother's hurt signified nothing, he completed the reconciliation by putting his arm, in familiar boyish fashion, round his neck. Thus, without a word spoken, the brief quarrel was at an end. It happened that the rain was over also, and the sun just beginning to shine out again. It was, indeed, an effect of the sunlight which had given Carlos a pretext for calling Juan again to his side.

"Look, Ruy," he said, "the sun shines on our father's words!"

These children had a secret of their own, carefully guarded, with the strange reticence[5] of childhood, even from Dolores, who had been the faithful nurse of their infancy, and who still cast upon their young lives the only shadow of motherly love they had ever known—a shadow, it is true, pale and faint, yet the best thing that had fallen to their lot: for even Juan could remember neither parent; while Carlos had never seen his father's face, and his mother had died at his birth.

Yet it happened that in the imaginary world which the children had created around them, and where they chiefly lived, their unknown father was by far the most important personage. All great nations in their childhood have their legends, their epics, written or unwritten, and their hero, one or many of them, upon whose exploits Fancy rings its changes at will during the ages when national language, literature, and character are in process of development.

So it is with individuals. Children of imagination—especially if they are brought up in seclusion, and guarded from coarse and worldly companionship—are sure to have their legends, perhaps their unwritten epic, certainly their hero. Nor are these dreams of childhood idle fancies. In their time they are good and beautiful

[5] The tendency not to communicate very much or not reveal everything.

gifts of God—healthful for the present, helpful for after-years. There is deep truth in the poet's words, "When thou art a man, reverence the dreams of thy youth."

The Cid Campeador,[6] the Charlemagne, and the King Arthur of our youthful Spanish brothers, was no other than Don Juan Alvarez de Meñaya, second and last Conde[7] de Nuera. And as the historical foundation of national romance is apt to be of the slightest—nay, the testimony of credible history is often ruthlessly set at defiance—so it is with the romances of children; nor did the present instance form any exception. All the world said that their father's bones lay bleaching on a wild Araucanian battle-field; but this went for nothing in the eyes of Juan and Carlos Alvarez. Quite enough to build their childish faith upon was a confidential whisper of Dolores—when she thought them sleeping—to the village barber-surgeon, who was helping her to tend them through some childish malady: "Dead? Would to all the Saints, and the blessed Queen of Heaven,[8] that we only had assurance of it!"

They had, however, more than this. Almost every day they read and re-read those mysterious words, traced with a diamond by their father's hand—as it never entered their heads to doubt—on the window of the room which had once been his favourite place of retirement:—

"*El Dorado*[9]
Yo hé trovado."

"I have found El Dorado."

No eyes but their own had ever noticed this inscription; and marvellous indeed was the superstructure their fancy contrived to raise on the slight and airy foundation of its enigmatical[10] five words. They had heard from the lips of Diego many of the fables current at the period about the "golden country" of which Spanish adventurers dreamed so wildly, and which they sought so vainly

[6] Lord conqueror; champion.
[7] A title of nobility in Spanish and Portuguese. In English, the title is count or earl.
[8] Catholic theology, prevalent in Spain, promoted the adoration of saints and Mary, "Queen of Heaven."
[9] A place of fabulous wealth or inordinately great opportunity.
[10] Difficult to interpret, understand, or explain; mysterious.

in the New World. They were aware that their father in his early days had actually made a voyage to the Indies: and they had thoroughly persuaded themselves, therefore, of nothing less than that he was the fortunate discoverer of El Dorado; that he had returned thither, and was reigning there as a king, rich and happy—only, perhaps, longing for his brave boys to come and join him. And join him one day they surely would, even though unheard of dangers (of which giants twelve feet high and fiery dragons—things in which they quite believed—were among the least) might lie in their way, thick as the leaves of the cork-trees when the autumn winds swept down through the mountain gorges.

"Look, Ruy," said Carlos, "the light is on our father's words!"

"So it is! What good fortune is coming now? Something always comes to us when they look like that."

"What do you wish for most?"

"A new bow, and a set of real arrows tipped with steel. And you?"

"Well—the 'Chronicles of the Cid,' I think."

"I should like that too. But I should like better still—"

"What?"

"That Fray Sebastian would fall ill of the rheum,[11] and find the mountain air too cold for his health; or get some kind of good place at his beloved Complutum."

"We might go farther and fare worse, like those that go to look for better bread than wheaten," returned Carlos, laughing. "Wish again, Juan; and truly this time—your wish of wishes."

"What else but to find my father?"

"I mean, next to that."

"Well, truly, to go once more to Seville, to see the shops, and the bull-fights, and the great Church; to tilt with our cousins, and dance the cachuca[12] with Doña Beatriz."

"That would not I. There be folk that go out for wool, and come home shorn. Though I like Doña Beatriz as well as any one."

---

[11] Watery discharge coming from the eyes, nose, or mouth.

[12] A dance in three/four time originating in Andalusia, Spain, and similar to the Bolero.

"Hush! here comes Dolores."

A tall, slender woman, robed in black serge, relieved by a neat white head-dress, entered the room. Dark hair, threaded with silver, and pale, sunken, care-worn features, made her look older than she really was. She had once been beautiful; and it seemed as though her beauty had been burned up in the glare of some fierce agony, rather than had faded gradually beneath the suns of passing years. With the silent strength of a deep, passionate heart that had nothing else left to cling to, Dolores loved the children of her idolised mistress and foster-sister. It was chiefly her talent and energy that kept together the poor remains of their fortune. She surrounded them with as many inexpensive comforts as possible; still, like a true Spaniard, she would at any moment have sacrificed their comfort to the maintenance of their rank, or the due upholding of their dignity. On this occasion she held an open letter in her hand.

"Young gentlemen," she said, using the formal style of address no familiarity ever induced her to drop, "I bring your worships good tidings. Your noble uncle, Don Manuel, is about to honour your castle with his presence."

"Good tidings indeed! I am as glad as if you had given me a satin doublet. He may take us back with him to Seville," cried Juan.

"He might have stayed at home, with good luck and my blessing," murmured Carlos.

"Whether you go to Seville or no, Señor Don Juan," said Dolores, gravely, "may very probably depend on the contentment you give your noble uncle respecting your progress in your Latin, your grammar, and your other humanities."

"A green fig for my noble uncle's contentment!" said Juan, irreverently. "I know already as much as any gentleman need, and ten times more than he does himself."

"Ay, truly," struck in Carlos, coming forward from the embrasure of the window; "my uncle thinks a man of learning—except he be a fellow of college, perchance—not worth his ears full of water. I heard him say such only trouble the world, and bring sorrow on themselves and all their kin. So, Juan, it is you who are likely to find favour in his sight, after all."

"Señor Don Carlos, what ails your face?" asked Dolores, noticing now for the first time the marks of the hurt he had received.

Both the boys spoke together.

"Only a blow caught in fencing; all through my own awkwardness. It is nothing," said Carlos, eagerly.

"I hurt him with my foil. It was a mischance. I am very sorry," said Juan, putting his hand on his brother's shoulder.

Dolores wisely abstained from exhorting them to greater carefulness. She only said, "Young gentlemen who mean to be knights and captains must learn to give hard blows and take them." Adding mentally—"Bless the lads! May they stand by each other as loyally ten or twenty years hence as they do now."

II.

The Monk's Letter.

"Quoth the good fat friar,
Wiping his own mouth—'twas refection time."
R. BROWNING.

RAY SEBASTIAN GOMEZ, to the Honourable Señor Felipe de Santa Maria, Licentiate of Theology, residing at Alcala de Henarez, commonly called Complutum.

Most Illustrious and Reverend Señor, "In my place of banishment, amidst these gloomy and inhospitable mountains, I frequently solace my mind by reflections upon the friends of my youth, and the happy period spent in those ancient halls of learning, where in the morning of our days you and I together attended the erudite prelections[1] of those noble and most orthodox Grecians, Demetrius Ducas and Nicetus Phaustus, or sat at the feet of that venerable patriarch of science, Don Fernando Nunez. Fortunate are you, O friend, in being able to pass your days amidst scenes so pleasant and occupations so congenial; while I, unhappy, am compelled by fate, and by the neglect of friends and patrons, to

[1] A lecture or discourse read in public or to a select company.

take what I may have, in place of having what I might wish. I am, alas! under the necessity of wearing out my days in the ungrateful occupation of instilling the rudiments of humane learning into the dull and careless minds of children, whom to instruct is truly to write upon sand or water. But not to weary your excellent and illustrious friendship with undue prolixity,[2] I shall briefly relate the circumstances which led to my sojourn here."

(The good friar proceeds with his personal narrative, but by no means briefly; and as it has, moreover, little or nothing to do with our story, it may be omitted with advantage.)

"In this desert, as I may truly style it" (he continues), "nutriment for the corporeal[3] frame is as poor and bare as nutriment for the intellectual part is altogether lacking. Alas! for the golden wine of Xerez, that ambery nectar wherewith we were wont to refresh our jaded spirits! I may not mention now our temperate banquets: the crisp red mullet, the succulent pasties, the delicious ham of Estremadura, the savoury olla podrida.[4] Here beef is rarely seen, veal never. Our olla is of lean mutton (if it be not rather of the flesh of goats), washed down with bad vinegar, called wine by courtesy, and supplemented by a few naughty figs or roasted chestnuts, with cheese of goat's milk, hard as the heads of the rustics who make it. Certainly I am experiencing the truth of the proverb, 'A bad cook is an inconvenient relation.' And marvellously would a cask of Xerez wine, if, through the kindness of my generous friends, it could find its way to these remote mountains, mend my fare, and in all probability prolong my days. The provider here is an antiquated, sour-faced duenna,[5] who rules everything in this old ruin of a castle, where poverty and pride are the only things to be found in plenty. She is an Asturian, and came hither in the train of the late unfortunate countess. Like all of that race, where the very shepherds style themselves nobles, she is proud; but it is just to add that she is also active, industrious, and thrifty to a miracle.

[2] Wordiness; verbosity.

[3] Relating to or involving the physical body rather than the mind or spirit.

[4] A popular dish in Spain. It dates back to the Middle Ages, when it was called *olla poderida*, where *poderida* meant "powerful" ("olla" refers to stew or to the stew pot), referring to the powerful ingredients that it included, or because only the rich powerful could get near this dish.

[5] A woman acting as a chaperone or governess to a younger woman, especially in Spain and Portugal.

"But to pass on to affairs of greater importance. I have presumed, on the part of my illustrious friend, some acquaintance with the sorrowful history of my young pupils' family. You will remember the sudden shadow that fell, like the eclipse of one of the bright orbs of heaven, upon the fame and fortunes of the Conde de Nuera, known, some fifteen years ago or more as a brilliant soldier and courtier, and personal favourite of his Imperial Majesty. There was a rumour of some black treason, I know not what, but men said it even struck at the life of the great Emperor, his friend and patron. It is supposed that the Emperor (whom God preserve!), in his just wrath remembered mercy, and generously saved the honour, while he punished the crime, of his ungrateful servant. At all events, the world was told that the Count had accepted a command in the Indies, and that he sailed thither from some port in the Low Countries to which the Emperor had summoned him, without returning to Spain. It is believed that, to save his neck from the axe and his name from dire disgrace, he signed away, by his own act, his large property to the Emperor and to the Holy Church, reserving only a pittance for his children. One year afterwards, his death, in battle with the Araucanian savages, was announced, and, if I am not mistaken, His Majesty was gracious enough to have masses said for his soul. But, at the time, the tongue of rumour whispered a far more dreadful ending to the tale. Men hinted that, upon the discovery of his treason, he despaired alike of human and divine compassion, and perished miserably by his own hand. But all possible pains were taken, for the sake of the family, to hush up the affair; and nothing certain has ever, or probably will ever, transpire. I am doubtful whether I am not a transgressor in having committed to paper what is written above. Still, as it is written, it shall stand. With you, most illustrious and honourable friend, all things are safe.

"The youths whom it is my task to instruct are not deficient in parts. But the elder, Don Juan, is idle and insolent; and withal, of so fiery a temper, that he will brook no manner of correction.

The younger, Don Carlos, is more toward[6] in disposition, and really apt at his humanities, were it not that his good-for-nothing brother is forever leading him into mischief. Don Manuel Alvarez, their uncle and guardian, who is a shrewd man of the world, will certainly cause him to enter the Church. But I pray, as I am bound in Christian charity, that it may not occur to him to make the lad a Minorite friar,[7] since, as I can testify from sorrowful experience, such go barely enough through this wicked and miserable world.

"In conclusion, I entreat of you, most illustrious friend, with the utmost despatch[8] and carefulness, to commit this writing to the flames; and so I pray our Lady and the blessed St. Luke, upon whose vigil I write, to have you in their good keeping.—Your unworthy brother,

"SEBASTIAN."

Thus, with averted face, or head shaken doubtfully, or murmured "Ay de the world spoke of him, of whom his own children, happy at least in this, knew scarce anything, save words that seemed like a cry of joy.

[6] *Archaic:* quick to learn; apt.
[7] The Order of Friars Minor (commonly called the Franciscans) is a religious order of men tracing their origin to Francis of Assisi and following the Rule of St. Francis. The Order forbids the ownership of property and encourages working or begging for a living.
[8] *Chiefly British:* dispatch; haste.

III.

Sword and Cassock.

"The helmet and the cap make houses strong."
SPANISH PROVERB.

ON MANUEL ALVAREZ stayed for several days at Nuera, as the half-ruined castle in the Sierra Morena was styled. Grievous, during this period, were the sufferings of Dolores, and unceasing her efforts to provide suitable accommodation, not merely for the stately and fastidious guest himself, but also for the troop of retainers he saw fit to bring with him, comprising three or four personal attendants, and half a score of men-at-arms—the last perhaps really necessary for a journey through that wild district. Don Manuel scarcely enjoyed the situation more than did his entertainers, but he esteemed it his duty to pay an occasional visit to the estate of his orphan nephews, to see that it was properly taken care of. Perhaps the only member of the party quite at his ease was the worthy Fray Sebastian, a good-natured, self-indulgent friar, with a better education and more refined tastes than the average of his order; fond of eating and drinking, fond of gossip, fond of a little superficial literature, and not fond of troubling himself about anything. He was comforted by the improved fare Don Manuel's visit introduced; and was, moreover, soon relieved from his very natural apprehensions that the guardian of his pupils might express discontent at the slowness of their progress. He speedily discovered that Don Manuel did not care to have his nephews made good scholars: he only cared to have them ready, in two or three years, to go to the University of Complutum, or to that of Salamanca, where they might remain until they were satisfactorily provided for—one in the Army, the other in the Church.

As for Juan and Carlos, they felt, with the sure instinct of children, in this respect something like that of animals, that their uncle had little love for them. Juan dreaded, more than under the circumstances he need have done, too careful inquiries into his progress; and Carlos, while he stood in great outward awe of his uncle, all the time contrived to despise him in his heart, because he neither knew Latin, nor could repeat any of the ballads of the Cid.

On the third day of his visit, after dinner, which was at noon, Don Manuel solemnly seated himself in the great carved armchair that stood on the estrada at one end of the hall, and summoned his nephews to his side. He was a tall, wiry-looking man, with a narrow forehead, thin lips, and a pointed beard. His dress was of the finest mulberry coloured cloth, turned back with velvet; everything about him was rich, handsome, and in good keeping, but without extravagance. His manner was dignified, perhaps a little pompous, like that of a man bent upon making the most of himself, as he had unquestionably made the most of his fortune.

He first addressed Juan, whom he gravely reminded that his father's imprudence had left him nothing save that poor ruin of a castle, and a few barren acres of rocky ground, at which the boy's eyes flashed, and he shrugged his shoulders and bit his lip. Don Manuel then proceeded, at some length, to extol the noble profession of arms as the road to fame and fortune. This kind of language proved much more acceptable to his nephew, and looking up, he said promptly, "Yes, señor my uncle, I will gladly be a soldier, as all my fathers were."

"Well spoken. And when thou art old enough, I promise to use my influence to obtain for thee a good appointment in His Imperial Majesty's army. I trust thou wilt honour thine ancient name."

"You may trust me," said Juan, in slow, earnest tones. Then raising his head, he went on more rapidly: "Beside his own name, Juan, my father gave me that of Rodrigo, borne by the Cid Ruy Diaz, the Campeador, meaning no doubt to show—"

"Peace, boy!" Don Manuel interrupted, cutting short the only words that his nephew had ever spoken really from his heart in his presence, with as much unconsciousness as a countryman might set his foot on a glow-worm. "Thou wert never named Rodrigo after thy Cid and his idle romances. Thy father called thee so after some madcap friend of his own, of whom the less spoken the better."

"My father's friend must have been good and noble, like himself," said Juan proudly, almost defiantly.

"Young man," returned Don Manuel severely, and lifting his eyebrows as if in surprise at his audacity, "learn that a humbler tone and more courteous manners would become thee in the presence of thy superiors." Then turning haughtily away from him, he addressed himself to Carlos: "As for thee, nephew Carlos, I hear with pleasure of thy progress in learning. Fray Sebastian reports of thee that thou hast a good ready wit and a retentive memory. Moreover, if I mistake not, sword cuts are less in thy way than in thy brother's. The service of Holy Mother Church will fit thee like a glove; and let me tell thee, boy, for thou art old enough to understand me, 'tis a right good service. Churchmen eat well and drink well—churchmen sleep soft—churchmen spend their days fingering the gold other folk toil and bleed for. For those who have fair interest in high places, and shuffle their own cards deftly, there be good fat benefices, comfortable canonries, and perhaps—who knows?—a rich bishopric at the end of all; with a matter of ten thousand hard ducats,[1] at the least, coming in every year to save or spend, or lend, if you like it better."

[1] A gold coin that was used as a trade currency throughout Europe before World War I.

"Ten thousand ducats!" said Carlos, who had been gazing in his uncle's face, his large blue eyes full of half-incredulous, half-uncomprehending wonder.

"Ay, my son, that is about the least. The Archbishop of Seville has sixty thousand every year, and more."

"Ten thousand ducats!" Carlos repeated again in a kind of awe-struck whisper. "That would buy a ship."

"Yes," said Don Manuel, highly pleased with what he considered an indication of precocious intelligence in money matters. "And an excellent thought that is of thine, my son. A good ship chartered for the Indies, and properly freighted, would bring thee back thy ducats *well perfumed.*[2] For a ship is sailing while you are sleeping. As the saying is, 'Let the idle man buy a ship or marry a wife.' I perceive thou art a youth of much ingenuity. What thinkest thou, then, of the Church?"

Carlos was still too much the child to say anything in answer except, "If it please you, señor my uncle, I should like it well."

And thus, with rather more than less consideration of their tastes and capacities than was usual at the time, the future of Juan and Carlos Alvarez was decided.

When the brothers were alone together, Juan said, "Dolores must have been praying Our Lady for us, Carlos. An appointment in the army is the very thing for me. I shall perform some great feat of arms, like Alphonso Vives, for instance, who took the Duke of Saxony prisoner; I shall win fame and promotion, and then come back and ask my uncle for the hand of his ward, Doña Beatriz."

"Ah, and I—if I enter the Church, I can never marry," said Carlos rather ruefully, and with a vague perception that his brother was to have some good thing from which he must be shut out for ever.

"Of course not; but you will not care."

"Never a whit," said the boy of twelve, very confidently. "I shall ever have thee, Juan. And all the gold my uncle says churchmen win so easily, I will save to buy our ship."

[2] With good interest.

"I will also say, so that one day we may sail together. I will be the captain, and thou shalt be the mass-priest, Carlos."

"But I marvel if it be true that churchmen grow rich so fast. The cura in the village must be very poor, for Diego told me he took old Pedro's cloak because he could not pay the dues for his wife's burial."

"More shame for him, the greedy vulture. Carlos, you and I have each half a ducat; let us buy it back."

"With all my heart. It will be worth something to see the old man's face."

"The cura is covetous rather than poor," said Juan. "But poor or no, no one dreams of *your* being a beggarly cura like that. It is only vulgar fellows of whom they make parish priests in the country. You will get some fine preferment, my uncle says. And he ought to know, for he has feathered his own nest well."

"Why is he rich when we are poor, Juan? Where does he get all his money?"

"The saints know best. He has places under Government. Something about the taxes, I think, that he buys and sells again."

"In truth, he's not one to measure oil without getting some on his fingers. How different from him our father must have been."

"Yes," said Juan. "His riches, won by his own sword and battle-axe, and his good right hand, will be worth having. Ay, and even worth seeing; will they not?"

So these children dreamed of the future—that future of which nothing was certain, except its unlikeness to their dreams. Nothing was certain; but what was only too probable? That the brave, free-hearted boy, who had never willingly injured any one, and who was ready to share his last coin with the poor man, would be hardened and brutalised into a soldier of fortune, like those who massacred tribes of trusting, unoffending Indians, or burned Flemish cities to the ground, amidst atrocities that even now make hearts quail and ears tingle. And yet worse, that the fair child beside him, whose life still shone with that child-like innocence which is truly the dew of youth, as bright and as fleeting, would be turned over, soul and spirit, to a system of training too surely calculated to obliterate the sense of truth, to deprave the moral taste, to make natural and healthful joys impossible, and unlawful and degrading ones fearfully easy and attainable; to teach the strong nature the love of power, the mean the love of money, and all alike falsehood, cowardice, and cruelty.

IV.

Alcala de Henarez.

"Give me back, give me back the wild freshness of morning,
Her tears and her smiles are worth evening's best light."

MOORE.

EW are the lives in which seven years come and go without witnessing any great event. But whether they are eventful or no, the years that change children into men must necessarily be important. Three years of these important seven, Juan and Carlos Alvarez spent in their mountain home, the remaining four at the University of Alcala, or Complutum. The university training was of course needful for the younger brother, who was intended for the Church. That the elder was allowed to share the privilege, although destined for the profession of arms, was the result of circumstances. His guardian, Don Manuel Alvarez, although worldly and selfish, still retained a lingering regard for the memory of that lost brother whose latest message to him had been, "Have my boy carefully educated." And, moreover, he could scarcely have left the high-spirited youth to wear out the years that must elapse before he could obtain his commission in the dreary solitude of his mountain home, with Diego and Dolores for companions, and for sole amusement, a horse and a few greyhounds. Better that he should take his chance at Alcala, and enjoy himself there as best he might, with no obligation to severe study, and but one duty strongly impressed on him—that of keeping out of debt.

He derived real benefit from the university training, though no academic laurels rested on his brow, nor did he take a degree. Fray Sebastian had taught him to read and write, and had even contrived to pass him through the Latin grammar, of which he afterwards remembered scarcely anything. To have urged him to learn more would have required severity only too popular at the time; but this Fray Sebastian was too timid, perhaps too prudent, to employ; while of interesting him in his studies he never thought. At Alcala, however, he was interested. He did not care, indeed, for the ordinary scholastic course; but he found in the college library all the books yet written in his native language, and it was then the palmy[1] age of Spanish literature. Beginning with the poems and romances relating to the history of his country, he read through everything; poetry, romance, history, science; nothing came amiss to him, except perhaps theology. He studied with especial care all that had reference to the story of the New World, whither he hoped one day to go. He attended lectures; he even acquired Latin enough to learn anything he really wanted to know, and could not find except in that language.

Thus, at the end of his four years' residence, he had acquired a good deal of useful though somewhat desultory[2] information; and he had gained the art of expressing himself in the purest Castilian, by tongue or pen, with energy, vigour, and precision.

The sixteenth century gives us many specimens of such men—and not a few of them were Spaniards—men of intelligence and general cultivation, whose profession was that of arms, but who can handle the pen with as much ease and dexterity as the sword; men who could not only do valiant deeds, but also describe them when done, and that often with singular effectiveness.

[1] Marked by prosperity; flourishing.
[2] Aimlessly passing from one thing to another; happening in a random, disorganised, or unmethodical way.

With his contemporaries Juan was popular, for his pride was inaggressive, and his fiery temper was counterbalanced by great generosity of disposition. During his residence at Alcala he fought three duels; one to chastise a fellow-student who had called his brother "Doña Carlotta," the other two on being provoked by the far more serious offence of covert sneers at his father's memory. He also caned severely a youth whom he did not think of sufficient rank to honour with his sword, merely for observing, when Carlos won a prize from him, "Don Carlos Alvarez unites genius and industry, as he would need to do, who is *the son of his own good works*." But afterwards, when the same student was in danger, through poverty, of having to give up his career and return home, Juan stole into his chamber during his absence, and furtively deposited four gold ducats (which he could ill spare) between the leaves of his breviary.[3]

Far more outwardly successful, but more really disastrous, was the academic career of Carlos. A student of theology, most of his days, and even some of his nights, were spent over the musty tomes[4] of the Schoolmen.[5] Like living water on the desert, his young bright intellect was poured out on the dreary sands of scholastic divinity (little else, in truth, than "bad metaphysics"), to no appreciable result, except its own utter waste. The kindred study of casuistry[6] was even worse than waste of intellect; it was positive defilement and degradation. It was bad enough to tread with painful steps through roads that led nowhere; but it became worse when the roads were miry, and the mud at every step clung to the traveller's feet. Though here the parallel must cease; for the moral defilement, alas! is most deadly and dangerous when least felt or heeded.

Fortunately, or unfortunately, according as we look on the things seen or the things not seen, Carlos offered to his instructors

[3] In the Roman Catholic Church, a book that contains hymns, psalms, and prayers prescribed for each day.
[4] A large heavy book on a serious subject.
[5] A scholar in one of the universities of the Middle Ages.
[6] The application of general rules and principles to questions of ethics and morals in order to resolve them.

admirable raw material out of which to fashion a successful, even a great Churchman. He came to them a stripling of fifteen, innocent, truthful, affectionate. He had "parts," as they styled them, and singularly good ones. He had just the acute perception, the fine and ready wit, which enabled him to cut his way through scholastic subtleties and conceits with ease and credit. And, to do his teachers justice, they sharpened his intellectual weapon well, until its temper grew as exquisite as that of the scimitar[7] of Saladin, which could divide a gauze kerchief by the thread at a single blow. But how would it fare with such a weapon, and with him who, having proved no other, could wield only that, in the great conflict with the Dragon that guarded the golden apples of truth? The question is idle, for truth was a luxury of which Carlos was not taught to dream. To find truth, to think truth, to speak truth, to act truth, was not placed before him as an object worth his attainment. Not the *true*, but the *best*, was always held up to him as the mark to be aimed at: the best for the Church, the best for his family, the best for himself.

He had much imagination, he was quick in invention and ready in expedients; good gifts in themselves, but very perilous where the sense of truth is lacking, or blunted. He was timid, as sensitive and reflective natures are apt to be, perhaps also from physical causes. And in those rough ages, the Church offered almost the only path in which the timid man could not only escape infamy, but actually attain to honour. In her service a strong head could more than atone for weak nerves. Power, fame, wealth, might be gained in abundance by the Churchman without stirring from his cell or chapel, or facing a single drawn sword or loaded musket. Always provided that his subtle, cultivated intellect could guide the rough hands that wielded the swords, or, better still, the crowned head that commanded them.

There may have been even then at that very university (there certainly were a few years earlier), a little band of students who had quite other aims, and who followed other studies than those

[7] An Arab or Turkish sword with a curved blade that broadens out as it nears the point.

from which Carlos hoped to reap worldly success and fame. These youths really desired to find the truth and to keep it; and therefore they turned from the pages of the Fathers and the Schoolmen to the Scriptures in the original languages. But the "Biblists," as they were called, were few and obscure. Carlos did not, during his whole term of residence, come in contact with any of them. The study of Hebrew, and even of Greek, was by this time discouraged; the breath of calumny[8] had blown upon it, linking it with all that was horrible in the eyes of Spanish Catholics, summed up in the one word, *heresy.* Carlos never even dreamed of any excursion out of the beaten path marked out for him, and which he was travelling so successfully as to distance nearly all his competitors.

Both Juan and Carlos still clung fondly to their early dream; though their wider knowledge had necessarily modified some of its details. Carlos, at least, was not quite so confident as he had once been about the existence of El Dorado; but he was as fully determined as Juan to search out the mystery of their father's fate, and either to clasp his living hand, or to stand beside his grave. The love of the brothers, and their trust in each other, had only strengthened with their years, and was beautiful to witness.

Occasional journeys to Seville, and brief intervals of making holiday there, varied the monotony of their college life, and were not without important results.

It was the summer of 1556. The great Carlos, so lately King and Kaiser, had laid down the heavy burden of sovereignty, and would soon be on his way to pleasant San Yuste, to mortify the flesh, and prepare for his approaching end, as the world believed; but in reality to eat, drink, and enjoy himself as well as his worn-out body and mind would allow him. Just then our young Juan, healthy, hearty, hopeful, and with the world before him, received the long wished-for appointment in the army of the new King of all the Spains, Don Felipe Segunde.

The brothers have eaten their last temperate meal together, in their handsome, though not very comfortable, lodging at Alcala.

[8] A slanderous statement or false accusation.

Juan pushes away the wine-cup that Carlos would fain have re-filled, and toys absently with the rind of a melon. "Carlos," he says, without looking his brother in the face, "remember that thing of which we spoke;" adding in lower and more earnest tones, "and so may God remember thee."

"Surely, brother. You have, however, little to fear."

"Little to fear!" and there was the old quick flash in the dark eyes. "Because, forsooth, to spare my aunt's selfishness and my cousin's vanity, she must not be seen at dance, of theatre, or bull-feast? It is enough for her to show her face on the Alameda or at mass to raise me up a host of rivals."

"Still, my uncle favours you; and Doña Beatriz herself will not be found of a different mind when you come home with your promotion and your glory, as you will, my Ruy!"

"Then, brother, watch thou in my absence, and fail not to speak the right word at the right moment, as thou canst so well. So shall I hold myself at ease, and give my whole mind to the noble task of breaking the heads of all the enemies of my liege lord the king."

Then, rising from the table, he girt on his new Toledo sword with its embroidered belt, threw over his shoulders his short scarlet cloak, and flung a gay velvet montero over his rich black curls. Don Carlos went out with him, and mounting the horses a lad from their country-home held in readiness, they rode together down the street and through the gate of Alcala; Don Juan followed by many an admiring gaze, and many a hearty "Vaya con Dios," from his late companions.

Go with God.

V.

Don Carlos Forgets Himself.

"A fair face and a tender voice had made me mad and blind."
E. B. BROWNING.

DON CARLOS ALVAREZ found Alcala, after his brother's departure, insupportably dull; moreover, he had now almost finished his brilliant university career. As soon, therefore, as he could, he took his degree as Licentiate of Theology. He then wrote to inform his uncle of the fact adding that he would be glad to spend part of the interval that must elapse before his ordination at Seville, where he might attend the lectures of the celebrated Fray Constantino Ponce de la Fuente, Professor of Divinity in the College of Doctrine in that city. But, in fact, a desire to fulfil his brother's last charge weighed more with him than an eagerness for further instruction; especially as rumours that his watchfulness was not unnecessary had reached his ears at Alcala.

He received a prompt and kind invitation from his uncle to make his house his home for as long a period as he might desire. Now, although Don Manuel was highly pleased with the genius and industry of his younger nephew, the hospitality he extended to him was not altogether disinterested. He thought Carlos capable of rendering what he deemed an essential service to a member of his own family.

That family consisted of a beautiful, gay, frivolous wife, three sons, two daughters, and his wife's orphan niece, Doña Beatriz de Lavella. The two elder sons were cast in their father's mould; which, to speak truth, was rather that of a merchant than of a cavalier. Had he been born of simple parents in the flats of Holland or the back streets of London, a vulgar Hans or Thomas, his tastes and capabilities might have brought him honest wealth. But since he had the misfortune to be Don Manuel Alvarez, of the bluest blood in Spain, he was taught to look on industry as ineffably degrading, and trade and commerce scarcely less so. Only one species of trade, one kind of commerce, was open to the needy and avaricious, but proud grandee. Unhappily it was almost the only kind that is really degrading—the traffic in public money, in places, and in taxes. "A sweeping rain leaving no food," such traffic was, in truth. The Government was defrauded; the people, especially the poorer classes, were cruelly oppressed. No one was enriched except the greedy jobber, whose birth rendered him infinitely too proud to work, but by no means too proud to cheat and steal.

Don Manuel the younger, and Don Balthazar Alvarez, were ready and longing to tread in their father's footsteps. Of the two pale-faced dark-eyed sisters, Doña Inez and Doña Sancha, one was already married, and the other had also plans satisfactory to her parents. But the person in the family who was not of it was the youngest son, Don Gonsalvo. He was the representative, not of his father, but of his grandfather; as we so often see types of character reproduced in the third generation. The first Conde de Nuera had been a wild soldier of fortune in the Moorish wars, fierce and fiery, with strong unbridled passions. At eighteen, Gonsalvo was his image; and there was scarcely any mischief possible to a youth of fortune in a great city, into which he had not already found his way. For two years he continued to scandalise his family, and to vex the soul of his prudent and decorous father.

Suddenly, however, a change came over him. He reformed; became quiet and regular in his conduct; gave himself up to study, making extraordinary progress in a very short time; and even showed what those around him called "a pious disposition." But these hopeful appearances passed as suddenly and as unaccountably as they came. After an interval of less than a year, he returned to his former habits, and plunged even more madly than ever into all kinds of vice and dissipation.

His father resolved to procure him a commission, and send him away to the wars. But an accident frustrated his intentions. In those days, cavaliers of rank frequently sought the dangerous triumphs of the bull-ring. The part of matador was performed, not, as now, by hired bravos of the lowest class, but often by scions of the most honourable houses. Gonsalvo had more than once distinguished himself in the bloody arena by courage and coolness. But he tempted his fate too often. Upon one occasion he was flung violently from his horse, and then gored by the furious bull, whose rage had been excited to the utmost pitch by the cruel arts usually practised. He escaped with life, but remained a crippled invalid, apparently condemned for the rest of his days to inaction, weakness, and suffering.

His father thought a good canonry would be a decent and comfortable provision for him, and pressed him accordingly to enter the Church. But the invalided youth manifested an intense repugnance to the step; and Don Manuel hoped that the influence of Carlos would help to overcome this feeling; believing that he would gladly endeavour to persuade his cousin that no way of life was so pleasant or so easy as that which he himself was about to adopt.

The good nature of Carlos led him to fall heartily into his uncle's plans. He really pitied his cousin, moreover, and gladly gave himself to the task of trying in every possible way to console and amuse him. But Gonsalvo rudely repelled all his efforts. In his eyes the destined priest was half a woman, with no knowledge of a man's aims or a man's passions, and consequently no right to speak of them.

"Turn priest!" he said to him one day; "I have as good a mind to turn Turk. Nay, cousin, I am not pious—you may present my orisons[1] to Our Lady with your own, if it so please you. Perhaps she may attend to them better than to those I offered before entering the bull-ring on that unlucky day of St. Thomas."

Carlos, though not particularly devout, was shocked by this language.

"Take care, cousin," he said; "your words sound rather like blasphemy."

"And yours sound like the words of what you are, half a priest already," retorted Gonsalvo. "It is ever the priest's cry, if you displease him, 'Open heresy! Rank blasphemy!' And next, 'the Holy Office, and a yellow Sanbenito.'[2] I marvel it did not occur to your sanctity to menace me with that."

The gentle-tempered Carlos did not answer; a forbearance which further exasperated Gonsalvo, who hated nothing so much as being, on account of his infirmities, borne with like a woman or a child. "But the saints help the churchmen," he went on ironically. "Good simple souls, they do not know even their own business! Else they would smell heresy close enough at hand. What doctrine does your Fray Constantino preach in the great Church every feast-day, since they made him canon-magistral?"

"The most orthodox and Catholic doctrine, and no other," said Carlos, roused, in his turn, by the attack upon his teacher: though he did not greatly care for his instructions, which turned principally upon subjects about which he had learned little or nothing in the schools. "But to hear thee discuss doctrine is to hear a blind man talking of colours."

[1] Petitions to a deity; prayers.
[2] A garment of sackcloth worn at an Auto-da-fé ("act of faith") of the Spanish Inquisition by condemned heretics, being yellow with red crosses for the penitent and black with painted flames and devils for the impenitent.

"If I be the blind man talking of colours, thou art the deaf prating of music," retorted his cousin. "Come and tell me, if thou canst, what are these doctrines of thy Fray Constantino, and wherein they differ from the Lutheran heresy? I wager my gold chain and medal against thy new velvet cloak, that thou wouldst fall thyself into as many heresies by the way as there are nuts in Barcelona."

Allowing for Gonsalvo's angry exaggeration, there was some truth in his assertion. Once out of the region of dialectic subtleties, the champion of the schools would have become weak as another man. And he could not have expounded Fray Constantino's preaching—because he did not understand it.

"What, cousin!" he exclaimed, affronted in his tenderest part, his reputation as a theological scholar. "Dost thou take me for a barefooted friar or a village cura? Me, who only two months ago was crowned victor in a debate upon the doctrines taught by Raymondus Lullius!"

But whatever chagrin Carlos may have felt at finding himself utterly unable to influence Gonsalvo, was soon effectually banished by the delight with which he watched the success of his diplomacy with Doña Beatriz.

Beatriz was almost a child in years, and entirely a child in mind and character. Hitherto, she had been studiously kept in the background, lest her brilliant beauty should throw her cousins into the shade. Indeed, she would probably have been consigned to a convent, had not her portion been too small to furnish the donative[3] usually bestowed by the friends of a novice upon any really aristocratic establishment. "And pity would it have been," thought Carlos, "that so fair a flower should wither in a convent garden."

He made the most of the limited opportunities of association which the ceremonious manners of the time and country afforded, even to inmates of the same house. He would stand beside her chair, and watch the quick flush mount to her olive, delicately-rounded cheek, as he talked eloquently of the absent Juan. He was never tired of relating stories of Juan's prowess, Juan's generosity.

[3] Donation.

In the last duel he fought, for instance, the ball had passed through his cap and grazed his head. But he only smiled, and re-arranged his locks, remarking, while he did so, that with the addition of a gold chain and medal, the spoiled cap would be as good, or better than ever. Then he would dilate[4] on his kindness to the vanquished; rejoicing in the effect produced, as a tribute as well to his own eloquence as to his brother's merit. The occupation was too fascinating not to be resorted to once and again, even had he not persuaded himself that he was fulfilling a sacred duty.

Moreover, he soon discovered that the bright dark eyes which were beginning to visit him nightly in his dreams, were pining all day for a sight of that gay world from which their owner was jealously and selfishly excluded. So he managed to procure for Doña Beatriz many a pleasure of the kind she most valued. He prevailed upon his aunt and cousins to bring her with them to places of public resort; and then he was always at hand, with the reverence of a loyal cavalier, and the freedom of a destined priest, to render her every quiet unobtrusive service in his power. At the theatre, at the dance, at the numerous Church ceremonies, on the promenade, Doña Beatriz was his especial charge.

Amidst such occupations, pleasant weeks and months glided by almost unnoticed by him. Never before had he been so happy. "Alcala was well enough," he thought; "but Seville is a thousand times better. All my life heretofore seems to me only like a dream, now I am awake."

Alas! he was not awake, but wrapped in a deep sleep, and cradling a bright delusive vision. As yet he was not even "as those that dream, and know the while they dream." His slumber was too profound even for this dim half-consciousness.

No one suspected, any more than he suspected himself, the enchantment that was stealing over him. But every one remarked his frank, genial manners, his cheerfulness, his good looks. Naturally, the name of Juan dropped gradually more and more out of his conversation; as at the same time the thought of Juan faded from his mind. His studies, too, were neglected; his attendance upon

[4] Expand.

the lectures of Fray Constantino became little more than a formality; while "receiving Orders" seemed a remote if not an uncertain contingency. In fact, he lived in the present, not caring to look either at the past or the future.

In the very midst of his intoxication, a slight incident affected him for a moment with such a chill as we feel when, on a warm spring day, the sun passes suddenly behind a cloud.

His cousin, Doña Inez, had been married more than a year to a wealthy gentleman of Seville, Don Garcia Ramirez. Carlos, calling one morning at the lady's house with some unimportant message from Doña Beatriz, found her in great trouble on account of the sudden illness of her babe.

"Shall I go and fetch a physician?" he asked, knowing well that Spanish servants can never be depended upon to make haste, however great the emergency may be.

"You will do a great kindness, amigo mio," said the anxious young mother.

"But which shall I summon?" asked Carlos. "Our family physician, or Don Garcia's?"

"Don Garcia's, by all means,—Dr. Cristobal Losada. I would not give a green fig for any other in Seville. Do you know his dwelling?"

"Yes. But should he be absent or engaged?"

"I must have him. Him, and no other. Once before he saved my darling's life. And if my poor brother would but consult him, it might fare better with him. Go quickly, cousin, and fetch him."

Carlos lost no time in complying; but on reaching the dwelling of the physician, found that though the hour was early he had already gone forth. After leaving a message, he went to visit a friend in the Triana suburb. He passed close by the Cathedral, with its hundred pinnacles, and that wonder of beauty, the old Moorish Giralda, soaring far up above it into the clear southern sky. It occurred to him that a few Ayes said within for the infant's recovery would be both a benefit to the child and a comfort to the mother. So he entered, and was making his way to a gaudy tinselled Virgin and Babe, when, happening to glance towards a different part of the building, his eyes rested on the physician, with whose person he was well acquainted, as he had often noticed him amongst Fray Constantino's hearers. Losada was now pacing up and down one of the side aisles, in company with a gentleman of very distinguished appearance.

As Carlos drew nearer, it occurred to him that he had never seen this personage in any place of public resort, and for this reason, as well as from certain slight indications in his dress of fashions current in the north of Spain, he gathered that he was a stranger in Seville, who might be visiting the Cathedral from motives of curiosity. Before he came up the two men paused in their walk, and turning their backs to him, stood gazing thoughtfully at the hideous row of red and yellow Sanbenitos, or penitential garments, that hung above them.

"Surely," thought Carlos, "they might find better objects of attention than these ugly memorials of sin and shame, which bear witness that their late miserable wearers—Jews, Moors, blasphemers, or sorcerers,—have ended their dreary lives of penance, if not of penitence."

The attention of the stranger seemed to be particularly attracted by one of them, the largest of all. Indeed, Carlos himself had been struck by its unusual size; and upon one occasion he had even had the curiosity to read the inscription, which he remembered because it contained Juan's favourite name. Rodrigo. It was this: "Rodrigo Valer, a citizen of Lebrixa and Seville; an apostate and false apostle, who pretended to be sent from God." And now, as he approached with light though hasty footsteps, he distinctly heard Dr. Cristobal Losada, still looking at the Sanbenito, say to his companion, "Yes, señor; and also the Conde de Nuera, Don Juan Alvarez."

Don Juan Alvarez! What possible tie could link his father's name with the hideous thing they were gazing at? And what could the physician know about him of whom his own children knew so little? Carlos stood amazed, and pale with sudden emotion.

And thus the physician saw him, happening to turn at that moment. Had he not exerted all his presence of mind (and he possessed a great deal), he would himself have started visibly. The unexpected appearance of the person of whom we speak is in itself disconcerting; but it deserves another name when we are saying that of him or his which, if overheard, might endanger life, or what is more precious still than life. Losada was equal to the occasion, however. The usual greetings having been exchanged, he asked quietly whether Señor Don Carlos had come in search of him, and hoped that he didn't owe the honour to any indisposition in his worship's noble family.

Carlos felt it rather a relief, under the circumstances, to have to say that his cousin's babe was alarmingly ill. "You will do us a great favour," he added, "by coming immediately. Doña Inez is very anxious."

The physician promised compliance; and turning to his companion, respectfully apologised for leaving him abruptly.

"A sick child's claim must not be postponed," said the stranger in reply. "Go, señor doctor, and God's blessing rest on your skill."

Carlos was struck by the noble bearing and courteous manner of the stranger, who, in his turn, was interested by the young man's anxiety about a sick babe. But with only a passing glance at the other, each went his different way, not dreaming that once again at least their paths were destined to cross.

The strange mention of his father's name that he had overheard filled the heart of Carlos with undefined uneasiness. He knew enough by that time to feel his childish belief in his father's stainless virtue a little shaken. What if a dreadful unexplained something, linking his fate with that of a convicted heretic, were yet to be learned? After all, the accursed arts of magic and sorcery were not so far removed from the alchemist's more legitimate labours, that a rash or presumptuous student might not very easily slide from one into the other. He had reason to believe that his father had played with alchemy, if he had not seriously devoted himself to its study.

Nay, the thought had sometimes flashed unbidden across his mind that the "El Dorado" found might after all have been no other than the philosopher's stone,[5] for he who has attained the power of producing gold at will may surely be said, without any stretch of metaphor, to have discovered a golden country. But at this period of his life the personal feelings of Carlos were so keen and absorbing that almost everything, consciously or unconsciously, was referred to them. And thus it was that an intense wish sprang up in his heart, that his father's secret might have descended to *him*.

Vain wish! The gold he needed or desired must be procured from a less inaccessible region than El Dorado, and without the aid of the philosopher's stone.

[5] The philosopher's stone, in Latin *philosophi lapis*, is a legendary substance that supposedly could turn inexpensive metals such as lead into gold and/or create an elixir that would make humans younger, thus delaying death.

VI.

Don Carlos Forgets Himself Still Further.

"The not so very false, as falsehood goes,
The spinning out and drawing fine, you know
Really mere novel-writing, of a sort,
Acting, improvising, make-believe,—
Surely not downright cheatery!"

R. Browning.

T cost Carlos some time and trouble to drive away the haunting thoughts which Losada's words had awakened. But he succeeded at length; or perhaps it would be more truthful to say the bright eyes and charming smiles of Doña Beatriz accomplished the work for him.

Every dream, however, must have a waking. Sometimes a slight sound, ludicrously trivial in its cause, dispels a slumber fraught with wondrous visions, in which we have been playing the part of kings and emperors.

"Nephew Don Carlos," said Don Manuel one day, "is it not time you thought of shaving your head? You are learned enough for your Orders long ago, and in a plentiful house supper is soon dressed."

"True, señor my uncle," murmured Carlos, looking suddenly aghast. "But I am under the canonical age."

"But you can get a dispensation."[1]

"Why such haste? There is time yet and to spare."

"That is not so sure. I hear the cura of San Lucar has one foot in the grave. The living is a good one, and I think I know where to go for it. So take care you lose not a heifer for want of a halter to hold it by."

With these words on his lips, Don Manuel went out. At the same moment Gonsalvo, who lay listlessly on a sofa at one end of the room, or rather court, reading "Lazarillo de Tormes," the first Spanish novel, burst into a loud paroxysm of laughter.

"What may be the theme of your merriment?" asked Carlos, turning his large dreamy eyes languidly towards him.

"Yourself, amigo mio. You would make the stone saints of the Cathedral laugh on their pedestals. There you stand, pale as marble, a living image of despair. Come, rouse yourself! What do you mean to do? Will you take what you wish, or let your chance slip by, and then sit and weep because you have it not? Will you be a priest or a man? Make your choice this hour, for one you must be, and both you cannot be."

Carlos answered him not; in truth, he dared not answer him. Every word was the voice of his own heart; perhaps it was also, though he knew it not, the voice of the great tempter. He withdrew to his chamber, and barred and bolted himself in it. This was the first time in his life that solitude was a necessity to him. His uncle's words had brought with them a terrible revelation. He knew himself now too well; he knew what he loved, what he desired, or rather what he hungered and thirsted for with agonising intensity. No; never the priest's frock for him. He must call Doña Beatriz de Lavella his—his before God's altar—or die.

Then came a thought, stinging him with sharp, sudden pain. It was a thought that should have come to him long ago,—"Juan!" And with the name, affection, memory, conscience, rose up together within him to combat the mad resolve of his passion.

Fiery passions slumbered in the heart of Carlos. Such are

[1] Exemption or release from a rule or obligation; especially a religious one.

sometimes found united with a gentle temper, a weak will, and sensitive nerves. Woe to their possessor when they are aroused in their strength!

Had Carlos been a plain soldier, like the brother he was tempted to betray, it is possible he might have come forth from this terrible conflict still holding fast his honour and his brotherly affection. It was his priestly training that turned the scale. He had been taught that simple truth between man and man was a thing of little consequence. He had been taught the art of making a hundred clever, plausible excuses for whatever he saw best to do. He had been taught, in short, every species of sophistry[2] by which, to the eyes of others, and to his own also, wrong might be made to seem right, and black to appear the purest white.

His subtle imagination forged in the fire of his kindled passions chains of reasoning in which no skill could detect a flaw. Juan had never loved as he did; Juan would not care; probably by this time he had forgotten Doña Beatriz. "Besides," the tempter whispered furtively within him, "he might never return at all; he might die in battle." But Carlos was not yet sunk so low as to give ear for a single instant to this wicked whisper; though certainly he could not henceforth look for his brother's return with the joy with which he had been wont to anticipate that event. But, in any case, Beatriz herself should be the judge between them. And he told himself that he knew (how did he know it?) that Beatriz preferred him. Then it would be only right and kind to prepare Juan for an inevitable disappointment. This he could easily do. Letters, carefully written, might gradually suggest to his brother that Beatriz had other views; and he knew Juan's pride and his fiery temper well enough to calculate that if his jealousy were once aroused, these would soon accomplish the rest.

Ere we, who have been taught from our cradles to "speak the truth from the heart," turn with loathing from the wiles of Carlos Alvarez, we ought to remember that he was a Spaniard—one of

[2] A method of argumentation that seems clever but is actually flawed or dishonest.

a nation whose genius and passion is for intrigue.[3] He was also a Spaniard of the sixteenth century; but, above all, he was a Spanish Catholic, educated for the priesthood.

The ability with which he laid his plans, and the enjoyment which its exercise gave him, served in itself to blind him to the treachery and ingratitude upon which those plans were founded.

He sought an interview with Fray Constantino, and implored from him a letter of recommendation to the imperial recluse at San Yuste, whose chaplain and personal favourite the canon magistral had been. But that eloquent preacher, though warmhearted and generous to a fault, hesitated to grant the request. He represented to Carlos that His Imperial Majesty did not choose his retreat to be invaded by applicants for favours, and that the journey to San Yuste would therefore be, in all probability, worse than useless. Carlos answered that he had fully weighed the difficulties of the case; but that if the line of conduct he adopted seemed peculiar, his circumstances were so also. He believed that his father (who died before his birth) had enjoyed the special regard of His Imperial Majesty, and he hoped that, for his sake, he might now be willing to show him some kindness. At all events, he was sure of an introduction to his presence through his mayor-domo, Don Luis Quixada, lord of Villagarçia, who was a friend of their house. What he desired to obtain, through the kindness of His Imperial Majesty, was a Latin secretaryship, or some similar office, at the court of the new king, where his knowledge of Latin, and the talents he hoped he possessed, might stand him in good stead, and enable him to support, though with modesty, the station to which his birth entitled him. For, although already a licentiate of theology, and with good prospects in the Church, he did not wish to take orders, as he had thoughts of marrying.

Fray Constantino felt a sympathy with the young man; and perhaps the rather because, if report speaks true, he had once been himself in a somewhat similar position. So he compromised matters by giving him a general letter of recommendation, in which

[3] Secret scheming or plotting.

he spoke of his talents and his blameless manners as warmly as he could, from the experience of the nine or ten months during which he had been acquainted with him. And although the attention paid by Carlos to his instructions had been slight, and of late almost perfunctory,[4] his great natural intelligence had enabled him to stand his ground more creditably than many far more diligent students. The Fray's letter Carlos thankfully added to the numerous laudatory epistles from the doctors and professors of Alcala that he already had in his possession.

All these he enclosed in a cedar box, which he carefully locked, and consigned in its turn to a travelling portmanteau, along with a fair stock of wearing apparel, sufficiently rich in material to suit his rank, but modest in colour and fashion. He then informed his uncle that before he took Orders it would be necessary for him, in his brother's absence, to take a journey to their little estate, and set its concerns in order.

His uncle, suspecting nothing, approved his plan, and insisted on providing him with the attendance of an armed guard to Nuera, whither he really intended to go in the first instance.

[4] Done as a matter of duty or custom, without thought, attention, or genuine feeling.

VII.

The Desengaño

"And I should evermore be vexed with thee
In vacant robe, or hanging ornament,
Or ghostly foot-fall lingering on the stair."
TENNYSON.

HE journey from the city of oranges to the green slopes of the Sierra Morena ought to have been a delightful one to Don Carlos Alvarez. It was certainly bright with hope. He scarcely harboured a doubt of the ultimate success of his plans, and the consequent attainment of all his wishes. Already he seemed to feel the soft hand of Doña Beatriz in his, and to stand by her side before the high altar of the great Cathedral.

And yet, as days passed on, the brightness within grew fainter, and an acknowledged shadow, ever deepening, began to take its place. At last he drew near his home, and rode through the little grove of cork-trees where he and Juan had played as children. When last they were there together the autumn winds were strewing the leaves, all dim and discoloured, about their paths. Now he looked through the fresh green foliage at the deep intense blue of the summer sky. But, though scarcely more than twenty, he felt at that moment old and worn and wished back the time of his boyish sports with his brother. Never again could he feel quite happy with Juan.

Soon, however, his sorrowful fancies were put to flight by the joyous greeting of the hounds, who rushed with much clamour from the cattle-yard to welcome him. There they were, all of them—Pedro, Zina, Pepe, Grullo, Butron—it was Juan who had named them, every one. And there, at the gate, stood Diego and Dolores, ready to give him joyful welcome. Throwing himself from his horse, he shook hands with these faithful old retainers, and answered their kindly but respectful inquiries both for himself and Señor Don Juan. Then, having caressed the dogs, inquired for each of the under-servants by name, and given orders for the due entertainment of his guard, he passed on slowly into the great deserted hall.

His arrival being unexpected, he merely surrendered his travelling cloak into the hands of Diego, and sat down to wait patiently while the servants, always dilatory,[1] prepared for him suitable accommodation. Dolores soon appeared with a flask of wine and some bread and grapes; but this was only a merienda, or slight afternoon luncheon, which she laid before her young master until she could make ready a supper fit for him to partake of. Carlos spent half an hour listening to her tidings of the household and the village, and felt sorry when she quitted the room and left him to his own reflections.

Every object on which his eyes rested reminded him of his brother. There hung the cross-bow with which, in old days, Juan had made such vigorous war on the rooks and the sparrows. There lay the foils and the canes with which they had so often fenced and played; Juan, in his unquestioned superiority, usually so patient with the younger brother's timidity and awkwardness. And upon that bench he had carved, with a hunting knife, his name in full, adding the title that had expired with his father, "Conde de Nuera."

---

[1] Tending to waste time or move slowly.

The memories these things recalled were becoming intrusive: he would fain[2] shake them off. Gladly would he have had recourse to his favourite pastime of reading, but there was not a book in the castle, to his knowledge, except the breviary he had brought with him. For lack of more congenial occupation, he went out at last to the stable to look at the horses, and to talk to those who were grooming and feeding them.

Later in the evening Dolores told him that supper was ready, adding that she had laid it in the small inner room, which she thought Señor Don Carlos would find more comfortable than the great hall.

That inner room was, even more than the hall, haunted by the shadowy presence of Juan. But it was usually daylight when the brothers were there together. Now, a tapestry curtain shaded the window, and a silver lamp shed its light on the well-spread table with its snowy drapery, and cover laid for one.

A lonely meal, however luxurious, is always apt to be somewhat dreary; it seems a provision for the lowest wants of our nature, and nothing more. Carlos sought to escape from the depressing influence by giving wings to his imagination, and dreaming of the time when wealth enough to repair and refurnish that half-ruinous old homestead might be his. He pleased himself with pictures of the long tables in the great hall, groaning beneath the weight of a bountiful provision for a merry company of guests, upon whom the sweet face of Doña Beatriz might beam a welcome. But how idle such fancies! The castle, after all, was Juan's, not his. Unless, indeed, more difficulties than one should be solved by Juan's death upon some French or Flemish battle-field. This thought he could not bear to entertain. Grown suddenly sick at heart, he pushed aside his plate of stewed pigeon, and, regardless of the feelings of Dolores, sent away untasted her dessert of sweet butter-cakes dipped in honey. He was weary, he said, and he would go to rest at once.

It was long before sleep would visit his eyelids; and when at last

[2] *Archaic:* with gladness or eagerness.

it came, his brother's dark reproachful eyes haunted him still. At daybreak he awoke with a start from a feverish dream that Juan, all pale and ghostlike, had come to his bedside, and laying his hand on his arm, said solemnly, "I claim the jewel I left thee in trust."

Further sleep was impossible. He rose, and wandered out into the fresh air. As yet no one was astir. Fair and sweet was all that met his gaze: the faint pearly light, the first blush of dawn in the quiet sky, the silvery dew that bathed his footsteps. But the storm within raged more fiercely for the calm without. There was first an agonising struggle to repress the rising thought, "Better, after all, not to do this thing." But, in spite of his passionate efforts, the thought gained a hearing; it seemed to cry aloud within him, "Better, after all, not to betray Juan!" "And give up Beatriz for ever? *For ever!*" he repeated over and over again, beating it

> "In upon his weary brain,
> As though it were the burden of a song."

He had climbed, almost unawares, to the top of a rocky hill; and now he stood, looking around him at the prospect, just as if he saw it. In truth, he saw nothing, felt nothing outward, until at last a misty mountain rain swept in his face, refreshing his burning brow with a touch as of cool fingers.

Then he descended mechanically. Exchanging salutations (as if nothing were amiss with him) with the milk-maid and the wood-boy, he crossed the open courtyard and re-entered the hall. There Dolores, and a girl who worked under her, were already busy, so he passed by them into the inner room.

Its darkness seemed to stifle him; with hasty hand he drew aside the heavy tapestry curtain. As he did so something caught his eye. For the hundredth time he re-read the mystic inscription on the glass:

"*El Dorado*

Yo hé trovado."

And, as an infant's touch words may open a sluice that lets in the mighty ocean, those simple words broke up the fountains of the great deep within. He gave full course to the emotions they awakened. Again he heard Juan's voice repeat them; again he saw Juan's deep earnest eyes look into his; not now reproachfully, but with full unshaken trust, as in the old days when first he said, "We will go forth together and find our father."

"Juan—brother!" he cried aloud, "I will never wrong thee, so help me God!" At that moment the morning sun, having scattered the mists with the glory of its rising, sent one of its early beams to kiss the handwriting on the window-pane. "Old token for good," thought Carlos, whose imaginative nature could play with fancies even in the hours of supreme emotion. "And true still even yet. Only the good is all for Juan; for me—nothing but despair."

And so Don Carlos found his "desengãno," or disenchantment, and it was a very thorough one.

Body and mind were well-nigh exhausted with the violence of the struggle. Perhaps this was fortunate, in so far that it won for the decision of his better nature a more rapid and easy acceptance. In a sense and for a season any decision was welcome to the weary, tempest-tossed soul.

It was afterwards that he asked himself how were long years to be dragged on without the face that was the joy of his heart and the life of his life? How was he to bear the never-ending pain, the aching loneliness, of such a lot? Better to die at once than to endure this slow, living death. He knew well that it was not in his nature to point the pistol or the dagger at his own breast. But he might pine away and die silently—as many thousands die—of blighted hopes and a ruined life. Or—and this was more likely, perhaps—as time passed on he might grow dead and hard in soul; until at last he would become a dry, cold, mechanical mass-priest, mumbling the Church's Latin with thin, bloodless lips, a keen eye to his dues, and a heart that might serve for a Church relic, so much faith would it require to believe that it had been warm and living once.

Still, laudably anxious to provide against possible future waverings of the decision so painfully attained, he wrote informing his uncle of his safe arrival; adding that he had fully made up his mind to take Orders at Christmas, but that he found it advisable to remain in his present quarters for a month or two. He at once dispatched two of the men-at-arms with the letter; and much was the thrifty Don Manuel surprised that his nephew should spend a handful of silver reals in order to inform him of what he knew already.

Gloomily the day wore on. The instinctive reserve of a sensitive nature made Carlos talk to the servants, receive the accounts, inspect the kine[3] and sheep—do everything, in short, except eat and drink—as he would have done if a great sorrow had not all the time been crushing his heart. It is true that Dolores, who loved him as her own son, was not deceived. It was for no trivial cause that the young master was pale as a corpse, restless and irritable, talking hurriedly by fitful snatches, and then relapsing into moody silence. But Dolores was a prudent woman, as well as a loving and faithful one; therefore she held her peace, and bided her time.

But Carlos noticed one effort she made to console him. Coming in towards evening from a consultation with Diego about some cork-trees which a Morisco merchantman wished to purchase and cut down, he saw upon his table a carefully sealed wine-flask, with a cup beside it. He knew whence it came. His father had left in the cellar a small quantity of choice wine of Xeres; and this relic of more prosperous times being, like most of their other possessions, in the care of Dolores, was only produced very sparingly, and on rare occasions. But she evidently thought "Señor Don Carlos" needed it now. Touched by her watchful, unobtrusive affection, he would have gratified her by drinking; but he had a peculiar dislike to drinking alone, while he knew he would only render his sanity doubtful by inviting either her or Diego to share the luxurious beverage. So he put it aside for the present, and drew towards him a sheet of figures, an inkhorn, and a pen. He could not work, however. With the silence and solitude, his great grief came back upon him again. But nature all this time had been silently working

[3] *Archaic:* cows or cattle.

for him. His despair was giving way to a more violent but less bitter sorrow. Tears came now: a long, passionate fit of weeping relieved his aching heart. Since his early childhood he had not wept thus.

An approaching footstep recalled him to himself. He rose with haste and shame, and stood beside the window, hoping that his position and the waning light might together shield him from observation. It was only Dolores.

"Señor," she said, entering somewhat hastily, "will it please you to see to those men of Seville that came with your Excellency? They are insulting a poor little muleteer, and threatening to rob his packages."

Yanguesian carriers and other muleteers, bringing goods across the Sierra Morena from the towns of La Mancha to those of Andalusia, often passed by the castle, and sometimes received hospitality there. Carlos rose at once at the summons, saying to Dolores, "Where is the boy?"

"He is not a boy, señor, he is a man; a very little man, but with a greater spirit, if I mistake not, than some twice his size."

It was true enough. On the green plot at the back of the castle, beside which the mountain pathway led, there were gathered the ten or twelve rough Seville pikemen, most of them of Moorish blood. In their midst, beside the foremost of his three mules, with one arm thrown round her neck and the other raised to give effect by animated gestures to his eager oratory, stood the muleteer. He was a very short, spare, active-looking man, clad from head to foot in chestnut-coloured leather. His mules were well laden; each with three large alforjas,[4] one at each side and one laid across the neck. But they were evidently well fed and cared for also; and they presented a gay appearance, with their adornments of bright-coloured worsted tassels and tiny bells.

"You know, my friends," the muleteer was saying, as Carlos came within hearing, "an arriero's[5] alforjas are like a soldier's colours,—it stands him upon his honour to guard them inviolate.

[4] Saddlebags.
[5] Muleteer.

No, no! Ask him for aught else—his purse, his blood—they are at your service; but never touch his colours, if you care for a long life."

"My honest friend, your colours, as you call them, shall be safe here," said Carlos, kindly.

The muleteer turned towards him a good-humoured, intelligent face, and, bowing low, thanked him heartily.

"What is your name?" asked Carlos; "and whence do you come?"

"I am Juliano; Juliano el Chico (Julian the Little) men generally call me—since, as your Excellency sees, I am not very great. And I come last from Toledo."

"Indeed! And what wares do you carry?"

"Some matters, small in bulk, yet costly, which I am bringing for a Seville merchant—Medel de Espinosa by name, if your worship has heard of him? I have mirrors, for example, of a new kind; excellent in workmanship, and true as steel, as well they may be."

"I know the shop of Espinosa well. I have been much in Seville," said Carlos, with a sudden pang, caused by the recollection of the many pretty trifles that he had purchased there for Doña Beatriz. "But follow me, my friend, and a good supper shall make you amends for the rudeness of these fellows.—Andres, take the best care thou canst of his mules; 'twill be only fair penance for thy sin in molesting their owner."

"A hundred thousand thanks, señor. Still, with your worship's good leave, and no offence to friend Andres, I had rather look to the beasts myself. We are old companions; they know my ways, and I know theirs."

"As you please, my good fellow. Andres will show you the stable, and I shall tell my mayor-domo to see that you lack nothing."

"Again I render to your Excellency my poor but hearty thanks."

Carlos went in, gave the necessary directions to Diego, and then returned to his solitary chamber.

VIII.

The Muleteer.

"Are ye resigned that they be spent
 In such world's help? The spirits bent
 Their awful brows, and said, 'Content.'

"Content! It sounded like Amen
 Said by a choir of mourning men:
 An affirmation full of pain

"And patience,—ay, of glorying,
 And adoration, as a king
 Might seal an oath for governing."

E. B. BROWNING.

HEN Carlos stood once more face to face with his sorrow—as he did as soon as he had closed the door—he found that it had somewhat changed its aspect. A trouble often does this when some interruption from the outer world makes us part company with it for a little while. We find on our return that it has developed quite a new phase, and seldom a more hopeful one.

It now entered the mind of Carlos, for the first time, that he had been acting very basely towards his brother. Not only had he planned and intended a treason, but by endeavouring to engage the affections of Doña Beatriz, he had actually committed one. Heaven grant it might not prove irreparable! Though the time that had passed since his better self gained the victory was only measured by hours, it represented to him a much longer period. Already it enabled him to look upon what had gone before from the vantage-ground that some degree of distance gives. He now beheld in true, perhaps even in exaggerated colours, the meanness and the treachery of his conduct. He, who prided himself upon the nobility of his nature matching that of his birth—he, Don Carlos Alvarez de Santillanos y Meñaya, the gentleman of stainless manners, of reputation untarnished by a single blot—he, who had never yet been ashamed of anything,—in his solitude he blushed and covered his face in shame, as the villany he had planned rose up before his mind. It would have broken his heart to be scorned by any man; and was it not worse a thousand-fold to be thus scorned by himself? He thought even more of the meanness of his plan than of its treachery. Of its sin he did not think at all. Sin was a theological term which he had been wont to handle in the schools, and to toss to and fro with the other materials upon which he showed off his dialectic skill; but it no more occurred to him to take it out of the scholastic world and to bring it into that in which he really lived and acted, than it did to talk Latin to Diego, or softly to whisper quotations from Thomas Aquinas into the ear of Doña Beatriz between the pauses of the dance.

Scarcely any consideration, however, could have made him more miserable than he was. Past and future—all alike seemed dreary. Not a happy memory, not a cheering anticipation could he find to comfort him. He was as one who goes forth to face the driving storm of a wintry night: not strong in hope and courage—a warm hearth behind him, and before him the pleasant starry glimmer that tells of another soon to be reached—but chilled, weary, forlorn, the wind whistling through thin garments, and nothing to meet his eye but the bare, bleak, shelterless moor stretching far out into the distance.

He sat long, too crushed in heart even to finish his slight, unimportant task. Sometimes he drew towards him the sheet of figures, and for a moment or two tried to fix his attention upon it; but soon he would push it away again, or make aimless dots and circles on its margin. While thus engaged, he heard a cheery and not unmelodious voice chanting a fragment of song in some foreign tongue. Listening more attentively, he believed the words were French, and supposed the singer must be his humble guest, the muleteer, on his way to the stable to take a last look at the beloved companions of his toils before he lay down to rest. The man had probably exercised his vocation at some former period in the passes of the Pyrenees, and had thus acquired some knowledge of French.

Half an hour's talk with any one seemed to Carlos at that moment a most desirable diversion from the gloom of his own thoughts. He might converse with this stranger when he dared not summon to his presence Diego or Dolores, because they knew and loved him well enough to discover in two minutes that something was seriously wrong with him. He waited until he heard the voice once more close beneath his window; then softly opening it, he called the muleteer. Juliano responded with ready alertness; and Carlos, going round to the door, admitted him, and led him into his sanctum.

"I believe," he said, "that was a French song I heard you sing. You have been in France, then?"

"Ay, señor; I have crossed the Pyrenees more than once. I have also been in Switzerland."

"You must, then, have visited many places worthy of note; and not with your eyes shut, I think. I wish you would tell me, for pastime, the story of your travels."

"Willingly, señor," said the muleteer, who, though perfectly respectful, had an ease and independence of manner that made Carlos suspect it was not the first time he had conversed with his superiors. "Where shall I begin?"

"Have you ever crossed the Santillanos, or visited the Asturias?"

"No, señor. A man cannot be everywhere; he that rings the bells does not walk in the procession. I am only master of the route from Lyons here; knowing a little also, as I have said, of Switzerland."

"Tell me first of Lyons, then. And be seated, my friend."

The muleteer sat down, and began his story, telling of the places he had seen with an intelligence that more and more engaged the attention of Carlos, who failed not to draw out his information by many pertinent questions. As they conversed, each observed the other with gradually increasing interest. Carlos admired the muleteer's courage and energy in the prosecution of his calling, and enjoyed his quaint and shrewd observations. Moreover, he was struck by certain indications of a degree of education and even of refinement not usual in his class. Especially he noticed the small, finely formed hand, which was sometimes in the warmth of conversation laid on the table, and which looked as if it had been accustomed to wield some implement far more delicate than a riding-whip. Another thing he took note of. Though Juliano's language abounded in proverbs, in provincialisms, in quaint and racy expressions, not a single oath escaped his lips. "I never saw an arriero before," thought Carlos, "who could get through two sentences without half a dozen of them."

Juliano, on the other hand, was observing his host, and with a far shrewder and deeper insight than Carlos could have imagined. During supper he had gathered from the servants that their young master was kind-hearted, gentle, easy-tempered, and had never injured any one in his life; and knowing all this, he was touched with genuine sympathy for the young noble, whose haggard face and sorrowful looks told but too plainly that some great grief was pressing on his heart.

"Your Excellency must be weary of my stories," he said at length. "It is time I left you to your repose."

And so indeed it was, for the hour was late.

"Ere you go," said Carlos kindly, "you shall drink a cup of wine with me."

He had no wine at hand but the costly beverage Dolores had

produced for his own especial use. Wondering a little what Juliano would think of such a luxurious beverage, he sought a second cup, for the proud Castilian gentleman was too "finely courteous" not to drink with his guest, although that guest was only a muleteer.

Juliano, evidently a temperate man, remonstrated: "But I have already tasted your Excellency's hospitality."

"That should not hinder your drinking to my good health," said Carlos, producing a small hunting-cup, forgotten until now, from the pocket of his doublet.

Then filling the larger cup, he handed it to Juliano. It was a very little thing, a trifling act of kindness. But to the last hour of his life, Carlos Alvarez thanked God that he had put it into his heart to offer that cup of wine.

The muleteer raised it to his lips, saying earnestly, "God grant you health and happiness, noble señor."

Carlos drank also, glad to relieve a painful feeling of exhaustion. As he set down the cup, a sudden impulse prompted him to say, with a bitter smile, "Happiness is not likely to come my way at present."

"Nay, señor, and wherefore not? With your good leave be it spoken, you are young, noble, amiable, with much learning and excellent parts, as they tell me."

"All these things may not prevent a man being very miserable," said Carlos frankly.

"God comfort you, señor."

"Thanks for the good wish," said Carlos, rather lightly, and conscious of having already said too much. "All men have their troubles, I suppose, but most men contrive to live through them. So shall I, no doubt."

"But God can comfort you," Juliano repeated with a kind of wistful earnestness.

Carlos, surprised at his manner, looked at him dreamily, but with some curiosity.

"Señor," said Juliano, leaning forward and speaking in a low tone full of meaning, "Let your worship excuse a plain man's plain question—Señor, do you know God?"

Carlos started visibly. Was the man mad? Certainly not; as all his previous conversation bore witness. He was evidently a very clever, half-educated man, who spoke with just the simplicity and unconsciousness of an intelligent child. And now he had asked a true child's question; one which it would exhaust a wise man's wisdom to answer. Thoroughly perplexed, Carlos at last determined to take it in its easiest sense. He said, "Yes; I have studied theology, and taken out my licentiate's degree at the University of Alcala."

"If it please your worship, what may that fine word theology mean?"

"You have said so many wise things, that I marvel you know not. Science about God."

"Then, señor, your Excellency knows about God. But is it not another thing to know God? I know much about the Emperor Carlos, now at San Yuste; I could tell you the story of all his campaigns. But I never saw him, still less spoke with him. And far indeed am I from knowing him to be my friend; and so trusting him that if my mules died, or the Alguazils seized me at Cordova for bringing over something contraband, or other mishap befell me, I should go or send to him, certain that he would help and save me."

"I begin to understand you," said Carlos; and a suspicion crossed his mind that the muleteer was a friar in disguise. But that could scarcely be, since his black abundant hair showed no marks of the tonsure.[1] "After the manner you speak only great saints know God."

"Indeed, señor! Can that be true? For I have heard that our Lord Christ"—(at the mention of the name Carlos crossed himself, a ceremony which the muleteer was so engrossed by his argument as to forget)—"that our Lord Christ came into the world to make men know the Father; and that, to all that believe on him, he truly reveals him."

"Where did you get this strange learning?"

"It is simple learning; and yet very blessed, señor," returned

[1] A shaved patch on the crown of the heads of priests and monks in some religious orders.

Juliano, evading the question. "For those who know God are happy. Whatever sorrows they have without, within they have joy and peace."

"You are advising me to seek peace in religion?"

It was singular certainly that a muleteer should advise *him*; but then this was a very uncommon muleteer. "And so I ought," he added, "since I am destined for the Church."

"No, señor; not to seek peace in religion, but to seek peace from God, and in Christ who reveals him."

"It is only the words that differ, the things are the same."

"Again I say, with all submission to your Excellency, not so. It is Christ Jesus himself—Christ Jesus, God and man—who alone can give the peace and happiness for which the heart aches. Are we oppressed with sin? He says, 'Thy sins are forgiven thee!'[2] Are we hungry? He is bread. Thirsty? He is living water. Weary? He says, 'Come unto me, all ye that are weary and heavy laden, and I will give you rest!'"[3]

"Man! who or what are you? You are quoting the Holy Scriptures to me. Do you then read Latin?"

"No, señor," said the muleteer humbly, casting his eyes down to the ground.

"No?"

"No, señor; in very truth. But—"

"Well? Go on!"

Juliano looked up again, a steady light in his eyes. "Will you promise, on the faith of a gentleman, not to betray me?" he asked.

"Most assuredly I will not betray you."

"I trust you, señor. I do not believe it would be possible for you to betray one who trusted you."

Carlos winced, and rather shrank from the muleteer's look of hearty, honest confidence.

"Though I cannot guess your reason for such precautions," he

[2] Possibly referring to Matthew 9:5, Luke 5:23, 7:48 or Mark 2:9.
[3] Matthew 11:28

said, "I am willing, if you wish it, to swear secrecy upon the holy crucifix."

"It needs not, señor; your word of honour is as much as your oath. Though I am putting my life in your hands when I tell you that I have dared to read the words of my Lord Christ in my own tongue."

"Are you then a heretic?" Carlos exclaimed, recoiling involuntarily, as one who suddenly sees the plague spot on the forehead of a friend whose hand he has been grasping.

"That depends upon your notion of a heretic, señor. Many a better man than I has been branded with the name. Even the great preacher Don Fray Constantino, whom all the fine lords and ladies in Seville flock to hear, has often been called heretic by his enemies."

"I have resided in Seville, and attended Fray Constantino's theological lectures," said Carlos.

"Then your worship knows there is not a better Christian in all the Spains. And yet men say that he narrowly escaped a prosecution for heresy. But enough of what men say. Let us hear what God says for once. His words cannot lead us astray."

"No; not the Holy Scriptures, properly expounded by learned and orthodox doctors. But heretics put their own construction upon the sacred text, which, moreover, they corrupt and interpolate."

"Señor, you are a scholar: you can consult the original, and judge for yourself how far that charge is true."

"But I do not want to read heretic writings."

"Nor I, señor. Yet I confess that I have read the words of my Saviour in my own tongue, which some misinformed or ignorant persons call heresy; and through them, to my soul's joy, I have learned to know Him and the Father. I am bold enough to wish the same knowledge yours, señor, that the same joy may be yours also." The poor man's eye kindled, and his features, otherwise homely enough, glowed with an enthusiasm that lent them true spiritual beauty.

Carlos was not unmoved. After a moment's pause he said, "If I could procure what you style God's Word in my own tongue, I do not say that I would refuse to read it. Should I discover any heretical mistranslation or interpolation, I could blot out the passage; or, if necessary, burn the book."

"I can place in your hands this very hour the New Testament of our Saviour Christ, lately translated into Castilian by Juan Perez, a learned man, well acquainted with the Greek."

"What! have you got it with you? In God's name bring it then; and at least I will look at it."

"Be it truly in God's name, señor," said Juliano, as he left the room.

During his absence Carlos pondered upon this singular adventure. Throughout his lengthened conversation with him, he had discerned no marks of heresy in the muleteer, except his possession of the Spanish New Testament. And being very proud of his dialectic acuteness, he thought he should certainly have discovered such had they existed. "He had need to be a clever heretic that would circumvent me," he said, with the vanity of a young and successful scholar. Moreover, his ten months' attendance on the lectures of Fray Constantino had, unconsciously to himself, somewhat imbued his mind with liberal ideas. He could have read the Vulgate at Alcala if he had cared to do so (only he never had); where then could be the harm of glancing, out of mere curiosity, at a Spanish translation from the same original?

He regarded the New Testament in the light of some very dangerous, though effective, weapon of the explosive kind; likely to overwhelm with terrible destruction the careless or ignorant meddler with its intricacies, and therefore wisely forbidden by the authorities; though in able and scientific hands, such as his own, it might be harmless—and even useful.

But it was a very different matter for the poor man who brought it to him. Was he, after all, a madman? Or was he a heretic? Or was he a great saint or holy hermit in disguise? But whatever his spiritual peril might or might not be, it was only too evident that he was incurring temporal dangers of a very awful kind. And perhaps he was doing so in the simplicity of ignorance. Carlos could not do less than warn him of them.

He soon returned; and drawing a small brown volume from beneath his leathern jerkin, handed it to the young nobleman.

"My friend," said Carlos kindly, as he took it from him, "do you know what you dare by offering this to me, or even by keeping it yourself?"

"I know it well, señor," was the calm reply; and the muleteer's dark eye met his undauntedly.

"You are playing a dangerous game. This time you are safe. But take care. You may try it once too often."

"I shall not, señor. I shall witness for my Lord just so often as he permits. When he has no more need of me, he will call me home."

"God help you. I fear you are throwing yourself into the fire. And for what?"

"For the joy of bringing food to the perishing, water to the thirsty, light to those that sit in darkness, rest to the weary and heavy-laden. Señor, I have counted the cost, and I shall pay the price right willingly."

After a moment's silence he continued: "I leave within your hands the treasure brought at such cost. But God alone, by his Divine Spirit, can reveal to you its true worth. Señor, seek that Spirit. Nay, be not offended. You are very noble and very learned; and it is a poor and ignorant man who speaks to you. But that poor man is risking his life for your soul's salvation; and thus he proves, at least, how true his desire to see you one day at the right hand of Christ, his King and Master. Adiõs, señor."

He bowed low; and before Carlos had sufficiently recovered from his astonishment to say a word in answer, he had left the room and closed the door behind him.

"Strange being!" thought Carlos; "but I shall talk with him again to-morrow." And ere he was aware, his eyelids were wet; for the courage and self-sacrifice of the poor muleteer had stirred some answering chord of emotion in his heart. Probably, in spite of all appearances to the contrary, he was a madman; or else he was a heretical fanatic. But he was a man willing to brave numberless sufferings (of which a death of torture was the last and least), to bring his fellow-men something which he imagined would make them happy. "The Church has no more orthodox son than I," said Don Carlos Alvarez; "but I shall read his book for all that."

Then, the hour being late, he retired to rest, and slept soundly.

He did not rise exactly with the sun, and when he came forth from his chamber breakfast was already in preparation.

"Where is the muleteer who was here last night?" he asked Dolores.

"He was up and away at sunrise," she answered. "Fortunately, it is not my custom to stop in bed and see the sunshine; so I just caught him loading his mules, and gave him a piece of bread and cheese and a draught of wine. A smart little man he is, and one who knows his business."

"I wish I had seen him ere he left," said Carlos aloud. "Shall I ever look upon his face again?" he added mentally.

Carlos Alvarez saw that face again, not by the ray of sun or moon, nor yet by the gleam of the student's lamp, but clear and distinct in a lurid awful light more terrible than Egyptian darkness, yet fraught with strange blessing, since it showed the way to the city of God, where the sun no more goes down, neither doth the moon withdraw herself.

Juliano el Chico, otherwise Julian Hernandez, is no fancy sketch, no "character of fiction." It is matter of history that, cunningly stowed away in his alforjas, amongst the ribbons, laces, and other trifles that formed their ostensible freight, there was a large supply of Spanish New Testaments, of the translation of Juan Perez. And that, in spite of all the difficulties and dangers of his self-imposed task, he succeeded in conveying his precious charge safely to Seville.

Our cheeks grow pale, our hearts shudder, at the thought of what he and others dared, that they might bring to the lips of their countrymen that living water which was truly "the blood of the men that went for it in jeopardy of their lives." More than jeopardy. Not alone did Juliano brave danger, he encountered certain death. Sooner or later, it was impossible that he should not fall into the pitiless grasp of that hideous engine of royal and priestly tyranny, called the Holy Inquisition.

We have no words in which to praise such heroism as his. We leave that—and we may be content to leave it—to Him whose lips shall one day pronounce the sublime award, "Well done, good and faithful servant; enter thou into the joy of thy Lord."[4] But in the view of such things done and suffered for his name's sake, there is another thought that presses on the mind. How real and great, nay, how unutterably precious, must be that treasure which men were found willing, at such cost, not only to secure for themselves, but even to impart to others.

[4] Matthew 25:21

IX.

El Dorado Found.

"So, the All-Great were the all-loving too
So, through the thunder comes a human voice,
Saying, O heart I made, a heart beats here!
Face my hands fashioned, see it in myself!
Thou hast no power, nor mayest conceive of mine
But love I gave thee with myself to love,
And thou must love me who have died for thee!"

R. BROWNING.

HREE silent months stole away in the old castle of Nuera. No outward event affecting the fortunes of its inmates marked their progress. And yet they were by far the most important months Don Carlos had ever seen, or perhaps would ever see. They witnessed a change in him, mysterious in its progress but momentous in its results. An influence passed over him, mighty as the wind in its azure pathway, but, like it, visible only by its effects; no man could tell "whence it cometh or whither it goeth."[1]

Again it was early morning, a bright Sunday morning in September. Already Carlos stood prepared to go forth. He had quite discarded his student's habit, and was dressed like any other young

[1] Referring to John 3:8.

nobleman, in a doublet and short cloak of Genoa velvet, with a sword by his side. His breviary was in his hand, however, and he was on the point of taking up his hat when Dolores entered the room, bearing a cup of wine and a manchet of bread.

Carlos shook his head, saying, "I intend to communicate. And you, Dolores," he added, "are you not also going to hear mass?"

"Surely, señor; we will all attend our duty. But there is still time to spare; your worship sets us an example in the matter of early rising."

"It were a shame to lose such fair hours as these. Prithee,[2] Dolores, and lest I forget, hast thou something savoury in the house for dinner?"

"Glad I am to hear you ask, señor. Hitherto it has seemed alike to your Excellency whether they served you with a pottage of lentils or a stew of partridges. But since Diego had the good fortune to kill that buck on Wednesday, we are better than well provided. Your worship shall dine on roast venison to-day."

"That will do. And if thou wouldst add some of the batter ware, in which thou art so skilful, it would be better still; for I intend to bring home a guest."

"Now, that is news! Without meaning offence, your worship might have told me before. Any noble caballero coming to these parts to visit you must needs have bed as well as board found him. And how can I, in three hours, more or less—"

"Nay, be not alarmed, Dolores; no stranger is coming here. Only I wish to bring the cura home to dinner."

Even the self-restrained Dolores could not repress an exclamation of surprise. For both the brothers had been accustomed to regard the ignorant vulgar cura of the neighbouring village with unmitigated dislike and contempt. In old times Dolores herself had sometimes tried to induce them to show him some trifling courtesies, "for their soul's health." They were willing enough to send "that beggar"—as Don Juan used to call him—presents of meat or game when they could, but these they would not have

[2] *Archaic:* used to introduce a request to somebody.

grudged to their worst enemy. To converse with him, or to seat him at their table, was a very different matter. He was "no fit associate for noblemen," said the boys; and Dolores, in her heart, agreed with them. She looked at her young master to see whether he was jesting.

"He likes a good dinner," Carlos added quietly. "Let us for once give him one."

"In good faith, Señor Don Carlos, I cannot tell what has come to you. You must be about doing penance for your sins, though I will say no young gentleman of your years has fewer to answer for. Still, to please your whim, the cura shall eat the best we have, though beans and bacon would be more fitting fare for him."

"Thank you, mother Dolores," said Carlos kindly. "In truth, neither Don Juan nor I had ever whim yet you did not strive to gratify."

"And who would not do more than that for so pleasant and kind a young master?" thought Dolores, as she withdrew to superintend the cooking operations. "God's blessing and Our Lady's rest on him, and in sooth[3] I think they do. Three months ago he came here looking like a corpse out of the grave, and fitter, as it seemed to me, to don his shroud than his priest's frock. But the free mountain air wherein he was born is bringing back the red to his cheek and the light to his eye, thank the holy Saints. Ah, if his lady mother could only see her gallant sons now!"

Meanwhile Don Carlos leisurely took his way down the hill. Having abundance of time to spare, he chose a solitary, devious path through the cork-trees and the pasture land belonging to the castle. His heart was alive to every pleasant sight and sound that met his eye and ear; although, or rather because, a low, sweet song of thankfulness was all the while chanting itself within him.

During his solitary walk he distinctly realised for the first time the stupendous change that had passed over him. For such changes cannot be understood or measured until afterwards, perhaps not always then. Drawing from his pocket Juliano's little book, he

[3] *Archaic:* truth.

clasped it in both hands. "This, God be thanked, has done it all, under him. And yet, at first, it added to my misery a hundred-fold." Then his mind ran back to the dreary days of helpless, almost hopeless wretchedness, when he first began its perusal. Much of it had then been quite unintelligible to him; but what he understood had only made his darkness darker still. He who had but just learned from that stern teacher, Life, the meaning of sorrow, learned from the pages of his book the awful significance of that other word, Sin. Bitter hours, never to be remembered without a shudder, were those that followed. Already prostrate on the ground beneath the weight of his selfish sorrow for the love that might never be his, cruel blows seemed rained upon him by the very hand to which he turned to lift him up. "All was his own fault," said conscience. But had conscience, enlightened by his book, said no more, he could have borne it. It was a different thing to recognise that all was his own *sin*—to feel more keenly every day that the whole current of his thoughts and affections was set in opposition to the will of God as revealed in that book, and illustrated in the life of him of whom it told.

But this sickness of heart, deadly though it seemed, was not unto death. The Word had indeed proved a mirror, in which he saw his own face reflected with the lines and colours of truth. But it had a farther use for him. As he did not fling it away in despair, but still gazed on, at length he saw in its clear depths another Face—a Face radiant with divine majesty, yet beaming with tender love and pity. He whom the mirror thus gave back to him had been "not far" from him all his life; had been standing over against him, watching and waiting for the moment in which to reveal himself. At last that moment came. He looked up from the mirror to the real Face; from the Word to him whom the Word revealed. He turned himself and said unto him, "Rabboni, which is to say, My Master." He laid his soul at his feet in love, in trust, in gratitude. And he knew then, not until then, that this was the "coming" to him, the "believing" on him, the receiving him, of which he spoke as the condition of life, of pardon, and of happiness.

From that hour he possessed life, he knew himself forgiven, he was *happy*. This was no theory, but a fact—a fact which changed all his present and was destined to change all his future.

He longed to impart the wonderful secret he had found. This longing overcame his contempt for the cura, and made him seek to win him by kindness to listen to words which perhaps might open for him also the same wonderful fountain of joy.

"Now I am going to worship my Lord, afterwards I shall speak of him," he said, as he crossed the threshold of the little village church.

In due season the service was over. Its ceremonies did not pain or offend Carlos in any way; he took part in them with much real devotion, as acts of homage paid to his Lord. Still, if he had analysed his feelings (which he did not), he would have found them like those of a king's child, who is obliged, on days of courtly ceremonial, to pay his father the same distant homage as the other peers of the realm, and yet knows that all this for him is but an idle show, and longs to throw aside its cumbrous pomp, and to rejoice once more in the free familiar association which is his habit and his privilege. But that the ceremonial itself could be otherwise than pleasing to his King, he had not the most distant suspicion.

He spoke kindly to the priest, and inquired by name after all the sick folk in the village, though in fact he knew more about them himself by this time than did Father Tomas.

The cura's heart was glad when the catechism came to a termination so satisfactory as an invitation to dine at the castle. Whatever the fare might be—and his expectations were not extravagantly high—it could scarce fail to be an improvement on the olla of which he had intended to make his Sunday repast. Moreover, one favour from the castle might be the earnest of others; and favours from the castle, poor though its lords might be, were not to be despised. Nor was he ill at ease in the society of an accomplished gentleman, as a man just a little better bred would probably have been. A wealthy peasant's son, and with but scanty education, Father Tomas was so hopelessly vulgar that he never once imagined he was vulgar at all.

Carlos bore as patiently as he could with his coarse manners, and conversation something worse than commonplace. Not until the repast was concluded did he find an opportunity of bringing forward the topic upon which he longed to speak. Then, with more tact than his guest could appreciate, he began by inquiring—as one himself intended for the priesthood might naturally do—whether he could always keep his thoughts from wandering while he was celebrating the holy mysteries of the faith.

Father Tomas crossed himself, and answered that he was a sinner like other men, but that he tried to do his duty to our holy Mother Church to the best of his ability.

Carlos remarked, that unless we ourselves know the love of God by experience we cannot love him, and that without love there is no acceptable service.

"Most true, señor," said the priest, turning his eyes upwards. "As the holy St. Augustine saith. Your worship quotes from him, I believe."

"I have quoted nothing," said Carlos, beginning to feel that he was speaking to the deaf; "but I know the words of Christ." And then he spoke, out of a full heart, of Christ's work for us, of his love to us, and of the pardon and peace which those receive that trust him.

But his listener's stolid face betrayed no interest, only a vague uneasiness, which increased as Carlos proceeded. The poor parish cura began to suspect that the clever young collegian meant to astonish and bewilder him by the exhibition of his learning and his "new ideas." Indeed, he was not quite sure whether his host was eloquently enlarging all the time upon Catholic truths, or now and then mischievously throwing out a few heretical propositions, in order to try whether he would have skill enough to detect them. Naturally, he did not greatly relish this style of entertainment. Nothing could be got from him save a cautious, "That is true, señor," or, "Very good, your worship;" and as soon as his notions of politeness would permit, he took his leave.

Carlos marvelled greatly at his dulness; but soon dismissed him from his mind, and took his Testament out to read under the shade of the cork-trees. Ere long the light began to fade, but he sat there still in the fast deepening twilight. Thoughts and fancies thronged upon his mind; and dreams of the past sought, as even yet they often did, to reassert their supremacy over his heart. One of those apparently unaccountable freaks of memory, which we all know by experience, brought back to him suddenly the luscious perfume of the orange-blossoms, called by the Spaniards the azahar. Such fragrance had filled the air, and such flowers had been strewed upon his pathway, when last he walked with Doña Beatriz in the gardens of the Alcazar of Seville.

Keen was the pang that shot through his heart at the remembrance. But it was conquered soon. As he went in-doors he repeated the words he had just been reading, "'He that cometh unto me shall never hunger; he that believeth on me shall never thirst.'[4] And *this* hunger of the soul, as well as every other, he can stay. Having him, I have all things.

'*El Dorado*
Yo hé trovado.'

"Father, dear, unknown father, I have found the golden country! Not in the sense thou didst fondly seek, and I as fondly dream to find it. Yet the only true land of gold I have found indeed—the treasure unfailing, the inheritance incorruptible, undefiled, and that fadeth not away, reserved in heaven for me."[5]

---

[4] John 6:35
[5] Referring to I Peter 1:4.

X.

Dolores.

> "Oh, hearts that break and give no sign,
> Save whitening lip and fading tresses;
> Till death pours out his cordial wine,
> Slow dropped from misery's crushing presses.
> If singing breath or echoing chord
> To every hidden pang were given,
> What endless melodies were poured,
> As sad as earth, as sweet as heaven."
>
> O. W. Holmes.

GREAT modern poet has compared the soul of man to a pilgrim who passes through the world staff in hand, never resting, ever pressing onwards to some point as yet unattained, ever sighing wearily, "Alas! that *there* is never *here*." And with deep significance adds his Christian commentator, "In Christ *there* is *here*."

He who has found Christ "is already at the goal." "For he stills our innermost fears, and fulfils our utmost longings." "In him the dry land, the mirage of the desert, becomes living water." "He who knows him knows the reason of all things." Passing all along the ages, we might gather from the silent lips of the dead such words as these, bearing emphatic witness to what human hearts have found in him. Yet, after all, we would come back to his own grand and simple words, as best expressing the truth: "I am the bread of life;"[1] "I will give you rest;"[2] "In me ye shall have peace."[3]

With the peace which he gave, there came to Carlos a strange new knowledge also. The Testament, from its first page to its last, became intelligible to him. From a mere sketch, partly dim and partly blurred and blotted, it grew into a transparency through which light shone upon his soul, every word being itself a star.

He often read his book to Dolores, though he allowed her to suppose it was Latin, and that he was improvising a translation for her benefit. She would listen attentively, though with a deeper shade of sadness on her melancholy face. Never did she volunteer an observation, but she always thanked him at the end in her usual respectful manner.

These readings were, in fact, a trouble to Dolores. They gave her pain, like the sharp throbs that accompany the first return of consciousness to a frozen member, for they awakened feelings that had long been dormant, and that she thought were dead for ever. But, on the other hand, she was gratified by the condescension of her young master in reading aloud for her edification. She had gone through the world giving very largely out of her own large loving heart, and expecting little or nothing in return. She would most gladly have laid down her life for Don Juan or Don Carlos; yet she did not imagine that the old servant of the house could be to them much more than one of the oak tables or the carved chairs. That "Señor Don Carlos" should take thought for her, and trouble himself to do her good, thrilled her with a sensation more like joy than any she had known for years. Little do those whose cups are so full of human love that they carry them carelessly, spilling many a precious drop as they pass along, dream how others cherish the few poor lees and remnants left to them.

Moreover Carlos, in the eyes of Dolores, was half a priest already, and this lent additional weight, and even sacredness, to all that he said and did.

[1] John 6:35
[2] Matthew 11:28
[3] Referring to John 16:33.

One evening he had been reading to her in the inner room by the light of the little silver lamp. He had just finished the story of Lazarus, and he made some remark on the grateful love of Mary, and the costly sacrifice by which she proved it. Tears gathered in the dark wistful eyes of Dolores, and she said with sudden and, for her, most unusual energy, "That was small wonder. Any one would do as much for him that brought the dear dead back from the grave."

"He has done a greater thing than even that for each of us," said Carlos.

But Dolores withdrew into her ordinary self again, as some timid creature might shrink into its shell from a touch. "I thank your Excellency," she said, rising to withdraw, "and I also make my acknowledgments to Our Lady, who has inspired you with such true piety, suitable to your holy calling."

"Stay a little, Dolores," said Carlos, as a sudden thought occurred to him; "I marvel it has so seldom come into my mind to ask you about my mother."

"Ay, señor. When you were both children, I used to wonder that you and Don Juan, while you talked often together of my lord your father, had scarce a thought at all of your lady mother. Yet if she had lived you would have been her favourite, señor."

"And Juan my father's," said Carlos, not without a slight pang of jealousy. "Was my noble father, then, more like what my brother is?"

"Yes, señor; he was bold and brave. No offence to your Excellency; for one you love I warrant me you could be brave enough. But he loved his sword and his lance and his good steed. Moreover, he loved travel and adventure greatly, and never could bear to abide long in the same place."

"Did he not make a voyage to the Indies in his youth?"

"He did; and then he fought under the Emperor, both in Italy, and in Africa against the Moors. Once His Imperial Majesty sent him on some errand to Leon, and there he first met my lady. Afterwards he crossed the mountains to our home, and wooed and won her. He brought her, the fairest young bride eyes could rest on, to Seville, where he had a stately palace on the Alameda."

"You must have grieved to leave your mountains for the southern city."

"No, señor, I did not grieve. Wherever your lady mother dwelt was home to me. Besides, 'a great grief kills all the rest.'"

"Then you had known sorrow before. I thought you lived with our house from your childhood."

"Not altogether; though my mother nursed yours, and we slept in the same cradle, and as we grew older shared each other's plays. At seven years old I went home to my father and mother, who were honest, well-to-do people, like all my forbears—good 'old Christians,' and noble—they could wear their caps in the presence of His Catholic Majesty. They had no girl but me, so they would fain have me ever in their sight. For ten years and more I was the light of their eyes; and no blither lass ever led the goats to the mountain in summer, or spun wool and roasted chestnuts at the winter fire. But, the year of the bad fever, both were stricken. Christmas morning, with the bells for early mass ringing in my ears, I closed my father's eyes; and three days afterwards, set the last kiss on my mother's cold lips. Nigh upon five-and-twenty years ago—but it seems like yesterday. Folks say there are many good things in the world, but I have known none so good as the love of father and mother. Ay de mi, señor, *you* never knew either."

"When your parents died, did you return to my mother?"

"For half a year I stayed with my brother. Though no daughter ever shed truer tears over the grave of better parents, I was not then quite broken-hearted. There was another love to whisper hope, and to keep me from desolation. He—Alphonso ('tis years and years since I uttered the name save in my prayers) had gone to the war, telling me he would come back and claim me for his bride. So I watched for him hour by hour, and toiled and spun, and spun and toiled, that I might not go home to him empty-handed. But at last a lad from our parish, who had been a comrade of his, returned and told me all. *He* was lying on the bloody field of Marignano, with a

French bullet in his heart. Señor, the sisters you read of could 'go to the grave and weep there.'[4] And yet the Lord pitied them."

"He pities all who weep," said Carlos.

"All good Christians, he may. But though an old Christian, I was not a good one. For I thought it bitter hard that my candle should be quenched in a moment, like a wax taper when the procession is done. And it came often into my mind how the Almighty, or Our Lady, or the Saints, could have helped me if they would. May they forgive me; it is hard to be religious."

"I do not think so."

"I suppose it is not hard to learned gentlemen who have been at the colleges. But how can simple men and women tell whether they are keeping all the commandments of God and Holy Church? It well may be that I had done something, or left something undone, whereby Our Lady was displeased."

"It is not Our Lady, but our Lord himself, who holds the keys of hell and of death," said Carlos, gaining at the moment a new truth for his own heart. "None enter the gates of death, as none shall come forth through them, save at his command. But go on, Dolores, and tell me how did comfort come to you?"

"Comfort never came to me, señor. But after a time there came a kind of numbness and hardness that helped me to live my life as if I cared for it. And your lady mother (God rest her soul!) showed me wondrous kindness in my sorrow. It was then she took me to be her own maiden. She had me taught many things, such as reading and various cunning kinds of embroidery, that I might serve her with them, she said; but I well knew they were meant to turn my heart away from its own aching. I went with her to Seville. I could be glad for her, señor, that God had given her the good thing he had denied to me. At last it came to be almost like joy to me to see the great deep love there was between your father and her."

This was a degree of unselfishness beyond the comprehension of Carlos just then. He felt his own wound throb painfully, and was not sorry to turn the conversation. "Did my parents reside long in Seville?" he asked.

[4] Referring to John 11:31.

"Not long, señor. Their life there was a gay one, as became their rank and wealth (for, as your worship knows, your father had a noble estate then). But soon they both grew tired of the gay world. My lady ever loved the free mountains, and my lord—I scarce can tell what change passed over him. He lost his care for the tourney and the dance, and betook himself instead to study. Both were glad to withdraw to this quiet spot. Here your brother Don Juan was born; and for nigh a year afterwards no lord and lady could have lived a happier and, at the same time, more pious and orderly life, than did your noble parents."

The thoughtful eye of Carlos turned to the inscription on the window, and kindled with a strange light. "Was not this room my father's favourite place of study?" he asked.

"It was, señor. Of course, the house was not then as it now is. Though simple enough, after the Seville palace with its fountains and marble statues, and doors grated with golden network, it was still a seemly dwelling-place for a noble lord and lady. There was glass in all the windows then, though through neglect and carelessness it has been broken (even your worship may remember how Don Juan sent an arrow through a quarrel-pane in the west window one day), so we thought it best to remove the traces."

"My parents led a pious life, you say?"

"Truly they did, señor. They were good and charitable to the poor; and they spent much of their time reading holy books, as you do now. Ay de mi! what was wrong with them I know not, save that perhaps they were scarce careful enough to give Holy Church all her dues. And I used sometimes to wish that my lady would show more devotion to the blessed Mother of God. But she *felt* it all, no doubt; only it was not her way, nor my lord's either, to be for ever running about on pilgrimage or offering wax candles, nor yet to keep the father confessor every instant with his ear to their lips."

Carlos started, and turned an earnest inquiring gaze upon her. "Did my mother ever read to you as I have done?" he asked.

"She sometimes read me good words out of the breviary, señor. All things went on thus, until one day when a letter came from the

Emperor himself (as I believe), desiring your father to go to him, to Antwerp. The matter was to be kept very private, but my lady used to tell me everything. My lord thought he was to be sent on some secret mission where skill was needed, and perchance peril was to be met. For it was well known that he loved such affairs, and was dexterous in the management of them. So he parted cheerily from my lady, she standing at the gate yonder, and making little Don Juan kiss hands to him as he rode down the path. Woe for the poor babe that never saw his father's face again. And worse woe for the mother! But death heals all things, except sin.

"After three weeks or a month, more or less, two monks of St. Dominic rode to the gates one day. The younger stayed without in the hall with us; while the elder, a man of stern and stately presence, had private audience of my lady in this chamber where we sit now—a place of death it has seemed to me ever since. For the audience had not lasted long until I heard a cry—such a cry!—it rings in my ears even now. I hastened to my lady. She had swooned—and long, long was it before sense returned again. Do not keep looking at me, señor, with eyes so like hers, or I cannot tell you more."

"Did she speak? Did she reveal anything to you?"

"Nothing, señor. During the days that followed, only things without meaning or connection, such as those in fever speak, or broken words of prayer, were on her lips. Until the very last, and then she was worn and weak, and could but receive the rites of the Church, and whisper a few directions about the poor babes. She bade us give you the name you bear, since he had said that his next boy should be called for the great Emperor. Then she prayed very earnestly, 'Lord, take him Thyself—take him Thyself!' Doctor Marco, who was present, thought she meant the poor little new-born babe—supposing, and no wonder, that it would be better tended in heaven by Our Lady and the angels, than here on earth. But I know it was not you she thought of."

"My poor mother—God rest her soul! Nay, I doubt not that now she rests in God," Carlos added, softly.

"And so the curse fell on your house, señor; and in such sorrow were you born. Yet you grew up merry lads, you and Don Juan."

"Thanks to thy care and kindness, well-beloved and faithful nurse. But, Dolores, tell me truly—have you never heard anything further of, or from, my father?"

"From him, never. Of him, that I believed, *never*."

"And what do you believe?" Carlos asked, eagerly.

"I know nothing, señor. I have heard all that your worship has heard, and no more."

"Do you think it is true—what we have all been told—of his death in the Indies?"

"I know nothing, señor," Dolores repeated, with the air of a person determined to say nothing.

But Carlos would not allow her to escape thus. Both had gone too far to leave the subject without probing it to its depths. And both felt instinctively that it was not likely again to be discussed between them. Laying his hand on her arm, and looking steadily in her face, he asked,—

"Dolores, are you sure my father is dead?"

Seemingly relieved by the form the question had taken, she met his gaze without flinching, and answered in tones of evident sincerity, "Sure as that I sit here." After a long pause she added, as she rose to go, "Señor Don Carlos, be not offended if I counsel you this once, since I held you a babe in my arms, and you will find none that loves you better—if a poor old woman may say so to a young and noble caballero."

"Say all you think to me, my dear and kind nurse."

"Then, señor, I say, leave vain thoughts and questions about your father's fate. 'There are no birds in last year's nests;' and 'Water that has run by will turn no mill.' And I entreat of you to repeat the same to your noble brother when you find opportunity. Look before you, señor, and not behind; and God's best blessings rest on you!"

Dolores turned to go, but turning back again, stood irresolute.

"What is it, Dolores?" Carlos asked; hoping, perhaps, for some further glimmer of light upon that dark past, from which she implored him to turn his thoughts.

"If it please you, Señor Don Carlos—" and she paused and hesitated.

"Can I do anything for you?" said Carlos, in a kind, encouraging tone.

"Ay, señor, that you can. With your learning and your good Book, surely you can tell me whether the soul of my poor Alphonso, dead on the battle-field without shrift[5] or sacrament, has yet found rest with God?"

Thus the true woman's heart, though so full of sympathy for others, still turned back to its own sorrow, which lay deepest of all.

Carlos felt himself unexpectedly involved in a difficulty.

"My book tells me nothing on the subject," he said, after some thought. "But I am sure you may be comforted, after all these years, during which you have diligently prayed, and sought the Church's prayers for him."

The long eager gaze of her wistful eyes asked mournfully, "Is this *all* you can tell me?" But her lips only said, "I thank your Excellency," as she withdrew.

[5] Confession to a priest.

XI.

The Light Enjoyed.

> "Doubt is slow to clear and sorrow is hard to bear,
> And each sufferer has his say, his scheme of the weal and the woe
> But God has a few of us whom he whispers in the ear;
> The rest may reason and welcome, 'tis we musicians know."
>
> R. Browning.

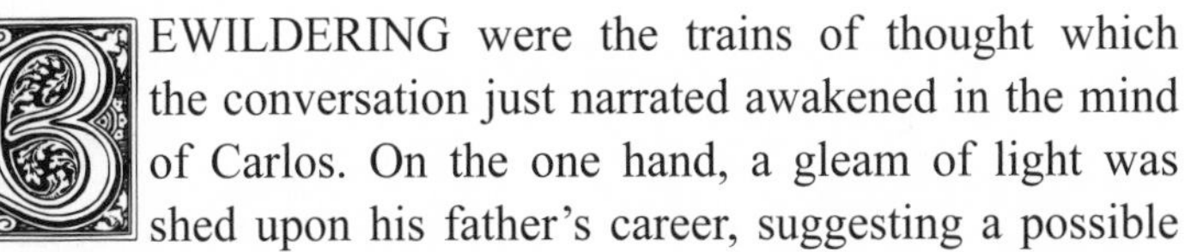

EWILDERING were the trains of thought which the conversation just narrated awakened in the mind of Carlos. On the one hand, a gleam of light was shed upon his father's career, suggesting a possible interpretation of the inscription on the window, that thrilled his heart with joy. On the other, the termination of that career was involved in even deeper obscurity than before; and he was made to feel, more keenly than ever, how childish and unreal were the dreams which he and his brother had been wont to cherish upon the subject.

Moreover, Dolores, just before she left him, had drawn a bow at a venture, and most unintentionally sent a sharp arrow through a joint in his harness. Why could he find no answer to a question so simple and natural as the one she had asked him? Why did the Book, which had solved so many mysteries for him, shed not a ray of light upon this one? Whence this ominous silence of the apostles and evangelists upon so many things that the Church most loudly proclaimed? Where, in his Book was purgatory to be found at all? Where was the adoration of the Virgin and the saints? Where were works of supererogation?[1] But here he started in horror, as one who suddenly saw himself on the brink of a precipice. Or rather, as one dwelling secure and contented within a little circle of light and warmth, to whom such questions came as intimations of a chaos surrounding it on every side, into which a chance step might at any moment plunge him.

Most earnestly he entreated that the Lord of his life, the Guide of his spirit, would not let him go forth to wander there. He prayed, expressly and repeatedly, that the doubts which began to trouble him might be laid and silenced. His prayer was answered, as all true prayer is sure to be, but it was not *granted.* He whose love is strong and deep enough to work out its good purpose in us even against the pleadings of our own hearts, saw that his child must needs pass through "a land of darkness" to reach the clearer light beyond. Conflicts fierce and terrible must be his portion, if indeed he were to take his place amongst those "called and chosen and faithful" ones who, having stood beside the Lamb in his contest with Antichrist, shall stand beside him on the sea of glass mingled with fire.

Already Carlos was in training for that contest—though as yet he knew not that there was any contest before him, save the general "striving against sin" in which all Christians have to take part. For the joy of the Lord is the Christian's strength in the day of battle. And he usually prepares those faithful soldiers whom he means to set in the forefront of the hottest battle, by previously bestowing that joy upon them in very full measure. He who is willing to "sell all that he hath," must first have found a treasure, and what "the joy thereof" is, none else may declare.

In this joy Carlos lived now; and it was as yet too fresh and new to be greatly disturbed by haunting doubts or perplexing questions. These, for the present, came and passed like a breath upon a surface of molten gold, scarcely dimming its lustre for a moment.

[1] The performance of work beyond what is required or expected.

It had become his great wish to receive Orders as soon as possible, that he might consecrate himself more entirely to the service of his Lord, and spread abroad the knowledge of his love more widely. With this view, he determined on returning to Seville early in October.

He left Nuera with regret, especially on account of Dolores, who had taken a new place in his consideration, and even in his affections, since he had begun to read to her from his Book. And, though usually very calm and impassive in manner, she could scarcely refrain from tears at the parting. She entreated him, with almost passionate earnestness, to be very prudent and careful of himself in the great city.

Carlos, who saw no special danger likely to menace him, save such as might arise from his own heart, felt tempted to smile at her foreboding tone, and asked her what she feared for him.

"Oh, Señor Don Carlos," she pleaded, with clasped hands, "take care; and do not be reading and telling your good words to every one you meet. For the world is an ill place, your worship, where good is ofttimes evil-spoken of."

"Never fear for me," returned Carlos, with his frank, pleasant smile. "I have found nothing in my Book but the most Catholic verities, which will be useful to all and hurtful to none. But of course I shall be prudent, and take due care of my words, lest by any extraordinary chance they might be misinterpreted. So that you may keep your mind at peace, dear Mother Dolores."

XII.

The Light Divided from the Darkness.

> "I felt and feel, whate'er befalls,
> The footsteps of thy life in mine."
> TENNYSON.

N the glorious autumn weather, Don Carlos rode joyfully through cork and chestnut groves, across bare brown plains, and amidst gardens of pale olives and golden orange globes shining through dark glossy leaves. He had long ago sent back to Seville the guard with which his uncle had furnished him, so that his only companion was a country youth, trained by Diego to act as his servant. But although he passed through the very district afterwards immortalised by the adventures of the renowned Don Quixote, no adventure fell to his lot. Unless it may count for an adventure that near the termination of his journey the weather suddenly changed, and torrents of rain, accompanied by unusual cold, drove him to seek shelter.

"Ride on quickly, Jorge," he said to his attendant, "for I remember there is a venta by the roadside not far off. A poor place truly, where we are little likely to find a supper. But we shall find a roof to shelter us and fire to warm us, and these at present are our most pressing needs."

Arrived at the venta, they were surprised to see the lazy landlord so far stirred out of his usual apathy as to busy himself in trying to secure the fastening of the outer door, that it might not swing backwards and forwards in the wind, to the great discomfort of all within the house. The proud indifferent Spaniard looked calmly up from his task, and remarked that he would do all in his power to accommodate his worship. "But unfortunately, señor and your Excellency, a *very* great and principal nobleman has just arrived here, with a most distinguished train of fine caballeros—his lordship's gentlemen and servants; and kitchen, hall, and chamber are as full of them as a hive is full of bees."

This was evil news to Carlos. Proud, sensitive, and shy, there could be nothing more foreign to his character than to throw himself into the society of a person who, though really only his equal in rank, was so much his superior in all that lends rank its charm in the eyes of the vulgar. "We had better push on to Ecija," said he to his reluctant attendant, bravely turning his face to the storm, and making up his mind to ten miles more in drenching rain.

At that moment, however, a tall figure emerged from the inner door, opening into the long room behind the stable and kitchen that formed the only tolerable accommodation the one-storied venta afforded.

"Surely, señor, you do not intend to go further in this storm," said the nobleman, whose fine thoughtful countenance Carlos could not but fancy that he had seen before.

"It is not far to Ecija, señor," returned Carlos, bowing. "And 'first come first served,' is an excellent proverb."

"The first-comer has certainly one privilege which I am not disposed to waive—that of hospitably welcoming the second. Do me the favour to come in, señor. You will find an excellent fire."

Carlos could not decline an invitation so courteously given.

He was soon seated by the wood fire that blazed on the hearth of the inner room, exchanging compliments, in true Spanish fashion, with the nobleman who had welcomed him so kindly.

Though no one could doubt for an instant the stranger's possession of the pure "Sangre azul,"[1] yet his manners were more frank and easy and less ceremonious than those to which Carlos had been accustomed in the exclusive and privileged class of Seville society—a fact accounted for by the discovery, afterwards made, that he was born and educated in Italy.

"I have the pleasure of recognising Don Carlos Alvarez de Santillanos y Meñaya," said he. "I hope the babe about whom his worship showed such amiable anxiety recovered from its indisposition?"

This then was the personage whom Carlos had seen in such close conversation with the physician Losada. The association of ideas immediately brought back the mysterious remark about his father he had overheard on that occasion. Putting that aside, however, for the present, he answered, "Perfectly, I thank your grace. We attribute the recovery mainly to the skill and care of the excellent Dr. Cristobal Losada."

"A gentleman whose medical skill cannot be praised too highly, except, indeed, it were exalted at the expense of his other excellent qualities, and particularly his charity to the poor."

Carlos heartily acquiesced, and added some instances of the physician's kindness to those who could not recompense him again. They were new to his companion, who listened with interest.

During this conversation supper was laid. As the principal guest had brought his own provisions with him, it was a comfortable and plentiful repast. Carlos, ere he sat down, left the room to re-arrange his dress, and found opportunity to ask the innkeeper if he knew the noble stranger's name.

"His Excellency is a great noble from Castile," returned the innkeeper, with an air of much importance. "His name, as I am informed, is Don Carlos de Seso; and his illustrious lady, Doña Isabella, is of the blood royal."

"Where does he reside? "

"His gentlemen tell me, principally at one of his fine estates in

[1] Blue blood; aristocracy.

the north, Villamediana they call it. He is also corregidor[2] of Toro. He has been visiting Seville upon business of importance, and is now returning home."

Pleased to be the guest of such a man (for in fact he was his guest), Carlos took his seat at the table, and thoroughly enjoyed the meal. An hour's interaction with a man who had read and travelled much, but had thought much more, was a rare treat to him. Moreover, De Seso showed him all that fine courtesy which a youth so highly appreciates from a senior, giving careful attention to every observation he hazarded, and manifestly bringing the best of his powers to bear on his own share of the conversation.

He spoke of Fray Constantino's preaching, with an enthusiasm that made Carlos regret that he had been hitherto such an inattentive hearer. "Have you seen a little treatise by the Fray, entitled 'The Confession of a Sinner'?" he asked.

Carlos having answered in the negative, his new friend drew a tract from the pocket of his doublet, and gave it to him to read while he wrote a letter.

Carlos, after the manner of eager, rapid readers, plunged at once into the heart of the matter, disdaining beginnings.

Almost the first words upon which his eyes fell arrested his attention and drew him irresistibly onwards. "Such has been the pride of man," he read, "that he aimed at being God; but so great was thy compassion towards him in his fallen state, that thou abasedst thyself to become not only of the rank of men, but a true man, and the least of men, taking upon thee the form of a servant, that thou mightest set me at liberty, and that by means of thy grace, wisdom, and righteousness, man might obtain more than he had lost by his ignorance and pride...Wast thou not chastised for the iniquity of others? Has not thy blood sufficient virtue to wash out the sins of all the human race? Are not thy treasures more able to enrich me than all the debt of Adam to impoverish me? Lord, although I had been the only person alive, or the only sinner in the world, thou wouldst not have failed to die for me. O my Saviour,

[2] Mayor.

I would say, and say it with truth, that I individually stand in need of those blessings which thou hast given to all. What though the guilt of all had been mine? Thy death is all mine. Even though I had committed all the sins of all, yet would I continue to trust thee, and to assure myself that thy sacrifice and pardon is all mine, though it belong to all."

So far he read in silence, then the tract fell from his hand, and an involuntary exclamation broke from his lips—"Passing strange!"

De Seso paused, pen in hand, and looked up surprised. "What find you 'passing strange,' señor?" he asked.

"That he—that Fray Constantino should have felt precisely what—what he describes here."

"That such a holy man should feel so deeply his own utter sinfulness? But you are doubtless aware that the holiest saints in all ages have shared this experience. St. Augustine, for instance, with whose writings so ripe a theological scholar is doubtless well acquainted."

"Such," returned Carlos, "are not worse than others; but they know what they are as others do not."

"True. Tried by the standard of God's perfect law, the purest life must appear a miserable failure. We may call the marble of our churches and dwellings white, until we see God's snow, pure and fresh from heaven, upon it."

"Ay, señor," said Carlos, with joyful eagerness; "but the Hand that points out the stains can cleanse them. No snow is half so pure as the linen clean and white which is the righteousness of saints."

It was De Seso's turn to be astonished now. In the look that, half leaning over the table, he bent upon the eager face of Carlos, surprise and emotion blended. For a moment their eyes met with a flash, like that which flint strikes from steel, of mutual intelligence and sympathy. But it passed again as quickly. De Seso said, "I suspect that I see in you, Señor Don Carlos, one of those admirable scholars who have devoted their talents to the study of that sacred language in which the words of the holy apostles are handed down to us. You are a Grecian?"

Carlos shook his head. "Greek is but little studied at Complutum now," he said, "and I confined myself to the usual theological course."

"In which, I have heard, your success has been brilliant. But it is a sore disgrace to us, and a heavy loss to the youth of our nation, that the language of St. John and St. Paul should be deemed unworthy of their attention."

"Your Excellency is aware that it was otherwise in former years," returned Carlos. "Perhaps the present neglect is owing to the suspicion of heresy which, truly or falsely, has attached itself to most of the accomplished Greek scholars of our time."

"A miserable misapprehension; the growth of monkish ignorance and envy, and popular superstition. Heresy is a convenient stigma with which men ofttimes brand as evil the good they are incapable of comprehending."

"Most true, señor. Even Fray Constantino has not escaped."

"His crime has been, that he has sought to turn the minds of men from outward acts and ceremonies to the great spiritual truths of which these are the symbols. To the vulgar, Religion is nothing but a series of shows and postures."

"Yes," answered Carlos; "but the heart that loves God and truly believes in our Lord and Saviour, is taught to put such in their proper place. These ought ye to have done, and not to leave the other undone.'"

"Señor Don Carlos," said De Seso, with surprise he could no longer suppress, "you are evidently a devout and earnest student of the Scriptures."

"I search the Scriptures; in them I think I have eternal life. And they testify of Christ,"[3] promptly responded the less cautious youth.

"I perceive that you do not quote the Vulgate."

Carlos smiled. "No, señor. To a man of your enlightened views I am not afraid to acknowledge the truth. I have seen—nay, why should I hesitate?—I possess a rare treasure—the New Testament

[3] Referring to John 5:39.

of our Lord and Saviour Jesus Christ in our own noble Castilian tongue."

Even through the calm and dignified deportment of his companion Carlos could perceive the thrill that this communication caused. There was a pause; then he said softly, "And your treasure is also mine." The low quiet words came from even greater depths of feeling than the eager tremulous tones of Carlos. For *his* convictions, slowly reached and dearly purchased, were "built below" the region of the soul that passions agitate,—

> "Based on the crystalline sea
> Of thought and its eternity."

The heart of Carlos glowed with sudden ardent love towards the man who shared his treasure, and, he doubted not, his faith also. He could joyfully have embraced him on the spot. But the force of habit and the sensitive reserve of his character checked this impetuous demonstrativeness. He only said, with a look that was worth an embrace, "I knew it. Your Excellency spoke as one who held our Lord and his truth in honour."

"Ella es pues honor a vosotros que creeis."[4]

It would have been hard to begin a verse that Carlos could not at this time have instantly completed. He went on: *"Mas para los que no creen, la piedra que los edificatores reprobaron."*[5]

"A sorrowful truth," said De Seso, "which my young friend must needs bear in mind. His Word, like himself, is rejected by the many. Its very mention may expose to obloquy[6] and danger."

"Only another instance, señor, of those lamentable prejudices about heresy about which we spoke anon. I am aware that there are those that would brand me (*me*, a scholar too!) with the odious name of heretic, merely for reading God's Word in my own tongue. But how utterly absurd the charge! The blessed Book has but confirmed my faith in all the doctrines of our holy Mother Church."

---

[4] Unto you who believe he is precious or an honour.
[5] But unto those that believe not, the stone that the builders reject.
[6] A state of disgrace brought about by being defamed.

"Has it?" said De Seso, quietly, perhaps a little dryly.

"Most assuredly, señor," Carlos rejoined, with warmth. "In fact I never understood, or, I may say, truly believed those holy verities until now. Beginning with the Credo itself, and the orthodox Catholic faith in our Lord's divinity and atonement."

Here their conversation was interrupted by the entrance of the attendants, who removed supper, replenished the lamp, and heaped fresh chestnut logs on the fire. But as soon as the room was cleared they returned eagerly to subjects so interesting to both.

"Our salvation rests," said De Seso, "upon the great cardinal truths you have named. By the faith which receives into your heart the atonement of Christ as a work done for you, you are justified."

"I am forgiven, and I shall be justified."

"Pardon me, señor; Scripture teaches that your justification is already complete. Therefore, *being justified by faith*, we have peace with God."[7]

"But that cannot surely be the apostle's meaning," said Carlos. "Ay de mi! I know too well that I am not yet completely justified. Far from it; evil thoughts throng my heart; and not with heart alone, but with lips, eyes, hands, I transgress daily."

"Yet, you see, peace can only be consequent on justification. And peace you have."

Carlos looked perplexed. Misled by the teaching of his Church, he confused justification with sanctification; consequently he could not legitimately enjoy the peace that ought to flow from the one as a complete and finished work, because the other necessarily remained imperfect.

De Seso explained that the word justify is never used in Scripture in its derivative sense, to *make* righteous; but always in its common and universally accepted sense, to *account* or *declare* righteous. Quite easily and naturally he glided into the teacher's place, whilst Carlos gladly took that of the learner; not, indeed, without astonishment at the layman's skill in divinity, but with too

---

[7] Romans 5:1

intense an interest in what he said to waste much thought upon his manner of saying it.

Hitherto he had been like an unlearned man, who, without guide or companion, explores the trackless shores of a newly-discovered land. Should such an one meet in his course a scientific explorer, who has mapped and named every mountain, rock, and bay, who has traced out the coast-line, and can tell what lies beyond the white hills in the distance, it is easy to understand the eagerness with which he would listen to his narrative, and the intentness with which he would bend over the chart in which the scene of his own journeyings lies portrayed.

Thus De Seso not only taught Carlos the true meaning of Scripture terms, and the connection of Scripture truths with each other; he also made clear to him the facts of his own experience, and gave names to them for him.

"I think I understand now," said Carlos after a lengthened conversation, in which, moving from point to point, he had suggested many doubts and not a few objections, and these in turn had been taken up and answered by his friend. "God be thanked, there is no more condemnation, no more punishment for us. Nothing, either in act or suffering, can be added to the work of Christ, which is complete."

"Ay, now you have grasped the truth which is the source of our joy and strength."

"It must then be our sanctification which suffering promotes, both in this life and in purgatory."

"All God's dealings with us in this life are meant to promote our sanctification. Joy may do it, by his grace, as well as sorrow. It is written, not alone, 'He humbled thee and suffered thee to hunger,'[8] but also, 'He fed thee with manna, to teach the secret of life in him, from him, and by him.'"

"But suffering is purifying—like fire."

"Not in itself. Criminals released from the galleys usually come forth hardened in their crimes by the lash and the oar."

[8] Deuteronomy 8:3

Having said this, De Seso rose and extinguished the expiring lamp, while Carlos remained thoughtfully gazing into the fire. "Señor," he said, after a long pause, during which the stream of thought ran continuously underground, to reappear consequently in an unexpected place—"Señor, do you think God's Word, which solves so many mysteries, can answer every question for us?"

"Scarcely. Some questions we may ask, of which the answers, in our present state, would be beyond our comprehension. And others may indeed be answered there, but we may miss the answers, because through weakness of faith we are not yet able to receive them."

"For instance?"

"I had rather not name an instance—at present," said De Seso, and Carlos thought his face had a sorrowful look as he gazed at it in the firelight.

"I would not willingly miss anything my Lord meant to teach. I desire to know all his will, and to follow it," Carlos rejoined earnestly.

"It may be that you know not what you desire. Still, name any question you wish; and I will tell you freely whether in my judgment God's Word contains an answer." Carlos stated the difficulty suggested by the inquiry of Dolores. Who can tell the exact moment when his bark leaves the gently flowing river for the great deep ocean? That of Carlos, on the instant when he put this question, was met by the first wave of the mighty sea upon which he was to be tossed by many a storm. But he did not know it.

"I agree with you as to the silence of God's Word about purgatory," returned his friend; and for some time both gazed into the fire without speaking.

"This and similar discoveries have sometimes given me, I own, a feeling of blank disappointment, and even of terror," said Carlos at length. For with him it was one of those rare hours in which a man can bear to translate into words the "dark misgivings "of the soul, usually unacknowledged even to himself.

"I cannot say," was the answer, "that the thought of passing through the gate of death into the immediate presence of my glorified Lord affects me with 'blank disappointment' or 'terror.'"

"How I—What do you say?" cried Carlos, starting visibly.

"'Absent from the body, present with the Lord.'[9] 'To depart and to be with Christ is far better.'"[10]

"But it was San Pablo, the great apostle and martyr, who said that. For us,—we have the Church's teaching," Carlos rejoined in quick, anxious tones.

"Nevertheless, I venture to think that, in the face of all you have learned from God's Word, you will find it a task somewhat of the hardest to prove purgatory."

"Not at all," said Carlos; and immediately he bounded into the arena of controversy, laid his lance in rest, and began an animated tilting-match with his new friend, who was willing (of course, thought Carlos, for argument's sake alone, and as an intellectual exercise) to personate a Lutheran antagonist.

But not a few doughty champions have met the stern reality of a bloody death in the mimic warfare of the tilting-field. At every turn Carlos found himself answered, baffled, confounded. Yet, how could he, how dared he, acknowledge defeat, even to himself, when with the imperilled doctrine so much else must fall? What would become of private masses, indulgences, prayers for the dead? Nay, what would become of the infallibility of Mother Church herself?

So he fought desperately. Fear, ever increasing, quickened his preceptions,[11] baptised his lips with eloquence, made his sense acute and his memory retentive. Driven at last from the ground of Scripture and reason, he took his stand upon that of scholastic divinity. Using the weapons with which he had been taught to play so deftly for once in terrible earnest, he spun clever syllogisms, in which he hoped to entangle his adversary. But De Seso caught the flimsy webs in the naked hand of his strong sense, and crushed them to atoms.

[9] II Corinthians 5:8
[10] Referring to Philippians 1:23.
[11] A rule, instruction, or principle that guides someone's actions, especially moral behavior; precept.

Then Carlos knew that the battle was lost. "I can say no more," he acknowledged, sorrowfully bowing his head.

"And what I have said—is it not in accordance with the Word of God?"

With a cry of dismay on his lips, Carlos turned and looked at him—"God help us! Are we then Lutherans?"

"It may be Christ is asking another question—Are we amongst those who follow him *whithersoever* he goeth?"

"Oh, not *there*—not to *that*!" cried Carlos, rising in his agitation and beginning to pace the room. "I abhor heresy—I eschew the thought. From my cradle I have done so. Anywhere but that!"

Pausing at last in his walk before the place where De Seso sat, he asked, "And, you, señor, have you considered whither this would lead?"

"I have. I do not ask thee to follow. But this I say: if Christ bids any man leave the ship and come to him upon these dark and stormy waters, he will stretch out his own right hand to uphold and sustain him."

"To leave the ship—his Church? That would be leaving him. And leaving him, I am lost, soul and body—lost—lost!"

"Fear not. At his feet, clinging to him, soul of man was never lost yet."

"I will cleave to him, and to the Church too."

"Still, if one must be forsaken, let not that one be Christ."

"Never, *never*!" After a pause he added, as if speaking to himself, "Lord, to whom shall we go? Thou hast the words of eternal life."

He stood motionless, wrapt in thought; while De Seso rose softly, and going to the window, put aside the rude shutter that had been fastened across it.

"The night is bright," said Carlos dreamily. "The moon must have risen."

"That is daylight you see," returned his companion with a smile. "Time for wayfarers to seek rest in sleep."

"Prayer is better than sleep."

"True, and we who own the same precious faith can well unite in prayer."

With the willing consent of Carlos, his new friend laid their common desires and perplexities before God. The prayer was in itself a revelation to him; he forgot even to wonder that it came from the lips of a layman. For De Seso spoke as one accustomed to converse with the Unseen, and to enter by faith to the inner sanctuary, the very presence of God himself. And Carlos found that it was good thus to draw nigh to God. He felt his troubled soul returning to its rest, to its quiet confidence in Him who, he knew, would guide him by his counsel, and afterwards receive him into glory.

When they rose, instinctively their right hands sought each other, and were locked in that strong grasp which is sometimes worth more than an embrace.

"We have confidence each in the other," said De Seso, so that we need exchange no pledge of faithfulness or secrecy."

Carlos bowed his head. "Pray for me, señor," he said. "Pray that God, who sent you here to teach me, may in his own time complete the work he has begun."

Then both lay down in their cloaks; one to sleep, the other to ponder and pray.

In the morning each went his several way. And never was it given to Carlos, in this world, to look upon that face or to grasp that hand again.

He who had thus crossed his path, as it were for a moment, was perhaps the noblest of all the heroic band of Spanish martyrs, that forlorn hope of Christ's army, who fought and fell "where Satan's seat was." His high birth and lofty station, his distinguished abilities, even those more superficial graces of person and manner which are not without their strong fascination, were all—like the precious ointment with the odour of which the house was filled—consecrated to the service of the Lord for whom he lived and died.

The eye of imagination lingers with special and reverential love upon that grand calm figure. But our simple story leads us far away amongst other scenes and other characters. We must now turn to a different part of the wide missionary harvest-field, in which the lowly muleteer Juliano Hernandez, and the great noble Don Carlos de Seso, were both labouring. Was their labour in vain?

XIII.

Seville.

> "There is a multitude around,
> Responsive to my prayer;
> I hear the voice of my desire
> Resounding everywhere."
>
> A. L. Waring.

ON CARLOS felt surprised, on returning to Seville, to find the circle in which he had been wont to move exactly as he left it. His absence appeared to him a great deal longer than it really was. Moreover, there lurked in his mind an undefined idea that a period so fraught with momentous change to him could not have passed without change over the heads of others. But the worldly only seemed more worldly, the frivolous more frivolous, the vain more vain than ever.

Around the presence of Doña Beatriz there still hung a sweet dangerous fascination, against which he struggled, and, in the strength of his new and mighty principle of action, struggled successfully. Still, for the sake of his own peace, he longed to find some fair pretext for making his home elsewhere than beneath his uncle's roof.

One great pleasure awaited his return—a letter from Juan. It was the second he had received; the first having merely told of his brother's safe arrival at the headquarters of the royal army at Cambray. Don Juan had obtained his commission just in time for active service in the brief war between France and Spain that immediately followed the accession of Philip II. And now, though he said not much of his own exploits, it was evident that he had already begun to distinguish himself by the prompt and energetic courage which was a part of his character. Moreover, a signal piece of good fortune had fallen to his lot. The Spaniards were then engaged in the siege of St. Quentin. Before the works were quite completed, the French General—the celebrated Admiral Coligny—managed to throw himself into the town by a brilliant and desperate *coup-de-main*.[1] Many of his heroic band were killed or taken prisoners, however; and amongst the latter was a gentleman of rank and fortune, a member of the admiral's suite, who surrendered his sword into the hands of young Don Juan Alvarez.

Juan was delighted with his prize, as he well might be. Not only was the distinction an honourable one for so young a soldier; but the ransom he might hope to receive would serve very materially to smooth his pathway to the attainment of his dearest wishes.

Carlos was now able to share his brother's joy with unselfish sympathy. With a peculiar kind of pleasure, not quite unmixed with superstition, he recalled Juan's boyish words, more than once repeated, "When I go to the wars, I shall make some great prince or duke my prisoner." They had found a fair, if not exactly literal, fulfilment, and that so early in his career. And a belief that had grown up with him from childhood was strengthened thereby. Juan would surely accomplish everything upon which his heart was set. Certainly he would find his father—if that father should prove to be after all in the land of the living.

Carlos was warmly welcomed back by his relatives—at least by all of them save one. To a mild temper and amiable disposition he united the great advantage of rivalling no man, and interfering with no man's career. At the same time, he had a well-defined and honourable career of his own, in which he bid fair to be successful; so that he was not despised, but regarded as a credit to the family.

[1] An attack without warning.

The solitary exception to the favourable sentiments he inspired was found in the bitter disdain which Gonsalvo, with scarcely any attempt at disguise, exhibited towards him.

This was painful to him, both because he was sensitively alive to the opinions of others; and also because he actually preferred Gonsalvo, notwithstanding his great and glaring faults, to his more calculating and worldly-minded brothers. Force of any kind possesses a real fascination for an intellectual and sympathetic, but rather weak character; and this fascination grows in intensity when the weaker has a reason to pity and a desire to help the stronger.

It was not altogether grace, therefore, which checked the proud words that often rose to the lips of Carlos in answer to his cousin's sneers or sarcasms. He was not ignorant of the cause of Gonsalvo's contempt for him. It was Gonsalvo's creed that a man who deserved the name always got what he wanted, or died in the attempt; unless, of course, absolutely insuperable physical obstacles interfered, as they did in his own case. As he knew well enough what Carlos wanted before his departure from Seville, the fact of his quietly resigning the prize, without even an effort to secure it, was final with him.

One day, when Carlos had returned a forbearing answer to some taunt, Doña Inez, who was present, took occasion to apologise for her brother, as soon as he had quitted the room. Carlos liked Doña Inez much better than her still unmarried sister, because she was more generous and considerate to Beatriz. "You are very good, amigo mio," she said, "to show so great forbearance to my poor brother. And I cannot think wherefore he should treat you so uncourteously. But he is often rude to his brothers, sometimes even to his father."

"I fear it is because he suffers. Though rather less helpless than he was six months ago, he seems really more frail and sickly."

"Ay de mi, that is too true. And have you heard his last whim? He tells us he has given up physicians for ever. He has almost as ill an opinion of them as—forgive me, cousin—of priests."

"Could you not persuade him to consult your friend, Doctor Cristobal?"

"I have tried, but in vain. To speak the truth, cousin," she added, drawing nearer to Carlos, and lowering her voice, "there is another cause that has helped to make him what he is. No one knows or even guesses aught of it but myself; I was ever his favourite sister. If I tell you, will you promise the strictest secrecy?"

Carlos did so; wondering a little what his cousin would think could she surmise the weightier secrets which were burdening his own heart.

"You have heard of the marriage of Doña Juana de Xeres y Bohorques with Don Francisco de Vargas?"

"Yes; and I account Don Francisco a very fortunate man."

"Are you acquainted with the young lady's sister, Doña Maria de Bohorques?"

"I have met her. A fair, pale, queenly girl. She is not fond of gaiety, but very learned and very pious, as I have been told."

"You will scarce believe me, Don Carlos, when I tell you that pale, quiet girl is Gonsalvo's choice, his dream, his idol. How she contrived to gain that fierce, eager young heart, I know not—but hers it is, and hers alone. Of course, he had passing fancies before; but she was his first serious passion, and she will be his last."

Carlos smiled. "Red fire and white marble," he said. "But, after all, the fiercest fire could not feed on marble. It must die out, in time."

"From the first, Gonsalvo had not the shadow of a chance," Doña Inez replied, with an expressive flutter of her fan. "I have not the least idea whether the young lady even knows he loves her. But it matters not. We are Alvarez de Meñaya; still we could not expect a grandee of the first order to give his daughter to a younger son of our house. Even before that unlucky bull-feast. *Now*, of course, he himself would be the first to say, 'Pine-apple kernels are not for monkeys,' nor fair ladies for crippled caballeros. And yet—you understand?"

"I do," said Carlos; and in truth he *did* understand, far better than Doña Inez imagined.

She turned to leave the room, but turned back again to say kindly, "I trust, my cousin, your own health has not suffered from your residence among those bleak inhospitable mountains? Don Garcia tells me he has seen you twice, since your return, coming forth late in the evening from the dwelling of our good Señor Doctor."

There was a sufficient reason for these visits. Before they parted, De Seso had asked Carlos if he would like an introduction to a person in Seville who could give him further instruction upon the subjects they had discussed together. The offer having been thankfully accepted, he was furnished with a note addressed, much to his surprise, to the physician Losada; and the connection thus begun was already proving a priceless boon to Carlos.

But nature had not designed him for a keeper of secrets. The colour mounted rapidly to his cheek, as he answered,—

"I am flattered by my lady cousin's solicitude for me. But, I thank God, my health is as good as ever. In truth, Doctor Cristobal is a man of learning and a pleasant companion, and I enjoy an hour's conversation with him. Moreover, he has some rare and valuable books, which he is kind enough to lend me."

"He is certainly very well-bred, for a man of his station," said Doña Inez, condescendingly.

Carlos did not resume his attendance upon the lectures of Fray Constantino at the College of Doctrine; but when the voice of the eloquent preacher was heard in the cathedral, he was never absent. He had no difficulty *now* in recognising the truths that he loved so well, covered with a thin veil of conventional phraseology. All mention, not absolutely necessary, of dogmas peculiarly Romish was avoided, unless when the congregation were warned earnestly, though in terms well-studied and jealously guarded, against "risking their salvation" upon indulgences or ecclesiastical pardons. The vanity of trusting to their own works was shown also; and in every sermon Christ was faithfully held up before the sinner as the one all-sufficient Saviour.

Carlos listened always with rapt attention, usually with keen delight. Often would he look around him upon the sea of earnest upturned faces, saying within himself, "Many of these my brethren and sisters have found Christ—many more are seeking him," and at the thought his heart would thrill with thankfulness. But even at that moment some word from the preacher's lips might change his joy into a chill of apprehension. It frequently happened that Fray Constantino, borne onward by the torrent of his own eloquence, was betrayed into uttering some sentiment so very nearly heretical as to make his hearer tingle with the peculiar sense of pain that is caused by seeing one rush heedlessly to the verge of a precipice.

"I often thank God for the stupidity of evil men and the simplicity of good ones," Carlos said to his new friend Losada, after one of these dangerous discourses.

For by this time, what De Seso had first led him to suspect, had become a certainty with him. He knew himself a *heretic*—a terrible consciousness to sink into the heart of any man in those days, especially in Catholic Spain. Fortunately the revelation had come to him gradually; and still more gradually came the knowledge of all that it involved. Yet those were sorrowful hours in which he first felt himself cut off from every hallowed association of his childhood and youth; from the long chain of revered tradition, which was all he knew of the past; from the vast brotherhood of the Church visible—that mighty organisation, pervading all society, leavening all thought, controlling all custom, ruling everything in this world, even if not in the next. His own past life was shattered: the ambitions he had cherished were gone—the studies he had excelled and delighted in were proved for the most part worse than vain. It is true that he believed, even still, that he might accept priestly ordination from the hands of Rome (for the idolatry of the mass was amongst the things not yet revealed to him); but he could no longer hope for honour or preferment, or what men call a career, in the Church. Joy enough would it be if he were permitted, in some obscure corner of the land, to tell his countrymen of a Saviour's love; and perpetual watchfulness, extreme caution, and the most judicious management would be necessary to preserve him—as hitherto they had preserved Fray Constantino—from the grasp of the Holy Inquisition.

To us who read that word in the lurid light that martyr fires kindled after this period, it may seem strange that Carlos was not more a prey to fear of the perils entailed by his heresy. But so slowly did he pass out of the stage in which he believed himself still a sincere Catholic into that in which he shudderingly acknowledged that he was in very truth a Lutheran, that the shock of the discovery was wonderfully broken to him. Nor did he think the danger that menaced him either near or pressing, so long as he conducted himself with reserve and prudence.

It is true that this reserve involved a degree of secrecy, if not of dissimulation,[2] that was fast becoming very irksome. Formerly the kind of fencing, feinting, and doubling into which he was often forced, would rather have pleased him, as affording scope for the exercise of ingenuity. But his moral nature was growing so much more sensitive, that he began to recoil from slight departures from truth, in which heretofore he would only have seen a proper exercise of the advantage which a keen and quick intellect possesses over dull ones. Moreover, he longed to be able to speak freely to others of the things which he himself found so precious.

Though quite sufficiently afraid of pain and danger, the thought of disgrace was still more intolerable to him. Keener than any suffering he had yet known—except the pang of renouncing Beatriz—was the consciousness that all those amongst whom he lived, and who now respected and loved him, would, if they guessed the truth, turn away from him with unutterable scorn and loathing.

One day, when walking in the city with his aunt and Doña Sancha, they turned down a side-street to avoid meeting the death procession of a murderer on his way to the scaffold. The crime for which he suffered had been notorious; and with the voluble exclamations of horror and congratulations at getting safely out of the way to which the ladies gave expression, were mingled prayers for the soul of the miserable man. "If they knew all," thought Carlos, as the slight, closely veiled forms clung trustingly to him for protection, "they would think *me* worse, more degraded, than yon wretched being. They pity *him*, they pray for *him*; *me* they would only loathe and execrate. And Juan, my beloved, my honoured

[2] A disguise or hiding of one's true feelings, thoughts, or intentions.

brother—what will he think?" This last thought was the one that haunted him most frequently and troubled him most deeply.

But had he nothing to counterbalance these pangs of fear and shame, these manifold dark misgivings? He had much. First and best, he had the peace that passeth all understanding shed abroad in his heart. Its light did not grow pale and faint with time; on the other hand, it increased in brightness and steadiness, as new truths arose like stars upon his soul, every new truth being in itself "a new joy" to him.

Moreover, he found keen enjoyment in the communion of saints. Great was his surprise when, after sufficiently instructing him in private, and satisfactorily testing his sincerity, Losada cautiously revealed to him the existence of a regularly organised Lutheran Church in Seville, of which he himself was actually the pastor. He invited Carlos to attend its meetings, which were held, with due precaution, and usually after nightfall, in the house of a lady of rank—Doña Isabella de Baena.

Carlos readily accepted the perilous invitation, and with deep emotion took his place amongst the band of "called, chosen, and faithful" men and women, every one of whom, as he believed, shared the same joys and hopes that he did. They were not at all such a "little band" as he expected to find them. Nor were they, with very few exceptions, of the poor of this world. If that bright southern land, so rich in all that kindles the imagination, eventually to her own ruin rejected the truth of God, at least she offered upon his altar some of her choicest and fairest flowers. Many of those who met in Doña Isabella's upper room were "chief men" and "devout and honourable women." Talent, learning, excellence of every kind was largely represented there; so also was the *sangre azul*, the boast of the proud Spanish grandees.[3] One of the first faces that Carlos recognised was the sweet, thoughtful one of the young Doña Maria de Bohorques, whose precocious learning and accomplishments had often been praised in his hearing, and in whom he had now a new and peculiar interest.

There were two noblemen of the first order—Don Domingo de

[3] A high-ranking Spanish nobleman.

Guzman, son of the Duke of Medina Sidonia, and Don Juan Ponce de Leon, son of the Count of Baylen. Carlos had often heard of the munificent charities of the latter, who had actually embarrassed his estates by his unbounded liberality to the poor. But while Ponce de Leon was thus labouring to relieve the sorrows of others, a deep sadness brooded over his own spirit. He was wont to go forth by night, and pace up and down the great stone platform in the Prado San Sebastian, that bore the ghastly name of the Quemadero,[4] or *Burning-place*, while in his heart the shadow of death—the darkest shadow of the dreadest death—was struggling with the light of immortality.

Did the rest of that devoted band share the agony of apprehension that filled those lonely midnight hours with passionate prayer? Some amongst them did, no doubt. But with most, the circumstances and occupations of daily life wove, with their multitudinous slender threads, a veil dense enough to hide, or at least to soften, the perils of their situation. The Protestants of Seville contrived to pass their lives and to do their work side by side with other men; they moved amongst their fellow-citizens and were not recognised; they even married and were given in marriage; though all the time there fell upon their daily paths the shadow of the grim old fortress where the Holy Inquisition held its awful secret court.

But then, at this period the Holy Inquisition was by no means exhibiting its usual terrible activity. The Inquisitor-General, Fernando de Valdez, Archbishop of Seville, was an old man of seventy-four, relentless when roused, but not particularly enterprising. Moreover, he was chiefly occupied in amassing enormous wealth from his rich and numerous Church preferments.[5] Hitherto, the fires of St. Dominic had been kindled for Jews and Moors; only one Protestant had suffered death in Spain, and Valladolid, not Seville, had been the scene of his martyrdom. Seville, indeed, had witnessed two notable prosecutions for Lutheranism—that of

[4] Place of execution built by the first inquisitors at Seville in 1481; it was decorated with four large statues representing prophets.
[5] An office, appointment, or position of high rank, especially one that brings social advancement or financial reward.

Rodrigo de Valer and that of Juan Gil, commonly called Dr. Egidius. But Valer had been only sent to a monastery to die, while, by a disgraceful artifice, retractation had been obtained from Egidius.

During the years that had passed since then, the Holy Office had appeared to slumber. Victims who refused to eat pork, or kept Sabbath on Saturday, were growing scarce for obvious reasons. And not yet had the wild beast "exceeding dreadful; whose teeth were of iron and his nails of brass,"[6] begun to devour a nobler prey. Did the monster, gorged with human blood, really slumber in his den; or did he only assume the attitude and appearance of slumber, as some wild beasts are said to do, to lure his unwary victims within the reach of his terrible crouch and spring?

No one can certainly tell; but however it may have been, we doubt not the Master used the breathing-time thus afforded his Church to prepare and polish many a precious gem, destined to shine through all ages in his crown of glory.

[6] Possibly referring to Daniel 7:19.

XIV.

The Monks of San Isodro.

"The earnest of eternal joy
In every prayer I trace;
I see the likeness of the Lord
In every patient face.
How oft, in still communion known,
Those spirits have been sent
To share the travail of my soul,
Or show me what it meant."

A. L. WARING.

T is amongst the perplexing conditions of our earthly life, that we cannot first reflect, then act; first form our opinions, then, and not till then, begin to carry them out into practise. Thought and action have usually to run beside each other in parallel lines; a terrible necessity, and never more terrible than during the progress of momentous inward changes.

A man becomes convinced that the star by which he has hitherto been steering is not the true pole-star, and that if he perseveres in his present course his barque[1] will inevitably be lost. At his peril, he must find out the one unerring guide; yet, while he seeks

[1] A sailing ship with three or more masts.

it, his hand must not for an instant quit his hold on the helm, for the winds of circumstance fill his sails, and he cannot choose whether he will go, he can only choose where. This lies at the root of much of the apparent inconsistency which has often been made a reproach to reformers.

Though Carlos did not feel this difficulty as keenly as some of his brethren in the faith, he yet felt it. His uncle was continually pressing him to take Orders, and to seek for this or that tempting preferment; whilst every day he had stronger doubts as to the possibility of his accepting any preferment in the Church, and was even beginning to entertain scruples about taking Orders at all.

During this period of deliberation and uncertainty, one of his new friends, Fray Cassiodoro, an eloquent Jeromite friar who assisted Losada in his ministrations, said to him, "If you intend embracing a religious life, Señor Don Carlos, you will find the white tunic and brown mantle of St. Jerome[2] more to your taste than any other habit."

Carlos pondered the hint; and shortly afterwards announced to his relatives that he intended to "go into retreat" for a season, at the Jeromite Convent of San Isodro del Campo, which was about two miles from Seville.

His uncle approved this resolution; and none the less, because he thought it was probably intended as a preparation for taking the cowl.[3] "After all, nephew, it may turn out that you have the longest head amongst us," he said. "In the race for wealth and honours, no man can doubt that the Regulars beat the Seculars now-a-days.[4] And there is not a saint in all the Spains so popular as St. Jerome. You know the proverb,—

'He who is a count, and to be a duke aspires,
Let him straight to Guadaloupe, and sing among the friars.'"

[2] Jerome's great work was the translation of the Bible into Latin, the edition known as the Vulgate.
[3] A monk's hooded cloak.
[4] In the eleventh century, it was natural to call those who added religious poverty to their common life Regulars, and those who gave up the common life, Seculars.

Gonsalvo, who was present, here looked up from his book and observed sharply, "No man will ever be a duke who changes his mind three times within three months."

"But I only changed my mind once," returned Carlos.

"You have never changed it at all, that I wot of," said Don Manuel. "And I would that thine were turned in the same profitable direction, son Gonsalvo."

"Oh yes! By all means. Offer the blind and the lame in sacrifice. Put heaven off with the wreck of a man that the world will not condescend to take into her service."

"Hold thy peace, son born to cross me!" said the father, losing his temper at by no means the worst of the many provocations he had recently received. "Is it not enough to look at thee lying there a useless log, and to suffer thy vile temper; but thou must set thyself against me, when I point out to thee the only path in which a cripple such as thou could earn green figs to eat with his bread, not to speak of supporting the rank of Alvarez de Meñaya as he ought."

Here Carlos, out of consideration for the feelings of Gonsalvo, left the room; but the angry altercation between the father and son lasted long after his departure.

The next day Don Carlos rode out, by a lonely path amidst the grey ruins of old Italica, to the stately castellated[5] convent of San Isodro. Amidst all his new interests, the young Castilian noble still remembered with due enthusiasm how the building had been reared, more than two hundred years ago, by the devotion of the heroic Alonzo Guzman the Good, who gave up his own son to death, under the walls of Tarifa, rather than surrender the city to the Moors.

Before he left Seville, he placed a copy of Fray Constantino's "Sum of Christian Doctrine" between two volumes of Gonsalvo's favourite "Lope de Vega." He had previously introduced to the notice of the ladies several of the Fray's little treatises, which contained a large amount of Scripture truth, so cautiously expressed

[5] With a serrated top edge like the walls of a castle.

as to have not only escaped the censure, but actually obtained the express approbation of the Holy Office. He had also induced them occasionally to accompany him to the preachings at the Cathedral. Further than this he dared not go; nor did he on other accounts think it advisable, as yet, to permit himself much communication with Doña Beatriz.

The monks of San Isodro welcomed him with that strong, peculiar love which springs up between the disciples of the same Lord, more especially when they are a little flock surrounded by enemies. They knew that he was already one of the initiated, a regular member of Losada's congregation. Both this fact, and the warm recommendations of Fray Cassiodoro, led them to trust him implicitly; and very quickly they made him a sharer in their secrets, their difficulties, and their perplexities.

To his astonishment, he found himself in the midst of a community, Protestant in heart almost to a man, and as far as possible acting out their convictions; while at the same time they retained (how could they discard them?) the outward ceremonies of their Church and their Order.

He soon fraternised with a gentle, pious young monk named Fray Fernando, and asked him to explain this extraordinary state of things.

"I am but just out of my novitiate, having been here little more than a year," said the young man, who was about his own age; "and already, when I came, the fathers carefully instructed the novices out of the Scriptures, exhorting us to lay no stress upon outward ceremonies, penances, crosses, holy water, and the like. But I have often heard them speak of the manner in which they were led to adopt these views."

"Who was their teacher? Fray Cassiodoro?"

"Latterly; not at first. It was Dr. Blanco who sowed the first seed of truth here."

"Whom do you mean? We in the city give the name of Dr. Blanco (the white doctor), from his silver hairs, to a man of your holy order, certainly, but one most zealous for the old faith. He is a friend and confidant of the Inquisitors, if indeed he is not himself a Qualificator of Heresy:[6] I speak of Dr. Garçias Arias."

"The same man. You are astonished, señor; nevertheless it is true. The elder brethren say that when he came to the convent all were sunk in ignorance and superstition. The monks cared for nothing but vain repetitions of unfelt prayers, and showy mummeries of idle ceremonial. But the white doctor told them all these would avail them nothing, unless their hearts were given to God, and they worshipped him in spirit and in truth. They listened, were convinced, began to study the Holy Scriptures as he recommended them, and truly to seek Him who is revealed therein."

"'Out of the eater came forth meat,'"[7] said Carlos. "I am truly amazed to hear of such teaching from the lips of Garçias Arias."

"Not more amazed than the brethren were by his after conduct," returned Fray Fernando. "Just when they had received the truth with joy, and were beginning heartily to follow it, their teacher suddenly changed his tone, and addressed himself diligently to the task of building up the things that he once destroyed. When Lent came round, the burden of his preaching was nothing but penance and mortification of the flesh. No less would content him than that the poor brethren should sleep on the bare ground, or standing; and wear sackcloth and iron girdles. They could not tell what to make of these bewildering instructions. Some followed them, others clung to the simpler faith they had learned to love, many tried to unite both. In fact, the convent was filled with confusion, and several of the brethren were driven half distracted. But at last God put it into their hearts to consult Dr. Egidius. Your Excellency is well acquainted with his history, doubtless?"

"Not so well as I should like to be. Still, for the present; let us keep to the brethren. Did Dr. Egidius confirm their faith?"

"That he did, señor; and in many ways he led them into a further acquaintance with the truth."

"And that enigma, Dr. Blanco?"

---

[6] One of the learned men who were appointed to assist the Inquisitors, and whose duty it was to decide whether doubtful propositions were, or were not, heretical.

[7] Judges 14:14

Fray Fernando shook his head. "Whether his mind was really changed, or whether he concealed his true opinions through fear, or through love of the present world, I know not. I should not judge him."

"No," said Carlos, softly. "It is not for us, who have never been tried, to judge those who have failed in the day of trial. But it must be a terrible thing to fail, Fray Fernando."

"As good Dr. Egidius did himself. Ah, señor, if you had but seen him when he came forth from his prison! His head was bowed, his hair was white; they who spoke with him say his heart was well-nigh broken. Still he was comforted, and thanked God, when he saw the progress the truth had made during his imprisonment, both in Valladolid and in Seville, especially amongst the brethren here. His visit was of great use to us. But the most precious boon we ever received was a supply of God's Word in our own tongue, which was brought to us some months ago."

Carlos looked at him eagerly. "I think I know whose hand brought it," he said.

"You cannot fail to know, señor. You have doubtless heard of Juliano El Chico?"

The colour rose to the cheek of Carlos as he answered. "I shall thank God all my life, and beyond it, that I have not heard of him alone, but met him. He it was who put this book into my hand," and he drew out his own Testament.

"We also have good cause to thank him. And we mean that others shall have it through us. For the books he brought we not only use ourselves; but diligently circulate far and wide, according to our ability."

"It is strange to know so little of a man, and yet to owe him so much. Can you tell me anything more than the name, Juliano Hernandez, which I repeat every day when I ask God in my prayers to bless and reward him?"

"I only know he is a poor, unlearned man, a native of Villaverda, in Campos. He went to Germany, and entered the service of Juan Peres, who, as you are aware, translated the Testament, and printed it, Juliano aiding in the work as compositor. He then undertook, of his own free will, the task of bringing a supply into this country; you well know how perilous a task, both the sea-ports and the passes of the Pyrenees being so closely watched by the emissaries of the Holy Office. Juliano chose the overland journey, since, knowing the mountains well, he thought he could manage to make his way unchallenged by some of their hazardous, unfrequented paths. God be thanked, he arrived in safety with his precious freight early last summer."

"Do you know where he is now?"

"No. Doubtless he is wandering somewhere, perhaps not far distant, carrying on, in darkness and silence, his noble missionary work."

"What would I give—rather, what would I not give—to see him once more, to take his hand in mine, and to thank him for what he has done for me!"

"Ah, there is the vesper bell. You know, señor, that Fray Cristobal is to lecture this evening on the Epistle to the Hebrews. That is why I love Tuesday best of all days in the week."

Fray Cristobal D'Arellano was a monk of San Isodro, remarkable for his great learning, which was consecrated to the task of explaining and spreading the Reformed doctrines. Carlos put himself under the tuition of this man, to perfect his knowledge of Greek, a language of which he had learned very little, and that little very imperfectly, at Alcala. He profited exceedingly by the teaching he received, and partially repaid the obligation by instructing the novices in Latin, a task which was very congenial to him, and which he performed with much success.

XV.

The Great Sanbenito.

"The thousands that, uncheered by praise,
Have made one offering of their days;
For Truth's, for Heaven's, for Freedom's sake,
Resigned the bitter cup to take."

HEMANS.

OUNG as was the Protestant Church in Seville, she already had her history. There was one name that Carlos had heard mentioned in connection with her first origin, round which there gathered in his thoughts a peculiar interest, or rather fascination. He knew now that the monks of San Isodro had been largely indebted to the instructions of Doctor Juan Gil, or Egidius. And he had been told previously that Egidius himself had learned the truth from an earlier and bolder witness, Rodrigo de Valer. This was the name that Losada once coupled in his hearing with that of his own father.

Why then had he not sought information, which might have proved so deeply interesting to him, directly from Losada himself, his friend and teacher? Several causes contributed to his reluctance to broach the subject. But by far the greatest was a kind of chivalrous, half romantic tenderness for that absent brother, whom he could now truly say that he loved best on earth. It is very difficult for us to put ourselves in the position of Spaniards of the sixteenth century, so far as at all to understand the way in which they were accustomed to look upon heresy. In their eyes it was not only a crime, infinitely more dreadful than that of murder; it was also a horrible disgrace, branding a man's whole lineage up and down for generations, and extending its baleful influence to his remotest kindred. Carlos asked himself, day by day, how would the high-hearted Don Juan Alvarez, whose idol was glory, and his dearest pride a noble and venerated name, endure to hear that his beloved and only brother was stained with that surpassing infamy? But at least it would be anguish enough to stab Juan once, as it were, with his own hand, without arming the dead hand of the father whose memory they both revered, and then driving home the weapon into his brother's heart. Rather would he let the matter remain in obscurity, even if (which was extremely doubtful) he could by any effort of his own shed a ray of light upon it.

Still he took occasion one day to inquire of his friend Fray Fernando, who had received full information on these subjects from the older monks, "Was not that Rodrigo de Valer, whose sanbenito hangs in the Cathedral, the first teacher of the pure faith in Seville?"

"True, señor, he taught many. While he himself, as I have heard, received the faith from none save God only."

"He must have been a remarkable man. Tell me all you know of him."

"Our Fray Cassiodoro has often heard Dr. Egidius speak of him; so that, though his lips were silenced long before your time or mine, señor, he seems still one of our company."

"Yes, already some of our number have joined the Church triumphant, but they are still one with us in Christ."

"Don Rodrigo de Valer," continued the young monk, "was of a noble family, and very wealthy. He was born at Lebrixa, but came to reside in Seville, a gay, light-hearted, brilliant young caballero, who was soon a leader in all the folly and fashion of the great city. But suddenly these things lost their charm for him. Much to the astonishment of the gay world, to which he had been such an ornament, he disappeared from the scenes of amusement and festivity he had been wont to love. His companions could not understand the change that came over him—but *we* can understand it well. God's arrows of conviction were sharp in his heart. And he led him to turn for comfort, not to penance and self-mortification, but to his own Word. Only in one form was that Word accessible to him. He gathered up the fragments of his old school studies—little cared for at the time, and well-nigh forgotten afterwards—to enable him to read the Vulgate. There he found justification by faith, and, through it, peace to his troubled conscience. But he did not find, as I need scarcely say to you, Don Carlos, purgatory, the worship of Our Lady and the saints, and certain other things our fathers taught us."

"How long since was all this?" asked Carlos, who was listening with much interest, and at the same time comparing the narrative with that other story he had heard from Dolores.

"Long enough, señor. Twenty years ago or more. When God had thus enlightened him, he returned to the world. But he returned to it a new man, determined henceforth to know nothing save Christ and him crucified. He addressed himself in the first instance to the priests and monks, whom, with a boldness truly amazing, he accosted wherever he met them, were it even in the most public places of the city, proving to them from Scripture that their doctrines were not the truth of God."

"It was no hopeful soil in which to sow the Word."

"No, truly; but it seemed laid upon him as a burden from God to speak what he felt and knew, whether men would hear or whether they would forbear. He very soon aroused the bitter enmity of those who hate the light because their deeds are evil. Had he been a poor man, he would have been burned at the stake, as that brave, honest-hearted young convert, Francisco de San Romano, was burned at Valladolid not so long ago, saying to those who offered him mercy at the last, 'Did you envy me my happiness?' But Don Rodrigo's rank and connections saved him from that fate. I have heard, too, that there were those in high places who shared, or at least favoured his opinions in secret. Such interceded for him."

"Then his words were received by some?" Carlos asked anxiously. "Have you ever heard the names of any of those who were his friends or patrons?"

Fray Fernando shook his head. "Even amongst ourselves, señor," he said, "names are not mentioned oftener than is needful. For 'a bird of the air will carry the matter;' and when life depends on our silence, it is no wonder if at last we become a trifle over-silent. In the lapse of years, some names that ought to be remembered amongst us may well chance to be forgotten, from this dread of breathing them, even in a whisper. Always excepting Dr. Egidius, Don Rodrigo's friends or converts are unknown to me. But I was about to say, the Inquisitors were prevailed upon, by those who interceded for him, to regard him as insane. They dismissed him, therefore, with no more severe penalty than the loss of his property, and with many cautions as to his future behaviour."

"I hold it scarce likely that he observed them."

"Very far otherwise, señor. For a short time, indeed, his friends prevailed on him to express his sentiments more privately; and Fray Cassiodoro says that during this interval he confirmed them in the faith by expounding the Epistle to the Romans. But he could not long hide the light he held. To all remonstrances he answered, that he was a soldier sent on a forlorn hope, and must needs press forward to the breach. If he fell, it mattered not; in his place God would raise up others, whose would be the glory and the joy of victory. So, once again, the Holy Office laid its grasp upon him. It was resolved that his voice should be heard no more on earth; and he was therefore consigned to the living death of perpetual imprisonment. And yet, in spite of all their care and all their malice, one more testimony for God and his truth was heard from his lips."

"How was that?"

"They led him, robed in that great sanbenito you have often seen, to the Church of San Salvador, to sit and listen, with the other weeping penitents, while some ignorant priest denounced their heresies and blasphemies. But he was not afraid after the sermon to stand up in his place, and warn the people against the preacher's erroneous doctrine, showing them where and how it differed from the Word of God. It is marvellous they did not burn him; but God restrained the remainder of their wrath. They sent him at last to the monastery of San Lucar, where he remained in solitary confinement until his death."

Carlos mused a little. Then he said, "What a blessed change, from solitary confinement to the company of just men made perfect; from the gloom of a convent prison to the glory of God's house, eternal in the heavens!"

"Some of the elder brethren say *we* may be called upon to pass through trials even more severe," remarked Fray Fernando. "I know not. Being amongst the youngest here, I should speak my mind with humility; still I cannot help looking around me, and seeing that everywhere men are receiving the Word of God with joy. Think of the learned and noble men and women in the city who have joined our band already, and are eager to gain others! New converts are won for us every day; not to speak of that great multitude among Fray Constantino's hearers who are really on our side, without dreaming it themselves. Moreover, your noble friend, Don Carlos de Seso, told us last summer that the signs in the north are equally encouraging. He thinks the Lutherans of Valladolid are more numerous than those of Seville. In Toro and Logrono also the light is spreading rapidly. And throughout the districts near the Pyrenees the Word has free course, thanks to the Huguenot traders from Beam."

"I have heard these things in Seville, and truly my heart rejoices at them. But yet—" here Carlos broke off suddenly, and remained silent, gazing mournfully into the fire, near which, as it was now winter, they had seated themselves.

At last Fray Fernando asked, "What do *you* think, señor?"

Carlos raised his dark blue eyes and fixed them on the questioner's face.

"Of the future," he said slowly, "I think—*nothing*. I dare not think of it. It is in God's hand, and he thinks for us. Still, one thing I cannot choose but see. Where we are we cannot remain. We are bound to a great wheel that is turning—turning—and turn with it, even in spite of ourselves, we must and do. But it is the wheel, not of chance, but of God's mighty purposes; that is all our comfort."

"And those purposes, are they not mercy and truth unto our beloved land?"

"They may be; but I know not. They are not revealed. 'Mercy and truth unto such as keep his covenant,'[1] that indeed is written."

"We are they that keep his covenant."

Carlos sighed, and resumed the thread of his own thought,—

"The wheel turns round, and we with it. Even since I came here it has turned perceptibly. And how it is to turn one step further without bringing us into contact with the solid frame of things as they are, and so crushing us, truly I see not. I see not; but I trust God."

"You allude to these discussions about the sacrifice of the mass now going on so continually amongst us?"

"I do. Hitherto we have been able to work underground; but if doubt must be thrown upon *that*, the thin shell of earth that has concealed and protected us, will break and fall in upon our heads. And then?"

"Already we are all asking, 'And then?'" said Fray Fernando. "There will be nothing before us but flight to some foreign land."

"And how is that to be accomplished? But God forgive me these words; and God keep me, and all of us, from the subtle snare of mixing with the question, 'What is his will?' that other question, 'What will be our fate if we try to do it?' As the noble De Seso said to me, all that matters to us is to be found amongst those who 'follow the Lamb whithersoever he goeth.' *But he went to Calvary.*"

The last words were spoken, in so low a tone that Fray Fernando heard them not.

"What did you say?" he asked.

---

[1] Referring to Psalm 25:10.

"No matter. Time enough to hear if God himself speaks it in our ears."

Their conversation was interrupted by the entrance of a lay brother, who informed Carlos that a visitor awaited him in the convent parlour. As it was one of the hours during which the rules of the house (which were quite liberal enough, without being lax) permitted the entertainment of visitors, Carlos went to receive his without much delay.

He knew that if the guest had been one of "their own," their loved brethren in the faith, even the attendant would have been well acquainted with his person, and would naturally have named him. He entered the room, therefore, with no very lively anticipations; expecting, at most, to see one of his cousins, who might have paid him the compliment of riding out from the city to visit him.

A tall, handsome, sunburnt man, who had his left arm in a sling, was standing with his back to the window. But in one moment more the other arm was flung round the neck of Carlos, and heart pressed to heart, the brothers stood together.

XVI.

Welcome Home.

> "We are so unlike each other,
> Thou and I, that none would guess
> We were children of one mother,
> But for mutual tenderness."
>
> E. B. BROWNING.

FTER the first tumult of greeting, in which affection was expressed rather by look and gesture than by word, the brothers sat down and talked. Eager questions rose to the lips of both, but especially to those of Carlos, whose surprise at Juan's unexpected appearance only equalled his delight.

"But you are wounded, my brother," he said. "Not seriously, I hope?"

"Oh no! Only a bullet through my arm. A piece of my usual good luck. I got it in The Battle."

No adjective was needed to specify the glorious day of St. Quentin, when Flemish Egmont's chivalrous courage, seconded by Castilian bravery, gained for King Philip such a brilliant victory over the arms of France. Carlos knew the story already from public sources. And it did not occur to Juan, nor indeed to Carlos either, that there had ever been, or would ever be again, a battle so worthy of being held in everlasting remembrance.

"But do you count the wound part of your good luck?" asked Carlos.

"Ay, truly, and well I may. It has brought me home; as you ought to have known ere this."

"I received but two letters from you—that written on your first arrival, and dated from Cambray; and that which told of your notable prize, the French prisoner."

"But I wrote two others: one, I entrusted to a soldier who was coming home invalided—I suppose the fellow lost it; the other (written just after the great St. Laurence's day) arrived in Seville the night before I made my own appearance there. His Majesty will need to look to his posts;[1] certes, they are the slowest carriers to be found in any Christian country." And Juan's merry laugh rang through the convent parlour, little enough used to echo such sounds.

"So I have heard almost nothing of you, brother; save what could be gathered from the public accounts," Carlos continued.

"All the better now. I have only such news as is pleasant for me to tell; and will not be ill, I think, for thee to hear. First, then, and in due order—I am promised my company!"

"Good news, indeed! My brother must have honoured our name by some special deed of valour. Was it at St. Quentin?" asked Carlos, looking at him with honest, brotherly pride. He was not much changed by his campaign, except that his dark cheek wore a deeper bronze, and his face was adorned with a formidable pair of *bigotes*.[2]

"That story must wait," returned Juan. "I have so much else to tell thee. Dost thou remember how I said, as a boy, that I should take a noble prisoner, like Alphonso Vives, and enrich myself by his ransom? And thou seest I have done it."

"In a good day! Still, he was not the Duke of Saxony."

"Like him, at least, in being a heretic, or Huguenot, if that be a

[1] A rider who covered the distance from one post to the next in a delivery system.
[2] Waxed and handlebar moustaches.

less unsavoury word to utter in these holy precincts. Moreover, he is a tried and trusted officer of Admiral Coligny's suite. It was that day when the admiral so gallantly threw himself into the besieged town. And, for my part, I am heartily obliged to him. But for his presence, there would have been no defence of St. Quentin, to speak of, at all; but for the defence, no battle; but for the battle, no grand victory for the Spains and King Philip. We cut off half of the admiral's troops, however, and it fell to my lot to save the life of a brave French officer whom I saw fighting alone amongst a crowd. He gave me his sword; and I led him to my tent, and provided him with all the solace and succour I could, for he was sorely wounded. He was the Sieur de Ramenais; a gentleman of Provence, and an honest, merry-hearted, valiant man, as it was ever my lot to meet withal. He shared my bed and board, a pleasant guest rather than a prisoner, until we took the town, making the admiral himself our captive, as you know already. By that time, his brother had raised the sum for his ransom, and sent it honourably to me. But, in any case, I should have dismissed him on parole, as soon as his wounds were healed. He was pleased to give me, beside the good gold pistoles, this diamond ring you see on my finger, in token of friendship."

Carlos took the costly trinket in his hand, and duly admired it. He did not fail to gather from Juan's simple narrative many things that he told not, and was little likely to tell. In the time of action, chivalrous daring; when the conflict was over, gentleness and generosity no less chivalrous, endearing him to all—even to the vanquished enemy. No wonder Carlos was proud of his brother! But beneath all the pride and joy there was, even already, a secret whisper of fear. How could he bear to see that noble brow clouded with anger—those bright confiding eyes averted from him in disdain? Turning from his own thoughts as if they had been guilty things, he asked quickly,—

"But how did you obtain leave of absence?"

"Through the kindness of his Highness."

"The Duke of Savoy?"

"Of course. And a braver general I would never ask to serve."

"I thought it might have been from the King himself, when he came to the camp after the battle."

Don Juan's cheek glowed with modest triumph. "His Highness was good enough to point me out to His Catholic Majesty," he said. "And the King spoke to me himself!"

It is difficult for us to understand how a few formal words of praise from the lips of one of the meanest and vilest of men could be looked upon by the really noble-hearted Don Juan Alvarez as almost the crowning joy of his life. With the enthusiastic loyalty of his age and country he honoured Philip the king; Philip the man being all the time a personage as utterly unknown to him as the Sultan of Turkey. But not choosing to expatiate upon a theme so flattering to himself, he continued,—

"The Duke contrived to send me home with despatches, saying kindly that he thought my wound required a little rest and care. Though I had affairs of importance" (and here the colour mounted to his brow) "to settle in Seville, I would not have quitted the camp, with my good-will, had we been about any enterprise likely to give us fair fighting. But in truth, Carlos, things have been abundantly dull since the fall of St. Quentin. Though we have our King with us, and Henry of France and the Duke of Guise have both joined the enemy, all are standing at gaze as if they were frozen, and doomed to stay there motionless till the day of judgment. I have no mind for that kind of sport, not I! I became a soldier to fight His Catholic Majesty's battles, not to stare at his enemies as if they were puppets paid to make a show for my amusement. So I was not sorry to take leave of absence."

"And your important business in Seville. May a brother ask what that means?"

"A brother may ask what he pleases, and be answered. Wish me joy, Carlos; I have arranged that little matter with Doña Beatriz." And his light words half hid, half revealed the great deep joy of his own strong heart. "My uncle," he continued, "is favourable to my views; indeed, I have never known him so friendly. We are to have our betrothal feast at Christmas, when your time of retreat here is over."

Carlos "wished him joy" most sincerely. Fervently did he thank God that it was in his power to do it; that the snare that had once wound itself so subtly around his footsteps was broken, and his soul escaped. He could now meet his brother's eye without self-reproach. Still, this seemed sudden. He said, "Certainly you did not lose time."

"Why should I?" asked Juan with simplicity. "'By-and-by is always too late,' as thou wert wont to say; and I would they learned that proverb at the camp. In truth," he added more gravely, "I often feared, during my stay there, that I might have lost all through my tardiness. But thou wert a good brother to me, Carlos."

"Mayest thou ever think so, brother mine," said Carlos, not without a pang, as his conscience told him how little he deserved the praise.

"But what in the world," asked Juan hastily, "has induced thee to bury thyself here, amongst these drowsy monks?"

"The brethren are excellent men, learned and pious. And I am not buried," Carlos returned with a smile.

"And if thou wert buried ten fathoms deep, thou shouldst come up out of the grave when I need thee to stand beside me."

"Do not fear for that. Now thou art come, I will not prolong my stay here, as otherwise I might have done. But I have been very happy here, Juan."

"I am glad to hear it," said the merry-hearted, unsuspecting Juan. "I am glad also that you are not in too great haste to tie yourself down to the Church's service; though our honoured uncle seems to wish you had a keener eye to your own interest, and a better look-out for fat benefices. But I believe his own sons have appropriated all the stock of worldly prudence meant for the whole family, leaving none over for thee and me, Carlos."

"That is true of Don Manuel and Don Balthazar, not of Gonsalvo."

"Gonsalvo! he is far the worst of the three," Juan exclaimed, with something like anger in his open, sunny face.

Carlos laughed. "I suppose he has been favouring you with his opinion of me," he said.

"If he were not a poor miserable weakling and cripple, I should answer him with the point of my good sword. However, this is idle talk. Little brother—" (Carlos being nearly as tall as himself, the diminutive was only a term of affection, recalling the days of their childhood, and more suited to masculine lips than its equivalent, dear)—"little brother, you look grave and pale, and ten years older than when we parted at Alcala."

"Do I? Much has happened with me since. I have been very sorrowful and very happy."

Don Juan laid his available hand on his brother's shoulder, and looked him earnestly in the face. "No secrets from me, little brother," he said. "If thou dost not like the service of Holy Church after all, speak out, and thou shalt go back with me to France, or to anywhere else in the known world that thou wilt. There may be some fair lady in the case," he added, with a keen and searching glance.

"No, brother—not that. I have indeed much to tell thee, but not now—not to-day."

"Choose thine own time; only remember, no secrets. That were the one unbrotherly act I could never forgive."

"But I am not yet satisfied about your wound," said Carlos, with perhaps a little moral cowardice, turning the conversation. "Was the bone broken?"

"No, fortunately; only grazed. It would not have signified, but for the treatment of the blundering barber-surgeon. I was advised to show it to some man of skill; and already my cousins have recommended to me one who is both physician and surgeon, and very able, they say."

"Dr. Cristobal Losada?"

"The same. Your favourite, Don Gonsalvo, has just been prevailed upon to make trial of his skill."

"I am heartily glad of it," returned Carlos. "There is a change of mind on his part, equal to any wherewith he can reproach me; and a change for the better, I have little doubt."

Thus the conversation wandered on; touching many subjects, exhausting none; and never again drawing dangerously near those deep places which one of the brothers knew must be thoroughly explored, and that at no distant day. For Juan's sake, for the sake of One whom he loved even more than Juan, he dared not—nay, he would not—avoid the task. But he needed, or thought he needed, consideration and prayer, that he might speak the truth wisely, as well as bravely, to that beloved brother.

XVII.

Disclosures.

> "No distance breaks the tie of blood;
> Brothers are brothers evermore;
> Nor wrong, nor wrath of deadliest mood,
> That magic may o'erpower."
>
> KEBLE.

HE opportunity for free converse with his brother which Carlos desired, yet dreaded, was unexpectedly postponed. It would have been in accordance neither with the ideas of the time nor with his own feelings to have shortened his period of retreat in the monastery, though he would not now prolong it. And though Don Juan did not fail to make his appearance upon every day when visitors were admitted, he was always accompanied by either of his cousins Don Manuel or Don Balthazar, or by both. These shallow, worldly-minded young men were little likely to allow for the many things, in which strangers might not intermeddle, that brothers long parted might find to say to each other; they only thought that they were conferring a high honour on their poorer relatives by their favour and notice. In their presence the conversation was necessarily confined to the incidents of Juan's campaign, and to family matters. Whether Don Balthazar would obtain a post he was seeking under Government;

whether Doña Sancha would eventually bestow the inestimable favour of her hand upon Don Beltran Vivarez or Don Alonso de Giron; and whether the disappointed suitor would stab himself or his successful rival;—these were questions of which Carlos soon grew heartily weary. But in all that concerned Beatriz he was deeply interested. Whatever he may once have allowed himself to fancy about the sentiments of a very young and childish girl, he never dreamed that she would make, or even desire to make, any opposition to the expressed wish of her guardian, who destined her for Juan. He was sure that she would learn quickly enough to love his brother as he deserved, even if she did not already do so. And it gave him keen pleasure that his sacrifice had not been in vain; that the wine-cup of joy which he had just tasted, then put steadily aside, was being drained to the dregs by the lips he loved best. It is true this pleasure was not yet unmixed with pain, but the pain was less than he would have believed possible a few months ago. The wound which he once thought deadly, was in process of being healed; nay, it was nearly healed already. But the scar would always remain.

Grand and mighty, but perplexing and mournful thoughts were filling his heart every day, more and more. Amongst the subjects eagerly and continually discussed with the brethren of San Isodro, the most prominent just now was the sole priesthood of Christ, with the impossibility of his one perfect and sufficient sacrifice being ever repeated.

But these truths, in themselves so glorious, had for those who dared to admit them one terrible consequence. Their full acknowledgment would transform the main altar's consummation, the sacrifice of the mass, from the highest act of Christian worship into a hideous lie, dishonouring to God, and ruinous to man.

To this conclusion the monks of San Isodro were drawing nearer slowly but surely every day. And Carlos was side by side with the most advanced of them in the path of progress. Though timid in action, he was bold in speculation. To his keen, quick intellect, to think and to reason was a necessity; he could not rest content with surface truths, nor leave any matter in which he was interested without probing it to its depths.

But as far at least as the monks were concerned, the conclusion now imminent was practically a most momentous one. It must transform the light that illuminated them into a fire that would burn and torture the hands that held and tried to conceal it. They could only guard themselves from loss and injury, perhaps from destruction, by setting it on the candlestick of a true and faithful profession.

"Better," said the brethren to each other, "leave behind us the rich lands and possessions of our order; what are these things in comparison to a conscience void of offence towards God and towards man? Let us go forth and seek shelter in some foreign land, destitute exiles but faithful witnesses for Christ, having purchased to ourselves the liberty of confessing his name before men." This plan was the most popular with the community; though there were some that objected to it, not because of the loss of worldly wealth it would entail, but because of its extreme difficulty, and the peril in which it would involve others.

That the question might be fully discussed and some course of action resolved upon, the monks of San Isodro convened a solemn chapter. Carlos had not, of course, the right to be present, though his friends would certainly inform him immediately afterwards of all that passed. So he whiled away part of the anxious hours by a walk in the orange grove belonging to the monastery. It was now December, and there had been a frost—not very usual in that mild climate. Every blade of grass was gemmed with tiny jewels, which were crushed by his footsteps as he passed along. He fancied them like the fair and sparkling, but unreal dreams of the creed in which he had been nurtured. They must perish; even should he weakly turn aside to spare them, God's sun would not fail ere long to dissolve them with the warmth of its beams. But wherefore mourn them? Would not the sun shine on still, and the blue sky, the emblem of eternal truth and love, still stretch above his head? Therefore he would look up—up, and not down.

Forgetting the things that were behind, and reaching forth unto those that were before, he would fain press forward towards the mark for the prize.[1] And then his heart went up in fervent prayer that not only he himself, but also all those who shared his faith, might be enabled so to do.

Turning into a path leading back through the grove to the monastery, he saw his brother coming towards him.

"I was seeking thee," said Don Juan.

"And always welcome. But why so early? On a Friday too!"

"Wherein is Friday worse than Thursday?" asked Juan with a laugh. "You are not a monk, or even a novice, to be bound by rules so strict that you may not say, 'Vaya con Dios' to your brother without asking leave of my lord Abbot."

Carlos had often noticed, not with displeasure, the freedom which Juan, since his return, assumed in speaking of churchmen and Church ordinances. He answered, "I am only bound by the general rules of the house, to which it is seemly that visitors should conform. To-day the brethren are holding a Chapter to confer upon matters pertaining to their discipline. I cannot well bring you indoors; but we do not need a better parlour than this."

"True. I care for no roof save God's sky; and as for glazed and grated windows, I abhor them. Were I thrown into prison, I should die in a week. I made an early start for San Isodro, on an unusual day, to get rid of the company of my excellent but tiresome cousins; for in truth I am sick unto death of their talk and their courtesies. Moreover, I have ten thousand things to tell you, brother."

"I have a few for your ear also."

"Let us sit down. Here is a pleasant seat which some of your brethren contrived to rest their weary limbs and enjoy the prospect. They know how to be comfortable, these monks."

They sat down accordingly. For more than an hour Don Juan was the chief speaker; and as he spoke out of the abundance of his heart, it was no wonder that the name oftenest on his lips was that of Doña Beatriz. Of the long and circumstantial story that he

[1] Referring to Philippians 3:14.

poured into the sympathising ear of Carlos no more than this is necessary to repeat—that Beatriz not only did not reject him (no well-bred Spanish girl would behave in such a singular manner to a suitor recommended by her guardian), but actually looked kindly, nay, even smiled upon him. His exhilaration was in consequence extreme; and its expression might have proved tedious to any listener not deeply interested in his welfare.

At last, however, the subject was dismissed. "So my path lies clear and plain before me," said Juan, his fine determined face glowing with resolution and hope. "A soldier's life, with its toils and prizes; and a happy home at Nuera, with a sweet face to welcome me when I return. And, sooner or later, *that* voyage to the Indies. But you, Carlos—speak out, for I confess you perplex me—what do *you* wish and intend?"

"Had you asked me that question a few months, I might almost say a few weeks, ago, I should not have hesitated, as now I do; for an answer."

"You were ever willing, more than willing, for Holy Church's service. I know but one cause which could alter your mind; and to the tender accusation you have already pleaded not guilty."

"The plea is a true one."

Certes; it cannot be that you have been seized with a sudden passion for a soldier's life," laughed Juan. "That was never your taste, little brother; and with all respect for you, I scarce think your achievements with sword and arquebus[2] would be specially brilliant. But there is something wrong with you," he said in an altered tone, as he gazed in his brother's anxious face.

"Not *wrong*, but—"

"I have it!" said Juan, joyously interrupting him. "You are in debt. That is soon mended, brother. In fact, it is my fault: I have had far too large a share already of what should have been for both of us alike. In future—"

"Hush, brother. I have always had enough, more than I needed. And thou hast many expenses, and wilt have more henceforward,

[2] An early type of portable gun supported on a tripod by a hook, or on a forked post.

whilst I shall only want a doublet[3] and hosen, and a pair of shoes."

"And a cassock[4] and gown?"

Carlos was silent.

"I vow it is a harder task to comprehend you than to chase Coligny's guard with my single arm! And you so pious, so good a Christian! If you were a dull rough soldier like me, and if you had had a Huguenot prisoner (and a very fine fellow, too) to share your bed and board for months, one could comprehend your not liking certain things over well, or even"—and Juan averted his face and lowered his voice—"your having certain evil thoughts you would scarcely care to breathe, in the ears of your father confessor."

"Brother, I too have had thoughts," said Carlos eagerly.

But Juan suddenly tossed off his montero,[5] and ran his finger through his black glossy hair. In old times this gesture used to be a sign that he was going to speak seriously. After a moment he began, but with a little hesitation, for in fact he held the *mind* of Carlos in as true and unfeigned reverence as Carlos held his *character*. And that is enough to say, without mentioning the additional respect with which he regarded him, as almost a priest. "Brother Carlos, you are good and pious. You were thus from childhood; and therefore it is that you are fit for the service of Holy Church. You rise and go to rest, you read your books, and tell your beads,[6] and say your prayers, all just as you are ordered. It is the best life for you, and for any man who *can* live it, and be content with it. You do not sin, you do not doubt; therefore you will never come into any grief or trouble. But let me tell you, little brother, you have a scant notion what men meet with who go forth into the great world and fight their way in it; seeing on every side of them things that, take them as they may, will *not* always square with the faith they have learned in childhood."

[3] A man's close-fitting jacket, with or without sleeves, popular in Europe between the 15th and 17th centuries.
[4] A full-length, usually black, robe worn by priests.
[5] A hunter's cap with sideflaps.
[6] Referring to rosary beads.

"Brother, I also have struggled and suffered. I also have doubted."

"Oh yes, a Churchman's doubts! You had only to tell yourself doubt was a sin, to make the sign of the cross, to say an Ave or two, then there was an end of your doubts. 'Twere a different matter if you had the evil one in the shape of an angel of light—at least in that of a courteous, well-bred Huguenot gentleman, with as nice a sense of honour as any Catholic Christian—at your side continually, to whisper that the priests are no better than they ought to be, that the Church needs reform; and heaven knows what more, and worse, beside. Now, my pious brother, if thou art going to curse me with bell, book, and candle, begin at once. I am ready, and prepared to be duly penitent. Let me first put on my cap though, for it is cold," and he suited the action to the word.

The voice in which Carlos answered him was low and tremulous with emotion. "Instead of cursing thee, brother beloved, I bless thee from my heart for words which give me courage to speak. I have doubted—nay, why should I shrink from the truth? I have learned, as I believe, from God himself, that some things which the Church teaches as her doctrines are only the commandments of men."

Don Juan started, and his colour changed. His vaguely liberal ideas were far from having prepared him for this. "What do you mean?" he cried, staring at his brother in amazement.

"That I am now, in very truth, what I think you would call—*a Huguenot*."

The die was cast. The avowal was made. Carlos waited its effects in breathless silence, as one who has fired a powder magazine[7] might await the explosion.

"May all the holy saints have mercy upon us!" cried Juan, in a voice that echoed through the grove. But after that one involuntary cry he was silent. The eyes of Carlos sought his face, but he turned away from him. At last he muttered, striking with his sword at the

---

[7] A detachable container for cartridges or bullets that can be quickly inserted or removed from a gun.

trunk of a tree that was near him, Huguenot—Protestant—*heretic!*"

"Brother," said Carlos, rising and standing before him—"brother, say what thou wilt, only speak to me. Reproach me, curse me, strike me, if it please thee, only speak to me."

Juan turned, gazed full in his imploring face, and slowly, very slowly, allowed the sword to fall from his hand. There was a moment of doubt, of hesitation. Then he stretched out that hand to his brother. "They who list may curse thee, but not I," he said.

Carlos strained the offered hand in so close a grasp that his own was cut by his brother's diamond ring, and the blood flowed.

For a long time both were silent, Juan in amazement, perhaps in consternation; Carlos in deep thankfulness. His confession was made, and his brother loved him still.

At last Juan spoke, slowly and as if half bewildered. "The Sieur de Ramenais believes in God, and in our Lord and his passion. And you?"

Carlos repeated the Apostles' Creed in the vulgar tongue.

"And in Our Lady, Mary, Mother of God?"

"I believe that she was the most blessed among women, the holiest among the holy saints. Yet I ask her intercession no more. I am too well assured of His love who says to me, and to all who keep his word, 'My brother, my sister, my mother.'"

"I thought devotion to Our Lady was the surest mark of piety," said Juan, in utter perplexity. "Then, I am only a man of the world. But oh, my brother, this is frightful!" He paused a moment, then added more calmly, "Still, I have learned that Huguenots are not beasts with horns and hoofs; but, possibly, brave and honourable men enough, as good, for this world, as their neighbours. And yet—the disgrace!" His dark cheek flushed, then grew pale, as there rose before his mind's eye an appalling vision—his brother robed in a hideous sanbenito, bearing a torch in the ghastly procession of an *Auto-da-fé*! "You have kept your secret as your life? My uncle and his family suspect nothing?" he asked anxiously.

"Nothing, thankfully."

"And who taught you this accursed—these doctrines?"

Carlos briefly told the story of his first acquaintance with the Spanish New Testament; suppressing, however, all mention of the personal sorrow that had made its teaching so precious to him; nor did he think it expedient to give the name of Juliano Hernandez.

"The Church may need reform. I am sure she does," Juan candidly admitted. "But Carlos, my brother," he added, while the expression of his face softened gradually into mournful, pitying tenderness, "little brother, in old times so gentle, so timid, hast thou dreamed—of the peril? I speak not now of the disgrace—that is hard enough to think of—hard enough," he repeated bitterly. "But the peril?"

Carlos was silent; his hands were clasped, his eyes raised upwards, full of thought, perhaps of prayer.

"What is that on thy hand?" asked Juan, with a sudden change of tone. "Blood? The Sieur de Ramenais' diamond ring has hurt thee."

Carlos glanced at the little wound, and smiled. "I never felt it," he said, "so glad was my heart, Ruy, for that brave grasp of faithful brotherhood." And there was a strange light in his eye as he added, "Perchance it may be thus with me, if Christ indeed should call me to suffer. Weak as I am, he can give, even to me, such blessed assurance of his love, that in the joy of it pain and fear shall be unfelt, or vanish."

Juan could not understand him, but he was awed and impressed. He had no heart for many words. He rose and walked towards the gate of the monastery grounds, slowly and in silence, Carlos accompanying him. When they had nearly reached the spot where they were to part, Carlos said, "You have heard Fray Constantino, as I asked you?"

"Yes, and I greatly admire him."

"He teaches God's truth."

"Why can you not rest content with his teaching, then, instead of going to look for better bread than wheaten, Heaven knows where?"

"When I return to the city next week I will explain all to thee."

"I hope so. In the meantime, Adiõs." He strode on a pace or two, then turned back to say, "Thou and I, Carlos; we will stand together against the world."

XVIII.

The Aged Monk.

"I will not boast a martyr's might
To leave my home without a sigh—
The dwelling of my past delight,
The shelter where I hoped to die."
ANON.

UCH was Carlos strengthened by the result of his interview with Don Juan. The thing that he greatly feared, his beloved brother's wrath and scorn, had not come upon him. Juan had shown, instead, a moderation, a candour, and a willingness to listen, which, while it really amazed him, inspired him with the happiest hopes. With a glad heart he repeated the Psalmist's exulting words: "The Lord is my strength and my shield; my heart hath trusted in him and I am helped; therefore my heart danceth for joy, and in my song will I praise him."[1]

He soon perceived that the Chapter was over; for figures, robed in white and brown, were moving here and there amongst the trees. He entered the house, and without happening to meet any one, made his way to the deserted Chapter-room. Its sole remaining occupant was a very aged monk, the oldest member of the

[1] Psalm 18:35

community. He was seated at the table, his face buried in his hands, and his frail, worn frame quivering as if with sobs.

Carlos went up to him and asked gently, "Father, what ails you?"

The old man slowly raised his head, and gazed at him with sad, tired eyes, which had watched the course of more than eighty years. "My son," he said, "if I weep, it is for joy."

Carlos wondered; for he saw no joy on the wrinkled brow or in the tearful face. But he merely asked, "What have the brethren resolved?"

"To await God's providence here. Praised be his holy name for that." And the old man bowed his silver head, and wept once more.

To Carlos also the determination was a cause for deep gratitude. He had all along regarded the proposed flight of the brethren with extreme dread, as an almost certain means of awakening the suspicions of the Holy Office, and thus exposing all who shared their faith to destruction. It was no light matter that the danger was now at least postponed, always provided that the respite was purchased by no sacrifice of principle.

"Thank God!" reiterated the old monk. "For here I have lived; and here I will die and be buried, beside the holy brethren of other days, in the chapel of Don Alonzo the Good. My son, I came hither a stripling as thou art—no, younger, younger—I know not how many years ago; one year is so like another, there is no telling. I could tell by looking at the great book, only my eyes are too dim to read it. They have grown dim very fast of late; when Doctor Egidius used to visit us, I could read my breviary with the youngest of them all. But no matter how many years. They were many enough to change a blooming, black-haired boy into an old man tottering on the grave's brink. And I to go forth now into that great, wicked world beyond the gate! I to look upon strange faces, and to live amongst strange men! Or to die amongst them, for to that it would come full soon! No, no, Señor Don Carlos. Here I took the cowl; here I lived; and here I will die and be buried, God and the saints helping me!"

"Yet for the Truth's sake, my father, would you not be willing to make even this sacrifice, and to go forth in your old age into exile?"

"If the brethren must needs go, so, I suppose, must I. But they are *not* going, St. Jerome be praised," the old man repeated.

"Going or staying, the presence of him whom they serve and for whom they witness will be with them."

"It may be, it may be, for aught I know. But in my young days so many fine words were not in use. We sang our matins,[2] our complines,[3] our vespers;[4] we said the holy mass and all our offices, and God and St. Jerome took care of the rest."

"But you would not have those days back again, would you, my father? You did not then know the glorious gospel of the grace of God."

"Gospel, gospel? We always read the gospel for the day. I know my breviary, young sir, just as well as another. And on festival days, some one always preached from the gospel. When Fray Domingo preached, plenty of great folks used to come out from the city to hear him. For he was very eloquent, and as much thought of, in his time, as Fray Cristobal is now. But they are forgotten in a little while, all of them. So will we, in a few years to come."

Carlos reproached himself for having named the gospel, instead of him whose words and works are the burden of the gospel story. For even to that dull ear, heavy with age, the name of Jesus was sweet. And that dull mind, drowsy with the slumber of a long life-time, had half awaked at least to the consciousness of his love.

"Dear father," he said gently, "I know you are well acquainted with the gospels. You remember what our blessed Lord saith of those who confess him before men, how he will not be ashamed to confess them before his Father in heaven? And, moreover, is it not a joy for us to show, in any way he points out to us, our love to him who loved us and gave himself for us?"

---

[2] In some Roman Catholic monastic communities, the hours before a vigil.
[3] The last of the seven separate hours that are set aside for prayer each day in the Roman Catholic Church.
[4] An evening church service.

"Yes, yes, we love him. And he knows I only wish to do what is right, and what is pleasing in his sight."

Afterwards, Carlos talked over the events of the day with the younger and more intelligent brethren; especially with his teacher, Fray Cristobal, and his particular friend, Fray Fernando. He could but admire the spirit that had guided their deliberations, and feel increased thankfulness for the decision at which they had arrived. The peace which the whole community of Spanish Protestants then enjoyed, perilous and unstable as it was, stood at the mercy of every individual belonging to that community. The unexplained flight of any obscure member of Losada's congregation would have been sufficient to give the alarm, and let loose the bloodhounds of persecution upon the Church; how much more the abandonment of a wealthy and honourable religious house by the greater part of its inmates?

The sword hung over their heads, suspended by a single hair, which a hasty or incautious movement, a word, a breath even, might suffice to break.

XIX.

Truth and Freedom.

"Man is greater than you thought him;
The bondage of long slumber he will break,
His just and ancient rights he will reclaim,
With Nero and Busiris he will rank
The name of Philip."

SCHILLER.

EVER before had it fallen to the lot of Don Juan Alvarez to experience such bewilderment as that which his brother's disclosure occasioned him. That brother, whom he had always regarded as the embodiment of goodness and piety, who was rendered illustrious in his eyes by all sorts of academic honours, and sanctified by the shadow of the coming priesthood, had actually confessed himself to be—what he had been taught to hold in deepest, deadliest abomination—a Lutheran heretic. But, on the other hand, from the wise, pious, and in every way unexceptionable manner in which Carlos had spoken, Juan could not help hoping that what, probably through some unaccountable aberration of mind, he himself persisted in styling Lutheranism, might prove in the end some very harmless and orthodox kind of devotion. Perhaps, eventually, his brother might found some new and holy order of monks and friars. Or even (he was so clever) he might take the lead in a Reformation of the Church, which, there was no use in an honest man's denying, was sorely needed. Still, he could not help admitting that the Sieur de Ramenais had sometimes expressed himself with nearly as much apparent orthodoxy; and he was undoubtedly a confirmed heretic—a Huguenot.

But if the recollection of this man, who for months had been his guest rather than his prisoner, served, from one point of view, to increase his difficulties, from another, it helped to clear away the most formidable of them. Don Juan had never been religious; but he had always been hotly orthodox, as became a Castilian gentleman of purest blood, and heir to all the traditions of an ancient house, foremost for generations in the great conflict with the infidel. He had been wont to look upon the Catholic faith as a thing bound up irrevocably with the knightly honour, the stainless fame, the noble pride of his race, and, consequently, with all that was dearest to his heart. Heresy he regarded as something unspeakably mean and degrading. It was associated in his mind with Jews and Moors, "caitiffs," "beggarly fellows;" all of them vulgar and unclean, some of them the hereditary enemies of his race. Heretics were Moslems, infidels, such as "my Cid" delighted in hewing down with his good sword Tizona, "for God and Our Lady's honour." Heretics kept the passover with mysterious, unhallowed rites, into which it would be best not to inquire; heretics killed (and perhaps ate) Christian children; they spat upon the cross; they had to wear ugly yellow sanbenitos at *Autos-da-fé*; and, to sum up all in one word, they "smelled of the fire." To give full weight to the last allusion, it must be remembered that in the eyes of Don Juan and his contemporaries, death by fire had no hallowed or ennobling associations to veil its horrors. The burning pile was to him what the cross was to our forefathers, and what the gibbet[1] is to us, only far more disgraceful. Thus it was not so much his conscience as his honour and his pride that were arrayed against the new faith.

[1] Gallows.

But, unconsciously to himself, opposition had been silently undermined by his association with the Sieur de Ramenais. It would probably have been fatal to Protestantism with Don Juan, had his first specimen of a Protestant been an humble muleteer. Fortunately, the new opinions had come to him represented by a noble and gallant knight, who

"In open battle or in tilting field
Forbore his own advantage;"

who was as careful of his "pundonor"[2] as any Castilian gentleman, and scarcely yielded even to himself in all those marks of good breeding, which, to say the truth, Don Juan Alvarez de Santillanos y Meñaya valued far more than any abstract dogmas of faith.

This circumstance produced a willingness on his part to give fair play to his brother's convictions. When Carlos returned to Seville, which he did about a week after the meeting of the Chapter, he was overjoyed to find Juan ready to hear all he had to say with patience and candour. Moreover, the young soldier was greatly attracted by the preaching of Fray Constantino, whom he pronounced, in language borrowed from the camp, "a right good camerado." Using these favourable dispositions to the best advantage, Carlos repeated to him passages from the New Testament; and with deep and prayerful earnestness explained and enforced the truths they taught, taking care, of course, not unnecessarily to shock his prejudices.

And, as time passed on, it became every day more and more apparent that Don Juan was receiving "the new ideas;" and that with far less difficulty and conflict than Carlos himself had done. For with him the Reformed faith had only prejudices, not convictions, to contend against. These once broken down, the rest was easy. And then it came to him so naturally to follow the guidance of Carlos in all that pertained to *thinking*.

Unmeasured was the joy of the affectionate brother when at last

[2] Point of honour.

he found that he might safely venture to introduce him privately to Losada as a promising inquirer.

In the meantime their outward life passed on smoothly and happily. With much feasting and rejoicing, Juan was betrothed to Doña Beatriz. He had loved her devotedly since boyhood; he loved her now more than ever. But his love was a deep, life-long passion—no sudden delirium of the fancy—so that it did not render him oblivious of every other tie, and callous to every other impression; it rather stimulated, and at the same time softened his whole nature. It made him not less, but more, sensitive to all the exciting and ennobling influences which were being brought to bear upon him.

Carlos perceived a change in Doña Beatriz that surprised him, while, at the same time, it made more evident than ever how great would have been his own mistake, had he accepted the passive gratitude of a child towards one who noticed and flattered her for the true deep love of a woman's heart. Doña Beatriz was a passive child no longer now. On the betrothal day, a proud and beautiful woman leaned on the arm of his handsome brother, and looked around her upon the assembled family, queen-like in air and mien, her cheek rivalling the crimson of the damask rose, her large dark eye beaming with passionate, exulting joy. Carlos compared her in thought to the fair, carved alabaster lamp that stood on the inlaid centre table of his aunt's state receiving-room. Love had wrought in her the change which light within always did in that, revealing its hidden transparency, and glorifying its pale, cold whiteness with tints so warmly beautiful, that the clouds of evening might have envied them.

The betrothal of Doña Sancha to Don Beltran Vivarez quickly followed. Don Balthazar also succeeded in obtaining the desired Government appointment, and henceforth enjoyed, much to his satisfaction, the honours and emoluments of an "*empleado*."[3] To crown the family good fortune, Doña Inez rejoiced in the birth of a son and heir, while even Don Gonsalvo, not to be left out, acknowledged some improvement in his health, which he attributed

[3] Bureaucratic official.

to the judicious treatment of Losada. The mind of an intelligent man can scarcely be deeply exercised upon one great subject, without the result making itself felt throughout the whole range of his occupations. Losada's patients could not fail to benefit by his habits of independent thought and searching investigation, and his freedom from vulgar prejudices. This freedom, so rare in his nation, led him occasionally, though very cautiously, even to hazard the adoption of a few remedies which were not altogether "*cosas de Espana*."[4]

The physician deserved less credit for his treatment of Juan's wounded arm, which nature healed, almost as soon as her beneficent operations ceased to be retarded by ignorant and blundering leech-craft.

Don Juan was occasionally heard to utter aspirations for the full restoration of his cousin Gonsalvo's health, more hearty in their expression than charitable in their motive. "I would give one of my fingers he could ride a horse and handle a sword, or at least a good foil with the button off, and I would soon make him repent his bearing and language to thee, Carlos. But what can a man do with a *thing* like that, save let him alone for very shame? Yet he is dastard enough to strike those whom his own infirmities hinder from returning the blow."

"If he could ride a horse or handle a sword, brother, I think you would find a marvellous change for the better in his bearing and language. That bitterness, what is it, after all, but the fruit of pain? Or of what is even worse than pain, repressed force and energy. He would be in the great world doing and daring; and behold, he is chained to a narrow room, or at best toils with difficulty a few hundred paces. No wonder that the strong winds, bound in their caverns, moan and shriek piteously at times. When I hear them I feel far too much compassion to think of anger. And I would give one of my fingers—nay, I would give my right hand," he added with a smile, "that he shared our blessed hope, Juan, my brother."

[4] Things of Spain.

"The most unlikely person of all our acquaintance to become a convert."

"So say not I. Do you know that he has given money—he that has so little—more than once to Señor Cristobal for the poor?"

"That is nothing," said Juan. "He was ever free-handed. Do you not remember, in our childhood, how he would strike us upon the least provocation, yet insist on our sharing his sweetmeats and his toys, and even sometimes fight us for refusing them? While the others knew the value of a ducat before they knew their Angelus,[5] and would sell and barter their small possessions like Dutch merchants."

"Which you spared not to call them, bearing yourself in the quarrels that naturally ensued with undaunted prowess; while I too often disgraced you by tearful entreaties for peace at all costs," returned Carlos, laughing. "But, my brother," he re sumed more gravely, "I often ask myself, are we doing all that is possible in our present circumstances to share with others the treasure we have found?"

"I trust it will soon be open to them all," said Juan, who had now come just far enough to grasp strongly his right to think and judge for himself, and with it the idea of emancipation from the control of a proud and domineering priesthood. "Great is truth, and shall prevail."

"Certainly, in the end. But much that looks like defeat to mortal eyes may come first."

"I think my learned brother, so much wiser than I upon many subjects, fails to read well the signs of the times. Whose Word saith, 'When ye see the fig-tree put forth her buds know ye that summer is nigh, even at the door'?[6] Everywhere the fig-trees are budding now."

"Still the frosts may return."

"Hold thy peace, too desponding brother. Thou shouldst have learned another lesson yesterday, when thou and I watched the

[5] A devotional prayer at morning, noon, and night to commemorate the Annunciation.
[6] Matthew 24:32-36; Mark 13:28-32; Luke 21:29-33

eager thousands as they hung breathless on the lips of our Fray Constantino. Are not those thousands really for *us*, and for truth and freedom?"

"No doubt Christ has his own amongst them."

"You always think of individuals, Carlos, rather than of our country. You forget we are sons of Spain, Castilian nobles. Of course we rejoice when even one man here and there is won for the truth. But our Spain! our glorious land, first and fairest of all the earth! our land of conquerors, whose arms reach to the ends of the world—one hand taming the infidel in his African stronghold, while the other crowns her with the gold and jewels of the far West! She who has led the nations in the path of discovery—whose fleets gem the ocean—whose armies rule the land,—shall she not also lead the way to the great city of God, and bring in the good coming time when all shall know him from the least to the greatest—when they shall know the truth, and the truth shall make them free?[7] Carlos, my brother, I do not dare to doubt it."

It was not often that Don Juan expressed himself in such a lengthened and energetic, not to say grandiloquent manner. But his love for Spain was a passion, and to extol her or to plead her cause, words were never lacking with him. In reply to this outburst of enthusiasm, Carlos only said gently, "Amen, and the Lord establish it in his time."

Don Juan looked keenly at him. "I thought you had faith, Carlos?" he said.

"Faith?" Carlos repeated inquiringly.

"Such faith," said Juan, "as I have. Faith in truth and freedom!" And he rang out the sonorous words, "*Verdad y libertad*," as if he thought, as indeed he did, that they had but to go forth through a submissive, rejoicing world, "conquering and to conquer."

"I have faith in *Christ*," Carlos answered quietly.

And in those two brief phrases each unconsciously revealed to the other the very depths of his soul, and told the secret of his history.

[7] Referring to John 8:32.

XX.

The First Drop of a Thunder Shower.

"Closed doorways that are folded
And prayed against in vain."
E. B. BROWNING.

EANWHILE the happy weeks glided on noiselessly and rapidly. They brought full occupation for head and heart, as well as varied and intense enjoyment. Don Juan's constant time spent with Doña Beatriz was not the less delightful because already he sought to imbue her mind with the truths which he himself was learning every day to love better. He thought her an apt and hopeful pupil, but, under the circumstances, he was scarcely the best possible judge.

Carlos was not so well satisfied with her attainments; he advised reserve and caution in imparting their secrets to her, lest through inadvertence she might betray them to her aunt and cousins. Juan considered this a mark of his constitutional timidity; yet he so far attended to his warnings, that Doña Beatriz was strongly impressed with the necessity of keeping their religious conversations a profound secret, whilst her sensibilities were not shocked by any mention of words so odious as heresy or Lutheranism.

But there could be no doubt as to Juan's own progress under the instructions of his brother, and of Losada and Fray Cassiodoro. He began, ere long, to accompany Carlos to the meetings of the Protestants, who welcomed the new acquisition to their ranks with affectionate enthusiasm. All were attracted by Don Juan's warmth and candour of disposition, and by his free, joyous, hopeful temperament; though he was not beloved by any as intensely as Carlos was by the few who really knew him, such as Losada, Don Juan Ponce de Leon, and the young monk, Fray Fernando.

Partly through the influence of his religious friends, and partly through the brilliant reputation he had brought from Alcala, Carlos now obtained a lectureship at the College of Doctrine, of which the provost,[1] Fernando de San Juan, was a decided and zealous Lutheran. This appointment was an honourable one, considered in no way derogatory to his social position, and useful as tending to convince his uncle that he was "doing something," not idly dreaming his time away.

Occupations of another kind opened out before him also. Amongst the many sincere and anxious inquirers who were troubled with perplexities concerning the relations of the old faith and the new, were some who turned to him, with an instinctive feeling that he could help them. This was just the work that best suited his abilities and his temperament. To sympathise, to counsel, to aid in conflict as only that man can do who has known conflict himself, was God's special gift to him. And he who goes through the world speaking, whenever he can, a word in season to the weary, will seldom be without some weary one ready to listen to him.

Upon one subject, and only one, the brothers still differed. Juan saw the future robed in the glowing hues borrowed from his own ardent, hopeful spirit. In his eyes the Spains were already won "for truth and freedom," as he loved to say. He anticipated nothing less than a glorious regeneration of Christendom, in which his beloved country would lead the van.

And there were many amongst Losada's congregation who

[1] A high-ranking administrative officer of a university.

shared these bright and beautiful, if delusive dreams, and the enthusiasm which had given them birth, and in its turn was nourished by them.

Again, there were others who rejoiced with much trembling over the good tidings that often reached them of the spread of the faith in distant parts of the country, and who welcomed each neophyte to their ranks as if they were adorning a victim for the sacrifice. They could not forget that name of terror, the Holy Inquisition. And from certain ominous indications they thought the sleeping monster was beginning to stir in his den. Else why had new and severe decrees against heresy been recently obtained from Rome? And above all, why had the Bishop of Terragona, Gonzales de Munebrãga, already known as a relentless persecutor of Jews and Moors, been appointed Vice-Inquisitor General at Seville?

Still, on the whole, hope and confidence predominated; and strange, nay, incredible as it may appear to us, beneath the very shadow of the Triana the Lutherans continued to hold their meetings "almost with open doors."

One evening Don Juan escorted Doña Beatriz to some festivity from which he could not very well excuse himself, whilst Carlos attended a re-union for prayer and mutual edification at the usual place—the house of Doña Isabella de Baena.

Don Juan returned at a late hour, but in high spirits. Going at once to the room where his brother sat awaiting him, he threw off his cloak, and stood before him, a gay, handsome figure, in his doublet of crimson satin, his gold chain, and well-used sword, now worn for ornament, with its embossed scabbard and embroidered belt.

"I never saw Doña Beatriz look so charming," he began eagerly. "Don Miguel de Santa Cruz was there, but he could not get so much as a single dance with her, and looked ready to die for envy. But save me from the impertinence of Luis Rotelo! I shall have to cane him one of these days, if no milder measures will teach him his place and station. *He*, the son of a simple hidalgo,[2] to dare lift his

[2] A man belonging to the lowest rank of Spanish nobility.

eyes to Doña Beatriz de Lavella? The caitiff's presumption!—But thou art not listening, brother. What is wrong with thee?"

No wonder he asked. The face of Carlos was pale; and the deep mournful eyes looked as if tears had been lately there. "A great sorrow, brother mine," he answered in a low voice.

"*My* sorrow too, then. Tell me, what is it?" asked Juan, his tone and manner changed in a moment.

"Juliano is taken."

Juliano! The muleteer who brought the books, and gave you that Testament?"

"The man who put into my hands this precious Book, to which I owe my joy now and my hope for eternity," said Carlos, his lip trembling.

"Ay de mi!—But perhaps it is not true."

"Too true. A smith, to whom he showed a copy of the Book, betrayed him. God forgive him—if there be forgiveness for such. It may have been a month ago, but we only heard it now. And he lies there—*there*."

"Who told you?"

"All were talking of it at the meeting when I entered. It is the sorrow of all; but I doubt if any have such cause to sorrow as I. For he is my father in the faith, Juan. And now," he added, after a long, sad pause, "I shall never tell him what he has done for me—at least on this side of the grave."

"There is no hope for him," said Juan mournfully, as one that mused.

"*Hope*! Only in the great mercy of God. Even those dreadful dungeon walls cannot shut him out."

"No; thank God."

"But the prolonged, the bitter, the horrible suffering! I have been trying to contemplate, to picture it—but I cannot. I dare not. And what I dare not think of, he must endure."

"He is a peasant, you are a noble—that makes some difference," said Don Juan, with whom the tie of brotherhood in Christ had not yet effaced all earthly distinctions. "But Carlos," he questioned suddenly, and with a look of alarm, "does not he know everything?"

"*Everything*," Carlos answered quietly. "One word from his lips, and the pile is kindled for us all. But that word will never be spoken. To-night not one heart amongst us trembled for ourselves, we only wept for him."

"You trust him, then, so completely? It is much to say. They in whose hands he is are cruel as fiends. No doubt they will—"

"Hush!" interrupted Carlos, with a look of such exceeding pain, that Juan was effectually silenced. "There are things we cannot speak of, save to God in prayer. Oh, my brother, pray for him, that Christ, for whom he has risked so much, may sustain him, and, if it may be, shorten his agony."

"Surely more than two or three will join in that prayer. But, my brother," he added, after a pause, "be not so downcast. Do you not know that every great cause must have its martyr? When was a victory won, and no brave man left dead on the field; a city stormed, and none fallen in the breach? Perhaps to that poor peasant may be given the glory—the great glory—of being honoured throughout all time as the sainted martyr whose death has consecrated our holy cause to victory. A grand lot truly worth suffering for!" And Juan's dark eye kindled, and his cheek glowed with enthusiasm.

Carlos was silent.

"Dost thou not think so, my brother?"

"I think that Christ is worth suffering for," said Carlos at last. "And that nothing short of his personal presence, realised by faith, can avail to bring any man victorious through such fearful trials. May that—may he be with his faithful servant now, when all human help and comfort are far away."

XXI.

By the Guadalquivir.

"There dwells my father, sinless and at rest,
Where the fierce murderer can no more pursue."
SCHILLER.

EXT Sunday evening the brothers attended the quiet service in Doña Isabella's upper room. It was more solemn than usual, because of the deep shadow that rested on the hearts of all the band assembled there. But Losada's calm voice spoke wise and loving words about life and death, and about him who, being the Lord of life, has conquered death for all who trust him. Then came prayer—true incense offered on the golden altar standing "before the mercy-seat," which only "the veil," still dropped between, hides from the eyes of the worshippers. But in such hours many a ray from the glory within shines through that veil.

"Do not let us return home yet, brother," said Carlos, when they had parted with their friends. "The night is fine."

"Whither shall we bend our steps?"

Carlos named a favourite walk through some olive-yards on the banks of the river, and Juan set his face towards one of the city gates.

"Why take such a circuit?" said Carlos, showing a disposition to turn in an opposite direction. "This is far the shorter way."

"True; but it is less pleasant."

Carlos looked at him gratefully. "My brother would spare my weakness," he said. "But it needs not. Twice of late, when you were engaged with Doña Beatriz, I went alone thither, and—to the Prado San Sebastian."

So they passed through the Puerta de Triana, and having crossed the bridge of boats, leisurely took their way beneath the walls of the grim old castle. As they did so, both prayed in silence for one who was pining in its dungeons. Don Juan, whose interest in the fate of Juliano was naturally far less intense than his brother's, was the first to break that silence. He remarked that the Dominican convent adjoining the Triana looked nearly as gloomy as the inquisitorial prison itself.

"I think it looks like all other convents," returned Carlos, with indifference.

They were soon in the shadow of the dark, ghost-like olive-trees. The moon was young, and gave but little light; but the large clear stars looked down through the southern air like lamps of fire, hanging not so much in the sky as from it. Were those bright watchers charged with a message from the land very far off, which seemed so near to *them* in the high places whence they ruled the night? Carlos drank in the spirit of the scene in silence. But this did not please his less meditative brother. "What art thou pondering?" he asked.

"'They that be wise shall shine as the brightness of the firmament, and they that turn many to righteousness as the stars for ever and ever.'"[1]

"Art thinking still of the prisoner in the Triana?"

"Of him, and also of another very dear to both of us, of whom I have for some time been purposing to speak to thee. What if thou and I have been, like children, seeking for a star on earth while all the time it was shining above us in God's glorious heaven?"

[1] Daniel 12:3

"Knowest thou not of old, little brother, that when thy parables begin I am left behind at once? I pray thee, let the stars alone, and speak the language of earth."

"What was the task to which thou and I vowed ourselves in childhood, brother?"

Juan looked at him keenly through the dim light. "I sometimes feared thou hadst forgotten," he said.

"No danger of that. But I had a reason—I think a good and sufficient one—for not speaking to thee until well and fully assured of thy sympathy."

"My sympathy? In aught that concerned the dream, the passion of my life!—of both our young lives! Carlos, how couldst thou even doubt of this?"

"I had reason to doubt at first whether a gleam of light which has been shed upon our father's fate would be regarded by his son as a blessing or a curse."

"Do not keep a man in suspense, brother. Speak at once."

"I doubt no longer *now*. It will be to thee, Juan, as to me, a joy exceeding great to think that our venerated father read God's Word for himself, and knew his truth and honoured it, as we have learned to do."

"Now, God be thanked!" cried Juan, pausing in his walk and clasping his hands together. "This indeed is joyful news. But speak, brother; how do you know it? Are you certain, or is it only dream, hope, conjecture?"

Carlos told him in detail, first the hint dropped by Losada to De Seso; then the story of Dolores; lastly, what he had heard at San Isodro about Don Rodrigo de Valer. And as he proceeded with his narrative, he welded the scattered links into a connected chain of evidence.

Juan, all eagerness, could hardly wait till he came to the end. "Why did you not speak to Losada?" he interrupted at last.

"Stay, brother, and hear me out; the best is to come. I have done so lately. But until assured how thou wouldst regard the matter, I cared not to ask questions, the answers to which might wound thy heart."

"You are in no doubt now. What heard you from Señor Cristobal?"

"I heard that Dr. Egidius named the Conde de Nuera as one of those who befriended Don Rodrigo. And that he had been present when that brave and faithful teacher privately expounded the Epistle to the Romans."

"There!" Juan exclaimed with a start. "There is the origin of my second and favourite name, Rodrigo. Brother, brother, these are the best tidings I have heard for years." And uncovering his head, he uttered fervent and solemn words of thanksgiving.

To which Carlos added a heartfelt "Amen," and resumed,—"Then, brother, you think we are justified in taking this joy to our hearts?"

"Without doubt," cried the sanguine Don Juan.

"And it follows that his crime—"

"Was what in our eyes constitutes the truest glory, the profession of a pure faith," said Juan with decision, leaping at once to the conclusion Carlos had reached by a far slower path.

"And those mystic words inscribed upon the window, the delight and wonder of our childhood—"

"Ah!" repeated Juan—

"'*El Dorado*
Yo hé trovado.'

But what they have to do with the matter I see not yet."

"You see not? Surely the knowledge of God in Christ, the kingdom of heaven opened up to us, is the true El Dorado, the golden country, which enriches those who find it for evermore."

"That is all very good," said Juan, with the air of a man not quite satisfied.

"I doubt not that was our father's meaning," Carlos continued.

"I doubt it, though. Up to that point I follow you, Carlos; but there we part. *Something* in the New World, I think, my father must have found."

A lengthened debate followed, in which Carlos discovered, rather to his surprise, that Juan still clung to his early faith in a literal land of gold. The more thoughtful and speculative brother sought in vain to reason him out of that belief. Nor was he much more successful when he came to state his own settled conviction that they should never see their father's face on earth. Not the slightest doubt remained on his own mind that, on account of his attachment to the Reformed faith, the Conde de Nuera had been, in the phraseology of the time, quietly "put out of the way." But whether this had been done during the voyage, or on the wild unknown shores of the New World, he believed his children would never know.

On this point, however, no argument availed with Juan. He seemed determined not to believe in his father's death. He confessed, indeed, that his heart bounded at the thought that he had been a sufferer "in the cause of truth and freedom." "He has suffered exile," he said, "and the loss of all things. But I see not wherefore he may not after all be living still, somewhere in that vast wonderful New World."

"I am content to think," Carlos replied, "that all these years he has been at rest with the dead in Christ. And that we shall see his face first with Christ when he appears in glory."

"But I am not content. We must learn something more."

"We shall never learn more. How can we?" asked Carlos.

"That is so like thee, little brother. Ever desponding, ever turned easily from thy purpose."

"Well; be it so," said Carlos meekly.

"But what *I* determine, that I do," said Juan. "At least will make my uncle speak out," he continued. "I have ever suspected that he knows something."

"But how is that to be done?" asked Carlos. "Nevertheless, do all thou canst, and God prosper thee. Only," he added with great earnestness, "remember the necessities of our present position; and for the sake of our friends, as well as of our own lives, use due prudence and caution."

"Fear not, my too prudent brother—the best and dearest brother in the world," he added kindly, "if he had but a little more courage."

Thus conversing they hastily retraced their steps to the city, the hour being already late.

Quiet weeks passed on after this, unmarked by any event of importance. Winter had now given place to spring; the time of the singing of birds was come. In spite of numerous and heavy anxieties, and of *one* sorrow that pressed more or less upon all, it was still spring-time in many a brave and hopeful heart amongst the adherents of the new faith in Seville. Certainly it was spring-time with Don Juan Alvarez.

One Sunday a letter arrived by special messenger from Nuera, containing the unwelcome tidings that the old and faithful servant of the house, Diego Montes, was dying. It was his last wish to resign his stewardship into the hands of his young master, Señor Don Juan. Juan could not hesitate. "I will go to-morrow morning," he said to Carlos; "but rest assured I will return hither as soon as possible; the days are too precious to be lost."

Together they repaired once more to Doña Isabella's house. Don Juan told the friends they met there of his intended departure, and ere they separated many a hand warmly grasped his, and many a voice spoke kindly the "Vaya con Dios"[2] for his journey.

"It needs not formal leave-takings, señores and my brethren," said Juan; "my absence will be very short; not next Sunday indeed, but possibly in a fortnight, and certainly this day month I shall meet you all here again."

"*God willing*," said Losada gravely. And so they parted.

[2] Meaning "Go with God."

XXII.

The Flood-Gates Opened.

"And they feared as they entered into the cloud."

OR the first stage of Don Juan's journey Carlos accompanied him. They spent the time in animated talk, chiefly about Nuera, Carlos sending kind messages to the dying man, to Dolores, and indeed to all the household. "Remember, brother," he said, "to give Dolores the little books I put into the alforjas, specially the 'Confession of a Sinner.'"

"I shall remember everything, even to bringing thee back tidings of all the sick folk in the village. Now, Carlos, here we agreed to part;—no, not one step further."

They clasped each other's hands. "It is not like a long parting," said Juan.

"No. Vaya con Dios, my Ruy."

"Quede con Dios[1] brother;" and he rode off, followed by his servant.

Carlos watched him wistfully; would he turn for a last look? He

[1] Remain with God.

did turn. Taking off his velvet montero, he gaily bowed farewell; thus allowing Carlos to gaze once more upon his dark, handsome, resolute features, keen, sparkling eyes and curling black hair.

Whilst Juan saw a scholar's face, thoughtful, refined, sensitive; a broad pale forehead, from which the breeze had blown the waving fair hair (fair to a southern eye, though really a bright soft brown), and lips that kept the old sweetness of expression, though, whether from the manly fringe that graced them or from some actual change, the weakness which marred them once had ceased to be apparent now.

Another moment, and both had turned their horses' heads. Carlos, when he reached the city, made a circuit to avoid one of the very frequent processions of the Host; since, as time passed on, he felt ever more and more disinclined to the absolutely necessary prostration. Afterwards he called upon Losada, to inquire the exact address of a person whom he had asked him to visit. He found him engaged in his character of physician, and sat down in the patio to await his leisure.

Ere long Dr. Cristobal passed through, politely accompanying to the gate a canon of the cathedral, for whose ailments he had just been prescribing. The Churchman, who was evidently on the best terms with his physician, was showing his good-nature and affability by giving him the current news of the city; to which Losada listened courteously, with a grave, quiet smile, and, when necessary, an appropriate question or comment. Only one item made any impression upon Carlos: it related to a pleasant estate by the sea-side which Munebrãga had just purchased, disappointing thereby a relative of the canon's who desired to possess it, but could not command the very large price readily offered by the Inquisitor.

At last the visitor was gone. In a moment the smile had faded from the physician's care-worn face. Turning to Carlos with a strangely altered look, he said, "The monks of San Isodro have fled."

"Fled!" Carlos repeated, in blank dismay.

"Yes; no fewer than twelve of them have abandoned the monastery."

"How did you hear it?"

"One of the lay brethren came in this morning to inform me. They held another solemn Chapter, in which it was determined that each one should follow the guidance of his own conscience, those, therefore, to whom it seemed best to go have gone, the rest remain."

For some moments they looked at each other in silence. So fearful was the peril in which this rash act involved them all, that it almost seemed as if they had heard a sentence of death.

The voice of Carlos faltered as he asked at last,—"Have Fray Cristobal or Fray Fernando gone?"

No; they are both amongst those, more generous if not more wise, who have chosen to remain and take what God will send them here. Stay, here is a letter from Fray Cristobal which the lay brother brought me; it will tell you as much as I know myself."

Carlos read it carefully. "It seems," he said, when he had finished, "that the consciences of those who fled would not allow them any longer to conform, even outwardly, to the rules of their order. Moreover, from the signs of the times, they believe that a storm is about to burst upon the company of the faithful."

"God grant it may prove that they have saved *themselves* from its violence," Losada answered, with a slight emphasis on "themselves."

"And for us?—God help us!" Carlos almost moaned, the paper falling from his trembling hand. "What shall we do?" "Be strong in the Lord, and in the power of his might,"[2] returned Losada bravely. "No other strength remains for us. But God grant none of us in the city may be so unadvised as to follow the example of the brethren. The flight of one might be the ruin of all."

"And those noble, devoted men who remain at San Isodro?"

"Are in God's hands, as we are."

"I will ride out and visit them, especially Fray Fernando."

[2] Ephesians 6:10

"Excuse me, Señor Don Carlos, but you will do nothing of the kind; that were to court suspicion. I will bear any message you choose to send."

"And you?"

Losada smiled, though sadly. "The physician has occasion to go," he said; "he is a very useful personage, who often covers with his ample cloak the *dogmatising heretic*."

Carlos recognised the official phraseology of the Holy Office. He repressed a shudder, but could not hide the look of terror that dilated his large blue eyes.

The older man, the more experienced Christian, could compassionate the youth. Losada, himself standing "face to face with death," spoke kind words of counsel and comfort to Carlos. He cautioned him strongly against losing his self-possession, and thereby running needlessly into danger. "Especially would I urge upon you, Señor Don Carlos," he said, "the duty of avoiding unnecessary risk, for already you are useful to us; and should God spare your life, you will be still more so. If I fall—"

"Do not speak of it, my beloved friend."

"It will be as God pleases," said the pastor calmly. "But I need not remind you, others stand in like peril with me. Especially Fray Cassiodoro, and Don Juan Ponce de Leon."

"The noblest heads, the likeliest to fall," Carlos murmured.

"Then must younger soldiers step forth from the ranks, and take up the standards dropped from their hands. Don Carlos Alvarez, we have high hopes of you. Your quiet words reach the heart; for you speak that which you know, and testify that which you have seen. And the good gifts of mind that God has given you enable you to speak with the greater acceptance. He may have much work for you in his harvest-field. But whether he should call you to work or to suffer, shrink not, but 'be strong and of good courage; be not afraid, neither be thou dismayed; for the Lord thy God is with thee whithersoever thou goest.'"[3]

"I will try to trust him; and may he make his strength perfect in

[3] Joshua 1:9

my weakness," said Carlos. "But for the present," he added, "give me any lowly work to do, whereby I may aid you or lighten your cares, my loved friend and teacher."

Losada gladly gave him, as indeed he had done several times before, instructions to visit certain secret inquirers, and persons in distress and perplexity of mind.

He passed the next two or three days in these ministrations, and in constant prayer, especially for the remaining monks of San Isodro, whose sore peril pressed heavily on his heart. He sought, as much as possible, to shut out other thoughts; or, when they would force an entrance, to cast their burden, which otherwise would have been intolerable, upon him who would surely care for his own Church, his few sheep in the wilderness. One morning he remained late in his chamber, writing a letter to his brother; and then went forth, intending to visit Losada. As it was a fast-day, and he kept the Church fasts rigorously, it happened that he had not previously met any of his uncle's family.

The entrance to the physician's house did not present its usual cheerful appearance. The gate was shut and bolted, and there was no sign of patients passing in or out. Carlos became alarmed. It was long before he obtained an answer to his repeated calls. At last, however, some one inside cried, "*Quien es*?"[4]

Carlos gave his name, well known to all the household. Then the door was half opened, and a mulatto serving-lad showed a terrified face behind it.

"Where is Señor Cristobal?"

"Gone, señor."

"Gone!—whither?"

The answer was a furtive, frightened whisper. "Last night—the Alguazils[5] of the Holy Office." And the door was shut and bolted in his face.

He stood rooted to the spot, speechless and motionless, in a trance of horror. At last he was startled by feeling some one grasp his arm without ceremony, indeed rather roughly.

---

[4] Who is there?

[5] Police officers.

"Are you moonstruck, Cousin Don Carlos?" asked the voice of Gonsalvo. "At least you might have had the courtesy to offer me the aid of your arm, without putting me to the shame of requesting it, miserable cripple that I am!" and he gave vent to a torrent of curses upon his own infirmities, using expressions profane and blasphemous enough to make Carlos shiver with pain.

Yet that very pain did him real service. It roused him from his stupor, as sharp anguish sometimes brings back a patient from a swoon. He said, "Pardon me, my cousin, I did not see you; but I hear you now—with sorrow."

Gonsalvo deigned no answer, except his usual short, bitter laugh.

"Whither do you wish to go?"

"Home. I am tired."

They walked along in silence; at last Gonsalvo asked, abruptly,—

"Have you heard the news?"

"What news?"

"The news that is in every one's mouth to-day. Indeed, the city has well nigh run mad with holy horror. And no wonder! Their reverences, the Lords Inquisitors, have just discovered a community of abominable Lutherans, a very viper's nest, in our midst. It is said the wretches have actually dared to carry on their worship somewhere in the town. Ah, no marvel you look horror-stricken, my pious cousin. *You* could never have dreamed that such a thing was possible, could you?" After one quick, keen glance, he did not look again in his cousin's face; but he might have felt the beating of his cousin's heart against his arm.

"I am told," he continued, "that nearly two hundred persons have been arrested already."

"*Two hundred!*" gasped Carlos.

"And the arrests are going on still."

"Who is taken?" Carlos forced his trembling lips to ask.

"Losada; more's the pity. A good physician, though a bad Christian."

"A good physician, and a good Christian too," said Carlos in the voice of one who tries to speak calmly in terrible bodily pain.

"An opinion you would do more wisely to keep to yourself, if a reprobate such as I may presume to counsel so learned and pious a personage."

"Who else?"

"One you would never guess. Don Juan Ponce de Leon, of all men. Think of the Count of Baylen's son being thus degraded! Also the master of the College of Doctrine, San Juan; and a number of Jeromite friars from San Isodro. Those are all I know worth a gentleman's taking account of. There are some beggarly tradesfolk, such as Medel d'Espinosa, the embroiderer; and Luis d'Abrego, from whom your brother bought that beautiful book of the Gospels he gave Doña Beatriz. But if only such cattle were concerned in it, no one would care."

"Some fools there be," Don Gonsalvo continued after a pause, "who have run to the Triana, and informed against themselves, thinking thereby to get off more easily. *Fools*, again I say, for their pains." And he emphasised his words by a pressure of the arm on which he was leaning.

At length they reached the door of Don Manuel's house.

"Thanks for your aid," said Gonsalvo. "Now that I remember it, Don Carlos, I hear also that we are to have a grand procession on Tuesday with banners and crosses, in honour of Our Lady, and of our holy patronesses Justina and Rufina, to beg pardon for the sin and scandal so long permitted in the midst of our most Catholic city. You, my pious cousin, licentiate of theology and all but consecrated priest—you will carry a taper, no doubt?"

Carlos would fain have left the question unanswered; but Gonsalvo meant to have an answer. "You will?" he repeated, laying his hand on his arm, and looking him in the face, though with a smile. "It would be very creditable to the family for one of us to appear. Seriously; I advise you to do it."

Then Carlos said quietly, "No;" and crossed the patio to the staircase which led to his own apartment.

Gonsalvo stood watching him, and mentally retracting, at his last word, the verdict formerly pronounced against him as "a coward," "not half a man."

XXIII.

The Reign of Terror.

"Though shining millions around thee stand,
For the sake of him at thy right hand
Think of the souls he died for here,
Thus wandering in darkness, in doubt and fear.

"The powers of darkness are all abroad—
They own no Saviour, and they fear no God;
And we are trembling in dumb dismay;
Oh, turn not thou thy face away."

HOGG.

T was late in the evening when Carlos emerged from his chamber. How the intervening hours had been passed he never told any one. But this much is certain,—he contended with and overcame a wild, almost uncontrollable impulse to seek refuge in flight. His reason told him that this would be to rush upon certain destruction: so sedulously guarded were all the ways of egress,[1] and so watchful and complete, in every city and village of the land, was the inquisitorial organisation; not to speak of the "Hermandad," or Brotherhood—a kind of civil police, always ready to co-operate with the ecclesiastical authorities.

[1] An exit.

Still, if he could not be saved, Juan might and should. This thought was growing gradually clearer and stronger in his bewildered brain and aching heart while he knelt in his chamber, finding a relief in the attitude of prayer, though few and broken were the words of prayer that passed his trembling lips. Indeed, the burden of his cry was this: "Lord, have mercy on us. Christ, have mercy on us. Thou that carest for us, forsake us not in our bitter need. For thine is the kingdom; even yet thou reignest."

This was all he could find to plead, either on his own behalf or on that of his imprisoned brethren; though for them his heart was wrung with unutterable anguish. Once and again did he repeat—"Thine is the kingdom and the power. Thine, O Father; thine, O Lord and Saviour. Thou *canst* deliver us."

It was well for him that he had Juan to save. He rose at last; and added to the letter previously written to his brother a few lines of most earnest entreaty that he would on no account return to Seville. But then, recollecting his own position, he marvelled greatly at his simplicity in purposing to send such a letter by the King's post—an institution which, strange to say, Spain possessed at an earlier period than any other country in Europe. If he should fall under suspicion, his letter would be liable to detention and examination, and might thus be the means of involving Juan in the very peril from which he sought to deliver him.

A better plan soon occurred to him. That he might carry it out, he descended late in the evening to the cool, marble-paved court, or *patio*, in the centre of which the fountain ever murmured and glistened, surrounded by tropical plants, some of them in gorgeous bloom.

As he had hoped, one solitary lamp burned like a star in a remote corner; and its light illumined the form of a young girl seated on a low chair, before an inlaid ebony table, writing busily. Doña Beatriz had excused herself from accompanying the family on an evening visit, that she might devote herself in undisturbed solitude to the composition of her first love-letter—indeed, her first letter of any kind: for short as he intended his absence to be, Juan had stipulated for this consolation, and induced her to promise it; and she knew that the King's post went northwards the next day, passing by Nuera on his way to the towns of La Mancha.

So engrossing was her occupation that she did not hear the step of Carlos. He drew near, and stood behind her. Pearls, golden Agni, and a scarlet flower or two, were twined with her glossy raven hair; and the lamp shed a subdued radiance over her fine features, which glowed through their delicate olive with the rosy light of joy. An exquisite though not very costly perfume, that Carlos in other days always associated with her presence, still continued a favourite with her, and filled the place around with fragrance. It brought back his memory to the past—to that wild, vain, yet enchanting dream; the brief romance of his life. But there was no time now even for "a dream within a dream." There was only time to thank God, from the depths of his soul, that in all the wide world there was no heart that would break for *him*.

"Doña Beatriz," he said gently.

She started, and half turned, a bright flush mounting to her cheek.

"You are writing to my brother."

"And how know you that, Señor Don Carlos?" asked the young lady, with a little innocent affectation.

But Carlos, standing face to face with terrible realities, pushed aside her pretty arts, as one hastening to succour a dying man might push aside a branch of wild roses that impeded his path.

"I most earnestly request of you, señora, to convey to him a message from me."

"And wherefore can you not write to him yourself, Señor Licentiate?"

"Is it possible, señora, that you know not what has happened?"

"Vaya, vaya, Don Carlos! how you startle one.—Do you mean these horrible arrests?"

Carlos found that a few strong, plain words were absolutely necessary in order to make Beatriz understand his brother's peril. She had listened hitherto to Don Juan's extracts from Scripture, and the arguments and exhortations founded thereon, conscious, indeed, that these were secrets which should be jealously guarded, yet unconscious that they were what the Church and the world branded as heresy. Consequently, although she heard of the arrest of Losada and his friends with vague regret and apprehension, she was far from distinctly associating the crime for which they suffered with the name dearest to her heart. She was still very young; and she had not thought much—she had only loved. And she blindly followed him she loved, without caring to ask whither he was going himself, or whither he was leading her. When at last Carlos made her comprehend that it was for reading the Scriptures, and talking of justification by faith alone, that Losada was thrown into the dungeons of the Triana, a thrilling cry of anguish broke from her lips.

"Hush, señora!" said Carlos; and for once his voice was stern. "If even your little black foot-page heard that cry, it might ruin all."

But Beatriz was unused to self-control. Another cry followed, and there were symptoms of hysterical tears and laughter. Carlos tried a more potent spell.

"Hush, señora!" he repeated. "We must be strong and silent, if we are to save Don Juan."

She looked piteously up at him, repeating, "Save Don Juan?"

"Yes, señora. Listen to me. *You*, at least, are a good Catholic. You have not compromised yourself in any way: you say your angelus; you make your vows; you bring flowers to Our Lady's shrine. *You* are safe."

She turned round and faced him—her cheek dyed crimson, and her eyes flashing,—

"I am safe! Is that all you have to say? Who cares for that? What is *my* life worth?"

"Patience, dear señora! Your safety aids in securing his. Listen.—You are writing to him. Tell him of the arrests; for hear of them he must. Use the language about heresy which will occur to you, but which I could not use. Then pass from the subject.

Write aught else that comes to your mind; but before closing your letter, say that I am well in mind and body, and would be heartily recommended to him. Add that I most earnestly request of him, for our common good and the better arrangement of our affairs, not to return to Seville, but to remain at Nuera. He will understand that. Lay your own commands upon him—your *commands*, remember, señora—to the same effect."

"I will do all that.—But here come my aunt and cousins."

It was true. Already the porter had opened for them the gloomy outer gate; and now the gilt and filagreed inner door was thrown open also, and the returning family party filled the court. They were talking together; not quite so gaily as usual, but still eagerly enough. Doña Sancha soon drew near to Beatriz, and began to rally her upon her occupation, threatening playfully to carry away and read the unfinished letter. No one addressed a word to Carlos; but that might have been mere accident.

It was, however, scarcely accidental that his aunt, as she passed him on her way to an inner room, drew her mantilla closer round her, lest its deep lace fringe might touch his clothing. Shortly afterwards Doña Sancha dropped her fan. According to custom, Carlos stooped for it, and handed it to her with a bow. The young lady took it mechanically, but almost immediately dropped it again with a look of scorn, as if polluted by its touch. Its delicate carved ivory, the work of Moorish hands, lay in fragments on the marble floor; and from that moment Carlos knew that he was under the ban, that he stood alone amidst his uncle's household—a suspected and degraded man.

It was not surprising. His intimacy with the monks of San Isodro, his friendship with Don Juan Ponce de Leon, and with the physician Losada, were all well-known facts. Moreover, had he not taught at the College of Doctrine, under the direct patronage of Fernando de San Juan, another of the victims? And there were other indications of his tendencies which could scarcely escape notice, once the suspicions of those who lived under the same roof with him were awakened.

For a time he stood silent, watching his uncle's countenance, and marking the frown that contracted his brow whenever his eye turned towards him. But when Don Manuel passed into a smaller saloon that opened upon the court, Carlos followed him boldly.

They stood face to face, but could hardly see each other. The room was darkness, save for a few struggling moonbeams.

"Señor my uncle," said Carlos, "I fear my presence here is displeasing to you."

Don Manuel paused before replying.

"Nephew," he said at length, "you have been lamentably imprudent. The saints grant you have been no worse."

A moment of strong emotion will sometimes bring out in a man's face characteristic lineaments of his family, in calmer seasons not traceable there. Thus it is with features of the soul. It was not the gentle timid Don Carlos who spoke now, it was Alvarez de Santillanos y Meñaya. There was both pride and courage in his tone.

"If it has been my misfortune to offend my honoured uncle, to whom I owe so many benefits, I am sorry, though I cannot charge myself with any fault. But I should be faulty indeed were I to prolong my stay in a house where I am no longer what, thanks to your kindness, señor my uncle, I have ever been hitherto, a welcome guest." Having spoken thus, he turned to go.

"Stay, young fool!" cried Don Manuel, who thought the better of him for his proud words. They raised him, in his estimation, from a mark for his scorn to a legitimate object for his indignation. "There spoke your father's voice. But I tell you, for all that, you shall not quit the shelter of my roof."

"I thank you."

"You may spare the pains. I ask you not, for I prefer to remain in ignorance, to what perilous and fool-hardy lengths your intimacy with heretics may have gone. Without being a Qualificator of heresy myself, I can tell that you smell of the fire. And indeed, young man, were you anything less than Alvarez de Meñaya, I would hardly scorch my own fingers to hold you out of it. The Devil—to whom, in spite of all your fair appearances, I fear you belong—might take care of his own. But since truth is the daughter of God, you shall have it from my lips. And the plain truth is, that I have no desire to hear every cur dog in Seville barking at me and mine; nor to see our ancient and honourable name dragged through the mire and filth of the streets."

"I have never disgraced that name."

"Have I not said that I desire no protestations from you? Whatever my private opinion may be, it stands upon our family honour to hold that yours is still unstained. Therefore, not from love, as I tell you plainly, but from motives that may perchance prove stronger in the end, I and mine extend to you our protection. I am a good Catholic, a faithful son of Mother Church; but I freely confess I am no hero of the Faith, to offer up upon its shrine those that bear my own name. I pretend not to such heights of sanctity, not I." And Don Manuel shrugged his shoulders.

"I entreat of you, señor my uncle, to allow me to explain—"

Don Manuel waved his hand with a forbidding gesture. "None of thy explanations for me," he said. "I am no silly cock, to scratch till I find the knife. Dangerous secrets had best be let alone. This I will say, however, that of all the contemptible follies of these evil times, this last one of heresy is the worst. If a man *will* lose his soul, in the name of common sense let him lose it for fine houses, broad lands, a duke's title, an archbishop's coffers, or something else good at least in this world. But to give all up, and to gain nothing, save fire here and fire again hereafter! It is sheer, blank idiocy."

"I *have* gained something," said Carlos firmly. "I have gained a treasure worth more than all I risk, more than life itself."

"What! Is there really a meaning in this madness? Have you and your friends a secret?" Don Manuel asked in a gentler voice, and not without curiosity. For he was the child of his age; and had Carlos told him that the heretics had made the discovery of the philosopher's stone, he would have seen nothing worthy of disbelief in the statement; he would only have asked him for proofs.

"The knowledge of God in Christ," began Carlos eagerly, "gives me joy and peace—"

"Is that all?" cried Don Manuel with an oath. "Fool that I was, to imagine, for half an idle minute, that there might be some grain of common sense still left in your crazy brain! But since it is only a question of words and names, and mystical doctrines, I have the honour to wish you good evening, Señor Don Carlos. Only I command you, as you value your life, and prefer a residence beneath my roof to a dungeon in the Triana, to keep your insanity within bounds, and to conduct yourself so as to avert suspicion. On these conditions we will shelter you. Eventually, if it can be done with safety, we may even ship you out of the Spains to some foreign country, where heretics, rogues, and thieves are permitted to go at large." So saying, he left the room.

Carlos was stung to the quick by his contempt; but remembered at last that it was a fragment of the true cross (really the first that had fallen to his lot), given him to wear in honour of his Master.

Sleep would not visit his eyes that night. The next day was the Sabbath, a day he had been wont to welcome and enjoy. But never again should the Reformed Church of Seville meet in the upper room which had been the scene of so much happy interaction. The next reunion was appointed for another place, a house not made with hands, eternal in the heavens.[2] Doña Isabella de Baena and Losada were in the dungeons of the Triana. Fray Cassiodoro de Reyna, singularly fortunate, had succeeded in making his escape. Fray Constantino, on the other hand, had been amongst the first arrested; but Carlos went as usual to the Cathedral, where that eloquent voice would never again be heard. A heavy silent gloom, like that which precedes a thunderstorm, seemed to fill the crowded aisles.

Yet it was there that the first gleam of comfort reached the breaking heart of Carlos. It came to him through the familiar words of the Latin service, loved from childhood.

[2] II Corinthians 5:1

He said afterwards to the trembling children of one of the victims, whose desolated home he dared to visit, "For myself, horror took hold of me. I dared not to think. I scarce dared to pray, save in broken words that were only like cries of pain. The first thing that helped me was that grand verse in the Te Deum, chanted by the sweet childish voices of the Cathedral choir—'Tu, devicto mortis aculeo, aperuesti credentibus regna coelorum.' Think, dear friends, not death alone, but its sting, its sharpness,—for us and our beloved,—He has overcome, and they and we in him. The gates of the kingdom of heaven stand open; opened by his hands, and neither men nor fiends can shut them again."

Such words as these did Carlos find opportunity to speak to many bereaved ones, from whom the desire of their eyes had been taken by a stroke far more bitter than death. This ministry of love did not greatly increase his own peril, since the less he deviated from his ordinary habits of life the less suspicion he was likely to awaken. But had it been otherwise, he was not now in a position to calculate. Perhaps he was too near heaven; at all events, he had already ventured too much for Christ's sake not to be willing, at his call, to venture a little more.

Meanwhile, the isolation of his position in his uncle's house grew overpowering. No one reproached him, no one taunted him, not even Gonsalvo. He often longed for some bitter word, ay, though it were a curse, to break the oppressive silence. Every eye looked upon him with hatred and scorn; every hand shrank from the slightest, most accidental contact with his. Almost he came to consider himself what all others considered him,—polluted, degraded—under the ban.

Once and again would he have sought escape by flight from an atmosphere in which it seemed more and more impossible to breathe. But flight meant arrest; and arrest, besides its overwhelming terrors for himself, meant the danger of betraying Juan. His uncle and his uncle's family, though they seemed now to scorn and hate him, had promised to save him if they could, and so far he trusted them.

XXIV.

A Gleam of Light.

"It is a weary task to school the heart,
Ere years or griefs have tamed its fiery throbbings,
Into that still and passive fortitude
Which is but learned from suffering."

HEMANS.

HORTLY afterwards, the son and heir of Doña Inez was baptised, with the usual amount of ceremony and rejoicing. After the event, the family and friends partook of a merienda of fruit, confectionery, and wine, in the patio of Don Garcia's house. Much against his inclination, Carlos was obliged to be present, as his absence would have occasioned remark and inquiry.

When the guests were beginning to disperse, the hostess drew near the spot where he stood, near to the fountain, admiring, or seeming to admire, a pure white azalia in glorious bloom.

"In good sooth, cousin Don Carlos," she said, "you forget old friends very easily. But I suppose it is because you are going so soon to take Orders. Every one knows how learned and pious you are. And no doubt you are right to wean yourself in good time from the concerns and amusements of this unprofitable world."

No word of this little speech was lost upon one of the greatest gossips in Seville, a lady of rank, who stood near leaning on the arm of Losada's former patient, the wealthy Canon. And this was what the speaker, in her good nature, probably intended.

Carlos raised to her face eyes beaming with gratitude for the friendly notice.

"No change of state, señora, can ever make me forget the kindness of my fair cousin," he responded with a bow.

"Your cousin's little daughter," said the lady, "had once a place in your affections. But with you, as with all the rest, I presume the boy is everything. As for my poor little Inez, her small person is of small account in the world now. It is well she has her mother."

"Nothing would give me greater pleasure than to renew my acquaintance with Doña Inez, if I may be permitted so to do."

This was evidently what the mother desired. "Go to the right then, amigo mio," she said promptly, indicating the place intended by a quick movement of her fan, "and I will send the child to you."

Carlos obeyed, and for a considerable time paced up and down a cool spacious apartment, only separated from the court by marble pillars, between which costly hangings were suspended. Being a Spaniard, and dwelling among Spaniards, he was neither surprised nor disconcerted by the long delay.

At last, however, he began to suspect that his cousin had forgotten him. But this was not the case. First a painted ivory ball rolled in over the smooth floor; then one of the hangings was hastily pushed aside, and the little Doña Inez bounded gaily into the room in search of her toy. She was a merry, healthy child, about two years old, and really very pretty, though her infantine charms were not set off to advantage by the miniature nun's habit in which she was dressed, on account of a vow made by her mother to "Our Lady of Carmel," during the serious illness for which Carlos had summoned Losada to her aid. She was followed almost immediately, not by the grave elderly nurse who usually waited on her, but by a girl of about sixteen, rather a beauty, whose quick dark eyes bestowed, from beneath their long lashes, bashful but evidently admiring glances on the handsome young nobleman.

Carlos, ever fond of children, and enjoying the momentary relief from the painful tension of his daily life, stooped for the ball and held it, just allowing its bright red to appear through his fingers. As the child was not in the least shy, he was soon engaged in a game with her.

Looking up in the midst of it, he saw that the mother had come in silently, and was watching him with searching anxious eyes that brought back in a moment all his troubles. He allowed the ball to slide to the ground, and then, with a touch of his foot, sent it rolling into one of the farthest corners of the spacious hall. The child ran gleefully after it; while the mother and the attendant exchanged glances. "You may take the noble child away, Juanita," said the former.

Juanita led off her charge without again allowing her to approach Carlos, thus rendering unnecessary the ceremony of a farewell. Was this the mother's contrivance, lest by spell of word or gesture, or even by a kiss, the heretic might pollute or endanger the innocent babe?

When they were alone together, Doña Inez was the first to speak. "I do not think you can be so wicked after all; since you love children, and play with them still," she said in a low, half-frightened tone.

"God bless you for those words, señora," answered Carlos with a trembling lip. He was learning to steel himself to scorn; but kindness tested his self-control more severely.

"Amigo mio," she resumed, drawing nearer and speaking more rapidly, "I cannot quite forget the past. It is very wrong, I know, and I am weak. Ay de mi. If it be true you really are that dreadful thing I do not care to name, I ought to have the courage to stand by and see you perish."

"But my kinsfolk," said Carlos, "do not intend me to perish. And for the protection they afford me I am grateful. More I could not have expected from them; less they might well have done for me. But I wish I could show them and you that I am not the foul dishonoured thing they deem me."

"If it had only been something respectable," said Doña Inez, with a sort of writhe, "such as some youthful irregularity, or stabbing or slaying somebody!—but what use in words? I would say, I counsel you to look to your own safety. Do you not know my brothers?"

"I think I do, señora. That an Alvarez de Meñaya should be defamed of heresy would be more than a disgrace—it would be a serious injury to them."

"There be more ways than one of avoiding the misfortune."

Carlos looked inquiringly at her. Something in her half-averted face and the quick shrug of her shoulders prompted him to ask, "Do you think they mean me mischief?"

"Daggers are sharp to cut knots," said the lady, playing with her fan and avoiding his eye.

With so many ghastlier terrors had the mind of Carlos grown familiar, that this one came to him in the guise of a relief. So "the sharpness of death" for him might mean no more than a dagger's thrust, after all! One moment here, the next in his Saviour's presence. Who that knew aught of the tender mercies of the Holy Office could do less than thank God on his bended knees for the prospect of such a fate!

"It is not *death* that I fear," he answered, looking at her steadily.

"But you may as well live; nay, you had better live. For you may repent, may save your unhappy soul. I shall pray for you."

"I thank you, dear and kind señora; but, through the grace of God, my soul is saved already. I believe in Jesus Christ—"

"Hush!" Doña Inez interrupted, dropping her fan and putting her fingers in her ears. "Hush! or ere I am aware I shall have listened to some dreadful heresy. The saints help me! How should I know just where the good Catholic words end, and the wicked ones begin? I might be caught in the web of the evil one; and then neither saint nor angel, no, nor even Our Lady herself, could deliver me. But listen to me, Don Carlos, for at all events I would save your life."

"I will listen gratefully to aught from your lips."

"I know that you dare not attempt flight from the city at present. But if you could lie concealed in some safe and quiet place within it till this storm has blown over, you might then steal away unobserved. Don Garcia says that now there is such a keen search made after the Lutherans, that every man who cannot give a good account of himself is like to be taken for one of the accursed sect. But that cannot last for ever; in six months or so the panic will be past. And those six months you may spend in safety, hidden away in the lodging of my lavandera."[1]

"You are kind—"

"Peace, and listen. I have arranged the whole matter. And once you are there, I will see that you lack nothing. It is in the Morrero;[2] a house hidden in a very labyrinth of lanes, a chamber in the house which a man would need to look for very particularly ere he found it."

"How shall *I* succeed in finding it?"

"You noticed the pretty girl who led in my little Inez? Pepe, the lavandera's son, is ready to die for the love of her. She will describe you to him, and engage his assistance in the adventure, telling him the story I have told her, that you wish to conceal yourself for a season, having stabbed your rival in a love affair."

"O Doña Inez! *I!*—almost a priest!"

"Well, well; do not look so horror-stricken, amigo mio. What could I do? I dared not give them a hint of the truth, or both my hands full of double ducats would not have tempted them to stir in the affair. So I thought no shame of inventing a crime for you that would win their interest and sympathy, and dispose them to aid you."

"Passing strange," said Carlos. "Had I only sinned against the law of God and the life of my neighbour, they would gladly help

[1] Washerwoman.

[2] Moorish quarter of the city.

me to escape; did they dream that I read his words in my own tongue, they would give me up to death."

"Juanita is a good little Christian," remarked Doña Inez; "and Pepe also is a very honest lad. But perhaps you may find some sympathy with the old crone of a lavandera, who is of Moorish blood, and, it is whispered, knows more of Mohammed than she does of her breviary."

Carlos disclaimed all connection with the followers of the false prophet.

"How should I know the difference?" said Doña Inez. "I thought it was all the same, heresy and heresy. But I was about to say, Pepe is a gallant lad, a regular *majo*; his hand knows its way either amongst the strings of a guitar, or on the hilt of a dagger. He has often served caballeros who were out of nights serenading their ladies; and he will go equipped as if for such an adventure. You, also, bind a guitar on your shoulder (you could use one in old times, and to good purpose too, if you have not forgotten all Christian accomplishments together); bribe old Sancho to leave the gates open, and sally forth to-morrow night when the clock strikes the midnight hour. Pepe will wait for you in the Calle del Candilejo until one."

"To-morrow night?"

"I would have named to-night, but Pepe has a dance to attend. Moreover, I knew not whether I could arrange this interview in sufficient time to prepare you. Now, cousin," she added anxiously, "you understand your part, and you will not fail in it."

"I understand everything, señora my cousin. From my heart I thank you for the noble effort to save me. Whether in its result it shall prove successful or no, already it is successful in giving me hope and strength, and renewing my faith in old familiar kindness."

"Hush! that step is Don Garcia's. It is best you should go."

"Only one word more, señora. Will my generous cousin add to her goodness by giving my brother, when it can be done with safety, a hint of how it has fared with me?"

"Yes; that shall be cared for. Now, Adiõs."

"I kiss your feet, señora."

She hastily extended her hand, upon which he pressed a kiss of friendship and gratitude. "God bless you, my cousin," he said.

"Vaya con Dios," she responded. "For it is our last meeting," she added mentally.

She stood and watched the retreating figure with tears in her bright eyes, and in her heart a memory that went back to old times, when she used to intercede with her rough brothers for the delicate shrinking child, who was younger, as well as frailer, than all the rest. "He was ever gentle and good, and fit to be a holy priest," she thought. "Ay de mi, for the strange, sad change! Yet, after all, I cannot see that he is so greatly changed. Playing with the child, talking with me, he is just the same Carlos as of old. But the devil is very cunning. God and Our Lady keep us from his wiles!"

XXV.

Waiting.

> "Our night is dreary, and dim our day,
> And if thou turn thy face away,
> We are sinful, feeble, and helpless dust,
> And have none to look to and none to trust. "
>
> HOGG.

HUS was Carlos roused from the dull apathy of forced inaction. With the courage and energy that are born of hope, he made the few and simple preparations for his flight that were in his power. He also visited as many as he could of his afflicted friends, feeling that his ministry among them was now drawing to a close.

He rejoined his uncle's family as usual at the evening meal. Don Balthazar, the empleado, was not present at its commencement, but soon came in, looking so much disturbed that his father asked, "What is amiss?"

"There is nothing amiss, señor and my father," answered the young man, as he raised a large cup of Manzanilla to his lips.

"Is there any news in the city?" asked his brother Don Manuel.

Don Balthazar set down the empty cup. "No great news," he answered. "A curse upon those Lutheran dogs that are setting the place in an uproar."

"What! more arrests," said Don Manuel the elder. "It is awful. The number reached eight hundred yesterday. Who is taken now?"

"A priest from the country, Doctor Juan Gonzalez, and a friar named Olmedo. But that is nothing. They might take all the churchmen in all the Spains, and fling them into the lowest dungeons of the Triana for me. It is a different matter when we come to speak of ladies—ladies, too, of the first families and highest consideration."

A slight shudder, and a kind of forward movement, as if to catch what was coming, passed round the table. But Don Balthazar seemed reluctant to say more.

"Is it any of our acquaintances?" asked the sharp, high-pitched voice of Doña Sancha at last.

"Every one is acquainted with Don Pedro Garcia de Xeres y Bohorques. It is—I tremble to tell you—his daughter."

"*Which?*" cried Gonsalvo, in tones that turned the gaze of all on his livid face and fierce eager eyes.

"St. Iago, brother! You need not look thus at me. Is it my fault?—It is the learned one, of course, Doña Maria. Poor lady, she may well wish now that she had never meddled with anything beyond her breviary."

"Our Lady and all the saints defend us! Doña Maria in prison for heresy—horrible! Who will be safe now?" the ladies exclaimed, crossing themselves shudderingly.

But the men used stronger language. Fierce and bitter were the anathemas they heaped upon heresy and heretics. Yet it is only just to say that, had they dared, they might have spoken differently. Probably in their secret hearts they meant the curses less for the victims than for their oppressors; and had Spain been a land in which men might speak what they thought, Gonzales de Munebrãga would have been devoted to a lower place in hell than Luther or Calvin.

Only two were silent. Before the eye of Carlos rose the sweet thoughtful face of the young girl, as he had seen it last, radiant with the faith and hope kindled by the sublime words of heavenly promise spoken by Losada. But the sight of another face—still, rigid, death-like—drove that vision away. Gonsalvo sat opposite to him at the table. And had he never heard the strange story Doña Inez told him, that look would have revealed it all.

Neither curse nor prayer passed the white lips of Gonsalvo. Not one of all the bitter words, found so readily on slighter occasions, came now to his aid. The fiercest outburst of passion would have seemed less terrible to Carlos than this unnatural silence.

Yet none of the others, after the first moment, appeared to notice it. Or if they did observe anything strange in the look and manner of Gonsalvo, it was imputed to physical pain, from which he often suffered, but for which he rejected, and even resented, sympathy, until at last it ceased to be offered him. Having given what expression they dared to their outraged feelings, they once more turned their attention to the unfinished repast. It was not at all a cheerful meal, yet it was duly partaken of, except by Gonsalvo and Carlos, both of whom left the table as soon as they could without attracting attention.

Willingly would Carlos have endeavoured to console his cousin; but he did not dare to speak to him, or even to allow him to guess that he saw the anguish of his soul.

One day still remained to him before his flight. In the morning, though not very early, he set out to finish his farewell visits to his friends. He had not gone many paces from the house, when he observed a gentleman in plain black clothing, with sword and cloak, look at him regardfully as he passed. A moment afterwards the same person, having apparently changed his mind as to the direction in which he wished to go, hurried by him at a rapid pace; and with a murmured "Pardon, señor," thrust a billet[1] into his hand.

Not doubting that one of his friends had sent an emissary to

[1] *Archaic:* A short letter; a note.

warn him of some danger, Carlos turned into one of the narrow winding lanes with which the semi-oriental city abounds, and finding himself safe from observation, cast a hasty glance at the billet.

His eye just caught the words, "His reverence the Lord Inquisitor—Don Gonsalvo—after midnight—revelations of importance—strict secrecy." What did it all mean? Did the writer wish to inform him that his cousin intended betraying him to the Inquisition? He did not believe it. But the sound of approaching footsteps made him thrust the paper hastily away; and in another moment his sleeve was grasped by Gonsalvo.

Give it to me," said his cousin in a breathless whisper.

"Give you what?"

"The paper that born idiot and marplot[2] put into thy hands, mistaking thee for me. Curse the fool! Did he not know I was lame?"

Carlos showed the note, still holding it. "Is this what you mean?" he asked.

"You have read it! Honourable!" cried Gonsalvo, with a bitter sneer.

"You are unjust to me. It bears no address; and I could not suppose otherwise than that it was intended for myself. However, I only read the few disconnected words upon which my eye first chanced to fall."

The cousins stood gazing in each other's faces; as those might do that meet in mortal combat, ere they close hand to hand. Each was pondering whether the other was capable of doing him a deadly injury. Yet, after all, each held, at the bottom of his heart, a conviction that the other might be trusted.

Carlos, though he had the greater cause for apprehension, was the first to come to a conclusion. Almost with a smile he handed the note to Gonsalvo. "Whatever yon mysterious billet may mean to Don Gonsalvo," he said, "I am convinced that he means no harm to any one bearing the name of Alvarez de Meñaya."

[2] An officious meddler whose interference compromises the success of an undertaking.

"You will never repent that word. And it is true—in the sense you speak it," returned Gonsalvo, taking the paper from his hand. At that moment he was irresolute whether to confide in Carlos or no. But the touch of his cousin's hand decided him. It was cold and trembling. One so weak in heart and nerve was obviously unfit to share the burden of a brave man's desperate resolve.

Carlos went his way, firmly believing that Gonsalvo intended no ill to him. But what then did he intend? Had he solicited the Inquisitor for a private midnight interview merely to throw himself at his feet, and with impassioned eloquence to plead the cause of Doña Maria? Were "important revelations"only a blind to procure his admission?

Impossible! who, past the age of infancy, would kneel to the storm to implore it to be still, or to the fire to ask it to subdue its rage? Perhaps some dreamy enthusiast, unacquainted with the world and its ways, might still be found sanguine enough for such a project, but certainly not Don Gonsalvo Alvarez de Meñaya.

Or had he a bribe to offer? Inquisitors, like other churchmen, were known to be subject to human frailties; of course they would not touch gold, but, according to a well-known Spanish proverb, you were invited to throw it into their cowls. And Munebrãga could scarcely have fed his numerous train of insolent retainers, decked his splendid barge with gold and purple, and brought rare plants and flowers from every known country to his magnificent gardens, without very large additions to the acknowledged income of the Inquisitor-General's deputy. But, again, not all the wealth of the Indies would avail to open the gates of the Triana to an obstinate heretic, however it might modify the views of "his Reverence" upon the merits of a doubtful case. And even to procure a few slight alleviations in the treatment of the accused, would have required a much deeper purse than Gonsalvo's.

Moreover, Carlos saw that the young man was "bitter of soul," ready for any desperate deed. What if he meant to accuse *himself.* Amidst the careless profanity in which he had been too wont to indulge, many a word had fallen from his lips that might be contrary to sound doctrine in the estimation of Inquisitors, comparatively lenient as they were to *blasphemers*. But what possible benefit to Doña Maria would be gained by his throwing himself into the jaws of death? And if it were really his resolve to commit suicide, by way of ending his own miseries, he could surely accomplish the act in a more direct and far less painful manner.

Thus Carlos pondered; but in whatever way he regarded the matter, he could not escape from the idea that his cousin intended some dangerous or fatal step. Gonsalvo was too still, too silent. This was an evil sign. Carlos would have felt comparatively easy about him had he made him shrink and shudder by an outburst of the fiercest, most indignant curses. For the less emotion is wasted in expression, the more remains, like pent-up steam, to drive the engine forward in its course. Moreover, there was an evil light in Gonsalvo's eye; a gleam like that of hope, but hope that was certainly not kindled from above.

Although the very crisis of his own fate was now approaching, and every faculty might have had full occupation nearer home, Carlos was haunted perpetually by the thought of his cousin. It continued to occupy him not only during his visits to his friends, but afterwards in the solitude and silence of his own apartment. We all know the strange perversity with which, in times of suspense and sorrow, the mind will sometimes run riot upon matters irrelevant, and even apparently trivial.

With slow footsteps the hours stole on; miserable hours to Carlos, except in so far as he could spend them in prayer, now his only resource and refuge. After pleading for himself; for Juan, for his dear imprisoned brethren and sisters, he named Gonsalvo; and was led most earnestly to implore God's mercy for his unhappy cousin. As he thought of his misery, so much greater than his own; his loneliness, without God in the world; his sorrow, without hope,—his pleading grew impassioned. And when at last he rose from his knees, it was with that sweet sense that God would hear—nay, that he *had* heard—which is one of the mysteries of the new life, the precious things that no man knoweth save he that receiveth them.

Then, believing it was nearly midnight, he quickly finished his simple preparations, took his guitar (which had now lain unused for a long time), and sallied forth from his chamber.

XXVI.

Don Gonsalvo's Revenge.

"Our God, the all just,
Unto himself reserves this royalty,
The secret chastening of the guilty heart:
The fiery touch, the scourge that purifies
Leave it with him. Yet make not that thy trust;
For that strong heart of thine—oh, listen yet!
Must in its depths o'ercome the very wish
Of death or torture to the guilty one,
Ere it can sleep again."

HEMANS.

ON MANUEL'S house had once belonged to a Moorish Cid, or lord. It had been assigned to the first Conde de Nuera, as one of the original *conquistadors*[1] of Seville; and he had bequeathed it to his second son. It had a turret, after the Moorish fashion, and the upper chamber of this had been given to Carlos on his first arrival in the city; from an idea that the theological student would require a solitary place for study and devotion, or, at least, that it would be decorous to suppose so. The room beneath had been occupied by Don Juan, but since his departure it was appropriated by Gonsalvo, who liked

[1] A Spanish conqueror or adventurer, especially one of those who conquered Mexico, Peru, and Central America in the 16th century.

solitude, and took advantage of his improved health to escape from the ground-floor, to which his infirmities had long confined him.

As Carlos stole noiselessly down the narrow winding stair, he noticed a light in his cousin's room. This in itself did not surprise him. But he certainly felt a little disconcerted when, just as he passed the door, Don Gonsalvo opened it, and met him face to face. He also was fully equipped in sword and cloak, and carried a torch in his hand.

"Vaya, vaya, Don Carlos," he said reproachfully; "after all, thou couldst not trust me."

"Nay, I did trust you."

From fear of being overheard, both entered the nearest room—Don Gonsalvo's—and its owner closed the door softly.

"You are stealing away from fear of me, and thereby throwing yourself into the fire. Do it not, Don Carlos; be advised, and do it not." He spoke earnestly, and without a shadow of the old bitterness and sarcasm.

"Nay, it is not thus. My flight was planned ere yesterday; and in concert with one who both can and will provide me with the means of safety. It is best I should go."

"Enough said then," returned Gonsalvo, more coldly. "Farewell; I seek not to detain you. Farewell; for though we may go forth together, our paths divide, and for ever, at the door."

"Your path is perhaps less safe than mine, Don Gonsalvo."

"Talk of what you understand, cousin. My path is safety itself. And now that I think of it (if you could be trusted), you might aid me perhaps. Did you know all, I dare not doubt that you would rejoice to do it."

"God knows how joyfully I would aid you if I could, Don Gonsalvo. But I fear you are bound on a useless, and worse than useless, errand."

"You know not my errand."

"But I know to whom you go this night. Oh, my cousin, is it possible you can dream that prayer of yours will soften hearts harder than the nether millstone?"

"I know the way to one heart; and though it be the hardest of all, I shall reach it."

Were you to pour the wealth of El Dorado at the feet of Gonzales de Munebrãga, he neither would nor could unloose one bolt of that prison."

Gonsalvo's wild look changed suddenly into one of wistful earnestness, almost of tenderness. He said, lowering his voice, "Near as death, the revealer of secrets may be to me, there are still some questions worth the asking. Perchance you can throw a gleam of light upon this horrible darkness. We are speaking frankly now, and as in God's presence. Tell me, *is that charge true?*"

"Frankly, and in the sense in which you ask—it is."

The last fatal words Carlos only whispered. Gonsalvo made no answer; but a kind of momentary spasm passed across his face.

Carlos at length went on in a low voice: "She knew the Evangel long before I did, though she is so young—not yet one-and-twenty. She was the pupil of Dr. Egidius; but he was wont to say he learned more from her than she did from him. Her keen, bright intellect cut through sophistries, and reached truth so quickly. And God gave her abundantly of his grace; making her willing, for that truth, to endure all things. Oft have I seen her sweet face kindle and glow whilst he who taught us spoke of the joy and strength given to those that suffer for the name of Christ. I am persuaded he is with her now, and will be with her even to the end. Could you gain access to her where she is, I think she would tell you she possesses a treasure of peace of which neither death nor suffering, neither cruelty of fiends nor worse cruelty of fiend-like men, can avail to rob her."

"She is a saint—she will be a blessed saint in heaven, let them say what they may," murmured Gonsalvo hoarsely. Then the fierce look returned to his face again. "But I think the old Christians of Castile, the men whose good swords made the infidels bite the dust, and planted the cross on their painted towers, are no better than curs and dastards."[2]

---

[2] *Archaic:* Somebody who is cowardly, mean, and treacherous.

"In that they suffer these things."

"Yes; a thousand times, yes. In the name of man's honour and woman's loveliness, are there, in our good city of Seville, neither fathers, nor brothers, nor lovers left alive? No man who thinks the sweetest eyes ever seen worth six inches of steel in five skilful fingers? No one man, save the poor forgotten cripple, Don Gonsalvo Alvarez. But he thanks God this night that he has spared his life, and left strength enough in his feeble limbs to bear him into a murderer's presence."

"Don Gonsalvo! what do you mean?" cried Carlos, shrinking from him.

"Lower thy voice, an' it please thee. But why should I fear to tell thee—*thee*, who hast good cause to be the death-foe of Inquisitors? If thou art not cur and dastard too, thou wilt applaud and pray for me. For I suppose heretics pray, at least as well as Inquisitors. I said I would reach the heart of Gonzales de Munebrãga this night. Not with gold. There is another metal of keener temper, which enters in where even gold cannot come."

"Then you mean—*murder?*" said Carlos, again drawing near him, and laying his hand on his arm. Gonsalvo sank into a seat, half mechanically, half from an instinct that led him to spare the strength he would need so sorely by-and-by.

In the momentary pause that followed, the clock of San Vicente tolled the midnight hour.

"Yes," replied Gonsalvo steadily; "I mean murder—as the shepherd does who strangles the wolf with his paw on the lamb."

"Oh, think—"

"I have thought of everything. And mark me, Don Carlos, I have but one regret. It is that my weapon deals an instantaneous death. Such revenge is poor and flavourless after all.

I have heard of poisons whose least drop, mingling with the blood, ensures a slow agonising death—time to learn what torture means, and to drain to the dregs the cup filled for others—to curse God and man ere he dies. For a phial of such, wherewith to anoint my blade, I would sell my soul to-night."

"O Gonsalvo, this is horrible! They are wild, wicked words you speak. Pray God to pardon you!"

"I adjure him by his justice to prosper me," said Gonsalvo, raising his head defiantly.

"He will not prosper you. And do you dream that such a mad achievement (suppose you even succeed in it) will open prison-doors and set captives free? Alas! alas! that we are not at the mercy of a tyrant's *will*. For tyrants, the worst of them, sometimes relent; and—they are mortal. That which is crushing us is not a living being, an organism with nerves, and brain, and blood. It is a system, a THING, a terrible engine, that moves on in its resistless way, cold and lifeless, without will or feeling. Strong as adamant, it kills, tortures, destroys; obeying laws far away out of our sight. Were Valdez and Munebrãga, and all the Board of Inquisitors, dead corpses by the morning light, not a single dungeon in the Triana would open its pitiless gate."

"I do not believe *that*," replied Gonsalvo, rather more quietly. "Surely there must be some confusion, of which advantage may be taken by friends of the prisoners. This, indeed, is the motive which now induces me to confide in you. *You* may know those who, if they had the chance, could strike a shrewd blow to save their dearest on earth from torture and death."

But Gonsalvo read no answer in the sorrowful face of Carlos to the searching look of inquiry with which he said this. After a silence he went on,—

"Suppose the worst, however. The Holy Office sorely needs a little blood-letting, and will be much the better for it. Whoever succeeds, Munebrãga will have my dagger flashing in his eyes, and will take care how he deals with his prisoners, and whom he arrests."

"I implore you to think of yourself," said Carlos.

Gonsalvo smiled. "I know I shall pay the forfeit," he said, "even as those who slew the Inquisitor Pedro Arbues before the high altar in Saragossa. But"—here the smile faded, and the stern set look returned to his face—"I shall not pay more, for a man's triumphant vengeance, than those fiends will dare to inflict upon a tender, delicately nurtured girl for the crime of a mystic meditation, or a few words of prayer not properly rounded off with an Ave."

"True. But then you will suffer alone. She has God with her."

"I *can* suffer alone."

For that word Carlos envied him. *He* shrank in terror from loneliness, from suffering, shuddering at the very thought of the dungeon and the torture-room. And just then the first quarter of his hour of grace chimed from the clock of San Vicente. What if he and Pepe should fail to meet? He would not think of that now. Whatever happened, Gonsalvo must be saved. He went on,—

"Here you can suffer alone and be strong. But how will you endure the loneliness of the long hereafter, away from God's presence, from light and life and hope? Are you content that you, and she for whom you give your life, should be sundered throughout eternity?"

"Nay; I am casting my lot in with hers. If the Church curses her (pure and holy as she ever was), its anathema shall fall on me too. If only the Church's key opens heaven, she and I will both stand without."

"Yet you know she will enter heaven. Shall *you*?"

Gonsalvo hesitated. "It will not be the blood of a villain that will bar my way," he said.

"God says, 'Thou shalt not kill.'"[3]

"Then what will he do with Gonzales de Munebrãga?"

"He will do that with him of which, if you but dreamed, it would change your fiercest hate into saddest, deepest pity. Have you realised what a span is our life here compared with the countless ages of eternity? Think! For God's chosen a few weeks, or months at most, of solitude and fear and pain, ended perhaps by—but that is as he pleases; *ended*, at all events. Then add up the million years, fill them with the joy of victory, and the presence and love of Christ himself. Can they not, and we for them, be content with this?"

"Are you content with it yourself?" Gonsalvo suddenly interrupted. "You seek flight."

---

[3] Exodus 20:13

The glow faded from the face of Carlos, and his eyes sank to the ground. "Christ has not called me yet," he answered in a lower tone. There was a silence; then he resumed: "Turn now to the other side. Would you change, even this hour, with Gonzales de Munebrãga? But take him from his wealth, and his pomp, and his sinful luxuries, all defiled with blood, and what remains for him? Everlasting fire, prepared for the devil and his angels."

"Everlasting fire!" Gonsalvo repeated, as if the thought pleased him.

"Leave him in God's hand. It is a stronger hand than yours, Don Gonsalvo."

"Everlasting fire! I would send him there to-night."

"And whither would you send your own sinful soul?"

"God might pardon, though the Church cursed."

"Possibly. But to enter God's heaven you need something besides pardon."

"What?" asked Gonsalvo, half wearily, half incredulously.

"'Holiness; without which no man can see the Lord.'"[4]

"Holiness?" Gonsalvo questioned, as if the word was strange to him, and he attached no meaning to it.

"Yes," Carlos went on, with intense and ever increasing earnestness; "unless, even from that passionate heart of yours, revenge and hatred are banished, you can never see God, never come where—"

"Hold thy peace, trifler!" Gonsalvo interrupted with angry impatience. "Too long have I tarried, listening to thine idle talk. Priests and women are content with words; brave men act. Farewell to thee!"

"One word more, only one." Carlos drew near and laid his hand on his cousin's arm. "Nay, you *shall* listen to me. Seemeth it to you a thing incredible that that heart of yours can be changed and softened to a love like his who prayed on the cross for his murderers? Yet it can be. *He* can do it. He gives pardon, holiness, peace. Peace of which you dream not now, but which she knows full well.

[4] Hebrews 12:14

O Don Gonsalvo, better join her where she is going, than wildly, rashly, and most uselessly peril your soul to avenge her!"

"Uselessly! Were that true indeed—"

"Ay de mi! who can doubt it?"

"Would I had time for thought!"

"Take it, in God's name, and pray him to keep you from a great crime."

For a few moments he sat still—still as the dead. Then he started suddenly. "Already the hour is passing," he exclaimed; "I shall be too late. Fool that I was, to be almost moved from my purpose by the idle words of a— The weakness is past now. Still, ere we part, give me thy hand, Don Carlos, for, on my faith, I never liked thee half so well."

Very sorrowfully Carlos extended it, rather wondering as he did so that the energetic Gonsalvo failed to spring from his seat and prepare to be gone.

Gonsalvo stirred not, even to take the offered hand. A death-like paleness overspread his face, and a cry of terror had well nigh broken from his lips. But he choked it back. "Something is strangely wrong with me," he faltered. "I cannot move. I feel dead—dead—from the waist down."

"God has spoken to you from heaven," said Carlos solemnly. He felt as if a miracle had been wrought in his presence. His Protestantism had not freed him from the superstitions of his age. Had he lived three centuries later, he would have seen nothing miraculous in the disease with which Gonsalvo was stricken, but rather have called it the natural result of intense agitation and excitement, acting upon a frame already weakened.

Yet the reckless Gonsalvo was the more superstitious of the two. He was at war with the creed in which he had been nurtured; but that older and deeper kind of superstition which has its root in human nature had, for this very reason, a stronger hold upon him.

"Dead—dead!" he repeated, the words falling from his lips in broken, awe-struck whispers. "The limbs I misused! The feet that led me into sin! God—God have mercy upon me! It is thy hand!"

"It is his hand; a sign he has not forsaken thee; that he means to bring thee back to himself. Oh, my cousin, do not despair. Hope yet in his mercy, for it is great."

Carlos knelt down beside him, took his passive hand in his, and spoke earnest, loving words of hope and comfort. The last quarter, ere the single stroke that should announce that the hour appointed for his own flight was past, chimed from the clock on the church tower. Yet he did not move—he had forgotten self. At last, however, he said, "But it may be something can be done to relieve you. You ought to have medical aid without delay. I should have thought of this before. I will rouse the household."

"No; that would endanger you. Go on your way, and bid the porter do it when you are gone."

It was too late; the household was roused. A loud authoritative knocking at the outer gate sent the blood back from the hearts of both with sudden and horrible fear.

There was a sound of opening gates, followed by footsteps—voices—cries.

Gonsalvo was the first to understand all. "The Alguazils of the Holy Office!" he exclaimed.

"I am lost!" cried Carlos, large drops gathering on his brow.

"Conceal yourself," said Gonsalvo; but he knew his words were vain. Already his quick ear had caught the sound of his cousin's name; and already footsteps were on the stairs.

Carlos glanced round the room. For a moment his eye rested on the window, eighty feet above the ground. Better spring from it and perish! No, that would be self-murder. In God's name he would await them manfully.

"You will be searched," Gonsalvo whispered hurriedly; "have you aught about your person that may add to your danger?"

Carlos drew from its place of concealment the heroic Juliano's treasured gift.

"I will hide it," said his cousin; and taking it hastily, he slipped it beneath his inner vest, where it lay in strange neighbourhood with a small, exquisitely tempered poniard,[5] destined never to be used.

The torch-light within, perhaps the voices, guided the Alguazils to that room. A hand was placed on the door. "They are coming, Don Carlos," cried Gonsalvo; "I am thy murderer."

"No—no fault of thine. Always remember that," said Carlos, in his sharpest anguish generous still. Then for one brief moment, that seemed an age, he was deaf to all outward things. Afterwards he was himself again.

And something more than himself perhaps. Now, as in other moments of intense excitement, the spirit of his race descended on him. When the Alguazils entered, it was Don Carlos Alvarez de Santilla nos y Meñaya who met them, with folded arms, with steadfast eye, and pale but dauntless forehead.

All was quiet, regular, and most orderly. Don Manuel, roused from his slumbers, appeared with the Alguazils, and respectfully requested a sight of the warrant upon which they proceeded.

It was produced; and all could see that it was duly signed, and sealed with the famous seal—the sword and olive branch, the dog with the flaming brand, the sorely outraged, "Justitia et misericordia."

Had Don Manuel Alvarez been king of all the Spains, and Carlos his heir-apparent, he dared not have offered the least resistance then. He had no wish to resist, however; he bowed obsequiously, and protested his own and his family's devotion to the Faith and the Holy Office. But he added (perhaps merely as a matter of form), that he could bring many witnesses of unimpeachable character to testify to his nephew's orthodoxy, and hoped to succeed in clearing him from whatever odious imputation had induced their Reverences to order his arrest.

Meanwhile Gonsalvo gnashed his teeth in impotent rage and despair. He would have bartered his life for two minutes of health and strength in which to rush suddenly on the Alguazils, and give Carlos time to escape, let the consequences of such frantic audacity be what they might. But the bands of disease, stronger than iron, made the body a prison for the indignant, tortured spirit.

[5] A small daggar with a slim blade, triangular or square in its cross section.

Carlos spoke for the first time. "I am ready to go with you," he said to the chief of the Alguazils. "Do you wish to examine my apartment? You are welcome. It is the chamber over this."

Having gone over every detail of such a scene a thousand times in imagination, he knew that the examination of papers and personal effects usually formed a part of it. And he had no fears for the result, as, in preparation for his flight, he had carefully destroyed everything that he thought could implicate himself or any one else.

"Don Carlos—cousin!" cried Gonsalvo suddenly, as surrounded by the officers he was about to leave the room. "Vaya con Dios! A braver man than you have I never seen."

Carlos turned on him one long, sorrowful gaze. "*Tell Ruy,*" he said. That was all.

Then there was trampling of footsteps overhead, and the sound of voices, not excited or angry, but cool, business-like, even courteous.

Then the footsteps descended, passed the door of Gonsalvo's room, sounded along the corridor, grew fainter on the great staircase, died away in the court.

Less than an hour afterwards, the great gate of the Triana opened to receive a new victim. The grave familiar held it, bowing low, until the prisoner and his guard had passed through. Then it was swung to again, and barred and bolted, shutting out from Don Carlos Alvarez all help and hope, all charity and all mercy—save only the mercy of God.

XXVII.

My Brother's Keeper.

"Since she loved him, he went carefully,
Bearing a thing so precious in his hand."
GEORGE ELIOT.

BOUT a week afterwards, Don Juan Alvarez dismounted at the door of his uncle's mansion. His shout soon brought the porter, a "pure and ancient Christian," who had spent nearly all his life in the service of the family.

"God save you, father," said Juan. "Is my brother in the house?"

"No, señor and your worship,"—the old man hesitated, and looked confused.

"Where shall I find him, then?" cried Juan; "speak at once, if you know."

"May it please your noble Excellency, I—I know nothing. At least—the Saints have mercy on us!" and he trembled from head to foot.

Juan thrust him aside, nearly knocking him down in his haste, and dashed breathless into his uncle's private room, on the right hand side of the patio.

Don Manuel was there, seated at a table, looking over some papers.

"Where is my brother?" asked Juan sternly and abruptly, searching his face with his keen dark eyes.

"Holy Saints defend us!" cried Don Manuel, nearly startled out of his ordinary decorum. "And what madness brings you here?"

"Where is my brother?" Juan repeated, in the same tone, and without moving a muscle.

"Be quiet—be reasonable, nephew Don Juan. Do not make a disturbance; it will be worse for all of us. We did all we could—"

"Señor, will you answer me?"

"Have patience. We did all we could for him, I was about to say; and more than we ought. The fault was his own, if he was suspected and taken—"

"*Taken!* Then I come too late." Sinking into the nearest seat, he covered his face with both hands, and groaned aloud.

Don Manuel Alvarez had never learned to reverence the sacredness of a great sorrow. Rushing in where such as he might well fear to tread, he presumed to offer consolation. "Come, then, nephew Don Juan," he said, "you know as well as I do that 'water that has run by will turn no mill,' and that 'there is no good in throwing the rope after the bucket.' No man can alter that which is past. All we can do is to avoid worse mischief in future."

"When was it?" asked Juan, without looking up.

"A week agone."

"Seven days and nights!"

"Thereabouts. But *you*—are you in love with destruction yourself, that, when you were safe and well at Nuera, you must needs come hither again?"

"I came to save him."

"Unheard of folly! If *you* have been meddling with these matters—and it is but too likely, seeing you were always with him (though, the Saints forbid I should suspect an honourable soldier like you of anything worse than imprudence)—do you not know they will wring the whole truth out of *him* with very little trouble, and your life is not worth a brass maravedì?"

Juan started to his feet, and glared scorn and defiance in his uncle's face. "Whoever dares to hint so vile a slander," he cried, "by my faith he shall repent it, were he my uncle ten times over. Don Carlos Alvarez never did, and never will, betray a trust, let those wretches deal with him as they may. But I know him; he will die, or worse,—they will make him mad." Here Juan's voice failed, and he stood in silent horror, gazing on the dread vision that rose before his mind.

Don Manuel was daunted by his vehemence. "You are the best judge yourself of what amount of danger you may be incurring," he said. "But let me tell you, Señor Don Juan, that I hold you rather a dangerous guest to harbour under the circumstances. To have the Alguazils of the Holy Office twice in my house would be enough to cost me all my places, not to mention the disgrace of it."

"You shall not lose a real by me or mine," returned Juan proudly.

"I did not mean, however, to refuse you hospitality," said Don Manuel, relieved, yet a little uneasy, perhaps even remorseful.

"But I mean to decline it, señor. I have only two favours to ask of you," he continued: "one, to allow me free association with my betrothed; the other, to permit me"—his voice faltered, stopped. With a great effort he resumed—"to permit me to examine my brother's room, and whatever effects he may have left there."

"Now you speak more rationally," said his uncle, mistaking the self-control of indignant pride for genuine calmness. "But as to your brother's effects, you may spare your pains; for the Alguazils set the seal of the Holy Office upon them on the night of his arrest, and they have since carried them away. As to the other matter, what Doña Beatriz may think of the connection, after the infamy in which your branch of the family is involved, I cannot tell."

A burning flush mounted to Juan's cheek as he answered, "I trust my betrothed; even as I trust my brother."

"You can see the lady herself. She may be better able than I to persuade you to consult for your own safety. For if you are not a madman, you will return at once to Nuera, which you ought never to have quitted; or you will take the earliest opportunity of rejoining the army."

"I shall not stir from Seville till I obtain my brother's deliverance; or—" Juan did not name the other alternative. Involuntarily he placed his hand on his belt, in which he had concealed certain old family jewels, which he believed would produce a considerable sum of money; for his last faint hope for Carlos lay in a judicious appeal to the all-powerful "Don Dinero."[1]

"You will *never* leave it, then," said Don Manuel. "And you must hold me excused from aiding and abetting your folly. Your brother's business has cost me and mine more than enough already. I had rather ten thousand times that a man had died of the plague in my house, were it for the scandal's sake alone! Nor, bad as it is, is the scandal all. Since that miserable night, my unhappy son Gonsalvo, in whose apartment the arrest took place, has been sick unto death, and out of his mind."

"Don Gonsalvo! What brought my brother to his room?"

"The devil, whose servant he is, may know; I do not. He was found there, in his sword and cloak, as if ready to go forth, when the officers came."

"Did he leave no message—no word for me?"

"Not one word. I know not if he spoke at all, save to offer to show the Alguazils his personal effects. To do him justice, nothing suspicious was found amongst them. But the less said on the subject the better. I wash my hands of it, and of him. I thought he would have done honour to the family; but he has proved its sorest disgrace."

"Señor, what you say of him you say of me also," said Juan, growing white with anger. "And already I have heard quite enough."

"That is as you please, Señor Don Juan."

"I shall only trespass upon you for the favour you have promised me—permission to wait upon Doña Beatriz."

[1] The Lord Dollar.

"I shall apprise her of your presence, and give her leave to act as she sees fit." And glad to put an end to the interview, Don Manuel left the room.

Juan sank into a seat once more, and gave himself up to an agony of grief for his brother.

So absorbed was he in his sorrow, that a light footstep entered and approached unheard by him. At last a small hand touched his arm. He started and looked up. Whatever his anguish of heart might be, he was still the loyal lover of Doña Beatriz. So the next moment found him on his knees saluting that hand with his lips. And then followed certain ceremonies abundantly interesting to those who enact them, but apt to prove tedious when described.

"My lady's devoted slave," said Don Juan, using the ordinary language of the time, "bears a breaking heart to-day. We knew neither father nor mother; there were but the two of us."

"Did you not receive my letter, praying you to remain at Nuera?" asked the lady.

"Pardon me, queen of my heart, in that I dared to disregard a wish of yours. But I knew *his* danger, and I came to save him. Alas! too late."

"I am not sure that I do pardon you, Don Juan."

"Then, I presume so far as to say, that I know Doña Beatriz better than she knows herself. Indeed, had I acted otherwise, she would scarce have pardoned me. How would it have been possible for me to consult for my own safety, leaving him, alone and unaided, in such fearful peril?"

"You acknowledge there is peril—*to you*?"

"There may be, señora."

"Ay de mi! Why, have you thus involved yourself? O Don Juan, you have dealt very cruelly with me!"

"Light of my eyes, life of my life, what mean you by these words?"

"Was it not cruel to allow your brother, with his gentle, winning ways, and his soft specious words, to lead you step by step from the faith of our fathers, until he had you entangled in I know not what horrible heresies, and made you put in peril your honour, your liberty, your life—everything?"

"We only sought Truth."

"Truth!" echoed the lady, with a contemptuous stamp of her small foot and twirl of her fan. "What is Truth? What good will Truth do me if those cruel men drag you from your bed at midnight, take you to that dreadful place, stretch you on the rack?" But that last horror was too much to bear; Doña Beatriz hid her face in her hands, and wept and sobbed passionately.

Juan soothed her with every tender, lover-like art. "I will be very prudent, dearest lady," he said at last; adding, as he gazed on her beautiful face, "I have too much to live for not to hold life very precious."

"Will you promise to fly—to leave the city *now*, before suspicions are awakened which may make flight impossible?"

"My first and my only love, I would die to fulfil your slightest wish. But this thing I cannot do."

"And wherefore not, Señor Don Juan?"

"Can you ask? I must hazard everything, spend everything, in the chance—if there be a chance—of saving him, or, at least, of softening his fate."

"Then God help us both," said Doña Beatriz.

"Amen! Pray to him day and night, señora. Perhaps he may have pity on us."

"There is no chance of saving Don Carlos. Know you not that of all the prisoners the Holy House receives, scarce one in a thousand goes forth again to take his place in the world?"

Juan shook his head. He knew well that his task was almost hopeless; yet, even by Doña Beatriz, he was not to be moved from his determination.

But he thanked her in strong, passionate words for her faith in him and her truth to him. "No sorrow can divide us, my beloved," he said, "nor even what they call shame, falsely as they speak therein. You are my star, that shines on me throughout the darkness."

"I have promised."

"My uncle's family may seek to divide us, and I think they will. But the lady of my heart will not heed their idle words?"

Doña Beatriz smiled. "I am a Lavella," she said. "Do you not know our motto?—'True unto death.'"

"It is a glorious motto. May it be mine too."

"Take heed what you do, Don Juan. If you love me, you will look well to your footsteps, since, wherever they lead, mine are bound to follow." Saying this, she rose, and stood gazing in his face with flushed cheek and kindling eyes.

The words were such as might thrill any lover's heart with joy and gratitude. Yet there was something in the look which accompanied them that changed joy and gratitude into vague fear and apprehension. The light in that dark eye seemed borrowed from the fire of some sublime but terrible resolve within. Juan's heart quailed, though he knew not why, as he said, "My queen should never tread except through flowery paths."

Doña Beatriz took up a little golden crucifix that, attached to a rosary of coral beads, hung from her girdle. "You see this cross, Don Juan?"

"Yes, señora mia."

"On that horrible night when they dragged your brother to prison, I swore a sacred oath upon it. You esteemed me a child, Don Juan, when you read me chapters from your book, and talked freely to me about God, and faith, and the soul's salvation. Perchance I was a child in some things. For I supposed them good words; how could they be otherwise, since you spoke them? I listened and believed, after a fashion; half thinking all the time of the pretty fans and trinkets you brought me, or of the pattern of such and such an one's mantilla that I had seen at mass. But your brother tore the veil from my eyes at last, and made me understand that those specious words, with which a child played childishly, were the crime that finds no pardon here or hereafter. Of the hereafter I know not; of the here I know too much. There be fair ladies, not more deeply involved than I, who have changed their gilded saloons for the dungeons of the Triana. But then it matters not so much about me. For I am not like other girls, who have fathers and mothers, sisters and brothers to care for them. Saving Don Carlos (who was good to me for your sake), no one ever gave me more than the half-sorrowful, half-pitying kindness one might give a pet parrot from the Indies. Therefore, thinking over all things, and knowing well your reckless nature, Señor Don Juan, I swore that night upon this holy cross, that if by evil hap *you* were attainted for heresy, *I* would go next day to the Triana and accuse myself of the same crime."

Juan did not for a moment doubt that she would do it; and thus a chain, light as silk but strong as adamant, was flung around him.

"Doña Beatriz, for my sake—" he began to plead.

"For my sake, Don Juan will take care of his life and liberty," she interrupted, with a smile that, if it had a little sadness, had very far more of triumph in it. She knew the power her resolve gave her over him: she had bought it dearly, and she meant to use it. "Is it *still* your wish to remain here," she continued; "or will you go abroad, and wait for better times?" Juan paused for a moment.

"No choice is left me while Carlos pines uncomforted in a dungeon," he said at last, firmly, though very sorrowfully.

"Then you know what you risk, that is all," answered the lady, whose will was a match for his.

In a marvellously short time had love and sorrow transformed the young and childish girl into a passionate, determined woman, with all the fire of her own southern skies in her heart.

Ere he departed, Juan pleaded for permission to visit her frequently. But here again she showed a keen-sighted apprehensiveness for *him*, which astonished him. She cautioned him against their cousins, Manuel and Balthazar; who, if they thought him in danger of arrest, were quite capable of informing against him themselves, to secure a share of his patrimony. Or they might gain the same end, without the disgrace of such a baseness, by putting him quietly out of the way with their daggers. On all accounts, his frequent presence at the house would be undesirable, and might be dangerous; but she agreed to inform him, by means of certain signals (which they arranged together), when he might pay a visit to her with safety. Then, having bidden her farewell, Don Juan turned his back on his uncle's house with a heavy heart.

XXVIII.

Reaping the Whirlwind.

"All is lost, except a little life."
BYRON.

EARLY a fortnight passed away before a tiny lace kerchief, fluttering at nightfall through the jealous grating of one of the few windows of Don Manuel's house that looked towards the street, told Juan that he was at liberty to seek admission the next day. He was permitted to enter; but he explored the patio and all the adjacent corridors and rooms without seeing the face of which he was in search. He did not, indeed, meet any one, not even a domestic; for it was the eve of the Feast of the Ascension, and nearly all the household had gone to see the great tabernacle carried in state to the Cathedral and set up there, in preparation for the solemnities of the following day.

He thought this a good opportunity for satisfying his longing to visit the apartment his brother had been wont to occupy. In spite of what his uncle had said to the contrary, and indeed of the dictates of his own reason, he could not relinquish the hope that something which belonged to him—perhaps even some word or line traced by his hand—might reward his careful search.

He ascended the stairs; not stealthily, or as if ashamed of his errand, for no one had the right to forbid him. He reached the turret without meeting any one, but had hardly placed his foot upon the stair that led to its upper apartment, when a voice called out, not very loudly,—

"Chien va?"

It was Gonsalvo's. Juan answered,—

"It is I—Don Juan."

"Come to me!"

A private interview with a madman is not generally thought particularly desirable. But Juan was a stranger to fear. He entered the room immediately, and was horror-stricken at the change in his cousin's appearance. A tangled mass of black hair mingled with his beard, and fell neglected over the pillow; while large, wild, melancholy eyes lit up the pallor of his wasted face. He lay, or rather reclined, on a couch, half covered by an embroidered quilt, but wearing a loose doublet, very carelessly thrown on.

Of late the cousins had been far from friendly. Still Juan from compassion stretched out his hand. But Gonsalvo would not touch it.

"Did you know all," he said, "you would stab me where I lie, and thus make an end at once of the most miserable life under God's heaven."

"I fear you are very ill, my cousin," said Juan, kindly; for he thought Gonsalvo's words the offspring of his wandering fancy.

"From the waist downwards I am dead. It is God's hand; and he is just."

"Does your physician give hope of your recovery from this seizure?"

With something like his old short, bitter laugh, Gonsalvo answered, "I have no physician."

"This must be one of his delusions," thought Juan; "or else, since he cannot have Losada, he has refused, with his usual obstinacy, to see any one else."

He said aloud, "That is not right, cousin Don Gonsalvo. You

ought not to neglect lawful means of cure. Señor Sylvester Areto is a very skilful physician; you might safely place yourself in his hands."

"Only there is one slight objection—my father and my brothers would not permit me to see him."

Juan was in no doubt how to regard this statement; but hoping to extract from him some additional information respecting his brother, he turned the conversation.

"When did this malady seize you?" he asked.

"Close the door gently, and I will tell you all. And oh! tread softly, lest my mother, who lies asleep in the room beneath, worn out with watching, should wake and separate us. Then must I bear my guilt and my anguish unconfessed to the grave."

Juan obeyed, and took a seat beside his cousin's couch.

"Sit where I can see your face," said Gonsalvo; "I will not shrink even from *that*. Don Juan, I am your brother's murderer."

Juan started, and his colour changed rapidly.

"If I did not think you were mad—"

"I am no more mad than you are," Gonsalvo interrupted "I was mad, indeed; but that horrible night, when God smote my body, I regained my reason. I see all things clearly now—too late."

"Am I to understand, then," said Juan, rising from his seat, and speaking in measured tones, though his eye was like a tiger's—"am I to understand that you—*you*—denounced my brother? If so, thank God that you are lying helpless there."

"I am not quite so vile a thing as that. I did not intend to harm a hair of his head; but I detained him here to his ruin. He had the means of escape provided, and but for me would have been in safety ere the Alguazils came."

"Well for both of us your guilt was not greater. Still, you cannot expect me—just yet—to forgive you."

"I expect no forgiveness from man," said Gonsalvo, who perhaps disdained to plead in his own exculpation the generous words of Carlos.

Juan had by this time changed his tone towards his cousin, and assumed his perfect sanity; though, engrossed by the thought of his brother, he was quite unconscious of the mental process by which he had arrived at this conclusion. He asked,—

"But why did you detain him? How did you come to know at all of his intended flight?"

"He had a safe asylum provided for him by some friend—I know not whom," said Gonsalvo, in reply. "He was going forth at midnight to seek it. At the same hour I also"—(for a moment he hesitated, but quickly went on) "was going forth—to plunge a dagger in my enemy's heart. We met face to face; and each confided his errand to the other. He sought, by argument and entreaty, to move me from a purpose which seemed to him a great crime. But ere our debate was ended, God laid his hand in judgment upon me; and whilst Don Carlos lingered, speaking words of comfort—brave and kind, though vain—the Alguazils came, and he was taken."

Juan listened in gloomy silence.

"Did he leave no message, not one word, for me?" he asked at last, in a low voice.

"Yes; one word. Filled with wonder at the calmness with which he met his terrible fate, I cried out, as they led him from the room, 'Vaya con Dios, Don Carlos, a braver man than you have I never seen!' With one long mournful look that haunts me still, he said, '*Tell Ruy!*'"

Strong man as he was, Don Juan Alvarez bowed his head and wept. They were the first tears the great sorrow had wrung from him—almost the first that he ever remembered shedding. Gonsalvo saw no shame in them.

"Weep on," he said—"weep on; and thank God that thy tears are for sorrow only, not for remorse."

Hoarse and heavy sobs shook the strong frame. For some time they were the only sounds that broke the stillness. At length Gonsalvo said slowly,—

"He gave me something to keep, which in right should belong to thee."

Juan looked up. Gonsalvo half raised himself; and drew a cushion from beneath his head. First he took off its outer cover of fine holland; then he inserted his hand into an opening that seemed like an accidental rip, and, not without some trouble, drew out a small volume. Juan seized it eagerly: well did he know his brother's Spanish Testament.

"Take it," said Gonsalvo; "but remember it is a dangerous treasure."

"Perhaps you are not sorry to part with it?"

"I deserve that you should say so," answered Gonsalvo, with unwonted gentleness. "But the truth is," he added, with a wan, sickly smile, "nothing can part me from it now, for I have learned almost every word of it by heart."

"How could you, in so short a time, accomplish such a task?" asked Juan, in surprise.

"Easily enough. I was alone long hours of the day, when I could read; and in the silent, sleepless nights I could recall and repeat what I read during the day. But for that I should be in truth what they call me—mad."

"Then you love its words?"

"I *fear* them," cried Gonsalvo, with strange energy, flinging out his wasted arm over the counterpane. "They are words of life—words of fire. They are, to the Church's words, the priest's threatenings, the priest's pardons, what your limbs, throbbing with healthy vigorous life, are to mine—cold, dead, impotent; or what the living champion—steel from head to heel, the Toledo blade in his strong right hand—is to the painted San Cristofro on the Cathedral door. Because I dare to say so much, my father pretends to think me mad; lest, wrecked as I am in mind and body, I should still find one terrible consolation,—that of flinging the truth for once in the face of the scribes and Pharisees, and then suffering for it—like Don Carlos."

He was silent from exhaustion, and lay with closed eyes and deathlike countenance. After a long pause, he resumed, in a low, weak voice,—

"Some words are good—perhaps. There was San Pablo, who was a blasphemer, and injurious."

"Don Gonsalvo, my brother once said he would give his right hand that you shared his faith."

"Oh, did he?" A quick flush overspread the wan face. "But hark! a step on the stairs! My mother's."

"I am neither afraid nor ashamed to be found here," said Don Juan.

"My poor mother! She has shown me more tenderness of late than I deserved at her hands. Do not let us involve her in trouble."

Juan greeted his aunt with due courtesy, and even attempted some words of condolence upon his cousin's illness. But he saw that the poor lady was terribly disconcerted, and indeed frightened, by his presence there. And not without cause, since mischief, even to bloodshed, might have followed had Don Manuel or either of his sons found Juan in communication with Gonsalvo. She conjured him to go, adding, by way of inducement,—

"Doña Beatriz is taking the air in the garden."

"Availing myself of your gracious permission, señora my aunt, I shall offer her my homage there; and so I kiss your feet.—Adiõs, Don Gonsalvo."

"Adiõs, my cousin."

Doña Katarina followed him out of the room.

"He is not sane," she whispered anxiously, laying her hand on his arm; "he is out of his mind. You perceive it clearly, Don Juan?"

"Certainly I shall not dispute it, señora," Juan answered, prudently.

XXIX.

A Friend at Court.

"I have a soul and body that exact
A comfortable care in many ways."
R. Browning.

ON JUAN'S peril was extreme. Well known as he was to many of the imprisoned Lutherans, it seemed a desperate chance that, amongst the numerous confessions wrung from them, no mention of his name should occur. He knew himself deeply implicated in the crime for which they were suffering—the one unpardonable crime in the eyes of Rome. Moreover, unlike his brother, whose temperament would have led him to avoid danger by every lawful means, he was by nature brave even to rashness, and bold even to recklessness. It was his custom to wear his heart on his lips; and though of late stern necessity had taught him to conceal what he thought, it was neither his inclination nor his habit to disguise what he felt. Probably, not even his desire to aid Carlos would have prevented his compromising himself by some rash word or deed, had not the soft hand of Doña Beatriz, strong in its weakness, held him back from destruction. Not for one instant could he forget her terrible vow. With this for ever before his eyes, it is little marvel if he was willing to do anything, to bear anything—ay, almost to feign anything—rather than involve the one he loved in a fate inconceivably horrible.

And—alas for the brave, honest-hearted, truthful Don Juan Alvarez!—it was often necessary to feign. If he meant to remain in Seville, and to avoid the dungeons of the Inquisition, he must obviate—or remove—suspicion by protesting, both by word and action, his devotion to the Catholic Church, and his hatred of heresy.

Could he stoop to this? Gradually, and more and more, as each day's emergency made it more and more necessary, he did stoop to it. He told himself it was all for his brother's sake. And though such a line of conduct was intensely repugnant to his character, it was not contrary to his principles. To conceal an opinion is one thing, to deny a friend quite another. And while Carlos had found a Friend, Juan had only embraced an opinion.

He himself would have said that he had found Truth—had devoted himself to the cause of Freedom. But where were truth and freedom now, with all the bright anticipations of their ultimate triumph which he had been wont to indulge? As far as his native land was concerned (and it must be owned that his mental eye scarcely reached beyond "the Spains"), a single day had blotted out his glowing visions for ever. Almost at the same moment, and as if by some secret preconcerted signal, the leading Protestants in Seville, in Valladolid, all over the kingdom, had been arrested and thrown into prison. Swiftly, silently, with the utmost order and regularity, had the whole thing been accomplished. Every name that Juan had heard Carlos mention with admiration and sympathy was now the name of a helpless captive. The Reformed Church of Spain existed no longer, or existed only in dungeons.

In what quarter the storm had first arisen, that burst so suddenly upon the community of the faithful, Don Juan never knew. It is probable the Holy Office had long been silently watching its prey, waiting for the moment of action to arrive. In Seville, it is said, a spy had been set upon some of Losada's congregation, who revealed their meeting to the Inquisitors. While in Valladolid, the foul treachery of the wife of one of the Protestants furnished the Holy Office with the means of bringing her husband and his friends to the stake.

Don Juan, whose young heart had lately beat so high with hope, now bowed his head in despair. And despairing of freedom, he lost his confidence in truth also. In opinion he was still a decided Lutheran. He accepted every doctrine of the Reformed as against the Roman Catholic creed. But the hold he once had upon these doctrines as living realities was slackened. He did not doubt that justification by faith was a scriptural dogma, but he did not think it necessary to die for it. Compared with the tremendous interest of the fate of Carlos and the peril of Beatriz, and amidst his desperate struggles to aid the one and shield the other, doctrinal questions grew pale and faint to him.

Nor had he yet learned to throw himself, in utter weakness, upon a strength greater than his own, and a love that knows no limits. He did not feel his weakness: he felt strong, in the strength of a brave heart struggling against cruel wrong; strong to resist, and, if it might be, to conquer his fate.

At first he cherished a hope that his brother was not actually in the secret dungeons of the Inquisition. For so great was the number of the captives, that the public gaols of the city and the convent prisons were full of them; and some had to be lodged even in private houses. As Carlos had been one of the last arrested, there seemed reason to suppose that he might be amongst those thus accommodated; in which case it would be much easier both to communicate with him, and to alleviate his fate, than if he were within the gloomy walls of the Triana; there might be, moreover, the possibility of forming some plan for his deliverance.

But Juan's diligent and persevering search resulted at last in the conviction that his brother was in the "Santa Casa" itself. This conviction sent a chill to his heart. He shuddered to think of his present suffering, whilst he feared the worst for the future, supposing that the Inquisitors would take care to lodge in their own especial fortress those whom they esteemed the most heinous transgressors.

He engaged a lodging in the Triana suburb, which the river, spanned by a bridge of boats, separated from the city. There were several reasons for this choice of residence; but by far the greatest was, that those who lingered beneath the walls of the grim old castle could sometimes see, behind its grated windows, spectral faces raised to catch the few scanty gleams of daylight which fell to their lot. Long weary hours did Juan watch there, hoping to recognise the face he loved. But always in vain.

When he went into the city, it was sometimes for other purposes than to visit Doña Beatriz. It was as often to seek the precincts of the magnificent Cathedral, and to pace up and down that terrace whose massive truncated pillars, raised when the Romans founded a heathen temple on the spot, had stood throughout the long ages of Moslem domination. Now the place was consecrated to Christian worship, and yet it was put to no hallowed use. Rich merchants, in many a varying garb that told of different nations, trod the stately colonnade, and bought and sold and made bargains there. For in those days (strange as seems to us the irreverence of the so-called "ages of faith") that terrace was the royal exchange of Seville, then a mercantile city of great importance. Don Juan Alvarez diligently resorted thither, and held many a close and earnest conversation with a keen-eyed, hawk-nosed Jew, whom he met there.

Isaac Osorio, or more properly, Isaac ben Osorio, was a notorious money-lender, who had often "obliged" Manuel's sons, not unfairly requiring heavy interest to counterbalance the hazardous nature of his investments. Callings branded as unlawful are apt to prove particularly gainful. The Jew was willing to "oblige" Don Juan also, upon certain conditions. He was not by any means ignorant of the purpose for which his money was needed. Of course he was himself a Christian in name, for none other would have been permitted to live upon Spanish ground. But by what wrongs, tortures, agonies worse than death, he and those like him had been forced to accept Christian baptism, will never be known until Christ comes again to judge the false Church that has slandered him. Will it be nothing in his sight that millions of the souls for whom he died have been driven to hate his Name—that Name so unutterably precious?

Osorio derived grim satisfaction from the thought that the Christians were now imprisoning, torturing, burning each other. It reminded him of the grand old days in his people's history, when the Lord of hosts was wont to stretch forth his mighty arm and trouble the armies of the aliens, turning every man's hand against his brother. Let the Gentiles bite and devour one another, the child of Abraham could look upon their quarrels with calm indifference. But if he had any sympathy, it was for the weaker side. He was rather disposed to help a Christian youth who was trying to save his brother from the same cruel fangs in which so many sons of Israel had writhed and struggled. Don Juan, therefore, found him accommodating, and even lenient. From time to time he advanced to him considerable sums, first upon the jewels he brought with him from Nuera, and then, alas upon his patrimony[1] itself.

Not without a keen pang did Juan thus mortgage the inheritance of his fathers. But he began to realise the bitter truth that a flight from Spain, and a new career in some foreign land, would eventually be the only course open to him—if indeed he escaped with life.

Nor would the armies of Spain henceforth be more free to him than her soil. Fortunately, the necessity for rejoining his regiment had not arisen. For the brief war in which he served was over now; and as the promised captaincy had not yet been assigned to him, he was at liberty for the present to remain at home.

He largely bribed the head-gaoler of the inquisitorial prison, besides supplying him liberally with necessaries and comforts for his brother's use. Gaspar Benevidio bore the worst of characters, both for cruelty and avarice;[2] still, Juan had no resource but to trust

---

[1] An inheritance from a father or male ancestor.
[2] An unreasonably strong desire to obtain and keep money.

implicitly to his honour, in the hope that at least some portion of what he gave would be allowed to reach the prisoner. But not a single gleam of information about him could be gained from Benevidio, who, like all other servants of the Inquisition, was bound by a solemn oath to reveal nothing that passed within its walls.

He also bribed some of the attendants and satellites of the all-powerful Inquisitor, Munebrãga. It was his desire to obtain a personal interview with the great man himself, that he might have the opportunity of trying the intercession of Don Dinero, to whose advances he was known to be not altogether obdurate.[3]

For the purpose of soliciting an audience, he repaired one evening to the splendid gardens belonging to the Triana, to await the Inquisitor, who was expected shortly to return from a sail for pleasure on the Guadalquivir. He was sick at heart of the gorgeous tropical plants that surrounded him, of the myrtle-blossoms that were showered on his path; of all that told of the hateful pomp and luxury in which the persecutor lived, while his victims pined unpitied in loathsome dungeons. Yet neither by word, look, nor sign dared he betray the rage that was gnawing his heart.

At length the shouts of the populace, who thronged the river's side, announced the approach of their idol; for such Munebrãga was for the time. Clad in costly silks and jewels, and surrounded by a brilliant little court, composed both of churchmen and laymen, the "Lord Inquisitor" stepped from his splendid purple-decked barge. Don Juan threw himself in his way, and modestly requested an audience. His bearing, though perfectly respectful, was certainly less obsequious than that to which Munebrãga had been accustomed of late. So the minister of the Holy Office turned from him haughtily, though, as Juan bitterly thought, "his father would have been proud to hold the stirrup for mine." "This is no fitting time to talk of business, señor," he said. "We are weary to-night, and need repose."

At that moment a Franciscan friar advanced from the group, and with his lowest bow and most reverent manner approached

[3] Obstinate; stubborn; inflexible.

the Inquisitor. "With the gracious permission of my very good lord, I shall address myself to the caballero, and report his errand to your sanctity. I have the honour of some acquaintance with his Excellency's noble family."

"As you please, Fray," said the voice accustomed to speak the terrible words that doomed to the rack and the pulley, though no one would have suspected this from the bland, careless good-nature of its tones. "But see that you tarry not so as to lose your supper. Howbeit, there is little need to caution you, or any other son of St. Francis, against undue neglecting of the body."

The son of St. Francis made no answer, either because it was not worth while, or because those who take the crumbs from the rich man's table must ofttimes take his taunts therewith. He disengaged himself from the group, and turned towards Juan a broad, good-humoured, not unintelligent face, which his former pupil recognised immediately.

"Fray Sebastian Gomez!" he exclaimed in astonishment.

"And very much at the service of my noble Señor Don Juan. Will your Excellency deign to bear me company for a little time? In yonder walk there are some rare flowers of rich colouring, which it were worth your while to observe."

They turned into the path he indicated, while the Lord Inquisitor's silken train swept towards that half of the Triana where godless luxury bore sway; the other half being consecrated to the twin demon, cruelty.

"Will it please your worship to look at these Indian pinks?" said the friar. "You will not see that flower elsewhere in all the Spains, save in the royal gardens. His Imperial Majesty brought it first from Tunis."

Juan all but cursed the innocent flowers; but recollected in time that God made them, though they belonged to Gonzales de Munebrãga. "What brings you here, Fray Sebastian?" he interrupted impatiently. "I thought to see only the black cowls of St. Dominic about the—the minister of the Holy Office."

"A little more softly, may I implore of your Excellency? Yonder casement is open.—Pues,[4] señor, I am here in the capacity of a guest. Nothing more."

"Every man to his taste," said Juan, drily, as with a heedless foot he kicked off the beautiful scarlet flower of a rare cactus.

"Have a care, señor and your Excellency; my lord is very proud of his cactus flowers."

"Then come with me to some spot of God's free earth where we can talk together, out of sight of him and his possessions."

"Nay, rest content, señor; and untire yourself in this fair arbour overlooking the river."

"At least, God made the river," said Juan, flinging himself, with a sigh of irritation and impatience, on the cushioned seat of the summer-house.

Fray Sebastian seated himself also. "My lord," he began to explain, "has received me with all courtesy, and is good enough to desire my continual attendance. The fact is, señor, his reverence is a man of literary taste."

Juan allowed himself the solace of a quiet sneer. "Oh, is he? Very creditable to him, no doubt."

"Especially he is a great lover of the divine art of poesy."[5]

No *genuine* love of the gentle art, whose great lesson is sympathy, did or could soften the Inquisitor's hard heart. Nor, had his wealth been doubled, could he have hired one real poet to sing his praise in strains worthy the ear of posterity. In an atmosphere so cold, the most ethereal spirit would have frozen. But it was in his power to buy flattery in rhyme, and it suited his inclination so to do. He liked the trick of rhyme, at once so easy and so charming in the sonorous Castilian tongue—it was a pleasure of the ear which he keenly appreciated, as he did also those of the eye and the palate.

"I addressed to him," Fray Sebastian continued with becoming modesty, "a little effort of my Muse—really a mere trifle—on the suppression of heresy, comparing the Lord Inquisitor to Michael the archangel, with the dragon beneath his feet. You understand, señor?"

---

[4] Well, or well then.

[5] *Archaic:* Writing poetry.

Juan understood so well that it was with difficulty he refrained from flinging the unlucky rhymester into the river. But of late he had learned many a lesson in prudence. Still, his words sounded almost fierce in their angry scorn. "I suppose he gave you in return—a good dinner."

But Fray Sebastian would not take offence. He answered mildly, "He was pleased to express his approval of my humble effort, and to admit me into his noble household; where, except my poor exertions to amuse and untire him by my conversation may be accounted a service, I am of no service to him whatever."

"So you are clad in purple and fine linen, and fare sumptuously every day," said Juan, with contempt that he cared not to conceal.

"As to purple and fine linen, señor, I am an unworthy son of St. Francis; and it is well known to your Excellency that by the rules of our Order not even one scrap of Holland— But you are laughing at me, as you used in old times, Señor Don Juan."

"God knows, I have little heart to laugh. In those old times you speak of, Fray, there was no great love between you and me; and no marvel, for I was a wild and idle lad. But I think you loved my gentle brother, Don Carlos!"

"That I did, señor, as did every one. Has any evil come upon him? St. Francis forbid!"

"Worse evil than I care to name. He lies in yonder tower."

"The blessed Virgin have pity on us!" cried Fray Sebastian, crossing himself.

"I thought you would have heard of his arrest," Juan continued, sadly.

"I, señor! Never a breath. Holy Saints defend us! How could I, or any one, dream that a young gentleman of noblest race, well learned, and of truly pious disposition, would have had the ill luck to fall under so foul a suspicion? Doubtless it is the work of some personal enemy. And—ah, woe is me! 'the clattering horse-shoe ever wants a nail'—here have I been naming heresy, 'talking of halters in the house of the hanged?'"

"Hold thy tongue about hanging," said Juan, testily, "and listen to me, if thou canst."

Fray Sebastian indicated, by a respectful gesture, his profound attention.

"It has been whispered to me that the door of his reverence's heart may be unlocked by a golden key."

Fray Sebastian assured him this was a foul slander; concluding a panegyric[6] on the purity of the Inquisitor's administration with the words, "You would forfeit his favour for ever by presuming so far as to offer a bribe."

"No doubt," answered Juan with a sneer, and a hard, worldly look in his face that of late was often seen there. "I should deserve to pay that penalty were I the fool to approach him with a bow, and, 'Here is a purse of gold for your sanctity.' But 'one take is worth two I give you's,' and there is a way of saying take to every man. And I ask you, for old kindness, to show me how to say it to his lordship."

Fray Sebastian pondered. After an interval he said, with some hesitation, "May I venture to inquire, señor, what means you possess of clearing the character of your noble brother?"

Juan only answered by a sorrowful shake of the head.

Darker and darker grew the friar's sensual but good-natured face.

"His excellent reputation, his brilliant success at college, his blameless life should tell in his favour," Juan said at length.

"Have you nothing more direct? If not, I fear it is a bad business. But 'silence is called holy,' so I hold my peace. Still, if indeed (which the Saints forbid) he has fallen inadvertently into error, it is a comfort to reflect that there will be little difficulty in reclaiming him."

Juan made no reply. Did he expect his brother to retract? Did he wish him to do it? These were questions he scarcely dared to ask himself. From any reply he could give to them he shrank in shuddering dread.

"He was ever gentle and tractable," Fray Sebastian continued, "and ofttimes but too easy to persuade."

[6] Extravagant praise delivered in formal speech or writing.

Juan rose, took up a stone, and threw it into the river. When the circles it made in the water had died away, he turned back to the friar. "But what can *I* do for him?" he asked, with an undertone of helpless sadness, touching from the lips of one so strong.

Fray Sebastian put his hand to his forehead, and looked as if he were composing another poem. "Let me see, your Excellency. There is my lord's nephew and pet page, Don Alonzo (where he has got the 'Don' I know not, but Don Dinero makes many a noble); I dare say it would not hurt the soft white hand to finger a purse of gold ducats, and those same ducats might help your brother's cause not a little."

"Manage the matter for me, and I will thank you heartily. Gold, to any extent that will serve *him*, shall be forthcoming; and, my good friend, see that you spare it not."

"Ah, Señor Don Juan, you were always generous."

"My brother's life is at stake," said Juan, softening a little. But the hard look returned as he added, "Those who live in great men's houses have many expenses, Fray. Always remember that I am your friend, and that my ducats are very much at your service also."

Fray Sebastian thanked him with his lowest bow. Juan's look changed again; this time more rapidly. "If it were possible," he added, in low, hurried tones—"if you could only bring me the least word of tidings from him—even one word to say if he lives, if he is well, how he is entreated. Three months it is now since he was taken, and I have heard no more than if they had carried him to his grave."

"It is a difficult matter, a *very* difficult matter that you ask of me. Were I a son of St. Dominic, I might indeed accomplish somewhat. For the black cowls are everything now. Still, I will do all I can, señor."

"I trust you, Fray. If under cover of seeking his conversion, of anything, you could but see him."

"Impossible, señor—utterly impossible."

"Why? They sometimes send friars to reason with the—the prisoners."

"Always Dominicans or Jesuits—men well-known and trusted by the Board of the Inquisition. However, señor, nothing that a man may do shall be wanting on my part. Will not that content your Excellency?"

"*Content* me? Well, as far as you are concerned, yes. But, in truth, I am haunted day and night by one horrible dread. What if—if they should *torture* him? My gentle brother, frail in mind and body, tender and sensitive as a woman! Terror and pain would drive him mad." The last words were a quick broken whisper. But outward expressions of emotion with Don Juan were always speedily repressed. Recovering apparent calmness, he stretched out his hand to Fray Sebastian, saying, with a faint smile, "I have kept you too long from my lord's supper-table—pardon me."

"Your Excellency's condescension in conversing with me deserves my profound gratitude," replied the monk, in true Castilian fashion. His residence at the Inquisitor's Court had certainly improved his manners.

Don Juan gave him his address, and it was agreed that he should call on him in a few days. Fray Sebastian then offered to bring him on his way through the garden and court of that part of the Triana which formed the Inquisitor's residence. But Juan declined the favour. He could not answer for himself when brought face to face with the impious pomp and luxury of the persecutor of the saints. He feared that, by some wild word or deed, he might imperil the cause he had at heart. So he hailed a waterman who was guiding his little boat down the tranquil stream in the waning light. The boat was soon brought to the place where the Inquisitor had landed from his barge; and Juan, after shaking the dust from his feet, both literally and metaphorically, sprang into it.

The popular ideal of a persecutor is very far from the truth. At the word there rises before most minds the vision of a lean, pale-faced, fierce-eyed monk, whose frame is worn with fasting, and his scourge red with his own blood. He is a fanatic—pitiless, passionate, narrow-minded, perhaps half insane—but penetrated to the very core of his being with intense zeal for his Church's interest, and prepared in her service both to inflict and to endure all things.

Very unlike this ideal were *most* of the great persecutors who carried out the behests of Antichrist. They were generally able men. But they were pre-eminently men wise in their generation, men *of* their generation, men who "loved this present world." They gave the Church the service of strong hand and skilful brain that she needed; and she gave *them*, in return, "gold, and silver, and precious stones, and pearls; and fine linen, and purple, and silk, and scarlet; and all sweet wood; and all manner of vessels of ivory, and all manner of vessels of most precious wood, and of brass, and of iron, and marble; and cinnamon, and odours, and ointment, and frankincense; and wine, and oil, and fine flour, and wheat; and beasts, and sheep, and horses and chariots, and slaves and souls of men." It was for these things, not for abstract ideas, not for high places in heaven, that they tortured and murdered the saints of God. Whilst the cry of the oppressed reached the ears of the Most High, those who were "wearing them out" lived in unhallowed luxury, in degrading sensuality. Gonzales de Munebrãga was a good specimen of the class to which he belonged—he was no exceptional case.

Nor was Fray Sebastian anything but an ordinary character. He was amiable, good-natured, free from gross vices—what is usually called "well disposed." But he "loved wine and oil," and to obtain what he loved he was willing to become the servant and the flatterer of worse men than himself, at the terrible risk of sinking to their level.

With all the force of his strong nature, Don Juan Alvarez loathed Munebrãga, and scorned Fray Sebastian. Gradually a strange alteration appeared to come over the little book he constantly studied—his brother's Spanish Testament. The words of promise, and hope, and comfort, in which he used to delight, seemed to be blotted from its pages; while ever more and more those pages were filled with fearful threatenings and denunciations of doom—against hypocritical scribes and Pharisees, false teachers and wicked high priests—against great Babylon, the mother of abominations. The peace-breathing, "Father, forgive them, for they know not what they do," grew fainter and more faint, until at last it faded completely from his memory; while there stood out before him night and day, in characters of fire, "Serpents, generation of vipers, how can ye escape the damnation of hell?"[7]

[7] Matthew 23:33

XXX.

The Captive.

"Ay, but for me—my name called—drawn
Like a conscript's lot from the lap's black yawn
He has dipped into on the battle dawn.
Bid out of life by a nod, a glance,
Stumbling, mute mazed, at Nature's chance
With a rapid finger circling round,
Fixed to the first poor inch of ground
To fight from, where his foot was found,
Whose ear but a moment since was free
To the wide camp's hum and gossipry—
Summoned, a solitary man,
To end his life where his life began,
From the safe glad rear to the awful van."

R. Browning.

N the night of his arrest, when Don Carlos Alvarez was left alone in his dungeon, he stood motionless as one in a dream. At length he raised his head, and began to look around him. A lamp had been left with him; and its light illumined a cell ten feet square, with a vaulted roof. Through a narrow grating, too high for him to reach, one or two stars were shining; but these he saw not. He only saw the inner door sheathed with iron; the mat of rushes on which he was to sleep; the stool that was to be his seat; the two earthen pitchers of water that completed his scanty furniture. From the first moment these things looked strangely familiar to him.

He threw himself on the mat to think and pray. He comprehended his situation perfectly. It seemed as if he had been all his life expecting this hour; as if he had been born for it, and led up to it gradually through all his previous experience. As yet he did not think that his fate was terrible; he only thought that it was inevitable—something that was to come upon him, and that in due course had come at last. It was his impression that he should always remain there, and never more see anything beyond that grated window and that iron door.

There was a degree of unreality about this mood. For the past fortnight, or more, his mind had been strained to its utmost tension. Suspense, more wearing even than sorrow, had held him on the rack. Sleep had seldom visited his eyes; and when it came, it had been broken and fitful.

Now the worst had befallen him. Suspense was over; certainty had come. This brought at first a kind of rest to the overtaxed mind and frame. He was as one who hears a sentence of death, but who is taken off the rack. No dread of the future could quite overpower the present unreasoning sense of relief.

Thus it happened that an hour afterwards he was sleeping the dreamless sleep of exhaustion. Well for him if, instead of "death's twin-brother," the angel of death himself had been sent to open the prison doors and set the captive free. And yet, after all, *would* it have been well for him?

So utter was his exhaustion, that when food was placed in his cell the next morning, he only awaked for a moment, then slept again as soundly as before. Not till some hours later did he finally shake off his slumber. He lay still for some time, examining with a strange kind of curiosity the little bolted aperture which was near the top of his door, and watching a solitary broken sunbeam which had struggled through the grating that served him for a window, and threw a gleam of light on the opposite wall.

Then, with a start, he asked himself, *"Where am I?"* The answer brought an agony of fear, of horror, of bitter pain, "Lost! lost! God have mercy on me! I am lost!" As one in intense bodily anguish, he writhed, moaned—ay, even cried aloud.

No wonder. Hope, love, life—alike in its noblest aims and its commonest joys—all were behind him. Before him were the dreary dungeon days and nights—it might be months or years; the death of agony and shame; and, worst of all, the unutterable horrors of the torture-room, from which he shrank as any one of us would shrink to-day.

Slowly and at last came the large burning tears. But very few of them fell; for his anguish was as yet too fierce for many tears. All that day the storm raged on. When the alcayde brought his evening meal, he lay still, his face covered with his cloak. But as night drew on he rose, and paced his narrow cell with hasty, irregular steps, like those of a caged wild animal.

How should he endure the horrible loneliness of the present, the maddening terror of all that was to come? And this life was to *last*. To last, until it should be succeeded by worse horrors and fiercer anguish. Words of prayer died on his lips. Or, even when he uttered them, it seemed as if God heard not—as if those thick walls and grated doors shut him out too.

Yet one thing was clear to him from the beginning. Deeper than all other fears within him lay the fear of denying his Lord. Again and again did he repeat, "When called in question, I will at once confess all." For he knew that, according to a law recently enacted by the Holy Office, and sanctioned by the Pope, no subsequent retractation could save a prisoner who had once confessed—he must die. And he desired finally and for ever to put it out of his own power to save his life and lose it.

As every dreary morning dawned upon him, he thought that ere its sun set he might be called to confess his Master's name before the solemn tribunal. At first he awaited the summons with a trembling heart. But as time passed on, the delay became more dreadful than the anticipated examination. At last he began to long for *any* change that might break the monotony of his prison-life.

The only person, with the exception of his gaoler, that ever entered his cell, was a member of the Board of Inquisitors, who was obliged by their rules to make a fortnightly inspection of the prisons. But the Dominican monk to whom this duty was relegated merely asked the prisoner a few formal questions: such as, whether he was well, whether he received his appointed provision, whether his warder used him with civility. To these Carlos always answered prudently that he had no complaint to make. At first he was wont to inquire, in his turn, when his case might be expected to come on. To this it would be answered, that there was no hurry about the matter. The Lords Inquisitors had much business on hand, and many more important cases than his to attend to; he must await their leisure and their pleasure.

At length a kind of lethargy stole over him; though it was broken frequently by sharp bursts of anguish. He ceased to take note of time, ceased to make fruitless inquiries of his gaoler, who would never tell him anything. Upon one occasion he asked this man for a breviary, since he sometimes found it difficult to recall even the gospel words that he knew so well. But he was answered in the set terms the Inquisitors taught their officials, that the book he ought now to study was the book of his own heart, which he should examine diligently, in order to the confession and repentance of his sins.

During the morning hours the outer door of his cell (there were two) was usually left open, in order to admit a little fresh air. At such times he often heard footsteps in the corridors, and doors opening and shutting. With a kind of sick yearning, not unmixed with hope, he longed that some visitant would enter his cell. But none ever came. Some of the Inquisitors were keen observers and good students of character. They had watched Carlos narrowly before his arrest, and they had arrived at the conclusion that utter and prolonged solitude was the best remedy for his disease.

Such solitude has driven many a weary tortured soul to insanity. But that divine compassion which no dungeon walls or prison bars avail to shut out, saved Carlos from such a fate.

One morning he knew from the stir outside that some of his fellow-captives had received a visit. But the deep stillness that followed the dying away of footsteps in the corridor was broken by a most unwonted sound. A loud, clear, and even cheerful voice sang out,—

"Vençidos van los frailes; vençidos van!
Corridos van los lobos; corridos van!"
*"There go the friars; there they run!
There go the wolves, the wolves are done!"*

Every nerve and fibre of the lonely captive's heart thrilled responsive to that strain. Evidently the song was one of triumph. But from whose lips? Who could dare to triumph in the abode of misery, the very seat of Satan?

Carlos Alvarez had heard that voice before. A striking peculiarity in the dialect rivetted this fact upon his mind. The words were neither the pure sonorous Castilian that he spoke himself, nor the soft gliding sibilant Andaluz that he heard in Seville, nor yet the patois of the Manchegan peasants around his mountain home. In such accents one, and one alone, had ever spoken in his hearing. And that was the man who said, "For the joy of bringing food to the perishing, water to the thirsty, light to those that sit in darkness, rest to the weary and heavy-laden, I have counted the cost, and I shall pay the price right willingly."

Whatever men had done to the body, it was evident that Juliano Hernandez was still unbroken in heart, strong in hope and courage. A fettered, tortured captive, he was yet enabled, not only to hold his own faith fast, but actually to minister to that of others. His rough rhyme intimated to his fellow-captives that "the wolves" of Rome were leaving his cell, vanquished by the sword of the Spirit. And that, as he overcame, so might they also.

Carlos heard, understood, and felt from that hour that he was not alone. Moreover, the grace and strength so richly given to his fellow-sufferer seemed to bring Christ nearer to himself. "Surely God is in this place—even here," he said, "and I knew it not." And then, bowing his head, he wept —wept such tears as bring help and healing with them.

Up to this time he had held Christ's hand indeed, else had he "utterly fainted." But he held it in the dark. He clung to him desperately, as if for mere life and reason. Now the light began to dawn upon him. He began to see the face of Him to whom he had been clinging. His good and gracious words—such words as, "Let not your heart be troubled," "My peace I give unto you"[1]—became again, as in old times, full of meaning, instinct with life. He "remembered the years of the right hand of the Most High;"[2] he thought of those days that now seemed so long ago, when, with such thrilling joy, he received the truth from Juliano's book. And he knew that the same joy might be his even in that dreary prison, because the same God was above him, and the same Lord was "rich unto all that call upon him."[3]

On the next occasion when Juliano raised his brave song of victory, Carlos had the courage to respond, by chanting in the vulgar tongue, "The Lord hear thee in the day of trouble; the name of the God of Jacob defend thee. Send thee help from the sanctuary, and strengthen thee out of Zion."[4]

But this brought him a visit from the alcayde, who commanded him to "forbear that noise."

"I only chanted a versicle from one of the Psalms," he explained.

"No matter. Prisoners are not permitted to disturb the Santa Casa," said Gasper Benevidio, as he quitted the cell.

The "Santa Casa," or Holy House, was the proper style and title of the prison of the Holy Inquisition. At first sight the name appears a hideous mockery. We seem to catch in it an echo of the laughter of fiends, as in that other kindred name, "The Society of Jesus." Yet, just then, the Triana was truly a holy house. Precious

[1] Referring to John 14:1 and John14:27.
[2] Referring to Psalm 77:10.
[3] Romans 10:12
[4] Psalm 20:1-2

in the sight of the Lord were those who crowded its dismal cells. Many a lonely captive wept and prayed and agonised there, who, though now forgotten on earth, shall one day shine with a brightness eclipsing kings and conquerors—"a star for ever and ever."

XXXI.

Ministering Angels.

"Thou wilt be near, and not forsake,
To turn the bitter pool
Into a bright and breezy lake,
The throbbing brow to cool;
Till, left awhile with Thee alone,
The wilful heart be fain to own
That he, by whom our bright hours shone,
Our darkness best may rule."

KEBLE.

HE overpowering heat of an Andalusian summer aggravated the physical sufferings of the captives. And so did the scanty and unwholesome provisions, which were all that reached them through the hands of the avaricious Benevidio.

But this last hardship was little felt by Carlos. Small as were the rations he received, they usually proved more than enough for him; indeed, the coarse food sometimes lay almost untested in his cell.

One morning, however, to his extreme surprise, something was pushed through the grating in the lower part of his inner door, the outer door being open, as was usual at that hour. The mysterious gift consisted of white bread and good meat, of which he partook with mingled astonishment and thankfulness. But the relief to the unvaried monotony of his life, and the occupation the little circumstance gave his thoughts, was much more to him than the welcome novelty of a wholesome meal.

The act of charity was repeated often, indeed almost daily. Sometimes bread and meat, sometimes fruit—the large luscious grapes or purple figs of that southern climate—were thus conveyed to him. Endless were the speculations these gifts awakened in his mind. He longed to discover his benefactor, not only to express his gratitude, but to supplicate that the same favours might be extended to his fellow-sufferers, especially to Juliano. Moreover, would not one so kindly disposed be willing to give him what he longed for far more than meat or drink—some word of tidings from the world without, or from his dear imprisoned brethren?

At first he suspected the under-gaoler, whose name was Herrera. This man was far more gentle and compassionate than Benevidio. Carlos often thought he would have shown him some kindness, or at least have spoken to him, if he dared. But dire would have been the penalty even the slightest transgression of the prison rules would have entailed. Carlos naturally feared to broach the matter, lest, if Herrera really had nothing to do with it, the unknown benefactor might be betrayed.

The same motive prevented his hazarding a question or exclamation at the time the little gifts were thrust in. How could he tell who might be within hearing? If it were safe to speak, surely the person outside would try the experiment.

It was generally very early in the morning, at the hour when the outer door was first opened, that the gifts came. Or, if delayed a little later, he would often notice something timid and even awkward in the way they were pushed through the grating, and the approaching and retreating footsteps, for which he used to listen so eagerly, would be quick and light, like those of a child.

At last a day came, marked indeed with white in the dark chronicle of prison life. Bread and meat were conveyed to him as usual; then there was a low knock upon the door. Carlos, who was standing close to it, responded by an eager "*Chien es*?"

"A friend. Kneel down, señor, and put your ear to the grating."

The captive obeyed, and a woman's voice whispered, "Do not lose heart, your worship. Friends outside are thinking of you."

"One friend is with me, even here," Carlos answered. "But," he added, "I entreat of you to tell me your name, that I may know whom to thank for the daily kindnesses which lighten my captivity."

"I am only a poor woman, señor, the alcayde's servant. And what I have brought you is your own, and but a small part of it."

"My own! How?"

"Robbed from you by my master, who defrauds and spoils the poor prisoners even of their necessary food. And if any one dares to complain to the Lords Inquisitors, he throws him into the Masmurra."

"The—what?"

"A deep, horrible cistern which he hath in his house." This was spoken in a still lower voice.

Carlos was not yet sufficiently naturalised to horrors to repress a shudder. He said, "Then I fear it is at great risk to yourself that you show kindness to me."

"It is for the dear Lord's sake, señor."

"Then you—you too—love his Name!" said Carlos, tears of joy starting to his eyes.

"*Chiton*,[1] señor! *chiton*! But as far as a poor woman may, I do love him," she added in a frightened whisper. "What I want now to tell you is, that the noble lord, your brother—"

"My brother!" cried Carlos; "what of him? Oh, tell me!"

"Let your Excellency speak lower. We may be overheard. I know he has seen my master once and again, and has given him much money to provide your worship with good food and other conveniences, which he, however, not having the fear of God before his eyes—" The rest of the sentence did not reach the ear of Carlos; but he could easily guess its import.

[1] Hush.

"That is little matter," he said. "But oh, kind friend, if I could send him a message, were it only one word."

Perhaps the wistful earnestness of his tone awakened latent mother instincts in the poor woman's heart. She knew that he was very young; that he had lain there for dreary months alone, away from the bright world into which he was just entering, and which was now shut to him for ever.

"I will do all I can for your Excellency," she said, in a tone that betrayed some emotion.

"Then," said Carlos, "tell him it is well with me. 'The Lord is my shepherd'[2]—all that psalm, bid him read it. But, above all things, say unto him to leave this place—to fly to Germany or England. For I fear, I fear—no, do not tell him what I fear. Only implore of him to go. You promise?"

"I promise, young sir, to do all I can. God comfort him and you."

"And God reward you, brave and kind friend. But one word more, if it may be without risk to you. Tell me of my dear fellow-prisoners. Especially of Dr. Cristobal Losada, Don Juan Ponce de Leon, Fray Constantino, and Juliano Hernandez, called Juliano El Chico."

"I do not know anything of Fray Constantino. I think he is not here. The others you name have—suffered."

"Not death!—surely not death!" said Carlos, in terror.

"There be worse things than death, señor," the poor woman answered. "Even my master, whose heart is iron, is astonished at the fortitude of Señor Juliano. He fears nothing—seems to feel nothing. No tortures have wrung from him a word that could harm any one."

"God sustain him! Oh, my friend," Carlos went on with passionate earnestness, "if by any deed of kindness, such as you have shown me, you could bring God's dear suffering servant so much comfort as a cup of cold water, truly your reward would be rich in heaven. For the day will come when that poor man will take his

[2] Psalm 23:1

station in the court of the King of kings, and at the right hand of Christ, in great glory and majesty."

"I know it, señor. I have tried—"

Just then an approaching footstep made Carlos start; but the poor woman said, "It is only the child, God bless her. But I must go, señor; for she comes to tell me her father has arisen, and is making ready to begin his daily rounds."

"Her father! Does Benevidio's own child help you to comfort his prisoners?"

Even so, thank the good God. I am her nurse. But I must not linger another moment. Adiõs, señor."

"Vaya con Dios, good mother. And God repay your kindness, as he surely will."

And surely he did repay it; but not on earth, unless the honour of being accounted worthy to suffer shame and stripes and cruel imprisonment for his sake be called a reward.[3]

[3] The story of the gaoler's servant and his little daughter is historical.

XXXII.

The Valley of the Shadow of Death.

"And shall I fear the coward fear of standing all alone
To testify of Zion's King and the glory of his throne?
My Father, O my Father, I am poor and frail and weak,
Let me not utter of my own, for idle words I speak;
But give me grace to wrestle now, and prompt my faltering tongue,
And name thy name upon my soul, and so shall I be strong."

MRS. STUART MENTEITH.

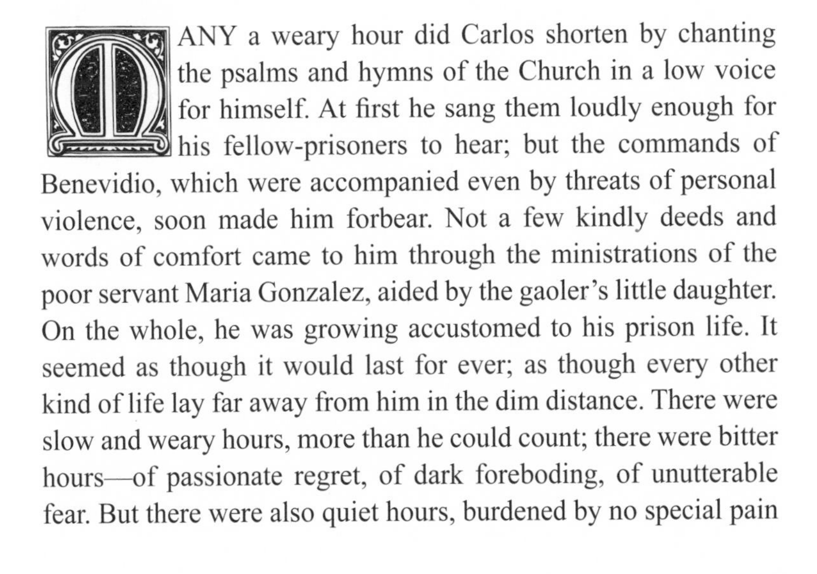

MANY a weary hour did Carlos shorten by chanting the psalms and hymns of the Church in a low voice for himself. At first he sang them loudly enough for his fellow-prisoners to hear; but the commands of Benevidio, which were accompanied even by threats of personal violence, soon made him forbear. Not a few kindly deeds and words of comfort came to him through the ministrations of the poor servant Maria Gonzalez, aided by the gaoler's little daughter. On the whole, he was growing accustomed to his prison life. It seemed as though it would last for ever; as though every other kind of life lay far away from him in the dim distance. There were slow and weary hours, more than he could count; there were bitter hours—of passionate regret, of dark foreboding, of unutterable fear. But there were also quiet hours, burdened by no special pain or sorrow; there were sometimes even happy hours, when Christ seemed very near, and his consolations were not small with his prisoner.

It was one of the quiet hours, when thoughts of the past, not full of the anguish of vain yearning, as they often were, but calm and even pleasant, were occupying his mind. He had been singing the Te Deum for himself; and thinking how sweetly the village choristers used to chant it at Nuera; not in the time of Father Tomas, but in that of his predecessor, a gentle old man with a special taste for music, whom he and his brother, then little children, loved, but used to tease. He was so deeply engaged in feeling over again his poignant distress upon one particular occasion when Juan had offended the aged priest, that all his present sorrows were forgotten for the moment, when he heard the large key grate harshly in the strong outer door of his cell.

Benevidio entered, bearing some articles of dress, which he ordered the prisoner to put on immediately.

Carlos obeyed in silence, though not without surprise, perhaps even a passing feeling of indignation. For the very form and fashion of the garments he was thus obliged to assume (a kind of jacket without sleeves, and long loose trowsers), meant to the Castilian noble keen insult and degradation.

"Take off your shoes," said the alcayde. "Prisoners always come before their reverences with uncovered head and feet. Now follow me."

It was, then, the summons to stand before his judges. A thrilling dread took possession of his soul. Heedless of the alcayde's presence, he threw himself for one brief moment on his knees. Then, though his cheek was pale, he could speak calmly. "I am ready," he said.

He followed his conductor through several long and gloomy corridors. At length he ventured to ask, "Whither are you leading me?"

"*Chiton*!" said Benevidio, placing his finger on his lips. Speech was not permitted there.

At last they drew near an open door. The alcayde quickened his pace, entered first, made a very low reverence, then drew back again, and motioned Carlos to go forward alone.

He did so; and found himself in the presence of his judges—the Board, or "Table of the Inquisition." He bowed, though rather from the habit of courtesy, than from any special respect to the tribunal, and stood silent.

Before any one addressed him, he had ample leisure for observation. The room was large, lofty, and surrounded by pillars, between which there were handsome hangings of gilt leather. At one end, the furthest from him, stood a great crucifix, larger than life. Around the long table on the estrada six or seven persons were seated. Of these, one alone was covered, he who sat nearest the door by which Carlos had entered, and facing the crucifix. He knew that this was Gonzales de Munebrãga, and the thought that he had once pleaded earnestly for that man's life, helped to give him boldness in his presence.

At Munebrãga's right hand sat a stern and stately man, whom Carlos, though he had never seen him before, knew, from his dress and the position he occupied, to be the prior of the Dominican convent adjoining the Triana. One or two of the subordinate members of the Board he had met occasionally in other days, and he had then considered them very far his own inferiors, both in education and in social position.

At length Munebrãga, half turning, motioned him to approach the table. He did so, and a person who sat at the opposite end, and appeared by his dress to be a notary, made him lay his hand on a missal, and administered an oath to him.

It bound him to speak the truth, and to keep everything secret which he might see or hear; and he took it without hesitation. A bench at the Inquisitor's left hand was then pointed out to him, and he was desired to be seated.

A member of the Board, who bore the title of the Promoter-fiscal, conducted the examination. After some merely formal questions, he asked him whether he knew the cause of his present imprisonment. Carlos answered immediately, "I do."

This was not the course usually taken by prisoners of the Holy Office. They commonly denied all knowledge of any offence that could have induced "their reverences" to order their arrest. With a slight elevation of the eyebrows, perhaps expressive of surprise, his examiner continued, gently enough, "Are you then aware of having erred from the faith, and by word or deed offended your own soul, and the consciences of good Christians? Speak boldly, my son; for to those who acknowledge their faults the Holy Office is full of tenderness and mercy."

"I have not erred, consciously, from the true faith, since I knew it."

Here the Dominican prior interposed. "You can ask for an advocate," he said; "and as you are under twenty-five years of age; you can also claim the assistance of a curator.[1] Furthermore, you can request a copy of the deposition against you, in order to prepare your defence."

"Always supposing," said Munebrãga himself, "that he formally denies the crime laid to his charge.—Do you?" he asked, turning to the prisoner.

"We understand you so to do," said the prior, looking earnestly at Carlos. "You plead not guilty?"

Carlos rose from his seat, and advanced a step or two nearer to the table where sat the men who held his life in their hands. Addressing himself chiefly to the prior, he said, "I know that by taking the course your reverence recommends to me, as I believe out of kindness, I may defer my fate for a little while. I may beat the air, fighting in the dark with witnesses whom you would refuse to name to me, still more to confront with me. Or, I may make you wring out the truth from me slowly, drop by drop. But what would that avail me? Neither for the truth, nor yet for any falsehood I might be base enough to utter, would you loose your hand from your prey. I prefer that straight road which is ever the shortest way. I stand before your reverences this day a professed Lutheran,

[1] Guardian.

despairing of mercy from man, but full of confidence in the mercy of God."

A movement of surprise ran around the Board at these daring words. The prior turned away from the prisoner with a pained, disconcerted look; but only to meet a half-triumphant, half-reproachful glance from his superior, Munebrãga. But Munebrãga was not displeased; far from it. It did not grieve him that the prisoner, a mere youth, "was throwing himself into the fire." That was his own concern. He was saving "their reverences" a great deal of trouble. Thanks to his hardihood, his folly, or his despair, a good piece of work was quickly and easily accomplished. For it was the business of the Inquisitors first to convict; retractations were an after consideration.

"Thou art a bold heretic, and fit for the fire," he said. "We know how to deal with such." And he placed his hand on the bell that was to signal the termination of the interview.

But the prior, recovering from his astonishment, once more interposed. "My lord and your reverence, be pleased to allow me a few minutes, in which I may set plainly before the prisoner both the wonted mercy and lenity of the Holy Office to the repentant, and the fatal consequences of obstinacy."

Munebrãga acquiesced by a nod, then leant back carelessly in his seat; this was not a part of the proceedings in which he felt much interest.

No one could doubt the sincerity with which the prior warned Carlos of the doom that awaited the impenitent heretic. The horrors of the death of fire, the deeper, darker horror of the fire that never dies, these were the theme of his discourse. If not actually eloquent, it had at least the earnestness of intense conviction. "But to the penitent," he added, and the hard face softened a little, "God is ever merciful, and his Church is merciful too."

Carlos listened in silence, his eyes bent on the ground. But when the Dominican concluded, he looked up again, glanced first at the great crucifix, then fixed his eyes steadily on the prior's face. "I cannot deny my Lord," he said. "I am in your hands, and you can do with me as you will. But God is mightier than you."

"Enough!" said Munebrãga, and he rang the hand-bell. After a very short delay, the alcayde reappeared, and led Carlos back to his cell.

As soon as he was gone, Munebrãga turned to the prior. "My lord," he said, "your wonted penetration is at fault for once. Is this the youth whom you assured us a few months of solitary confinement would render pliant as a reed and plastic as wax? Whereas we find him as bold a heretic as Losada, or D'Arellano, or that imp of darkness, little Juliano."

"Nay, my lord, I do not despair of him. Far from it. He is much less firm than he seems. Give him time, with a due mixture of kindness and severity, and, I trust in our Lord and St. Dominic, we will see him a hopeful penitent."

"I am of your mind, reverend father," said the Promoter-fiscal. "It is probable he confessed only to avoid the Question. Many of them fear it more than death."

"You are right," answered Munebrãga quickly.

The notary looked up from his papers. "Please your lordships," he said, "I think it is the sangre azul that makes him so bold. He is Alvarez de Meñaya."

"Keep to thy quires and thine ink-horn, man of law," interposed Munebrãga angrily. "Thy part is to write down what wiser men say, not to prate thyself." It was well known that the Inquisitor, far from boasting the sangre azul himself, had not even what the Spaniards call "good red blood" flowing in his veins; hence his irritation at the notary's speech.

There is often a great apparent similarity in the effects of quite opposite causes. That which results from a degree of weakness of character may sometimes wear the aspect of transcendent courage. A bolder man than Don Carlos Alvarez might, in his circumstances, have made a struggle for life. He might have fought over every point as it arose; have availed himself of every loophole for escape; have thrown upon his persecutors the onus of proving his crime. But such a course would not have been possible to Carlos. As a running leap is far more easy than a standing one, so to sensitive temperaments it is easier to rush forward to meet pain or danger than to stand still and fight it off, knowing all the time that it must come at last.

He would have been astonished had he guessed the impression made upon his examiners. To himself it seemed that he had confessed his Lord in much weakness. Still, he had confessed him. And shut out as he was from all ordinary "means of grace," the act of confession became a kind of sacrament to him. It was a token and an evidence of Christ's presence with him, and Christ's power working in him. He could say now, "In the day that I called upon thee thou answeredst me and strengthenedst me with strength in my soul." And from that hour he seemed to live in greater nearness to Christ, and more intimate communion with him, than he had ever done before.

It was well that he had strong consolation, for his need was great. Two other examinations followed after a short interval; and in both of these Munebrãga took a far more active part than he had done in the first. The Inquisitors were at that time extremely anxious to procure evidence upon which to condemn Fray Constantino, who up to this point had steadily resisted every effort they had made to induce him to criminate himself. They thought it probable that Don Carlos Alvarez could assist them if he would, especially since there had been found amongst his papers a highly laudatory letter of recommendation from the late Canon Magistral.

Still, his assistance was needed even more in other matters. It is scarcely necessary to say that Munebrãga, who forgot nothing, had not forgotten the mysterious appointment made with him, but never kept, by a cousin of the prisoner's, who was now stated to be hopelessly insane. What did that mean? Was the story true; or were the family keeping back evidence which might compromise one or more of its remaining members?

But Carlos was expected to resolve a yet graver question; or, at least, one that touched him more nearly. His own arrest had been decreed in consequence of two depositions against him. First, a member of Losada's congregation had named him as one of the habitual attendants; then a monk of San Isodro had fatally compromised him under the torture. The monk's testimony was clear and explicit, and was afterwards confirmed by others. But the first witness had deposed that two gentlemen of the name of Meñaya had been wont to attend the conventicle.[2] Who was the second? Hitherto this problem had baffled the Inquisitors. Don Manuel Alvarez and his sons were noted for orthodoxy; and the only other Meñaya known to them was the prisoner's brother. But in his favour there was every presumption, both from his character as a gallant officer in the army of the most Catholic king, and from the fact of his voluntary return to Seville; where, instead of shunning, he seemed to court observation, by throwing himself continually in the Inquisitor's way, and soliciting audience of him.

Still, of course, his guilt was possible. But, in the absence of anything suspicious in his conduct, some clearer evidence than the vague deposition alluded to was absolutely necessary, in order to warrant proceedings against him. According to the inquisitorial laws, what they styled "full half proof"of a crime must be obtained before ordering the arrest of the supposed criminal.

And the key to all these perplexities had now to be wrung from the unwilling hands of Carlos. This needed "half proof" could, and must, be furnished by him. "He must speak out," said those stern, pitiless men, who held him in their hands.

But here he was stronger than they. Neither arts, persuasions, threats, nor promises, availed to unseal those pale, silent lips. Would torture do it? He was told plainly, that unless he would answer every question put to him freely and distinctly, he must undergo its worst horrors.

His heart throbbed wildly, then grew sick and faint. A dread far keener than the dread of death prompted one short sharp struggle against the inevitable. He said, "It is against your own law to torture a confessed criminal for information concerning others. For the law presumes that a man loves himself better than his neighbour; and, therefore, that he who has informed against himself would more readily inform against other heretics if he knew them."

[2] An unlawful or secret religious gathering or the building where it is held.

He was right. His early studies had enabled him to quote correctly one of the rules laid down by the highest authority for the regulation of the inquisitorial proceedings. But what mattered rules and canons to the members of a secret and irresponsible tribunal?

Munebrãga covered his momentary embarrassment with a sneer. "That rule was framed for delinquents of another sort," he said. "You Lutheran heretics have the command, 'Thou shalt love thy neighbour as thyself,' so deeply rooted in your hearts, that the very flesh must needs be torn from your bones ere you will inform against your brethren. I overrule your objection as frivolous."

And then a sentence, more dreaded than the terrible death-sentence itself, received the formal sanction of the Board.

Once more alone in his cell, Carlos flung himself on his knees, and pressing his burning brow against the cold damp stone, cried aloud in his anguish, "Let this cup—only this—pass from me!"[3]

His was just the nature to which the thought of physical suffering is most appalling. Keenly sensitive in mind and body, he shrank in unspeakable dread from what stronger characters might brave or defy. His vivid imagination intensified every pang he felt or feared. His mind was like a room hung round with mirrors, in which every terrible thing, reflected a hundred times, became a hundred terrors instead of one. What another would have endured once, he endured over and over again in agonised anticipation.

At times the nervous horror grew absolutely insupportable. Fearfulness and trembling took hold upon him. He felt ready to pray that God in his great mercy would take away his life, and let the bearer of the dreaded summons find him beyond all their malice.

One thought haunted him like a demon, whispering words of despair. It had begun to haunt him from the hour when poor Maria Gonzalez told him she had seen his brother. What if they dragged that loved name from his lips! What if, in his weakness, he became Juan's betrayer! Once it had been in his heart to betray him from selfish love; perhaps in judgment for that sin he was now to betray

[3] Referring to Matthew 26:39, Jesus' words in Gethsemane.

him through sharp bodily anguish. Even if his will were kept firm all through (which he scarcely dared to hope), would not reason give way, and wild words be wrung from his lips that would too surely ruin all?

He tried to think of his Saviour's death and passion; tried to pray for strength and patience to drink of his cup. Sometimes he prayed that prayer with strong crying and tears; sometimes with cold mute lips, too weary to cry any longer. If he was heard and answered, he knew it not then.

Days of suspense wore on. They were only less dreary than the nights, when sleep fled from his eyes, and horrible visions (which yet he knew were less horrible than the truth) rose in quick succession before his mind.

One evening, seated on his bench in the twilight, he fell into an uneasy slumber. The dark dread that never left him, mingling with the sunny gleam of old memories, wove a vivid dream of Nuera, and of that summer morning when the first great conflict of his life found an ending in the strong resolve, Juan, brother! I will never wrong thee, never!"

The grating of the key in the door and the sudden flash of the lamp aroused him. He started to his feet at the alcayde's entrance. This time no change of dress was prescribed him. He knew his doom. He cried, but to no human ear. From the very depths of his being the prayer arose, "Father, save—sustain me; *I am thine!*"

XXXIII.

On the Other Side.

"Happy are they who learn at last,—
Though silent suffering teach
The secret of enduring strength,
And praise too deep for speech,—
Peace that no pressure from without,
No storm within can reach.

"There is no death for me to fear,
For Christ my Lord hath died:
There is no curse in all my pain,
For he was crucified;
And it is fellowship with him
That keeps me near his aide."

A. L. WARING.

HEN the light of the next morning streamed in through the narrow grating of his cell, Carlos was there once more, lying on his bed of rushes. But was it indeed the next morning, or was it ten years, twenty years afterwards? Without a painful effort of thought and memory, he himself could scarcely have told. That last night was like a great gulf, fixed between his present and all his past. The moment when he entered that torch-lit subterranean room seemed a sharp, black dividing line, sundering his life into two halves. And the latter half seemed longer than that which had gone before.

Nor could years of suffering have left a sadder impress on the young face, out of which the look of youth had passed, apparently for ever. Brow and lips were pale; but two crimson spots, still telling of feverish pain, burned on the hollow cheeks, while the large lustrous eyes beamed with even unnatural brilliance.

The poor woman, who was doing the work of God's bright angels in that dismal prison, came softly in. How she obtained entrance there Carlos did not know, and was far too weak to ask, or even to wonder. But probably she was sent by Benevidio, who knew that, in his present condition, some human help was indispensable to the prisoner.

Maria Gonzalez was too well accustomed to scenes of horror to be over-much surprised or shocked by what she saw. Silently, though with a heart full of compassion, she rendered the few little services in her power. She placed the broken frame in as easy a position as she could, and once and again she raised to the parched lips the "cup of cold water" so eagerly desired.

He roused himself to murmur a word of thanks; then, as she prepared to leave him, his eyes followed her wistfully.

"Can I do anything more for you, señor?" she asked.

"Yes, mother. Tell me—have you spoken to my brother?"

"Ay de mi! no, señor," said the poor woman, whose ability was not equal to her good-will. "I have tried, but I could not get from my master the name of the place where he lives without making him suspect something, and never since have I had the good fortune to see his face."

"I know you have done—what you could. My message does not matter now. Not so much. Still, best he should go. Tell him so, when you find him. But, remember, tell him nought of this. You promise, mother? He must never know it—*never!*"

She spoke a few words of pity and condolence.

"It *was* horrible!" he faltered, in faint, broken tones.

"Worst of all—the return to life. For I thought all was over, and that I should awake face to face with Christ. But—I cannot speak of it."

There was a long silence; then his eye kindled, and a look of joy—ay, even of triumph—flashed across the wasted, suffering face. "But *I have overcome!* No; not I. Christ has overcome in me, the weakest of his members. Now I am beyond it—on the other side."

To the poor tortured captive there had been given a foretaste, strange and sweet, of what they feel who stand on the sea of glass, having the harps of God in their hands. Men had done their worst—their very worst. He knew now all "the dread mystery of pain;" all that flesh could accomplish in its fiercest conflict with spirit. Yet not one word that could injure any one he loved had been wrung from his lips.

All was over now. In that there was mercy—far more mercy than was shown to others. He had been permitted to drain the cup at a single draught. *Now* he could feel grateful to the physicians, who with truly kind cruelty (and not without some risk to themselves) had prevented, in his case, that fiendish device, "the suspension of the torture." Even according to the execrable[1] laws of the Inquisition, he had won his right to die in peace.

As time passed on, a blessed sense that he was now out of the hands of man, and in those of God alone, sank like balm upon his weary spirit. Fear was gone; grief had passed away; even memory had almost ceased to give him a pang. For how could he long for the loved faces of former days, when day and night Christ himself was near him? So strangely near, so intimately present, that he sometimes thought that if, through some wonderful relenting of his persecutors, Juan were permitted to come and stand beside him, that loved brother would still seem further away, less real, than the unseen Friend who was keeping watch by his couch. And even the bodily pain, that so seldom left him, was not hard to bear, for it was only the touch of His finger.

He had passed into the clear air upon the mountain top, where

[1] Appalling; repulsive.

the sun shines ever, and the storm winds cannot come. Nothing hurt him; nothing disturbed him now. He had visitors; for what had really placed him beyond the reach of his enemies was, not unnaturally, supposed by them to have brought him into a fitting state to receive their exhortations. So Inquisitors, monks, and friars—"persons of good learning and honest repute"—came in due course to his lonely cell, armed with persuasions and arguments, which were always weighted with threats and promises.

Their voices seemed to reach him faintly, from a great distance. Into "the secret place of the Lord," where he dwelt now, they could not enter. Threats and promises fell powerless on his ear. What more could they do to him? As far as the mere facts of the case were concerned, this security may have been misplaced—nay, it was misplaced; but it saved him from much suffering. And as for promises, had they thrown open the door of his dungeon and bid him go forth free, only that one intense longing to see his brother's face would have nerved him to make the effort.

Arguments he was glad to answer when permitted. It was a joy to speak for his Lord, who had done, and was doing, such great things for him. As far as he could, he made use of those Scripture words with which his memory was so richly stored. But more than once it happened that he was forced to take up the weapons which he had learned in the schools to use so skilfully. He tore sophisms to pieces with the dexterity of one who knew how they were constructed, and astonished the students of Aristotle and Thomas Aquinas by vanquishing them on their own ground.

Reproach and insult he met with a fearless meekness that nothing could ruffle. Why should he feel anger? Rather did he pity those who stood without in the darkness, not seeing the Face he saw, not hearing the Voice he heard. Usually, however, those who visited him yielded to the spell of his own sweet and perfect courtesy, and were kinder than they intended to be to the "professed impenitent heretic."

His heart, now "at leisure from itself," was filled with sympathy for his imprisoned brethren and sisters. But, except to Maria

Gonzalez, he dared not speak of them, lest the simplest remark or question might give rise to some new suspicion, or supply some link, hitherto missing, in the chain of evidence against them. But those who came to visit him sometimes gave him unasked intelligence about them. He could not, however, rely upon the truth of what reached him in this way. He was told that Losada had retracted; he did not believe it. Equally did he disbelieve a similar story of Don Juan Ponce de Leon, in which, unhappily, there was some truth. The constancy of that gentle, generous-hearted nobleman had yielded under torture and cruel imprisonment, and concessions had been wrung from him that dimmed the brightness of his martyr crown. On the other hand, the waverer, Garçias Arias, known as the "White Doctor," had come forward with a hardihood truly marvellous, and not only confessed his own faith, but mocked and defied the Inquisitors.

Of Fray Constantino, the most contradictory stories were told him. At one time he was assured that the great preacher had not only admitted his own guilt, but also, on the rack, had informed against his brethren. Again he was told, and this time with truth, that the Emperor's former chaplain and favourite had been spared the horrors of the Question, but that the eagerly desired evidence against him had been obtained by accident. A lady of rank, one of his chief friends, was amongst the prisoners; and the Inquisitors sent an Alguazil to her house to demand possession of her jewels. Her son, without waiting to ascertain the precise object of the officer's visit, surrendered to him in a panic some books which Fray Constantino had given his mother to conceal. Amongst them was a volume in his own handwriting, containing the most explicit avowal of the principles of the Reformation. On this being shown to the prisoner, he struggled no longer. "You have there a full and candid confession of my belief," he said. And he was now in one of the dark and loathsome subterranean cells of the Triana.

Amongst those who most frequently visited Carlos was the prior of the Dominican convent. This man seemed to take a peculiar interest in the young heretic's fate. He was a good specimen of a character oftener talked about than met with in real life,—the genuine fanatic. When he threatened Carlos, as he spared not to do, with the fire that is never quenched, at least he believed with all his heart that he was in danger of it. Carlos soon perceived this, and accepting his honest intention to benefit him, came to regard him with a kind of friendliness. Besides, the prior listened to what he said with more attention than did most of the others, and even in the prison of the Inquisition a man likes to be listened to, especially when his opportunities of speaking are few and brief.

Many weeks passed by, and still Carlos lay on his mat, in weakness and suffering of body, though in calm gladness of spirit. Surgical and medical aid had been afforded him in due course. And it was not the fault of either surgeon or physician that he did not recover. They could stanch wounds and set dislocated joints, but when the springs of life were sapped, how could they renew them? How could they quicken the feeble pulse, or send back life and energy into the broken, exhausted frame? At this time Carlos himself felt certain—even more certain than did his physician—that never again would his footsteps pass the limits of that narrow cell.

Once, indeed, there came to him a brief and fleeting pang of regret. It was in the spring-time; everywhere else so bright and fair, but making little change in those gloomy cells. Maria Gonzalez now sometimes obtained access to him, partly through Benevidio's increased inattention to all his duties, partly because, any attempt at escape on the part of the captive being obviously out of the question, he was somewhat less jealously watched. And more than once the gaoler's little daughter stole in timidly beside her nurse, bearing some trifling gift for the sick prisoner. To Carlos these visits came like sunbeams; and in a very short time he succeeded in establishing quite an intimate friendship with the child.

One morning she entered his cell with Maria, carrying a basket, from which she produced, with shy pleasure, a few golden oranges. "Look, señor," she said, "they are good to eat now, for the blossoms are out.[2] I gathered some to show you;" and filling both her hands with the luscious wealth of the orange flowers, she flung them carelessly down on the mat beside him. In her eyes they were of no value compared with the fruit.

With Carlos it was far otherwise. The rich perfume that filled the cell filled his heart also with sweet sad dreams, which lasted long after his kindly visitors had left him. The orange-trees had just been in flower last spring when all God's free earth and sky were shut out from his sight for ever. Only a year ago! What a long, long year it seemed! And only one year further back he was walking in the orange gardens with Doña Beatriz, in all the delicious intoxication of his first and last dream of youthful love. "Better here than there, better now than then," he murmured, though the tears gathered in his eyes. "But oh, for one hour of the old free life, one look at orange-trees in flower, or blue skies, or the grassy slopes and cork-trees of Nuera! Or"—and more painfully intense the yearning grew—"one familiar face, belonging to the past, to show me it was not all a dream, as I am sometimes tempted to think it. Thine, Ruy, if it might be.—O Ruy, Ruy!—But, thank God, I have not betrayed thee!"

In the afternoon of that day visitors were announced. Carlos was not surprised to see the stern narrow face and white hair of the Dominican prior. But he was a little surprised to observe that the person who followed him wore the grey cowl of St. Francis. The prior merely bestowed the customary salutation upon him, and then, stepping aside, allowed his companion to approach.

But as soon as Carlos saw his face, he raised himself eagerly, and stretching out both his hands, grasped those of the Franciscan. "Dear Fray Sebastian!" he cried; "my good, kind tutor!"

"My lord the prior has been graciously pleased to allow me to visit your Excellency."

"It is truly kind of you, my lord. I thank you heartily," said Carlos, frankly and promptly turning towards the Dominican,

[2] The people of Seville do not think the oranges fit to eat until the new blossoms come out in spring.

who looked at him with somewhat the air of one who is trying to be stern with a child.

"I have ventured to allow you this indulgence," he said, "in the hope that the counsels of one whom you hold in honour may lead you to repentance."

Carlos turned once more to Fray Sebastian, whose hand he still held. "It is a great joy to see you," he said. "Only to-day I had been longing for a familiar face. And you are changed never a whit since you used to teach me my humanities. How have you come hither? Where have you been all these years?"

Poor Fray Sebastian vainly tried to frame an answer to these simple questions. He had come to that prison straight from Munebrãga's splendid patio, where, amidst the gleam of azulejos and of many-coloured marbles, the scent of rare exotics and the music of rippling fountains, he had partaken of a sumptuous mid-day repast. In this dark foul dungeon there was nothing to please the senses, not even God's free air and light. Everything on which his eye rested was coarse, painful, loathsome. By the prisoner's side lay the remains of a meal, in great contrast to his. And the sleeve, fallen back from the hand that held his own, showed deep scars on the wrist. He knew whence they were. Yet the face that was looking in his, with kindling eyes, and a smile on the parted lips, might have been the face of the boy Carlos, when he praised him for a successful task, only for the pain in it, and, far deeper than pain, a look of assured peace that boyhood could scarcely know.

Repressing a choking sensation, he faltered, "Señor Don Carlos, it grieves me to the heart to see you here."

"Do not grieve for me, dear Fray Sebastian; for I tell you truly, I have never known such happy hours as since I came here. At first, indeed, I suffered; there was storm and darkness. But then"—here for a moment his voice failed, and his flushed cheek and quivering lip betrayed the anguish a too hasty movement cost the broken frame. But, recovering himself quickly, he went on: "Then he arose and rebuked the wind and the sea; and there was a great calm. That calm lasts still. And oftentimes this narrow room seems to me the house of God, the very gate of heaven. Moreover," he added, with a smile of strange brightness, "there is heaven itself beyond."

"But, señor and your Excellency, consider the disgrace and sorrow of your noble family—that is, I mean"—here the speaker paused in perplexity, and met the keen eye of the prior, fixed somewhat scornfully, as he thought, upon him. He was quite conscious that the Dominican was thinking him incapable, and incompetent to the task he had so earnestly solicited. He had sedulously prepared himself for this important interview, had gone through it in imagination beforehand, laying up in his memory several convincing and most pertinent exhortations, which could not fail to benefit his old pupil. But these were of no avail now; in fact, they all vanished from his recollection. He had just begun something rather vague and incoherent about Holy Church, when the prior broke in.

"Honoured brother," he said, addressing with scrupulous politeness the member of a rival fraternity, "the prisoner may be more willing to listen to your pious exhortations, and you may have more freedom in addressing him, if you are left for a brief space alone together. Therefore, though it is scarcely regular, I will visit a prisoner in a neighbouring apartment, and return hither for you in due time."

Fray Sebastian thanked him, and he withdrew, saying as he did so, "It is not necessary for me to remind my reverend brother that conversation upon worldly matters is strictly forbidden in the Holy House."

Whether the prior visited the other prisoner or no, it is not for us to inquire; but if he did, his visit was a short one; for it is certain that for some time he paced the gloomy corridor with troubled footsteps. He was thinking of a woman's face, a fair young face, to which that of Don Carlos Alvarez wore a startling likeness. "Too harsh, needlessly harsh," he murmured; "for, after all, she was no heretic. But which of us is always in the right? Ave Maria Sanctissima, ora pro me![3] But if I can, I would fain make some reparation—to *him*. If ever there was a true and sincere penitent,

[3] Meaning "pray for me."

he is one."

After a little further delay, he summoned Fray Sebastian by a peremptory knock at the inner door, the outer one of course remaining open. The Franciscan came, his broad, good-humoured face bathed in tears, which he scarcely made an effort to conceal.

The prior glanced at him for a moment, then signed to Herrera, who was waiting in the gallery, to come and make the door fast. They walked on together in silence, until at length Fray Sebastian said, in a trembling voice, "My lord, you are very powerful here; can *you* do nothing for him?"

"I *have* done much. At my intercession he had nine months of solitude, in which to recollect himself and ponder his situation, ere he was called on to make answer at all. Judge my amazement when, instead of entering upon his defence, or calling witnesses to his character, he at once confessed all.

Judge my greater amazement at his continued obstinacy since. When a man has broken a giant oak in two, he may feel some surprise at being baffled by a sapling."

"He will not relent," said Fray Sebastian, hardly restraining his sobs. "He will die."

"I see one chance to save him," returned the prior; "but it is a hazardous experiment. The consent of the Supreme Council is necessary, as well as that of my Lord Vice-Inquisitor, and neither may be very easy to obtain."

"To save his body or his soul?" Fray Sebastian asked anxiously.

"Both, if it succeeds. But I can say no more," he added rather haughtily; "for my plan is bound up with a secret, of which few living men, save myself, are in possession."

XXXIV.

Fray Sebastian's Trouble.

"Now, with fainting frame,
With soul just lingering on the flight begun,
To bind for thee its last dim thoughts in one,
I bless thee. Peace be on thy noble head,
Years of bright fame, when I am with the dead!
I bid this prayer survive me, and retain
Its power again to bless thee, and again.
Thou hast been gathered into my dark fate
Too much; too long for my sake desolate
Hath been thine exiled youth;
but now take back
From dying hands thy freedom."

HEMANS.

T was late in August. All day long the sky had been molten fire, and the earth brass. Every one had dozed away the sultry noontide hours in the coolest recesses of dwellings made to exclude heat, as ours to exclude cold. But when at last the sun sank in flame beneath the horizon, people began to creep out languidly to woo the refreshment of the evening breeze.

The beautiful gardens of the Triana were still deserted, save by two persons. One of these, a young lad—we beg pardon, a young gentleman—of fifteen or sixteen, sat, or rather reclined, by the river-side, eating slices from an enormous melon, which he cut with a small silver-hilted dagger. A plumed cap, and a gay velvet jerkin lined with satin, had been thrown aside for coolness' sake, and lay near him on the ground; so that his present dress consisted merely of a mass of the finest white holland, delicately starched and frilled, velvet hosen, long silk stockings, and fashionable square-toed shoes. Curls of scented hair were thrown back from a face beautiful as that of a girl, but bold and insolent in its expression as that of a spoiled and mischievous boy.

The other person was seated in the arbour mentioned once before, with a book in his hand, of which, however, he did not in the course of an hour turn over a single leaf. A look of chronic discontent and dejection had replaced the good-humoured smiles of Fray Sebastian Gomez. Everything was wrong with the poor Franciscan now. Even the delicacies of his patron's table ceased to please him; and he, in his turn, was fast ceasing to please his patron. How could it be otherwise, when he had lost not only his happy art of indirect ingenious flattery, but his power to be commonly agreeable or amusing? No more poems—not so much as the briefest sonnet—on the suppression of heresy were to be had from him; and he was fast becoming incapable of turning a jest or telling a story.

It is said that idiots[1] often manifest peculiar pain and terror at the sound of music, because it awakens within them faint stirrings of that higher life from which God's mysterious dispensation has shut them out. And it is true that the first stirrings of higher life usually come to all of us with pain and terror. Moreover, if we do not crush them out, but cherish and foster them, they are very apt to take away the brightness and pleasantness of the old lower life altogether, and to make it seem worthless and distasteful.

A new and higher life had begun for Fray Sebastian. It was not his conscience that was quickened, only his heart. Hitherto he had chiefly cared for himself. He was a good-natured man, in

[1] One destitute of reason, or the ordinary intellectual powers of man.

the ordinary acceptation of the term; yet no sympathy for others had ever spoiled his appetite or hindered his digestion. But for the past three months he had been feeling as he had not felt since he clung weeping to the mother who left him in the parlour of the Franciscan convent—a child of eight years old. The patient suffering face of the young prisoner in the Triana had laid upon him a spell that he could not break.

To say that he would have done anything in his power to save Don Carlos, is to say little. Willingly would he have lived for a month on black bread and brackish water, if that could have even mitigated his fate. But the very intensity of his desire to help him was fast making him incapable of rendering him the smallest service. Munebrãga's flatterer and favourite might possibly, by dint of the utmost self-possession and the most adroit management, have accomplished some little good. But Fray Sebastian was now consciously forfeiting even the miserable fragment of power that had once been his. He thought himself like the salt that had lost its savour, and was fit neither for the land nor yet for the dunghill.

Absorbed in his mournful reflections, he continued unconscious of the presence of such an important personage as Don Alonzo de Munebrãga, the Lord Vice-Inquisitor's favourite page. At length, however, he was made aware of the fact by a loud angry shout, "Off with you, varlets, scum of the people! How dare you put your accursed fishing-smack to shore in my lord's garden, and under his very eyes?"

Fray Sebastian looked up, and saw no fishing-boat, but a decent covered barge, from which, in spite of the page's remonstrance, two persons were landing: an elderly female clad in deep mourning, and her attendant, apparently a tradesman's apprentice, or serving-man.

Fray Sebastian knew well haw many distracted petitioners daily sought access to Munebrãga, to plead (alas, how vainly!) for the lives of parents, husbands, sons, or daughters. This was doubtless one of them. He heard her plead, "Dear young gentleman, hinder me not. Have you a mother? My only son lies—"

"Out upon thee, woman!" interrupted the page; "and the foul fiend take thee and thy only son together."

"Hush, Don Alonzo!" Fray Sebastian interposed, coming forward towards the spot; and perhaps for the first time in his life there was something like dignity in his tone and manner. "You must be aware, señora," he said, turning to the woman, "that the right of using this landing-place is restricted to my lord's household. You will be admitted at the gate of the Triana, if you present yourself at a proper hour."

"Alas! good father, once and again have I sought admission to my lord's presence. I am "the unhappy mother of Luis D'Abrego, he who used to paint and illuminate the Church missals so beautifully. More than a year agone they tore him from me, and carried him away to yonder tower, and since then, never a word of him have I heard. Whether he is living or dead, this day I know not."

"Oh, a Lutheran dog! Serve him right," cried the page, "I hope they have put him on the pulley."

Fray Sebastian turned suddenly, and dealt the lad a stinging blow on the side of his face. To the latest hour of his life this act of passion remained incomprehensible to himself. He could only ascribe it to the direct agency of the evil one. "I was tempted by the Devil," he would say with a sigh. "Vade retro me, Satana."

Crimson to the roots of his perfumed hair, the boy sought his dagger. "Vile caitiff! beggarly trencher-scraping Franciscan!" he cried, "you shall repent of this."

But apparently changing his mind the next moment, he allowed the dagger to drop from his hand, and snatching up his jerkin, ran at full speed towards the house.

Fray Sebastian crossed himself, and gazed after him bewildered; his unwonted passion dying as suddenly as it had flamed up, and giving place to fear.

Meanwhile the mother of Abrego, to whom it did not occur that the buffet bestowed on the page could have any serious consequences, resumed her pleadings. "Your reverence seems to have a heart that can feel for the unhappy," she said. "Refuse not the prayer of the most unhappy woman in the world. Only let me see his lordship—let me throw myself at his feet and tell him the whole truth. My poor lad had nothing at all to do with the Lutherans; he was a good, true Christian, and an old one, like all his family."

"Nay, nay, my good woman; I fear I can do nothing to help you. And I entreat of you to leave this place, else some of my lord's household are sure to come and compel you. Ay, there they are."

It was true enough. Don Alonzo, as he ran through the porch, shouted to the numerous idle attendants who were lounging about, and some of them immediately rushed out into the garden.

In justice to Fray Sebastian, it must be recorded, that before he consulted for his personal safety, he led the poor woman back to the barge, and saw her depart in it. Then he made good his own retreat, going straight to the lodging of Don Juan Alvarez.

He found Juan lying asleep on a settle. The day was hot; he had nothing to do; and, moreover, the fiery energy of his southern blood was dashed by the southern taint of occasional torpor.[2] Starting up suddenly, and seeing Fray Sebastian standing before him with a look of terror, he asked in alarm, "Any tidings, Fray? Speak—tell me quickly."

"None, Señor Don Juan. But I must leave this place at once." And the friar briefly narrated the scene that had just taken place, adding mournfully, "Ay de mi! I cannot tell what came over me—*me*, the mildest-tempered man in all the Spains!"

"And what of all that?" asked Juan rather contemptuously.

"I see nothing to regret, save that you did not give the insolent lad what he deserved, a sound beating."

"But, Señor Don Juan, you don't understand," gasped the poor friar. "I must fly immediately. If I stay here over to-night I shall find myself before the morning—*there*." And with a significant gesture he pointed to the grim fortress that loomed above them.

"Nonsense. They cannot suspect a man of heresy, even *de levi*,[3] for boxing the ear of an impudent serving-lad."

[2] Lack of mental or physical energy.
[3] Lightly.

"Ay, and can they not, your worship? Do you not know that the gardener of the Triana has lain for many a weary month in one of those dismal cells; and all for the grave offence of snatching a reed out of the hand of one of my lord's lackeys so roughly as to make it bleed?"

"Truly? Now are things come to a strange pass in our free and royal land of Spain! A beggarly upstart, such as this Munebrãga, who could not, to save himself from the rack, tell you the name of his own great-grandfather, drags the sons and brothers—ay, and the wives and daughters—of our knights and nobles to the dungeon and the stake before our eyes. And it is not enough for him to set his own heel on our necks. His minions—his very grooms and pages—must lord it over us, and woe to him who dares to chastise their insolence. Nathless, I would feel it a comfort to make every bone in that urchin's body ache soundly. I have a mind—but this is folly. I believe you are right, Fray. You should go."

"Moreover," said the friar mournfully, "I am doing no good here."

"No one can do good now," returned Juan, in a tone of deep dejection. "And to-day the last blow has fallen. The poor woman who showed him kindness, and sometimes told us how he fared, is herself a prisoner."

"What! she has been discovered?"

"Even so: and with those fiends mercy is the greatest of all crimes. The child met me to-day (whether by accident or design, I know not), and told me, weeping bitterly."

"God help her!"

"Some would gladly endure her punishment if they might commit her crime," said Don Juan. There was a pause; then he resumed, "I had been about to ask you to apply once more to the prior."

Fray Sebastian shook his head. "That were of no use," he said; "for it is certain that my lord the Vice-Inquisitor and the prior have had a misunderstanding about the matter. And the prior, so far from obtaining permission to deal with him as he desired, is not even allowed to see him now."

"And yourself?—whither do you mean to go?" asked Juan, rather abruptly.

"In sooth, I know not, señor. I have had no time to think. But go I must."

"I will tell you what to do. Go to Nuera. There for the present you will be safe. And if any man inquire your business, you have a fair and ready answer. *I* send you to look after my affairs. Stay; I will write by you to Dolores. Poor, true-hearted Dolores!" Don Juan seemed to fall into a reverie, so long did he sit motionless, his face shaded by his hand.

His mournful air, his unwonted listlessness, his attenuated frame—all struck Fray Sebastian painfully. After musing a while in silence, he said at last, very suddenly, "Señor Don Juan!" Juan looked up.

"Have you ever thought since on the message he sent you by me?"

Don Juan looked as though that question were worse than needless. Was not every word of his brother's message burned into his heart? This it was: "My Ruy, thou hast done all for me that the best of brothers could. Leave me now to God, unto whom I am going quickly, and in peace. Quit the country as soon as thou canst; and God's best blessings surround thy path and guard thee evermore."

One fact Carlos had most earnestly entreated Fray Sebastian to withhold from his brother. Juan must never know that he had endured the horrors of the Question. The monk would have promised almost anything that could bring a glow of pleasure to that pale, patient face. And he had kept his promise, though at the expense of a few falsehoods, that did not greatly embarrass his conscience. He had conveyed the impression to Don Juan that it was merely from the effects of his long and cruel imprisonment that his brother was sinking into the only refuge that remained to him—a quiet grave.

After a pause, he resumed, looking earnestly at Juan—"*He* wished you to go."

"Do you not know that next month they say there will be—*an*

Auto?"

"Yes; but it is not likely—"

They gazed at each other in silence, neither saying *what* was not likely.

"Any horror is *possible*," said Juan at last. "But no more of this. Until after the Auto, with its chances of *some* termination to this dreadful suspense, I stir not from Seville. Now, we must think for you. I know where to find a boat, the owner of which will take you some miles on your way up the river to-night. Then you can hire a horse."

Fray Sebastian groaned. Neither the journey itself, its cause, nor its manner were anything but disagreeable to the poor friar. But there was no help for him. Juan gave him some further directions about his way; then set food and wine before him.

"Eat and drink," he said. "Meanwhile I will secure the boat. When I return, I can write to Dolores."

All was done as he planned; and ere the morning broke, Fray Sebastian was far on his way to Nuera, with the letter to Dolores stitched into the lining of his doublet.

XXXV.

The Eve of the Auto.

"It is good for a man that he bear the yoke in his youth
He sitteth alone and keepeth silence, because he hath borne it upon him.
He putteth his mouth in the dust, if so be there may be hope."
LAMENTATIONS 3:27-29.

N the 21st of September 1559, all Seville wore a festive appearance. The shops were closed, and the streets were filled with idle loiterers in their gay holiday apparel. For it was the eve of the great Auto, and the preliminary ceremonies were going forward amidst the admiration of gazing thousands. Two stately scaffolds, in the form of an amphitheatre, had been erected in the great square of the city, then called the Square of St. Francis; and thither, when the work was completed, flags and crosses were borne in solemn procession, with music and singing.

But a still more significant ceremonial was enacted in another place. Outside the walls, on the Prado San Sebastian, stood the ghastly Quemadero—the great altar upon which, for generations, men had offered human sacrifices to the God of peace and love. Thither came long files of barefooted friars, carrying bushes and faggots,[1] which they laid in order on the place of death, while, in sweet yet solemn tones, they chanted the "Miserere" and "De Profundis."

Very close together on those festive days were "strong light and deep shadow." But our way leads us, for the present, into the light. Turning away from the Square of St. Francis, and the Prado San Sebastian, we enter a cool upper room in the stately mansion of Don Garçia Ramirez. There, in the midst of gold and gems, and of silk and lace, Doña Inez is standing, busily engaged in the task of selecting the fairest treasures of her wardrobe to grace the grand festival of the following day. Doña Beatriz de Lavella, and the young waiting-woman who had been employed in the vain though generous effort to save Don Carlos, are both aiding her in the choice.

"Please your ladyship," said the girl, "I should recommend rose colour for the basquina.[2] Then, with those beautiful pearls, my lord's late gift, my lady will be as fine as a duchess; of whom, I hear, many will be there.—But what will Señora Doña Beatriz please to wear?"

"I do not intend to go, Juanita," said Doña Beatriz, with a little embarrassment.

"Not intend to go!" cried the girl, crossing herself in surprise. "Not go to see the grandest sight there has been in Seville for many a year! Worth a hundred bull-feasts! Ay de mi! what a pity!"

"Juanita," interposed her mistress, "I think I hear the señorita's voice in the garden. It is far too hot for her to be out of doors. Oblige me by bringing her in at once."

As soon as the attendant was gone, Doña Inez turned to her cousin. "It is really most unreasonable of Don Juan," she said, "to keep you shut up here, whilst all Seville is making holiday."

"I am glad—I have no heart to go forth," said Doña Beatriz, with a quivering lip.

"Nor have I too much, for that matter. My poor brother is so

[1] A bundle of sticks or twigs, especially wood to be burned as fuel.
[2] A short-sleeved overdress for outdoor wear.

weak and ill to-day, it grieves me to the heart. Moreover, he is still so thoughtless about his poor soul. That is the worst of all. I never cease praying Our Lady to bring him to a better mind. If he would only consent to see a priest; but he was ever obstinate. And if I urge the point too strongly, he will think I suppose him dying."

"I thought his health had improved since you had him brought over here."

"Certainly he is happier here than he was in his father's house. But of late he seems to me to be sinking, and that quickly. And now, the Auto—"

"What of that?" asked Doña Beatriz, with a quick look, half suspicious and half frightened.

Doña Inez closed the door carefully, and drew nearer to her cousin. "They say she will be amongst the relaxed,"[3] she whispered.

"Does he know it?" asked Beatriz.

"I fear he suspects something; and what to tell him, or not to tell him, I know not—Our Lady help me! Ay de mi! 'Tis a horrible business from beginning to end. And the last thing—the arrest of the sister, Doña Juana! A duke's daughter—a noble's bride. But—best be silent.

'Con el re e la Inquisicion,
Chiton! Chiton!'"[4]

Thus, only in a few hurried words, spoken with 'bated breath, did Doña Inez venture to allude to the darkest and saddest of the horrible tragedies in that time of horrors. Nor shall we do more.

"Still, you know, amiga mia," she continued, "one must do like one's neighbours. It would be so ridiculous to look gloomy on a festival day. Besides, every one would talk."

"That is why I say I am glad Don Juan made it his prayer to me that I would not go. For not to look sorrowful, when thy father, Don Manuel, and my aunt, Doña Katarina, are both doing their utmost to drive me out of my senses, would be past my power."

"Have they been urging the suit of Señor Luis upon thee again?

[3] Those delivered over to the secular arm—that is, to death.
[4] "With the King or the Inquisition. Hush! Hush!" A Spanish Proverb.

My poor Beatriz, I am truly sorrow for thee," said Doña Inez, with genuine sympathy.

"Urging it again!" Beatriz repeated with flashing eyes. "Nay; but they have never ceased to urge it. And they spare not to say such wicked, cruel words. They tell me Don Juan is dishonoured by his brother's crime. Dishonoured, forsooth! Think of dishonour touching him! After the day of St. Quentin, the Duke of Savoy was not of that mind, nor our Catholic King himself. And they have the audacity to say that I can easily get absolved of my troth to him. Absolved of a solemn promise made in the sight of God and of Our Lady, and all the holy Saints! If *that* be not heresy, as bad as—"

"Hush!" interrupted Doña Inez. "These are dangerous subjects. Moreover, I hear some one knocking at the door." It proved to be a page bearing a message.

"If it please Doña Beatriz de Lavella, Don Juan Alvarez de Santillanos y Meñaya kisses the señora's feet, and most humbly desires the favour of an audience."

"I go," said Beatriz.

"Request Señor Don Juan to have the goodness to untire himself a little, and bring his Excellency fruit and wine," added Doña Inez. "My cousin," she said, turning to Beatriz as soon as the page left the room, "do you not know your cheeks are all aflame? Don Juan will think we have quarrelled. Rest you here a minute, and let me bathe them for you with this water of orange-flowers."

Beatriz submitted, though reluctantly, to her cousin's good offices. While she performed them she whispered, "And be not so downcast, amiga mia. There is a remedy for most troubles. And as for yours, I see not why Don Juan himself should not save you out of them once for all." She added, in a whisper, two or three words that more than undid all the benefit which the cheeks of Beatriz might otherwise have derived from the application of the fragrant water.

"No use," was the agitated reply. "Even were it possible, *they* would not permit it."

"You can come to visit me. Then trust me to manage the rest.

The truth is, amiga mia," Doña Inez continued hurriedly, as she smoothed her cousin's dark glossy hair, "what between sickness, and quarrelling, and the Faith, and heresy, and prisons, there is so much trouble in the world that no one can help, it seems a pity not to help all one can. So you may tell Don Juan that if Doña Inez can do him a good turn she will not be found wanting. There, I despair of your cheeks. Yet I must allow that their crimson becomes you well. But you would rather hear that from Don Juan's lips than from mine. Go to him, my cousin." And with a parting kiss Beatriz was dismissed.

But if she expected any flattery that day from the lips of Don Juan, she was disappointed. His heart was far too sorrowful. He had merely come to tell his betrothed what he intended to do on the morrow—that dreadful morrow! "I have secured a station," he said, "from whence I can watch the whole procession, as it issues from the gate of the Triana. If *he* is there, I shall dare everything for a last look and word. And a desperate man is seldom baffled. If even his dust is there, I shall stand beside it till all is over. If not—" Here he broke off, leaving his sentence unfinished, as if in that case it did not matter what he did.

Just then Doña Inez entered. After customary salutations, she said, "I have a request to make of you, my cousin, on the part of my brother, Don Gonsalvo. He desires to see you for a few moments."

"Señora my cousin, I am very much at your service, and at his."

Juan was accordingly conducted to the upper room where Gonsalvo lay. And at the special request of the sick man, they were left alone together.

He stretched out a wasted hand to his cousin, who took it in silence, but with a look of compassion. For it needed only a glance at his face to show that death was there.

"I should be glad to think you forgave me," he said.

"I do forgive you," Juan answered. "You intended no evil."

"Will you, then, do me a great kindness? It is the last I shall ask.

Tell me the names of any of the—the victims that have come to your knowledge."

"It is only through rumour one can hear these things. Not yet have I succeeded in discovering whether the name dearest to me is amongst them."

"Tell me—has rumour named in your hearing—Doña Maria de Xeres y Bohorques?"

Juan was still ignorant of the secret which Doña Inez had but recently confided to his betrothed. He therefore answered, without hesitation, though in a low, sad tone, "Yes; they say she is to die to-morrow."

Don Gonsalvo flung his hand across his face, and there was a great silence, which the awed and wondering Juan broke at last. Guessing at the truth, he said, "It may be I have done wrong to tell you."

"No; you have done right. I knew it ere you told me. It is well—for her."

"A brave word, bravely spoken."

"Nigh upon eighteen months—long slow months of grief and pain. All ended now. To-morrow night she will see the glory of God."

There was another long pause. At last Juan said,—

"Perhaps, if you could, you would gladly share her fate?"

Gonsalvo half raised himself, and a flush overspread the wan face that already wore the ashy hue of approaching death. "Share *that* fate?" he cried, with an eagerness contrasting strangely with his former slow and measured utterance. "Change with *them?* Ask the beggar, who sits all day at the King's gate, waiting for his dole of crumbs, would he gladly change with the King's children, when he sees the golden gate flung open before them, and watches them pass in robed and crowned, to the presence-chamber of the King himself."

"Your faith is greater than mine," said Juan in surprise.

"In one way, yes," replied Gonsalvo, sinking back, and resuming his low, quiet tone. "For the beggar dares to hope that the King has looked with pity even on *him*."

"You do well to hope in the mercy of God."

"Cousin, do you know what my life has been?"

"I think I do."

"I am past disguise now. Standing on the brink of the grave, I dare speak the truth, though it be to my own shame. There was no evil, no sin—stay, I will sum up all in one word. *One* pure, blameless life—a man's life, too—I have watched from day to day, from childhood to manhood. All that your brother Don Carlos was, I was not; all he was not, I was."

"Yet you once thought that life incomplete, unmanly," said Juan, remembering the taunts that in past days had so often aroused his wrath.

"I was a fool. It is just retribution that I—I who called him coward—should see him march in there triumphant, with the palm of victory in his hand. But let me end; for I think it is the last time I shall speak of myself in any human ear. I sowed to the flesh, and of the flesh I have reaped—*corruption*. It is an awful word, Don Juan. All the life in me turned to death; all the good in me (what God meant for good, such as force, fire, passion) turned to evil. What availed it me that I loved a star in heaven—a bright, lonely, distant star—while I was earthy, of the earth? Because I could not (and thank God for that!) pluck down my star from the sky and hold it in my hand, even that love became corruption too. I fulfilled my course, the earthly grew sensual, the sensual grew devilish. And then God smote me, though not then for the first time. The stroke of his hand was heavy. My heart was crushed, my frame left powerless." He paused for a while, then slowly resumed. "The stroke of his hand, your brother's words, your brother's book—by these he taught me. There is deliverance even from the bondage of corruption, through him who came to call not the righteous, but sinners. One day—and that soon—I, even I, shall kneel at his feet, and thank him for saving the lost. And then I shall see my star, shining far above me in his glorious heaven, and be content and glad."

"God has been very gracious to you, my cousin," said Juan in a tone of emotion. "And what he has cleansed I dare not call common. Were my brother here to-day, I think he would stretch out to you the right hand, not of forgiveness, but of fellowship. I have told you how he longed for your soul."

"God can fulfil more desires of his than that, Don Juan, and I doubt not he will. What know we of his dealings? we who all these dreary months have been mourning for and pitying his prisoners, to-morrow to be his crowned and sainted martyrs? It were a small thing with him to flood the dungeon's gloom with light, and give—even here, even now—all their hearts long for to those who suffer for him."

Juan was silent. Truly the last was first, and the first last now. Gonsalvo had reached some truths which were still far beyond *his* ken.[5] He did not know how their seed had been sown in his heart by his own brother's hand. At length he answered, in a low and faltering voice, "There is much in what you say. Fray Sebastian told me—"

"Ay," cried Gonsalvo eagerly, "what did Fray Sebastian tell you of *him*?"

"That he found him in perfect peace, though ill and weak in body. It is my hope that God himself has delivered him ere now out of their cruel hands. And I ought to tell you that he spoke of all his relatives with affection, and made special inquiry after your health."

Gonsalvo said quietly, "It is likely I shall see him before you."

Juan sighed. "To-morrow will reveal something," he said.

"Many things, perhaps," Gonsalvo returned. "Well—Doña Beatriz waits you now. There is no poison in that wine, though it be of an earthly vintage; and God himself puts the cup in your hand; so take it, and be comforted. Yet stay, have you patience for one word more?"

"For a thousand, if you will, my cousin."

"I know that in heart you share his—our faith."

Juan shrank a little from his gaze.

[5] Knowledge or understanding.

"Of course," he replied, "I have been obliged to conceal my opinions; and, indeed, of late all things have seemed to grow dim and uncertain with me. Sometimes, in my heart of hearts, I cannot tell what truth is."

"He came not to call the righteous, but sinners,"[6] said Gonsalvo. "And the sinner who has heard his call must believe, let others doubt as they may. Thank God, the sinner may not only believe, but love. Yes; in that the beggar at the gate may take his stand beside the king's children unreproved. Even I dare to say, 'Lord, thou knowest all things; thou knowest that I love thee.'[7] Only to them it is given to prove it while I—ay, there was the bitter thought. Long it haunted me. At last I prayed that if indeed he deigned to accept me, all sinful as I was, he would give me for a sign something to do, to suffer, or to give up, whereby I might prove my love."

"And did he hear you?"

"Yes. He showed me one thing harder to give up than life; one thing harder to do than to brave the torture and the death of fire."

"What is that?"

Once more Gonsalvo veiled his face. Then he murmured, "Harder to give up—vengeance, hatred; harder to do—to pray for *their* murderers."

"*I* could never do it," said Juan, starting.

"And if at last—at last—*I* can,—I, whose anger was fierce, and whose wrath was cruel, even unto death,—is not that His own work in me?"

Juan half turned away, and did not answer immediately. In his heart many thoughts were struggling. Far, indeed, was he from praying for his brother's murderers; almost as far from wishing to do it. Rather would he invoke God's vengeance upon them. Had Gonsalvo, in the depths of his misery, remorse, and penitence, actually found something which Don Juan Alvarez still lacked? He said at last, with a humility new and strange to him,—

"My cousin, you are nearer heaven than I."

[6] Referring to Mark 2:17.
[7] Referring to John 21:17.

"As to time—yes," said Gonsalvo, with a faint smile. "Now farewell, cousin; and thank you."

"Can I do nothing more for you?"

"Yes; tell my sister that I know all. Now, God bless you, and deliver you from the evils that beset your path, and bring you and yours to some land where you may worship him in peace and safety."

And so the cousins parted, never to meet again upon earth.

XXXVI.

"The Horrible and Tremendous Spectacle."

"All have passed:
The fearful, and the desperate, and the strong.
Some like the barque that rushes with the blast:
Some like the leaf borne tremblingly along;
And some like men who have but one more field
To fight, and then may slumber on their shield—
Therefore they arm in hope.

HEMANS.

T earliest dawn next morning, Juan established himself in an upper room of one of the high houses which overlooked the gate of the Triana. He had hired it from the owners for the purpose, stipulating for sole possession and perfect loneliness.

At sunrise the great Cathedral bell tolled out solemnly, and all the bells in the city responded. Through the crowd, which had already gathered in the street, richly dressed citizens were threading their way on foot. He knew they were those who, out of zeal for the faith, had volunteered to act as *patrinos*, or god-fathers, to the prisoners, walking beside them in the procession. Amongst them he recognised his cousins, Don Manuel and Don Balthazar. They were all admitted into the castle by a private door.

Ere long the great gate was flung open. Juan's eyes were rivetted to the spot. There was a sound of singing, sweet and low, as of childish voices; for the first to issue from those gloomy portals were the boys of the College of Doctrine, dressed in white surplices, and chanting litanies to the saints. Clear and full at intervals rose from their lips the "Ora pro nobis"[1] of the response; and tears gathered unconsciously in the eyes of Juan at the old familiar words.

In great contrast with the white-robed children came the next in order. Juan drew his breath hard, for here were the penitents: pale, melancholy faces, "ghastly and disconsolate beyond what can be imagined;"[2] forms clothed in black, without sleeves, and barefooted—hands carrying extinguished tapers.

Those who walked foremost in the procession had only been convicted of such *minor* offences as blasphemy, sorcery, or polygamy. But by-and-by there came others, wearing ugly san-benitos—yellow, with red crosses—and conical paper mitres on their heads. Juan's eye kindled with intenser interest; for he knew that these were Lutherans. Not without a wild dream—hope, perhaps—that the near approach of death might have subdued his brother's fortitude, did he scan in turn every mournful face. There was Luis D'Abrego, the illuminator of church books; there, walking long afterwards, as far more guilty, was Medel D'Espinosa, the dealer in embroidery, who had received the Testaments brought by Juliano. There were many others of much higher rank, with whom he was well acquainted. Altogether more than eighty in number, the long and melancholy train swept by, every man or woman attended by two monks and a patrino. But Carlos was not amongst them.

Then came the great Cross of the Inquisition; the face turned towards the penitent, the back to the *impenitent*—those devoted to the death of fire. And now Juan's breath came and went—his lips trembled; all his soul was in his eager, straining eyes. Now first he saw the hideous zamarra—a black robe, painted all over

[1] Meaning "pray for us."

[2] Report of De Pegna; commentaries of Pegna was long the standing guide of the Inquisition.

with saffron-coloured flames, into which devils and serpents, rudely represented, were thrusting the impenitent heretic. A paper crown, or carroza, similarly adorned, covered the victim's head. But the face of the wearer was unknown to Juan. He was a poor artisan—Juan de Leon by name—who had made his escape by flight, but had been afterwards apprehended in the Low Countries. Torture and cruel imprisonment had almost killed him already; but his heart was strong to suffer for the Lord he loved, and though the pallor of death was on his cheek, there was no fear there.

But the countenances of those that followed Juan knew too well. Never afterwards could he exactly recall the order in which they walked; yet every individual face stamped itself indelibly on his memory. He would carry those looks in his heart until his dying hour.

No less than four of the victims wore the white tunic and brown mantle of St. Jerome. One of these was an old man—leaning on his staff for very age, but with joy and confidence beaming in his countenance. The white locks, from which Garçias Arias had gained the name of Doctor Blanco, had been shorn away; but Juan easily recognised the waverer of past days, now strengthened with all might, according to the glorious power of him whom at last he had learned to trust. The accomplished Cristobal D'Arellano, and Fernando de San Juan, Master of the College of Doctrine, followed calm and dauntless. Steadfast, too, though not without a little natural shrinking from the doom of fire, was a mere youth—Juan Crisostomo.

Then came one clad in a doctor's robe, with the step of a conqueror and the mien of a king. As he issued from the Triana he chanted, in a clear and steady voice, the words of the Hundred and ninth Psalm: "Hold not thy peace, O God of my praise; for the mouth of the ungodly, yea, the mouth of the deceitful, is opened upon me: and they have spoken against me with false tongues. They compassed me about also with words of hatred, and fought against me without a cause . . . Help me, O Lord my God: O save me according to thy mercy; and they shall know how that this is thine hand, and that thou, Lord, hast done it. Though they curse, yet bless thou." So died away the voice of Juan Gonzalez, one of the noblest of Christ's noble band of witnesses in Spain.

All these were arrayed in the garments of their ecclesiastical orders, to be solemnly degraded on the scaffold in the Square of St. Francis. But there followed one already in the full infamy, or glory, of the zamarra and carroza, with painted flames and demons;—with a thrill of emotion, Juan recognised his friend and teacher, Cristobal Losada—looking calm and fearless—a hero marching to his last battle, conquering and to conquer.

Yet even that face soon faded from Juan's thoughts. For there walked in that gloomy death procession six females—persons of rank; nearly all of them young and beautiful, but worn by imprisonment, and more than one amongst them maimed by torture. Yet if man was cruel, Christ, for whom they suffered, was pitiful. Their countenances, calm and even radiant, revealed the hidden power by which they were sustained. Their names—which deserve a place beside those of the women of old who were last at his cross and first beside his open sepulchre—were, Doña Isabella de Baena, in whose house the church was wont to meet; the two sisters of Juan Gonzalez; Doña Maria de Virves; Doña Maria de Cornel; and, last of all, Doña Maria de Bohorques, whose face shone as the first martyr's, looking up into heaven. She alone, of all the female martyr band, appeared wearing the gag, an honour due to her heroic efforts to console and sustain her companions in the court of the Triana.

Juan's brave heart well-nigh burst with impotent, indignant anguish. "Ay de mi, my Spain!" he cried; "thou seest these things, and endurest them. Lucifer, son of the morning, thou art fallen—fallen from thy high place amongst the nations."

It was true. From the man, or nation, "that hath not," shall be taken "even that which he seemeth to have." Had the spirit of chivalry, Spain's boast and pride, been faithful to its own dim light, it might even then have saved Spain. But its light became darkness; its trust was betrayed into the hand of superstition. Therefore, in the just judgment of God, its own degradation quickly followed. Spain's chivalry lost gradually all that was genuine, all that was noble in it; until it became only a faint and ghastly mockery, a sign of corruption, like the phosphoric light that flickers above the grave.

Absorbed in his bitter thoughts, Juan well-nigh missed the last of the doomed ones—last because highest in worldly rank. Sad and slow, with eyes bent down, Don Juan Ponce de Leon walked along. The flames on his zamarra were reversed; poor symbol of the poor mercy for which he sold his joy and triumph and dimmed the brightness of his martyr crown. Yet surely he did not lose the glad welcome that awaited him at the close of that terrible day; nor the right to say, with the erring restored apostle, "Lord, thou knowest all things; thou knowest that I love thee."[3]

All the living victims had passed now. And Don Carlos Alvarez was not amongst them. Juan breathed a sigh of relief; but not yet did his straining eyes relax their gaze. For Rome's vengeance reached even to the grave. Next, there were borne along the statues of those who had died in heresy, robed in the hideous zamarra, and followed by black chests containing their bones to be burned.

Not there!—No—not there! At last Juan's trembling hands let go the framework of the window to which they had been clinging; and, the intense strain over, he fell back exhausted.

The stately pageant swept by, unwatched by him. He never saw, what all Seville was gazing on with admiration, the grand procession of the judges and counsellors of the city, in their robes of office; the chapter of the Cathedral; the long slow train of priests and monks that followed. And then, in a space left empty out of reverence, the great green standard of the Inquisition was borne aloft, and over it a gilded crucifix. Then came the Inquisitors themselves, in their splendid official dresses. And lastly, on horseback and in gorgeous apparel, the familiars of the Inquisition.

It was well that Juan's eyes were turned from that sight. What avails it for lips white with passion to heap wild curses on the heads

[3] John 21:17

of those for whom God's curse already "waits in calm shadow," until the day of reckoning be fully come? Curses, after all, are weapons dangerous to use, and apt to pierce the hand that wields them.

His first feeling was one of intense relief, almost of joy. He had escaped the maddening torture of seeing his brother dragged before his eyes to the death of anguish and shame. But to that succeeded the bitter thought, growing soon into full, mournful conviction, "I shall see his face no more on earth. He is dead—or dying."

Yet that day the deep, strong current of his brotherly love was crossed by another tide of emotion. Those heroic men and women, whom he watched as they passed along so calmly to their doom, had he no bond of sympathy with them? Was it so long since he had pressed Losada's hand in grateful friendship, and thanked Doña Isabella de Baena for the teaching received beneath her roof? With a thrill of keen and sudden shame the gallant soldier saw himself a recreant, who had flaunted his gay uniform on the parade and at the field-day, but when the hour of conflict came, had stepped aside, and let the sword and the bullet find out braver and truer hearts.

He could not die thus for his faith. On the contrary, it cost him but little to conceal it, to live in every respect like an orthodox Catholic. What, then, had they which he had not? Something that enabled his young brother—the boy who used to weep for a blow—to stand and look fearless in the face of a horrible death. Something that enabled even poor, wild, passionate Gonsalvo to forgive and pray for the murderers of the woman he loved. What was it?

XXXVII.

Something Ended and Something Begun.

"O sweet and strange it is to think that ere this day is done,
The voice that now is speaking may be beyond the sun
For ever and for ever with those just souls and true
And what is life that we should mourn, why make we such ado?"

TENNYSON.

ATE in the afternoon of that day, Doña Inez entered her sick brother's room. A glitter of silk rose-coloured and black, of costly lace and of gems and gold, seemed to surround her. But as she threw aside the mantilla that partially shaded her face, and almost sank on a seat beside the bed, it was easy to see that she was very faint and weary, if not also very sick at heart.

"Santa Maria! I am tired to death," she murmured. "The heat was killing; and the whole business interminably long."

Gonsalvo gazed at her with eager eyes, as a man dying of thirst might gaze on one who holds a cup of water; but for a while he did not speak. At last he said, pointing to some wine that lay near, beside an untasted meal, "Drink, then."

"What, my brother!" said Doña Inez, reproachfully, "you have not touched food to-day! You—so ill and weak!"

"I am a man—even still," said Gonsalvo with a little bitterness in his tone.

Doña Inez drank, and for a few moments fanned herself in silence, distress and embarrassment in her face.

At last Gonsalvo, who had never withdrawn his eager gaze, said in a low voice,—

"Sister, remember your promise."

"I am afraid—for you."

"You need not," he gasped. "Only tell me all."

Doña Inez passed her hand wearily across her brow.

"Everything floats before me," she said. "What with the music, and the mass, and the incense; and the crosses, and banners, and gorgeous robes; and then the taking of the oaths, and the sermon of the faith."

"Still—you kept my charge?"

"I did, brother." She lowered her voice. "Hard as it was, I looked at *her*. If it comforts you to know that, all through that long day, her face was as calm as ever I have seen it listening to Fray Constantino's sermons, you may take that comfort to your heart. When her sentence had been read, she was asked to recant; and I heard her answer rise clear and distinct, 'I neither can nor will recant.' Ave Maria Sanctissima! it is all a great mystery."

There was a silence, then she resumed,—

"And Señor Cristobal Losada—" but the thought of the kind and skilful physician who had watched beside her own sick-bed, and brought back her babe from the gates of the grave, almost overcame her. Turning quickly to other victims, she went on—

"There were four monks of St. Jerome. Think of the White Doctor, that every one believed so good a man, so pious and orthodox! Another of them, Fray Cristobal D'Arellano, was accused in his sentence of some wicked words against Our Lady which, it would seem, he never said. He cried out boldly, before them all, 'It is false! I never advanced such a blasphemy; and I am ready to prove the contrary with the Bible in my hand.' Every one seemed too much amazed even to think of ordering him to be gagged: and, for my part, I am glad the poor wretch had his word for the last time. I cannot help wishing they had equally forgotten to silence Doctor Juan Gonzales; for it does not appear that he was speaking any blasphemy, but merely a word of comfort to a poor pale girl, his sister, as they told me. Two of them are to die with him—God help them!—Holy Saints forgive me; I forgot we were told not to pray for them," and she crossed herself.

"Does my sister really believe that compassionate word a sin in God's sight?"

"How am I to know? I believe whatever the Church says, of course. And surely there is enough in these days to inspire us with a pious horror of heresy. *Pues*," she resumed, "there was that long and terrible ceremony of degrading from the priesthood. And yet that Gonzalez passed through it all as calm and unmoved as though he were but putting on his robes to say mass. His mother and his two brothers are still in prison, it is said, awaiting their doom. Of all the relaxed, I am told that only Don Juan Ponce de Leon showed any sign of penitence. For the sake of his noble house, one is glad to think he is not so hardened as the rest. Ay de mi! Whether it be right or wrong, I cannot help pitying their unhappy souls."

"Pity your own soul, not theirs," said Gonsalvo. "For I tell you Christ himself, in all his glory and majesty, at the right hand of the Father, will *stand up* to receive them this night, as he did to welcome St. Stephen long ago."

"Oh, my poor brother, what dreadful words you speak! It is a mortal sin even to listen to you. Take thought, I implore you, of your own situation."

"I *have* taken thought," interrupted Gonsalvo, faintly. "But I can bear no more—just now. Leave me, I pray you, alone with God."

"If you would even try to say an Ave!—But I fear you are ill—suffering. I do not like to leave you thus."

"Do not heed me; I shall be better soon. And a vow is upon me that I must keep to-day." Once more he flung the wasted hand across his face to conceal it.

Irresolute whether to go or stay, she stood for some minutes watching him silently. At length she caught a low murmur, and hoping that he prayed, she bent over him to hear. Only three words reached her ear. They were these—"Father, forgive them."

After an interval, Gonsalvo looked up again. "I thought you were gone," he said. "Go now, I entreat of you. But so soon as you know *the end*, spare not to come and tell me. For I wait for that."

Thus entreated, Doña Inez had no choice but to leave him alone, which she did.

Evening had worn to night, and night was beginning to wear towards daybreak, when at last Don Garçia Ramirez, and those of his servants who had accompanied him to the Prado San Sebastian to see the end, returned home.

Doña Inez sat awaiting her husband in the patio. She looked pale and languid; apparently the great holiday of Seville had been anything but a joyful day to her.

Don Garçia divested himself of his cloak and sword, and dismissed the servants to their beds. But when his wife invited him to partake of the supper she had prepared, he turned upon her with very unusual ill-humour. "It is little like thy wonted wit, señora mia, to bid a man to his breakfast at midnight," he said. Yet he drank deeply of the Xeres wine that stood on the board beside the venison pasty and the manchet bread.

At last, after long patience, Doña Inez won from his lips what she desired to hear. "Oh yes; all is over. Our Lady defend us! I have never seen such obstinacy; nor could I have believed it possible unless I had seen it. The criminals encouraged each other to the very last. Those girls, the sisters of Gonzalez, repeated their Credo at the stake; whereupon the attendant Brethren entreated them to have so much pity on their own souls as to say, 'I believe in the *Roman* Catholic Church.' They answered, 'We will do as our brother does.' So the gag was removed, and Doctor Juan cried aloud, 'Add nothing to the good confession you have made already.' But for all that, order was given to strangle them; and one of the friars told us they died in the true faith. I suppose it is not a sin to hope they did."

After a pause, he continued, in a deeper tone, "Señor Cristobal amazed me as much as any of them. At the very stake, some of the Brethren undertook to argue with him. But seeing that we were all listening, and might hear somewhat to the hurt of our souls, they began to speak in the Latin tongue. Our physician immediately did the same. I am no scholar myself; but there were learned men there who marked every word, and one of them told me afterwards that the doomed man spoke with as much elegance and propriety as if he had been contending for an academic prize, instead of waiting for the lighting of the fire which was to consume him. This unheard-of calmness and composure, whence is it? The devil's own work, or"—he broke off suddenly and resumed in a different tone, "Señora mia, have you thought of the hour? Let us to our beds!"

"I cannot go to rest until you tell me one thing more. Doña Maria de Bohorques?"

"Vaya, vaya! have we not had enough of it all?"

"Nay; I have made a promise. I must entreat you to tell me how Doña Maria de Bohorques met her doom."

"With unflinching hardihood. Don Juan Ponce tried to urge her to yield somewhat. But she refused, saying it was not now a time for reasoning, and that they ought rather to meditate on the Lord's death and passion. (They believe in *that*, it seems.) When she was bound to the stake, the monks and friars crowded round her, and pressed her only to repeat the Credo. She did so; but began to add some explanations, which, I suppose, were heretical. Then immediately the command was given to strangle her; and so, in one moment, while she was yet speaking, death came to her."

"Then she did not suffer. She escaped the fire! Thank God!"

Five minutes afterwards, Doña Inez stood by her brother's bed. He lay in the same posture, his face still shaded by his hand.

"Brother," she said gently– "brother, all is over. She did not suffer. It was done in one moment."

There was no answer.

"Brother, are you not glad she did not feel the fire? Can you not thank God for it? Speak to me."

Still no answer.

He could not be asleep! Impossible!— "Speak to me, Gonsalvo!—*Brother!*"

She drew close to him; she touched his hand to remove it from his face. The next moment a cry of horror rang through the house. It brought the servants and Don Garçia himself to the room.

"He is dead! God and Our Lady have mercy on his soul!" said Don Garçia, after a brief examination.

"If only he had had the Holy Sacrament, I could have borne it!" said Doña Inez; and then, kneeling down beside the couch, she wept bitterly.

So passed the beggar with the King's sons, through the golden gate into the King's own presence-chamber. His wrecked and troublous life over, his passionate heart at rest for ever, the erring, repentant Gonsalvo found entrance into the same heaven as D'Arellano, and Gonzalez, and Losada, with their radiant martyr-crowns. In the many mansions there was a place for him, as for those heroic and triumphant ones. He wore the same robe as they—a robe washed and made white, not in the blood of martyrs, but in the blood of the Lamb.

XXXVIII.

Nuera Again.

"Happy places have grown holy;
If ye went where once ye went,
Only tears would fall down slowly,
As at solemn Sacrament.
Household names, that used to flutter
Through your laughter unawares,
God's divine one ye can utter
With less trembling in your prayers."
E. B. BROWNING.

CHILL and dreary torpor stole over Juan's fiery spirit after the Auto. The settled conviction that his brother was dead took possession of his mind. Moreover, his soul had lost its hold upon the faith which he once embraced so warmly. He had consciously ceased to be true to his best convictions, and those convictions, in turn, had ceased to support him. His confidence in himself, his trust in his own heart, had been shaken to its foundations. And he was very far from having gained in its stead that strong confidence in God which would have infinitely more than counterbalanced its loss.

Thus two or three slow and melancholy months wore away. Then, fortunately for him, events happened that forced him, in spite of himself, to the exertion that saves from the deadly slumber of despair. It became evident, that if he did not wish to see the last earthly treasure that remained to him swept out of his reach for ever, he must rouse himself from his lethargy so far as to grasp and hold it; for now Don Manuel *commanded* his ward to bestow her hand upon his rival, Señor Luis Rotelo.

In her anguish and dismay, Beatriz fled for refuge to her kind-hearted cousin, Doña Inez.

Doña Inez received her into her house, where she soothed and comforted her; and soon found means to despatch an "esquelita," or billet, to Don Juan, to the following effect: "Doña Beatriz is here. Remember, my cousin, 'that a leap over a ditch is better than another man's prayer.'"

To which Juan replied immediately:—

"Señora and my cousin, I kiss your feet. Lend me a helping hand, and I take the leap."

Doña Inez desired nothing better. Being a Spanish lady, she loved an intrigue for its own sake; being a very kindly disposed lady, she loved an intrigue for a benevolent object. With her active co-operation and assistance, and her husband's connivance, it was quickly arranged that Don Juan should carry off Doña Beatriz from their house to a little country chapel in the neighbourhood, where a priest would be in readiness to perform the solemn rite which should unite them for ever. Thence they were to proceed at once to Nuera, Don Juan disguising himself for the journey as the lady's attendant. Doña Inez did not anticipate that her father and brothers would take any hostile steps after the conclusion of the affair—glad though they might have been to prevent it—since there was nothing which they hated and dreaded so much as a public scandal.

All Juan's latent fire and energy woke up again to meet the peril and to secure the prize. He was successful in everything; the plan had been well laid, and was well and promptly carried out. And thus it happened, that amidst December snows he bore his beautiful bride home to Nuera in triumph. If triumph it could be called, overcast by the ever-present memory of the one who "was not," which rested like a deep shadow upon all joy, and subdued and chastened it. Few things in life are sadder than a great, long-expected blessing coming thus;—like a friend from a foreign land whose return has been eagerly anticipated, but who, after years of absence, meets us changed in countenance and in heart, unrecognising and unrecognised.

Dolores welcomed her young master and his bride with affection and thankfulness. But he noticed that the dark hair, at the time of his last visit still only threaded with silver, had grown white as the mountain snows. In former days Dolores could not have told which of the noble youths, her lady's gallant sons, had been the dearer to her. But now she knew full well. Her heart was in the grave with the boy she had taken a helpless babe from his dying mother's arms. But, after all, *was* he in the grave? This was the question which she asked herself day by day, and many times a day. She was not quite so sure of the answer as Señor Don Juan seemed to be. Since the day of the Auto, he had assumed all the outward signs of mourning for his brother.

Fray Sebastian was also at Nuera, and proved a real help and comfort to its inmates. His very presence served to shield the household from any suspicions that might have been awakened with regard to their faith. For who could doubt the orthodoxy of Don Juan Alvarez, while he not only contributed liberally to the support of his parish church, but also kept a pious Franciscan in his family, in the capacity of private chaplain? Though it must be confessed that the Fray's duties were anything but onerous; now, as in former days, he showed himself a man fond of quiet, who for the most part held his peace, and let every one do what was right in his own eyes.

He was now on far more cordial terms with Dolores than he had ever been before. This was partly because he had learned that worse physical evils than ollas of lean mutton, or cheese of goat's milk, *might* be borne with patience, even with thankfulness. But partly also because Dolores now really tried to consult his tastes and to promote his comfort. Many a savoury dish "which the Fray used to like" did she trouble herself to prepare; many a flask of wine from their diminishing store did she gladly produce, "for the kind words that he spake to him in his sorrow and loneliness."

In spite of the depressing influences around her, Doña Beatriz could not but be very happy. For was not Don Juan hers, all her own, her own for ever? And with the zeal love inspires, and the skill love imparts, she applied herself to the task of brightening his darkened life. Not quite without effect. Even from that stern and gloomy brow the shadows at length began to roll away.

Don Juan could not speak of his sorrow. For weeks indeed after his return to Nuera his brother's name did not pass his lips. Better had it been otherwise, both for himself and for Dolores. Her heart, aching with its own lonely anguish and its vague, dark surmisings, often longed to know her young master's true innermost thought about his brother's fate. But she did not dare to ask him.

At last, however, this painful silence was partially broken through. One morning the old servant accosted her master with an air of some displeasure. It was in the inner room within the hall. Holding in her hand a little book, she said, "May it please your Excellency to pardon my freedom, but it is not well done of you to leave this lying open on your table. I am a simple woman; still I am at no loss to know what and whence it is. If you will not destroy it, and cannot keep it safe and secret, I implore of your worship to give it to me."

Juan held out his hand for it. "It is dearer to me than any earthly possession," he said briefly.

"It had need to be dearer than your life, señor, if you mean to leave it about in that fashion."

"I have lost the right to say so much," Juan answered. "And yet, Dolores—tell me, would it break your heart if I sold this place—you know it is mortgaged heavily already—and quitted the country?"

Juan expected a start, if not a cry of surprise and dismay. That Alvarez de Meñaya should sell the inheritance of his fathers seemed indeed a monstrous proposal. In the eyes of the world it would be an act of insanity, if not a crime. What then would it appear to one who loved the name of Santillanos y Meñaya far better than her life?

But the still face of Dolores never changed. "Nothing would break my heart now," she said calmly.

"You would come with us?"

She did not even ask *whither*. She did not care: all her thoughts were in the past.

"That is of course, señor," she answered. "If I had but first assurance of *one* thing."

"Name it; and if I can assure you, I will."

Instead of naming it she turned silently away. But presently turning again, she asked, "Will your Excellency please to tell me, is it that book that is driving you into exile?"

"It is. I am bound to confess the truth before men; and that is impossible here."

"But are you sure then that it is the truth?"

"Sure. I have read God's message both in the darkness and in the light. I have seen it traced in characters of blood—and fire."

"But—forgive the question, señor—does it make you happy?"

"Why do you ask?"

"Because, Señor Don Juan"—she spoke with an effort, but firmly, and fixing her eyes on his face—"he who gave you yon book found therein that which made him happy. I know it; he was here, and I watched him. When he came first, he was ill, or else very sorrowful, I know not why. But he learned from that book that God Almighty loved him, and that the Lord and Saviour Christ was his friend; and then his sorrow passed away, and his heart grew full of joy, so full that he must needs be telling me—ay, and even that poor dolt of a cura down there in the village—about the good news. And I think"—but here she stopped, frightened at her own boldness.

"What think you?" asked Juan, with difficulty restraining his emotion.

"Well, Señor Don Juan, I think that if that good news be true, it would not be so hard to suffer for it. Blessed Virgin! Could it be aught but joy to me, for instance, to lie in a dark dungeon, or even to be hanged or burned, if that could work out his deliverance? There be worse things in the world than pain or prisons. For where there's love, señor—Moreover, it comes upon me sometimes that the Lords Inquisitors may have mistaken his case. Wise and learned they may be, and good and holy they are, of course—'twere sin to doubt it—yet they may mistake sometimes. 'Twas but the other day, my old eyes growing dim apace, that I took a blessed gleam of sunlight that had fallen on yon oak table for a stain, and set to work to rub it off; the Lord forgive me for meddling with one of the best of his works! And, for aught we know, just so may they be doing, mistaking God's light upon the soul for the devil's stain of heresy. But the sunlight is stronger than they, after all."

"Dolores, you are half a Lutheran already yourself," answered Juan in surprise.

"I, señor! The Lord forbid! I am an old Christian, and a good Catholic, and so I hope to die. But if you must hear all the truth, I would walk in a yellow sanbenito, with a taper in my hand, before I would acknowledge that *he* ever said one word or thought one thought that was not Catholic and Christian too. All his crime was to find out that the good Lord loved him, and to be happy on account of it. If that be your religion also, Señor Don Juan, I have nothing to say against it. And, as I have said, God granting me, in his great mercy, one assurance first, I am ready to follow you and your lady to the world's end."

With these words on her lips she left the room. For a time Juan sat silent in deep thought. Then he opened the Testament, and turned over its leaves until he found the parable of the sower. "'Some fell upon stony places,'" he read, "'where they had not much earth; and forthwith they sprung up, because they had no deepness of earth: and when the sun was up, they were scorched; and, because they had no root, they withered away.'[1] There," he said within himself, "in those words is written the history of my life, from the day my

[1] Matthew 13:5-6

brother confessed his faith to me in the garden of San Isodro. God help me, and forgive my backsliding! But at least it is not too late to go humbly back to the beginning, and to ask him who alone can do it to break up the fallow ground."

He closed the book, walked to the window and looked out. Presently his eye was attracted to those dear mystic words on the pane, which both the brothers had loved and dreamed over from their childhood,—

"*El Dorado*
Yo hé trovado."

And at that moment the sun was shining on them as brightly as it used to do in those old days gone by for ever.

No vague dream of any good, foreshadowed by the omen to him or to his house, crossed the mind of the practical Don Juan. But he seemed to hear once more the voice of his young brother saying close beside him, "Look, Ruy, the light is on our father's words." And memory bore him back to a morning long ago, when some slight boyish quarrel had been ended thus.

Over his stern, handsome face there passed a look that shaded and softened it, and his eyes grew dim—dim with tears. But just then Doña Beatriz, radiant from a morning walk, and with her hands full of early spring flowers, tripped in, singing a Spanish ballad,—

"Ye men that row the galleys.
I see my lady fair;
She gazes at the fountain
That leaps for pleasure there."

Beatriz was a child of the city; and, moreover, her life hitherto had been an unloved and unloving one. Now her nature was expanding under the wholesome influences of home life and home love, and of simple healthful pleasures. "Look, Don Juan, what pretty things grow in your fields here! I have never seen the like," she said, breaking off in her song to exhibit her treasures.

Don Juan looked carelessly at them, lovingly at her. "I would fain hear a morning hymn from those sweet, tuneful lips," he pleaded.

"Most willingly, amigo mio,—

'Ave Sanctissima—'"

"Hush, my beloved; hush, I entreat of you." And laying his hand lightly on her shoulder, he gazed in her face with a mixture of fond and tender admiration and of gentle reproach difficult to describe. "*Not that*. For the sake of all that lies between us and the old faith, not that. Rather let us sing together,—

'Vezina Regis prodeunt.'

For you know that between us and our King there stands, and there needs to stand, no human mediator. Do you not, my beloved?"

"I know that you are right," answered Beatriz, still reading her faith in Don Juan's eyes. "But we can sing afterwards, whatever you like, and as much as you will. I pray you let us come forth now into the sunshine together. Look, what a glorious morning it is!"

XXXIX.

Left Behind.

"They are all gone into a world of light,
And I alone am lingering here."
HENRY VAUGHAN.

HE change of seasons brought little change to those dark cells in the Triana, where neither the glory of summer nor the breath of spring could come. While the world, with its living interests, its hopes and fears, its joys and sorrows, kept surging round them, not even an echo of its many voices reached the doomed ones within, who lay so near, yet so far from all, "fast bound in misery and iron."

Not yet had the Deliverer come to Carlos. More than once he had seemed very near. During the summer heats, so terrible in that prison, fever had wasted the captive's already enfeebled frame; but this was the means of prolonging his life, for the eve of the Auto found him unable to walk across his cell. Still he heard without very keen sorrow the fate of his beloved friends, so soon did he hope to follow them.

And yet, month after month, life lingered on. In his circumstances restoration to health was simply impossible. Not that he endured more than others, or even as much as some. He was not loaded with fetters, or buried in one of the frightful subterranean cells where daylight never entered. Still, when to the many physical sufferings his position entailed was added the weight of sickness, weakness, and utter loneliness, they formed together a burden heavy enough to have crushed even a strong heart to despair.

Long ago the last gleam of human sympathy and kindness had faded from him. Maria Gonzalez was herself a prisoner, receiving such payment as men had to give her for her brave deeds of charity. God's payment, however, was yet to come, and would be of another sort. Herrera, the under-gaoler, was humane, but very timid; moreover, his duties seldom led him to that part of the prison where Carlos lay. So that he was left dependent upon the tender mercies of Gaspar Benevidio, which were indeed cruel.

And yet, in spite of all, he was not crushed, not despairing. The lamp of patient endurance burned on steadily, because it was continually fed with oil by an unseen Hand.

It has been beautifully said, "The personal love of Christ to you, felt, delighted in, returned, is factually, truly, simply, without exaggeration, the deepest joy and the deepest feeling that the heart of man or woman can know. It will absolutely satisfy your heart. It would satisfy your heart if it were his will that you should spend the rest of your life alone in a dungeon."

Just this, nothing else, nothing less, sustained Carlos throughout those long slow months of suffering, which had now come to "add themselves and make the years." It proved sufficient for him. It has proved sufficient for thousands—God's unknown saints and martyrs, whose names we shall learn first in heaven.

Those who still occasionally sought access to him, in the hope of transforming the obstinate heretic into a penitent, marvelled greatly at the cheerful calm with which he was wont to receive them and to answer their arguments.

Sometimes he would even brave all the wrath of Benevidio, and raising his voice as loud as he could, he would make the gloomy vaults re-echo to such words as these: "The Lord is my light and my salvation; whom shall I fear? The Lord is the strength of my life; of whom shall I be afraid?"[1] Or these: "Whom have I in heaven but thee? and there is none upon earth that I desire beside thee. My flesh and my heart faileth; but God is the strength of my heart, and my portion for ever."[2]

But still it was not in Christ's promise, nor was it to be expected, that his prisoner should never know hours of sorrow, weariness, and heart-sinking. Such hours came sometimes. And on the very morning when Don Juan and Doña Beatriz were going forth together into the spring sunshine through the castle gate of Nuera, Carlos, in his dungeon, was passing through one of the darkest of these. He lay on his mat, his face covered with his wasted hands, through which tears were slowly falling. It was but very seldom that he wept now; tears had grown rare and scarce with him.

The evening before, he had received a visit from two Jesuits, bound on the only errand which would have procured their admission there. Irritated by his bold and ready answers to the usual arguments, they had recourse to declamation. And one of them bethought himself of mentioning the fate of the Lutherans who suffered at the two great Autos of Valladolid. "Most of the heretics," said the Jesuit, "though when they were in prison they were as obstinate as thou art now, yet had their eyes opened in the end to the error of their ways, and accepted reconciliation at the stake. At the last great Act of Faith, held in the presence of King Philip, only Don Carlos de Seso—" Here he stopped, surprised at the agitation of the prisoner, who had heard their threatenings against himself so calmly.

"De Seso! De Seso! Have they murdered him too?" moaned Carlos, and for a few brief moments he gave way to natural emotion. But quickly recovering himself, he said, "I shall only see him the sooner."

"Were you acquainted with him?" asked the Jesuit.

"I loved and honoured him. My avowing that cannot hurt him *now*," answered Carlos, who had grown used to the bitter thought

[1] Psalm 27:1
[2] Psalm 73:25-26

that any name would be disgraced, and its owner imperilled, by his mentioning it with affection.

"But if you will do me so much kindness," he added, "I pray you to tell me anything you know of his last hours. Any word he spoke."

"He could speak nothing," said the younger of his two visitors. "Before he left the prison he had uttered so many horrible blasphemies against Holy Church and Our Lady that he was obliged to wear the gag during the whole ceremony, lest he should offend the little ones."[3]

This last cruel wrong—the refusal of leave to the dying to speak one word in defence of the truths he died for—stung Carlos to the quick. It wrung from lips so patient hitherto words of indignant threatening. "God will judge your cruelty," he said. "Go on, fill up the measure of your guilt, for your time is short. One day, and that soon, there will be a grand spectacle, grander than your Autos. Then shall you, torturers of God's saints, call upon the mountains and rocks to cover you, and to hide you from the wrath of the Lamb."

Once more alone, his passionate anger died away. And it was well. Surrounded as he was on every side by strong, cold, relentless wrong and cruelty, if his spirit had beaten its wings against those bars of iron, it would soon have fallen to the ground faint and helpless, with crushed pinions. It was not in such vain strivings that he could find, or keep, the deep calm peace with which his heart was filled; it was in the quiet place at his Saviour's feet, from whence, if he looked at his enemies at all, it was only to pity and forgive them.

But though anger was gone, a heavy burden of sorrow remained. De Seso's noble form, shrouded in the hideous zamarra, his head crowned with the carroza, his face disfigured by the gag,—these were ever before his eyes. He well-nigh forgot that all this was over now—that for him the conflict was ended and the triumph begun.

[3] A genuine inquisitorial expression.

Could he have known even as much as we know now of the close of that heroic life, it might have comforted him.

Don Carlos de Seso met his doom at the second of the two great Autos celebrated at Valladolid during the year 1559. At the first, the most steadfast sufferers were Francisco de Vibero Cazalla, one of a family of confessors; and Antonio Herezuelo, whose pathetic story—the most thrilling episode of Spanish martyrology—would need an abler pen than ours.

During his lingering imprisonment of a year and a half, De Seso never varied in his own clear testimony to the truth, never compromised any of his brethren. Informed at last that he was to die the next day, he requested writing materials. These being furnished him, he placed on record a confession of his faith, which Llorente, the historian of the Inquisition, thus describes:—"It would be difficult to convey an idea of the uncommon vigour of sentiment with which he filled two sheets of paper, though he was then in the presence of death. He handed what he had written to the Alguazil, with these words: 'This is the true faith of the gospel, as opposed to that of the Church of Rome, which has been corrupted for ages. In this faith I wish to die, and in the remembrance and lively belief of the passion of Jesus Christ, to offer to God my body, now reduced so low.'"

All that night and the next morning were spent by the friars in vain endeavours to induce him to recant. During the Auto, though he could not speak, his countenance showed the steadfastness of his soul—a steadfastness which even the sight of his beloved wife amongst those condemned to perpetual imprisonment failed to disturb. When at last, as he was bound to the stake, the gag was removed, he said to those who stood around him, still urging him to yield, "I could show you that you ruin yourselves by not following my example; but there is no time. Executioners, light the fire that is to consume me."

Even in the act of death it was given him, though unconsciously, to strengthen the faith of another. In the martyr band was a poor man, Juan Sanchez, who had been a servant of the Cazallas, and was apprehended in Flanders with Juan de Leon. He had borne himself bravely throughout; but when the fire was kindled, the ropes that bound him to the stake having given way, the instinct of self-preservation made him rush from the flames, and, not knowing what he did, spring upon the scaffold where those who yielded at the last were wont to receive absolution. The attendant monks at once surrounded him, offering him the alternative of the milder death. Recovering self-possession, he looked around him. At one side knelt the penitents, at the other, motionless amidst the flames, De Seso stood,

> "As standing in his own high hall."

His choice was made. "I will die like De Seso," he said calmly; and then walked deliberately back to the stake, where he met his doom with joy.

Another brave sufferer at this Auto, Don Domingo de Roxas, ventured to make appeal to the justice of the King, only to receive the memorable reply, never to be read without a shudder,—"I would carry wood to burn my son, if he were such a wretch as thou!"

All these circumstances Carlos never heard on this side of the grave. But in the quiet Sabbath-keeping that remaineth for the people of God, there will surely be leisure enough to talk over past trials and triumphs. At present, however, he only saw the dark side—only knew the bare and bitter facts of suffering and death. He had not merely loved De Seso as his instructor; he had admired him with the generous enthusiasm of a young man for a senior in whom he recognises his ideal—all that he himself would fain become. If the Spains had but known the day of their visitation, he doubted not that man would have been their leader in the path of reform. But they knew it not; and so, instead, the chariot of fire had come for him. For him, and for nearly all the men and women whose hands Carlos had been wont to clasp in loving brotherhood. Losada, D'Arellano, Ponce de Leon, Doña Isabella de Baena, Doña Maria de Bohorques,—all these honoured names, and many more, did he repeat, adding after each one of them, "At rest with Christ." Somewhere in the depths of those dreary dungeons it might be that the heroic Juliano, his father in the faith, was lingering still; and also Fray Constantino, and the young monk of San Isodro, Fray Fernando. But the prison walls sundered them quite as hopelessly from him as the River of Death itself.

Earlier ties sometimes seemed to him only like things he had read or dreamed of. During his fever, indeed, old familiar faces had often flitted round him. Dolores sat beside him, laying her hand on his burning brow; Fray Sebastian taught him disjointed, meaningless fragments from the Schoolmen; Juan himself either spoke cheerful words of hope and trust, or else talked idly of long-forgotten trifles.

But all this was over now: neither dream nor fancy came to break his utter, terrible loneliness. He knew that he was never to see Juan again, nor Dolores, nor even Fray Sebastian. The world was dead to him, and he to it. And as for his brethren in the faith, they had gone "to the light beyond the clouds, and the rest beyond the storms," where he would so gladly be. Why, then, was he left so long, like one standing without in the cold? Why did not the golden gate open for him as well as for them? What was he doing in this place?—what *could* he do for his Master's cause or his Master's honour? He did not murmur. By this time his Saviour's prayer, "Not my will, but thine be done,"[4] had been wrought into the texture of his being with the scarlet, purple, and golden threads of pain, of patience, and of faith. But it is well for Christ's tried ones that he knows longing is not murmuring. Very full of longing were the words—words rather of pleading than of prayer—that rose continually from the lips of Carlos that day,—"And now, Lord, *what* wait I for?"

[4] Luke 22:42

XL.

"A Satisfactory Penitent."

> "How long in thraldom's grasp I lay
> I knew not; for my soul was black,
> And knew no change of night or day."
> CAMPBELL.

ARLOS was sleeping tranquilly in his dungeon on the following night, when the opening of the door aroused him. He started with sickening dread, the horrors of the torture-room rising in an instant before his imagination. Benevidio entered, followed by Herrera, and commanded him to rise and dress immediately. Long experience of the Santa Casa had taught him that he might as well make an inquiry of its doors and walls as of any of its officials. So he obeyed in silence, and slowly and painfully enough. But he was soon relieved from his worst fear by seeing Herrera fold together the few articles of clothing he had been allowed to have with him, preparatory to carrying them away. "It is only, then, a change of prison," he thought; "and wherever they bring me, heaven will be equally near."

His limbs, enfeebled by two years of close confinement, and lame from the effects of one terrible night, were sorely tried by what he thought an almost interminable walk through corridors and down narrow winding stairs. But at last he was conducted to a small postern door, which, greatly to his surprise, Benevidio proceeded to unlock. The kind-hearted Herrera took advantage of the moment when Benevidio was thus occupied to whisper,—

"We are bringing you to the Dominican prison, señor; you will be better used there."

Carlos thanked him by a grateful look and a pressure of the hand. But an instant afterwards he had forgotten his words. He had forgotten everything save that he stood once more in God's free air, and that God's own boundless heaven, spangled with ten thousand stars, was over him, no dungeon roof between. For one rapturous moment he gazed upwards, thanking God in his heart. But the fresh air he breathed seemed to intoxicate him like strong wine. He grew faint, and leaned for support on Herrera.

"Courage, señor; it is not far—only a few paces," said the under-gaoler, kindly.

Weak as he was, Carlos wished the distance a hundred times greater. But it proved quite long enough for his strength. By the time he was delivered over into the keeping of a couple of lay brothers, and locked by them into a cell in the Dominican monastery, he was scarcely conscious of anything save excessive fatigue.

The next morning was pretty far advanced before any one came to him; but at last he was honoured with a visit from the prior himself. He said frankly, and with perfect truth,—

"I am glad to find myself in your hands, my lord."

To one accustomed to feel himself an object of terror, it is a new and pleasant sensation to be trusted. Even a wild beast will sometimes spare the weak but fearless creature that ventures to play with it: and Don Fray Ricardo was not a wild beast; he was only a stern, narrow, conscientious man, the willing and efficient agent of a terrible system. His brow relaxed visibly as he said,—

"I have always sought your true good, my son."

"I am well aware of it, father."

"And you must acknowledge," the prior resumed, "that great forbearance and lenity have been shown towards you. But your infatuation has been such that you have deliberately and persistently sought your own ruin. You have resisted the wisest arguments, the gentlest persuasions, and that with an obstinacy, which time and discipline seem only to increase. And now at last, as another Auto-da-fé may not be celebrated for some time, my Lord Vice-Inquisitor-General, justly incensed at your contumacy,[1] would fain have thrown you into one of the underground dungeons, where, believe me, you would not live a month. But I have interceded for you."

"I thank your kindness, my lord. But I cannot see that it matters much how you deal with me now. Sooner or later, in one form or other, it must be death; and I thank God it can be no more."

While a man might count twenty, the prior looked silently in that steadfast sorrowful young face. Then he said,—

"My son, do not yield to despair; for I come to thee this day with a message of hope. I have also made intercession for thee with the Supreme Council of the Holy Office; and I have succeeded in obtaining from that august tribunal a great and unusual grace."

Carlos looked up, a sudden flush on his cheek. He hoped this unusual grace might be permission to see some familiar face ere he died; but the prior's next words disappointed him. Alas! it was only the offer of escape from death on terms that he might not accept. And yet such an offer really deserved the name the prior gave it—a great and unusual grace. For, as has been already intimated, by the laws of the Inquisition at that time in force, the man who had *once* professed heretical doctrines, however sincerely he might have retracted them, was doomed to die. His penitence would procure him the favour of absolution—the mercy of the garotte[2] instead of the stake, that was all.

The prior went on to explain to Carlos, that upon the ground of his youth, and the supposition that he had been led into error by others, his judges had consented to show him singular favour. "Moreover," he added, "there are other reasons for this course of action, upon which it would be needless, and might be inexpedient, to enter at present; but they have their weight, especially with

[1] Flagrant disobedience or rebelliousness.
[2] An instrument of torture used in Spain.

me. For the preservation, therefore, both of your soul and your body—upon which I take more compassion than you do yourself—I have, in the first place, obtained permission to remove you to a more easy and more healthful confinement, where, besides other favours, you will enjoy the great privilege of a companion, constant interaction with whom can scarcely fail to benefit you."

Carlos thought this last a doubtful boon; but as it was kindly intended, he was bound to be grateful. He thanked the prior accordingly; adding, "May I be permitted to ask the name of this companion?"

"You will probably find out ere long, if you conduct yourself so as to deserve it,"—an answer Carlos found so enigmatical, that after several vain endeavours to comprehend it, he gave up the task in despair, and not without some apprehension that his long imprisonment had dulled his perceptions. "Amongst us he is called Don Juan," the prior continued. "And this much I will tell you. He is a very honourable person, who had many years ago the great misfortune to be led astray by the same errors to which you cling with such obstinacy. God was pleased, however, to make use of my poor instrumentality to lead him back to the bosom of the Church. He is now a true and sincere penitent, diligent in prayer and penance, and heartily detesting his former evil ways. It is my last hope for you that his wise and faithful counsels may bring you to the same mind."

Carlos did not particularly like the prospect. He feared that this vaunted penitent would prove a noisy apostate, who would seek to obtain the favour of the monks by vilifying his former associates. Nor, on the other hand, did he think it honest to accept without protest kindnesses offered him on the supposition that he might even yet be induced to recant. He said,—

"I ought to tell you, señor, that my mind will never change, God helping me. Rather than lead you to imagine otherwise, I would go at once to the darkest cell in the Triana. My faith is based on the Word of God, which can never be overthrown."

"The penitent of whom I speak used such words as these, until

God and Our Lady opened his eyes. Now he sees all things differently. So will you, if God is pleased to give you the inestimable benefit of his divine grace; for it is not of him that willeth, nor of him that runneth, but of God that showeth mercy,"[3] said the Dominican, who, like others of his order, ingeniously managed to combine strong predestinarian theories with the creed of Rome.

"That is most true, señor," Carlos responded.

"But to resume," said the prior; "for I have yet more to say. Should you be favoured with the grace of repentance, I am authorised to hold out to you a well-grounded hope, that, in consideration of your youth, your life may even yet be spared."

"And then, if I were strong enough, I might live out ten or twenty years—like the last two," Carlos answered, not without a touch of bitterness.

"It is not so, my son," returned the prior mildly. "I cannot promise, indeed, under any circumstances, to restore you to the world. For that would be to promise what could not be performed; and the laws of the Holy Office expressly forbid us to delude prisoners with false hopes.[4] But this much I will say, your restraint shall be rendered so light and easy, that your position will be preferable to that of many a monk, who has taken the vows of his own free will. And if you like the society of the penitent of whom I spoke anon, you shall continue to enjoy it."

Carlos began to feel a somewhat unreasonable antipathy to this penitent, whose face he had never seen. But what mattered the antipathies of a prisoner of the Holy Office? He only said, "Permit me again to thank you, my lord, for the kindness you have shown me. Though my fellow-men cast out my name as evil, and deny me my share of God's free air and sky, and my right to live in his world, I still take thankfully every word or deed of pity and gentleness they give me by the way. For they know not what they do."

The prior turned away, but turned back again a moment afterwards, to ask—what for the credit of his humanity he ought to have

[3] Romans 9:16
[4] But these laws were often broken or evaded.

asked a year before—"Do you stand in need of any thing? or have you any request you wish to make?"

Carlos hesitated a moment. Then he said, "Of things within your power to grant, my lord, there is but one that I care to ask. Two brethren of the Society of Jesus visited me the day before yesterday. I spoke hastily to one of them, who was named Fray Isodor, I think. Had I the opportunity, I should be glad to offer him my hand."

"Now, of all mysterious things in heaven or earth," said the prior, "a heretic's conscience is the most difficult to comprehend. Truly you strain at a gnat and swallow a camel. But as for Fray Isodor, you may rest content. For good and sufficient reasons, he cannot visit you here. But I will repeat to him what you have said. And I know well that his own tongue is a sharp weapon enough when used in the defence of the faith."

The prior withdrew; and shortly afterwards one of the monks appeared, and silently conducted Carlos to a cell, or chamber, in the highest story of the building. Like the cells in the Triana, it had two doors—the outer one secured by strong bolts and bars, the inner one furnished with an aperture through which food or other things could be passed.

But here the resemblance ceased. Carlos found himself, on entering, in what seemed to him more like a hall than a cell; though, indeed, it must be remembered that his eye was accustomed to ten feet square. It was furnished as comfortably as any room needed to be in that warm climate; and it was tolerably clean, a small mercy which he noted with no small gratitude. Best perhaps of all, it had a good window, looking down on the courtyard, but strongly barred, of course. Near the window was a table, upon which stood an ivory crucifix, and a picture of the Madonna and child.

But even before his eye took in all these objects, it turned to the penitent, whose companionship had been granted him as so great a boon. He was utterly unlike all that he had expected. Instead of a fussy, noisy deviant, he saw a serene and stately old man, with long white hair and beard, and still, clearly chiselled, handsome features. He was dressed in a kind of mantle, of a nondescript colour, made like a monk's cowl without the hood, and bearing two large St. Andrew's crosses, one on the breast and the other on the back; in fact, it was a compromised sanbenito.

As Carlos entered, he rose (showing a tall, spare figure, slightly stooped), and greeted his new companion with a courteous and elaborate bow, but did not speak.

Shortly afterwards, food was handed through the aperture in the door; and the half-starved prisoner from the Triana sat down with his fellow-captive to what he esteemed a really luxurious repast. He had intended to be silent until obliged to speak, but the aspect and bearing of the penitent quite disarranged his preconceived ideas. During the meal, he tried once and again to open a conversation by some slight courteous observation.

All in vain. The penitent did the honours of the table like a prince in disguise, and never failed to bow and answer, "Yes, señor," or "No, señor," to everything Carlos said. But he seemed either unable or unwilling to do more.

As the day wore on, this silence grew oppressive to Carlos; and he marvelled increasingly at his companion's want of ordinary interest in him, or curiosity about him. Until at length a probable solution of the mystery dawned upon his mind. As he considered the penitent an agent of the monks deputed to convert him, very likely the penitent, on his side, regarded *him* in the light of a spy commissioned to watch his proceedings.

But this, if it was true at all, was only a small part of the truth. Carlos failed to take into account the terrible effect of long years of solitude, crushing down all the faculties of the mind and heart. It is told of some monastery, where the rules were so severe that the brethren were only allowed to converse with each other during one hour in the week, that they usually sat for that hour in perfect silence: they had nothing to say. So it was with the penitent of the Dominican convent. He had nothing to say, nothing to ask;

curiosity and interest were dead within him—dead long ago, of absolute starvation.

Yet Carlos could not help observing him with a strange kind of fascination. His face was too still, too coldly calm, like a white marble statue; and yet it was a noble face. It was, although not a thoughtful face, the face of a thoughtful man asleep. It did not lack expressiveness, though it lacked expression. Moreover, there was in it a look that awakened dim, undefined memories—shadowy things, that fled away like ghosts whenever he tried to grasp them, yet persistently rose again, and mingled with all his thoughts.

He told himself many times that he had never seen the man before. Was it, then, an accidental likeness to some familiar face that so fixed and haunted him? Certainly there was something which belonged to his past, and which, even while it perplexed and baffled, strangely soothed and pleased him.

At each of the canonical hours (which were announced to them by the tolling of the convent bells), the penitent did not fail to kneel before the crucifix, and, with the aid of a book and a rosary, to read or repeat long Latin prayers, in a half audible voice. He retired to rest early, leaving his fellow-prisoner supremely happy in the enjoyment of his lamp and his Book of Hours. For it was two years since the eyes of the once enthusiastic young scholar had rested on a printed page, or since the kindly gleam of lamp or fire had cheered his solitude. The privilege of refreshing his memory with the passages of Scripture contained in the Romish book of devotion now appeared an unspeakable boon to him. And although, accustomed as he was to a life of unbroken monotony, the varied impressions of the day had produced extreme weariness of mind and body, it was near midnight before he could prevail upon himself to close the volume, and lie down to rest on the comfortable pallet prepared for him.

He was just falling asleep, when the midnight bell tolled out heavily. He saw his companion rise, throw his mantle over his shoulders, and betake himself to his devotions. How long these lasted he could not tell, for the stately kneeling figure soon mingled with his dreams—strange dreams of Juan as a penitent, dressed in a sanbenito, and with white hair and an old man's face, kneeling devoutly before the altar in the church at Nuera, but reciting one of the songs of the Cid instead of De Profundis.

XLI.

More about the Penitent.

"Ay, thus thy mother looked,
With such a sad, yet half-triumphant smile,
All radiant with deep meaning."

HEMANS.

SLIGHT incident that occurred the following morning, partially broke down the barrier of reserve between the two prisoners. After his early devotions, the penitent laid aside his mantle, took up a besom made of long slips of cane, and proceeded, with great deliberation and gravity, to sweep out the room. The contrast that his stately figure, his noble air, and the dignity of all his movements, offered to the menial occupation in which he was engaged, was far too pathetic to be ludicrous. Carlos could not but think that he wielded the lowly implement as if it were a chamberlain's staff of office, or a grand marshal's baton.

He himself was well accustomed to such tasks; for every prisoner of the Santa Casa, no matter what his rank might be, was his own servant. And it spoke much for the revolution that had taken place in his ideas and feelings, that though taught to look on all servile occupations as ineffably degrading, he had never associated a thought of degradation with anything laid upon him to do or to suffer as the prisoner of Christ.

And yet he could not endure to see his aged and stately fellow-prisoner thus occupied. He rose immediately, and earnestly entreated to be allowed to relieve him of the task, pleading that all such duties ought to devolve on him as the younger. At first the penitent resisted, saying that it was part of his penance. But when Carlos continued to urge the point, he yielded; perhaps the more readily because his will, like his other faculties, was weakened for want of exercise. Then, with more apparent interest than he had shown in any of his previous proceedings, he watched the rather slow and difficult movements of his young companion.

"You are lame, señor," he said, a little abruptly, when Carlos, having finished his work, sat down to rest.

"From the pulley," Carlos answered quietly; and then his face beamed with a sudden smile, for the secret of the Lord was with him, and he tasted the sweet, strange joy that springs out of suffering borne for Him.

That look was the wire that drew an electric flash of memory from the clouds that veiled the old man's soul. What that sudden flash revealed was a castle gate, at which stood a stately yet slender form robed in silk. In the fair young face tears and smiles were contending; but a smile won the victory, as a little child was held up, and made to kiss a baby-hand in farewell to its father.

In a moment all was gone; only a vague trouble and uneasiness remained, accompanied by that strange sense of having seen or felt just the same thing before, with which most of us are familiar. Accustomed to solitude, the penitent spoke aloud, perchance unconsciously.

"Why did they bring you here?" he said, in a half fretful tone. "You hurt me. I have done very well alone all these years."

"I am sorry to incommode[1] you, señor," returned Carlos. "But I did not come here of my own will; neither, unhappily, can I go. I am a prisoner like yourself; but, unlike you, I am a prisoner under sentence of death."

[1] To bother or inconvenience.

For several minutes the penitent did not answer. Then he rose, and taking a step or two towards the place where Carlos sat, gravely extended his hand. "I fear I have spoken uncourteously," he said. "So many years have passed since I have conversed with my fellows, that I have well-nigh forgotten how I ought to address them. Do me the favour, señor and my brother, to grant me your pardon."

Carlos warmly assured him no offence had been given; and taking the offered hand, he pressed it reverently to his lips. From that moment he loved his fellow-prisoner in his heart.

There was an interval of silence, then the penitent of his own accord resumed the conversation. "Did I hear you say you are under sentence of death?" he asked.

"I am so actually, though not formally," Carlos replied. "In the language of the Holy Office, I am a professed impenitent heretic."

"And you so young!"

"To be a heretic?"

"No; I meant so young to die."

"Do I look young—even yet? I should not have thought it. To me the last two years seem like a long life-time."

"Have you been two years, then, in prison? Poor boy! Yet I have been here ten, fifteen, twenty years—I cannot tell how many. I have lost the account of them."

Carlos sighed. And such a life was before him, should he be weak enough to surrender his hope. He said, "Do you really think, señor, that these long years of lonely suffering are less hard to bear than a speedy though violent death?"

"I do not think it matters, as to that," was the penitent's not very apposite[2] reply. In fact, his mind was not capable, at the time, of dealing with such a question; so he turned from it instinctively. But in the meantime he was remembering, every moment more and more clearly, that a duty had been laid upon him by the authority to which his soul held itself in absolute subjection. And that duty had reference to his fellow-prisoner.

[2] Appropriate; pertinent.

"I am commanded," he said at last, "to counsel you to seek the salvation of your soul, by returning to the bosom of the one true Catholic and Apostolic Church, out of which there is no peace and no salvation."

Carlos saw that he spoke by rote; that his words echoed the thought of another, not his own. It seemed to him, under the circumstances, scarcely generous to argue. He spared to put forth his mental powers against the aged and broken man, as Juan in like case would have spared to use his strong right arm.

After a moment's thought, he replied,—

"May I ask of your courtesy, señor and my father, to bear with me for a little while, that I may frankly disclose to you my real belief?"

Appeal could never be made in vain to that penitent's courtesy. No heresy, that could have been proposed, would have shocked him half so much as the supposition that one Castilian gentleman could be uncourteous to another, upon any account. "Do me the favour to state your opinions, señor," he responded, with a bow, "and I will honour myself by giving them my best attention."

Carlos was little used to language such as this. It induced him to speak his mind more freely than he had been able to do for the last two years. But, mindful of his experience with old Father Bernardo at San Isodro, he did not speak of doctrines; he spoke of a Person. In words simple enough for a child to understand, but with a heart glowing with faith and love, he told of what he was when he walked on earth, of what he is at the right hand of the Father, of what he has done and is doing still for every soul that trusts him.

Certainly the faded eye brightened; and something like a look of interest began to dawn in the mournfully still and passive countenance. For a time Carlos was aware that his listener followed every word, and he spoke slowly on purpose to allow him so to do. But then there came a change. The listening look passed out of the eyes; and yet they did not wander once from the speaker's face. The expression of the whole countenance was gradually altered, from one of rather painful attention to the dreamy look of a man who hears sweet music, and gives free course to the emotions it is calculated to awaken. In truth, the voice of Carlos was sweet music in his fellow-captive's ear; and he would willingly have sat thus for ever, gazing at him and enjoying it.

Carlos thought that if this was their reverences' idea of "a satisfactory penitent," they were not difficult to satisfy. And he marvelled increasingly that so astute a man as the Dominican prior should have put the task of his conversion into such hands. For the piety so lauded in the penitent appeared to him mere passiveness—the submission of a soul out of which all resisting forces had been crushed. "It is only life that resists," he thought; "the dead they can move whithersoever they will."

Intolerance always sets a premium on mental stagnation. Nay, it actually produces it; it "makes a desert, and calls it peace." And what the Inquisition did for the penitent, that it has done also for the penitent's fair fatherland. Was the resurrection of dead and buried faculties possible for *him*? Is such a resurrection possible for *it*?

And yet, in spite of the deadness of heart and brain, which he doubted not was the result of cruel suffering, Carlos loved his fellow-prisoner every hour more and more. He could not tell why; he only knew that "his soul was knit" to his.

When Carlos, for fear of fatiguing him, brought his explanations to a close, both relapsed into silence; and the remainder of the day passed without much further conversation, but with a constant interchange of little kindnesses and courtesies. The first sight that greeted the eyes of Carlos when he awoke the next morning was that of the penitent kneeling before the pictured Madonna, his lips motionless, his hands crossed on his breast, and his face far more earnest with feeling—it might be thought with devotion—than he had ever seen it yet.

Carlos was moved, but saddened. It grieved him sore that his aged fellow-prisoner should pour out the last costly libation of love and trust left in his desolated heart before the shrine of that which was no god. And a great longing awoke within him to lead back this weary and heavy-laden one to the only Being who could give him true rest.

"If, indeed, he is one of God's chosen, of his loved and redeemed ones, he will be led back," thought Carlos, who had spent the past two years in thinking out many things for himself. Certain aspects of truth, which may be either strong cordials or rank poisons, as they are used, had grown gradually clear to him. Opposed to the Dominican prior upon most subjects, he was at one with him upon that of predestination. For he had need to be assured, when the great water floods prevailed, that the chain which kept him from drifting away with them was a strong one. And therefore he had followed it up, link by link, until he came at last to that eternal purpose of God in which it was fast anchored. Since the day that he first learned it, he had lived in the light of that great centre truth, "I have loved thee"—*thee* individually. But as he lay in the gloomy prison, sentenced to die, something more was revealed to him. "I have loved thee *with an everlasting love, therefore* with loving-kindness have I drawn thee."[3] The value of this truth, to him as to others, lay in the double aspect of that word "everlasting;" its look forward to the boundless future, as well as backward on the mysterious past. The one was a pledge and assurance of the other. And now he was taking to his heart the comfort it gave, for the penitent as well as for himself. But it made him, not less, but more anxious to be God's fellow-worker in bringing him back to the truth.

In the meantime, however, he was quite mistaken as to the feelings with which the old man knelt before the pictured Virgin and Child. His heart was stirred by no mystic devotion to the Queen of Heaven, but by some very human feelings, which had long lain dormant, but which were now being gradually awakened there. He was thinking not of heaven, but of earth, and of "earth's warm beating joy and dole." And what attracted him to that spot was only the representation of womanhood and childhood, recalling, though

[3] Jeremiah 31:3

far off and faintly, the fair young wife and babe from whom he had been cruelly torn years and years ago.

A little later, as the two prisoners sat over the bread and fruit that formed their morning meal, the penitent began to speak more frankly than he had done before. “I was quite afraid of you, señor, when you first came,” he said.

“And perhaps I was not guiltless of the same feeling towards you,” Carlos answered. “It is no marvel. Companions in sorrow, such as we are, have great power either to help or to hurt one another.”

“You may truly say that,” returned the penitent. “In fact, I once suffered so cruelly from the treachery of a fellow-prisoner, that it is not unnatural I should be suspicious.” “How was that, señor?”

“It was very long ago, soon after my arrest. And yet, not soon. For weary months of darkness and solitude, I cannot tell how many, I held out—I mean to say, I continued impenitent.”

“Did you?” asked Carlos with interest. “I thought as much.”

“Do not think ill of me, I entreat of you, señor,” said the penitent anxiously. “I am *reconciled.* I have returned to the bosom of the true Church, and I belong to her. I have confessed and received absolution. I have even had the Holy Sacrament; and if ill, or in danger of death, it is promised I shall receive ‘suma jestad’[4] at any time. And I have abjured and detested all the heresies I learned from De Valero.”

“From De Valero! Did you learn from him?” The pale cheek of Carlos crimsoned for a moment, then grew paler than before. “Tell me, señor, if I may ask it, how long have you been here?”

“That is just what I cannot tell. The first year stands out clearly; but all the after years are like a dream to me. It was in that first year that the caitiff I spoke of anon, who was imprisoned with me—you observe, señor, I had already asked for reconciliation. It was promised me. I was to perform penance; to be forgiven; to have my freedom. *Pues*, señor, I spoke to that man as I might to you, freely and from my heart. For I supposed him a gentleman. I

[4] “His Majesty,” the ordinary term applied by Spaniards to the Host.

dared to say that their reverences had dealt somewhat hardly with me, and the like. Idle words, no doubt—idle and wicked. God knows, I have had time enough to repent them since. For that man, my fellow-prisoner, he who knew what prison was, went forth straightway and delated me to the Lords Inquisitors for those idle words—God in heaven forgive him! And thus the door was shut upon me—shut—shut for ever. Ay de mi! Ay de mi!"

Carlos heard but little of this speech. He was gazing at him with eager, kindling eyes. "Were there left behind in the world any that it wrung your heart to part from?" he asked, in a trembling voice.

"There were: And since you came, their looks have never ceased to haunt me. Why, I know not. My wife, my child!" And the old man shaded his face, while in his eyes, long unused to tears, there rose a mist, like the cloud in form as a man's hand, that foretold the approach of the beneficent rain, which should refresh and soften the thirsty soil, making all things young again.

"Señor," said Carlos, trying to speak calmly, and to keep down the wild tumultuous throbbing of his heart—"señor, a boon, I entreat of you. Tell me the name you bore amongst men. It was a noble one, I know."

"True. They promised to save it from disgrace. But it was part of my penance not to utter it; if possible, to forget it."

"Yet, this once. I do not ask idly—this once—have pity on me, and speak it," pleaded Carlos, with intense tremulous earnestness.

"Your face and your voice move me strangely; it seems to me that I could not deny you anything. I am—I ought to say, I *was*—Don Juan Alvarez de Santillanos y Meñaya."

Before the sentence was concluded, Carlos lay senseless at his feet.

XLII.

Quiet Days.

"I think that by-and-by all things
Which were perplexed a while ago
And life's long, vain conjecturings,
Will simple, calm, and quiet grow.
Already round about me, some
August and solemn sunset seems
Deep sleeping in a dewy dome,
And bending o'er a world of dreams."
OWEN MEREDITH.

HE penitent laid Carlos gently on his pallet (he still possessed a measure of physical strength, and the worn frame was easy to lift); then he knocked loudly on the door for help, as he had been instructed to do in any case of need. But no one heard, or at least no one heeded him, which was not remarkable, since during more than twenty years he had not, on a single occasion, thus summoned his gaolers. Then, in utter ignorance what next to do, and in very great distress, he bent over his young companion, helplessly wringing his hands.

Carlos stirred at last, and murmured, "Where am I? What is it?" But even before full consciousness returned, there came the sense, taught by the bitter experience of the last two years, that he must look within for aid—he could expect none from any fellow-creature. He tried to recollect himself. Some bewildering, awful joy had fallen upon him, striking him to the earth. Was he free? Was he permitted to see Juan?

Slowly, very slowly, all grew clear to him. He half raised himself, grasped the penitent's hand, and cried aloud, "*My father*!"

"Are you better, señor?" asked the old man with solicitude. "Do me the favour to drink this wine."

"Father, my father! I am your son. I am Carlos Alvarez de Santillanos y Meñaya. Do you not understand me, father?"

"I do not understand you, señor," said the penitent, moving a little away from him, with a mixture of dignified courtesy and utter amazement in his manner strange to behold. "Who is it that I have the honour to address?"

"O my father, I am your son—your very son Carlos!"

"I have never seen you till—ere yesterday."

"That is quite true; and yet—"

"Nay, nay," interrupted the old man; "you are speaking wild words to me. I had but one boy—Juan—Juan Rodrigo. The heir of the house of Alvarez de Meñaya was always called Juan."

"He lives. He is Captain Don Juan now, the bravest soldier, and the best, truest-hearted man on earth. How you would love him! Would you could see him face to face! Yet no; thank God you cannot."

"My babe a captain in His Imperial Majesty's army!" said Don Juan, in whose thoughts the great Emperor was reigning still.

"And I," Carlos continued, in a broken, agitated voice—"I, born when they thought you dead—I, who opened my young eyes on this sad world the day God took my mother home from all its sin and sorrow—I am brought here, in his mysterious providence, to comfort you, after your long dreary years of suffering."

"Your mother? Did you say your mother? My wife, *Costanza mia*. Oh, let me see your face!"

Carlos raised himself to a kneeling attitude, and the old man laid his hand on his shoulder, and gazed at him long and earnestly. At length Carlos removed the hand, and drawing it gently upwards, placed it on his head. "Father," he said, "you will love your son? you will bless him, will you not? He has dwelt long amongst those who hated him, and never spoke to him save in wrath and scorn, and his heart pines for human love and tenderness."

Don Juan did not answer for a while; but he ran his fingers through the soft fine hair. "So like hers," he murmured dreamily. "Thine eyes are hers too—*zarca.*[1] Yes, yes; I do bless thee—But who am I to bless? God bless thee, my son!"

In the long, long silence that followed, the great convent bell rang out. It was noon. For the first time for twenty years the penitent did not hear that sound.

Carlos heard it, however. Agitated as he was, he yet feared the consequences that might follow should the penitent omit any part of the penance he was bound by oath to perform. So he gently reminded him of it. "Father—(how strangely sweet the name sounded!)—"father, at this hour you always recite the penitential psalms. When you have finished, we will talk together. I have ten thousand things to tell you."

With the silent, unreasoning submission that had become a part of his nature, the penitent obeyed; and, going to his usual station before the crucifix, began his monotonous task. The fresh life newly awakened in his heart and brain was far from being strong enough, as yet, to burst the bonds of habit. And this was well. Those bonds were his safeguard; but for their wholesome restraint, mind or body, or both, might have been shattered by the tumultuous rush of new thoughts and feelings.

But the familiar Latin words, repeated without thought, almost without consciousness, soothed the weary brain like a slumber.

Meanwhile, Carlos thanked God with a full heart. Here, then—*here*, in the dark prison, the very abode of misery—had God given him the desire of his heart, fulfilled the longing of his early years. Now the wilderness and the solitary place were glad; the desert rejoiced and blossomed as the rose. Now his life seemed

[1] Blue; a word applied by the Spaniards only to blue eyes.

complete, its end answering its beginning; all its meaning lying clear and plain before him. He was satisfied.

"Ruy, Ruy, I have found our father!—Oh, that I could but tell thee, my Ruy!"—was the cry of his heart, though he forced his lips to silence. Nor could the tears of joy, that sprang unbidden to his eyes, be permitted to overflow, since they might perplex and trouble his fellow-captive—*his father*.

He had still a task to perform; and to that task his mind soon bent itself; perhaps instinctively taking refuge in practical detail from emotions that might otherwise have proved too strong for his weakened frame. He set himself to consider how best he could revive the past, and make the present comprehensible to the aged and broken man, without overpowering or bewildering him.

He planned to tell him, in the first instance, all that he could about Nuera. And this he accomplished gradually, as he was able to bear the strain of conversation. He talked of Dolores and Diego; described both the exterior and interior of the castle; in fact, made him see again the scenes to which his eye had been accustomed in past days. With special minuteness did he picture the little room within the hall, both because it was less changed since his father's time than the others, and because it had been his favourite apartment. "And on the window," he said, "there were some words, written with a diamond, doubtless by your hand, my father. My brother and I used to read them in our childhood; we loved them, and dreamed many a wondrous dream about them. Do you not remember them?"

But the old man shook his head.

Then Carlos began,—

"'*El Dorado—*

Yo hé trovado.'"

"Yes, I remember now," said Don Juan promptly.

"And the golden country you had discovered—was it not the truth as revealed in Scripture?" asked Carlos, perhaps a little too eagerly.

The penitent mused a space; grew bewildered; said at last

sorrowfully, "I know not. I cannot now recall what moved me to write those lines, or even when I wrote them."

In the next place, Carlos ventured to tell all he had heard from Dolores about his mother. The fact of his wife's death had been communicated to the prisoner; but this was the only fragment of intelligence about his family that had reached him during all these years. When she was spoken of, he showed emotion, slight in the beginning, but increasing at every succeeding mention of her name, until Carlos, who had at first been glad to find that the slumbering chords of feeling responded to his touch, came at last to dread laying his hands upon them, they were apt to moan so piteously. And once and again did his father say, gazing at him with ever-increasing fondness, "Thy face is hers, risen anew before me."

Carlos tried hard to awaken Don Juan's interest in his firstborn. It is true that he cherished an almost passionate love for Juanito the babe, but it was such a love as we feel for children whom God has taken to himself in infancy. Juan the youth, Juan the man, seemed to him a stranger, difficult to conceive of or to care about. Yet, in time, Carlos did succeed in establishing a bond between the long-imprisoned father and the brave, noble, free-hearted son, who was so like what that father had been in his early manhood. He was never weary of telling of Juan's courage, Juan's truthfulness, Juan's generosity; often concluding with the words, "*He* would have been your favourite son, had you known him, my father."

As time wore on, he won from his father's lips the principal facts of his own story. His past was like a picture from which the colouring, once bright and varied, has faded away, leaving only the bare outlines of fact, and here and there the shadows of pain still faintly visible. What he remembered, that he told his son; but gradually, and often in very disjointed fragments, which Carlos carefully pieced together in his thoughts, until he formed out of them a tolerably connected whole.

Just three-and-twenty years before; on his arrival in Seville, in obedience to what he believed to be a summons from the Emperor, the Conde de Nuera had been arrested and thrown into the secret dungeons of the Inquisition. He well knew his offence: he had been the friend and associate of De Valero; he had read and studied the Scriptures; he had even advocated, in the presence of several witnesses, the doctrine of justification by faith alone. Nor was he unprepared to pay the terrible penalty. Had he, at the time of his arrest, been led at once to the rack or the stake, it is probable he would have suffered with a constancy that might have placed his name beside that of the most heroic martyrs.

But he was allowed to wear out long months in suspense and solitude, and in what his eager spirit found even harder to bear, absolute inaction. Excitement, motion, stirring occupation for mind and body, had all his life been a necessity to him. In the absence of these he pined—grew melancholy, listless, morbid. His faith was genuine, and would have been strong enough to enable him for anything in the line of his character; but it failed under trials purposely and sedulously contrived to assail that character through its weak points.

When already worn-out with dreary imprisonment, he was beset by arguments, clever, ingenious, sophistical, framed by men who made argument the business of their lives. Thus attacked, he was like a brave but unskilful man fencing with adepts in the noble science. He *knew* he was right; and with the Vulgate in his hand, he thought he could have proved it. But they assured him they proved the contrary; nor could he detect a flaw in their syllogisms when he came to examine them. If not convinced, then surely he ought to have been. They conjured him not to let pride and vain-glory seduce him into self-opinionated obstinacy, but to submit his private judgment to that of the Holy Catholic Church. And they promised that he should go forth free, only chastised by a suitable and not disgraceful penance, and by a pecuniary fine.

The hope of freedom burned in his heart like fire; and by this time there was sufficient confusion in his brain for his will to find arguments there against the voice of his conscience. So he yielded, though not without conflict, fierce and bitter. His retractation was drawn up in as mild a form as possible by the Inquisitors, and duly signed by him. No public act of penance was required, as strict secrecy was to be observed in the whole transaction.

But the Inquisitor-General, Valdez, felt a well-grounded distrust of the penitent's sincerity, which was quickened perhaps by a desire to appropriate to the use of the Holy Office a larger share of his possessions than the moderate fine alluded to. Probably, too, he dreaded the disclosures that might have followed had the Count been restored to the world. He had recourse, therefore, to an artifice often employed by the Inquisitors, and seriously recommended by their standard authorities. The "fly" (for such traitors were common enough to have a technical name as well as a recognised existence) reported that the Conde de Nuera railed at the Holy Office, blasphemed the Catholic faith, and still adhered in his heart to all his abominable heresies. The result was a sentence of perpetual imprisonment.

Don Juan's condition was truly pitiable then. Like Samson, he was shorn of the locks in which his strength lay, bound hand and foot, and delivered over to his enemies. Because he could not bear perpetual imprisonment he had renounced his faith, and denied his Lord. And now, without the faith he had renounced, without the Lord he had denied, he must bear it. It told upon him as it would have told on nine men out of ten, perhaps on ninety-nine out of a hundred. His mind lost its activity, its vigour, its tone. It became, in time, almost a passive instrument in the hands of others.

And then the Dominican monk, Fray Ricardo, brought his powerful intellect and his strong will to bear upon him. He had been sent by his superiors (he was not prior until long afterwards) to impart the terrible story of her husband's arrest to the Lady of Nuera, with secret instructions to ascertain whether her own faith had been tampered with. In his fanatical zeal he performed a cruel task cruelly. But he had a conscience, and its fault was not insensibility. When he heard the tale of the lady's death, a few days after his visit, he was profoundly affected. Accustomed, however, to a religion of weights and balances, it came naturally to him to set one thing against another, by way of making the scales even.

If he could be the means of saving the husband's soul, he would feel, to say the least, much more comfortable about his conduct to the wife.

He spared no pains upon the task he had set himself; and a measure of success crowned his efforts. Having first reduced the mind of the penitent to a cold, blank calm, agitated by no wave of restless thought or feeling, he had at length the delight of seeing his own image reflected there, as in a mirror. He mistook that spectral reflection for a reality, and great was his triumph when, day by day, he saw it move responsive to every motion of his own.

But the arrest of his penitent's son broke in upon his self-satisfaction. It seemed as though a dark doom hung over the family, which even the father's repentance was powerless to avert. He wished to save the youth, and he had tried to do it after his fashion; but his efforts only resulted in bringing up before him the pale accusing face of the Lady of Nuera, and in interesting him more than he cared to acknowledge in the impenitent heretic, who seemed to him such a strange mixture of gentleness and obstinacy. Surely the father's influence would prevail with the son, originally a much less courageous and determined character, and now already wrought upon by a long period of loneliness and suffering.

Perhaps also—monk, fanatic, and inquisitor though he was—the pleasantness of trying the experiment, and cheering thereby the last days of the pious and docile penitent, his own especial convert, weighed a little with him; for he was still a man. Moreover, like many hard men, he was capable of great kindness towards those whom he liked. And, with the full approbation of his conscience, he liked his penitent; whilst, rather in spite of his conscience, he liked his penitent's son.

Carlos did not trouble himself overmuch about the prior's motives. He was too content in his new-found joy, too engrossed in his absorbing task—the concern and occupation of his every hour, almost of his every moment. He was as one who toils patiently to clear away the moss and lichen that has grown over a memorial stone; that he may bring out once more, in all their freshness, the precious words engraven upon it. The inscription was there, and there it had been always (so he told himself); all that he had to do was to remove that which covered and obscured it.

He had his reward. Life returned, first through love for him, to the heart; then, through the heart, to the brain. Not rapidly and with tingling pain, as it returns to a frozen limb, but gradually and insensibly, as it comes to the dry trees in spring.

But, in the trees, life shows itself first in the extremities; it is slowest in appearing in those parts which are really nearest the sources of all life. So the penitent's interest in other subjects, and his care for them, revived; yet in one thing, the greatest of all, these seemed lacking still. There did not return the spiritual light and life, which Carlos could not doubt he had enjoyed in past days. Sometimes, it is true, he would startle his son by unexpected reminiscences, disjointed fragments of the truth for which he had suffered so much. He would occasionally interrupt Carlos, when he was repeating to him passages from the Testament, to tell him "something Don Rodrigo said about that, when he expounded the Epistle to the Romans." But these were only like the rich flowers that surprise the explorer amidst the tangled weeds of a waste ground, showing that a carefully tended garden has flourished there once—very long ago.

"It is not that I desire him above all things to hold this doctrine or that," thought Carlos; "I desire him to find Christ again, and to rejoice in his love, as doubtless he did in the old days. And surely he will, since Christ found him—chose him for his own even before the foundation of the world."

But in order to bring this about, perhaps it was necessary that the faded colours of his soul should be steeped in the strong and bitter waters of a great agony, that they might regain thereby their full freshness.

XLIII.

El Dorado Found Again.

"And every power was used, and every art,
To bend to falsehood one determined heart,
Assailed, in patience it received the shock,
Soft as the wave, unbroken as the rock."
CRABBE.

HAT are you doing, my father?" Carlos asked one morning.

Don Juan had produced from some private receptacle a small ink-horn, and was moistening its long-dried contents with water.

"I was thinking that I should like to write down somewhat," he said.

"But whereto will ink serve us without pen and paper?"

The penitent smiled; and presently pulled out from within his pallet a little faded writing-book, and a pen that looked—what it was—more than twenty years old.

"Long ago," he said, "I used to be weary, weary of sitting idle all the day; so I bribed one of the lay brothers with my last ducat to bring me this, only that I might set down therein whatever happened, for pastime."

"May I read it, my father?"

"And welcome, if thou wilt;" and he gave the book into the hand of his son. "At first, as you see, there be many things written therein. I cannot tell what they are now; I have forgotten them all;—but I suppose I thought them, or felt them—once. Or sometimes the brethren would come to visit me, and talk, and afterwards I would write what they said. But by degrees I set down less and less in it. Many days passed in which I wrote nothing, because nothing was to write. Nothing ever happened."

Carlos was soon absorbed in the perusal of the little book. The records of his father's earlier prison life he scanned with great interest and with deep emotion; but coming rather suddenly upon the last entry, he could not forbear a smile. He read aloud:

"'A feast day. Had a capon for dinner, and a measure of red wine.'"

"Did I not judge well," asked the father, "that it was time to give over writing, when I could stoop low enough to record such trifles? Yes; I think I can recall the bitterness of heart with which I laid the book aside. I despised myself for what I wrote therein; and yet I had nothing else to write—would never have anything else, I thought. But now God has given me my son. I will write that down."

Looking up, after a little while, from his self-imposed task, he asked, with an air of perplexity,—

"But when was it? How long is it since you came here, Carlos?"

Carlos in his turn was perplexed. The quiet days had glided on swiftly and noiselessly, leaving no trace behind.

"To me it seems to have been all one long Sabbath," he said. "But let me think. The summer heats had not come; I suppose it must have been March or April—April, perhaps. I remember thinking I had been just two years in prison."

"And now it is growing cool again. I suppose it may have been four months—six months ago. What think you?"

Carlos thought it nearer the latter period than the former.

"I believe we have been visited six times by the brethren," he said. "No; only five times."

These visits of inspection had been made by command of the prior—himself absent from Seville on important business during most of the time—and the result had been duly reported to him. The monks to whom the duty had been deputed were aged and respectable members of the community; in fact, the only persons in the monastery who were acquainted with Don Juan's real name and history. It was their opinion that matters were progressing favourably with the prisoners. They found the penitent as usual—docile, obedient, submissive, only more inclined to converse than formerly; and they thought the young man very gentle and courteous, grateful for the smallest kindness, and ready to listen attentively, and with apparent interest, to everything that was said.

For more definite results the prior was content to wait: he had great faith in waiting. Still, even to him six months seemed long enough for the experiment he was trying. At the end of that time—which happened to be the day after the conversation just related—he himself made a visit to the prisoners.

Both most warmly expressed their gratitude for the singular grace he had shown them. Carlos, whose health had greatly improved, said that he had not dreamed so much earthly happiness could remain for him still.

"Then, my son," said the prior, "give evidence of thy gratitude in the only way possible to thee, or acceptable to me. Do not reject the mercy still offered thee by Holy Church. Ask for reconciliation."

"My lord," replied Carlos, firmly, "I can but repeat what I told you six months agone—that is impossible."

The prior argued, expostulated, threatened—in vain. At length he reminded Carlos that he was already condemned to death—the death of fire; and that he was now putting from him his last chance of mercy. But when he still remained steadfast, he turned away from him with an air of deep disappointment, though more in sorrow than in anger, as one pained by keen and unexpected ingratitude.

"I speak to thee no more," he said. "I believe there is in thy father's heart some little spark, not only of natural feeling but of the grace of God. I address myself to him."

Whether Don Juan had never fully comprehended the statement of Carlos that he was under sentence of death, or whether the tide of emotion caused by finding in him his own son had swept the terrible fact from his remembrance, it is impossible to say; but it certainly came to him, from the lips of the prior, as a dreadful, unexpected blow. So keen was his anguish that Fray Ricardo himself was moved; and the rather, because it was impossible to the aged and broken man to maintain the outward self-restraint a younger and stronger person might have done.

More touched, at the moment, by his father's condition than by all the horrors that menaced himself, Carlos came to his side, and gently tried to soothe him.

"Cease!" said the prior, sternly. "It is but mockery to pretend sympathy with the sorrow thine own obstinacy has caused. If in truth thou lovest him, save him this cruel pain. For three days still," he added, "the door of grace shall stand open to thee. After that term has expired, I dare not promise thy life." Then turning to the agitated father—"If you can make this unhappy youth hear the voice of divine and human compassion," he said, "you will save both his body and his soul alive. You know how to send me a message. God comfort you, and incline his heart to repentance." And with these words he departed, leaving Carlos to undergo the sharpest trial that had come upon him since his imprisonment.

All that day, and the greater part of the night that followed it, the two wills strove together. Prayers, tears, entreaties, seemed to the agonised father to fall on the strong heart of his son like drops of rain on the rock. He did not know that all the time they were falling on that heart like sparks of living fire; for Carlos, once so weak, had learned now to endure pain, both of mind and body, with brow and lip that "gave no sign." Passing tender was the love that had sprung up between those two, so strangely brought together. And now Carlos, by his own act, must sever that sweet bond—must leave his newly-found father in a solitude doubly terrible, where the feeble lamp of his life would soon go out in obscure darkness. Was not this bitterness enough, without the anguish of seeing that father bow his white head before him, and teach his aged lips words of broken, passionate entreaty that his son—his one earthly treasure—would not forsake him thus?

"My father," Carlos said at last, as they sat together in the moonlight, for their light had gone out unheeded—"my father, you have often told me that my face is like my mother's."

"Ay de mi!" moaned the penitent—"and truly it is. Is that why it must leave me as hers did? Ay de mi, Costanza mia! Ay de mi, my son!"

"Father, tell me, I pray you, to escape what anguish of mind or body would you set your seal to a falsehood told to her dishonour?"

"Boy, how can you ask? Never!—nothing could force me to that." And from the faded eye there shot a gleam almost like the fire of old days.

"Father, there is One I love better than ever you loved her. Not to save myself, not even to save you, from this bitter pain, can I deny him or dishonour his name. Father, I cannot!—Though this is worse than the torture," he added.

The anguish of the last words pierced to the very core of the old man's heart. He said no more; but he covered his face, and wept long and passionately, as a man weeps whose heart is broken, and who has no longer any power left him to struggle against his doom.

Their last meal lay untasted. Some wine had formed part of it; and this Carlos now brought, and, with a few gentle, loving words, offered to his father. Don Juan put it aside, but drew his son closer, and looked at him in the moonlight long and earnestly.

"How can I give thee up?" he murmured.

As Carlos tried to return his gaze, it flashed for the first time across his mind that his father was changed. He looked older, feebler, more wan than he had done at his coming. Was the newly awakened spirit wearing out the body? He said,—

"It may be, my father, that God will not call you to the trial. Perhaps months may elapse before they arrange another Auto."

How calmly he could speak of it;—for he had forgotten himself. Courage, with him, always had its root in self-forgetting love.

Don Juan caught at the gleam of hope, though not exactly as Carlos intended. "Ay, truly," he said, "many things may happen before then."

"And nothing can happen save at the will of Him who loves and cares for us. Let us trust him, my beloved father. He will not allow us to be tempted above that we are able to bear. For he is good—oh, how good!—to the soul that seeketh him. Long ago I believed that; but since he has honoured me to suffer for him, once and again have I proved it true, true as life or death. Father, I once thought the strongest thing on earth—that which reached deepest into our nature—was pain. But I have lived to learn that his love is stronger, his peace is deeper, than all pain."

With many such words—words of faith, and hope, and tenderness—did he soothe his weary, broken-hearted father. And at last, though not till towards morning, he succeeded in inducing him to lie down and seek the rest he so sorely needed.

Then came his own hour; the hour of bitter, lonely conflict. He had grown accustomed to the thought, to the *expectation*, of a silent, peaceful death within the prison walls. He had hoped, nay, certainly believed, that in the slow hours of some quiet day or night, undistinguished from other days and nights, God's messenger would steal noiselessly to his gloomy cell, and heart and brain would thrill with rapture at the summons, "The Master calleth thee."

Now, indeed, it was true that the Master called him. But he called him to go to Him through the scornful gaze of ten thousand eyes; through reproach, and shame, and mockery; the hideous zamarra and carroza; the long agony of the Auto, spun out from daybreak till midnight; and, last of all, through the torture of the doom of fire. How could he bear it? Sharp were the pangs of fear that wrung his heart, and dread was the struggle that followed.

It was over at last. Raising to the cold moonlight a steadfast though sorrowful face, Carlos murmured audibly, "What time I am afraid I will put my trust in thee.[1] Lord, I am ready to go with thee, whithersoever thou wilt; only—with thee."

He woke, late the following morning, from the sleep of exhaustion to the painful consciousness of something terrible to come upon him. But he was soon roused from thoughts of self by seeing his father kneel before the crucifix, not quietly reciting his appointed penance, but uttering broken words of prayer and lamentation, accompanied by bitter weeping. As far as he could gather, the burden of the cry was this, "God help me! God forgive me! I have lost it!" Over and over again did he moan those piteous words, "I have lost it!" as if they were the burden of some dreary song. They seemed to contain the sum of all his sorrow.

Carlos, yearning to comfort him, still did not feel that he could interrupt him then. He waited quietly until they were both ready for their usual reading or repetition of Scripture; for Carlos, every morning, either read from the Book of Hours to his father, or recited passages from memory, as suited his inclination at the time.

He knew all the Gospel of John by heart. And this day he began with those blessed words, dear in all ages to the tried and sorrowing, "'Let not your heart be troubled: ye believe in God, believe also in me. In my Father's house are many mansions: if it were not so, I would have told you. I go to prepare a place for you.'"[2] He continued without pause to the close of the sixteenth chapter, "These things I have spoken unto you, that in me ye might have peace. In the world ye shall have tribulation: but be of good cheer; I have overcome the world."[3]

Then once more Don Juan uttered that cry of bitter pain, "Ay de mi! I have lost it!"

Carlos thought he understood him now. "Lost that peace, my father?" he questioned gently.

The old man bowed his head sorrowfully.

[1] Psalm 56:3
[2] John 14:2
[3] John 16:33

"But it is in him. 'In me ye might have peace.' And him you have," said Carlos.

Don Juan drew his hand across his brow, was silent for a few moments, then said slowly, "I will try to tell you how it is with me. There is one thing I could do, even yet; one path left open to my footsteps in which none could part us.—What hinders my refusing to perform my penance, and boldly taking my stand beside thee, Carlos?"

Carlos started, flushed, grew pale again with emotion. He had not dreamed of this, and his heart shrank from it in terror. "My beloved father!" he exclaimed in a trembling voice. "But no—God has not called you. Each one of us must wait to see his guiding hand."

"Once I could have done it bravely, nay, joyfully," said the penitent. "*Not now.*" And there was a silence.

At last Don Juan resumed, "My boy, thy courage shames my weakness. What hast thou seen, what dost thou see, that makes this thing possible to thee?"

"My father knows. I see him who died for me, who rose again for me, who lives at the right hand of God to intercede for me."

"*For me?*"

"Yes; it is this thought that gives strength and peace."

"Peace—which I have lost for ever."

"Not for ever, my honoured father. No; you are his, and of such it is written, 'Neither shall any man pluck them out of my hand.'[4] Though your tired hand has relaxed its grasp of him, his has never ceased to hold you, and never can cease."

"I was at peace and happy long ago, when I believed, as Don Rodrigo said, that I was justified by faith in him."

"Once justified, justified for ever," said Carlos.

"Don Rodrigo used to say so too, but—I cannot understand it now," and a look of perplexity passed over his face.

Carlos spoke more simply. "No! Then come to him now, my father, just as if you had never come before. You may not know that

[4] John 10:28

you are justified; you know well that you are weary and heavy laden. And to such he says, 'Come.' He says it with outstretched arms, with a heart full of love and tenderness. He is as willing to save you from sin and sorrow as you are this hour to save me from pain and death. Only, you cannot, and he can."

"Come—that is—believe?"

"It is believe, and more. Come, as your heart came out to me, and mine to you, when we knew the great bond between us. But with far stronger trust and deeper love; for he is more than son or father. He fulfils all relationships, satisfies all wants."

"But then, what of those long years in which I forgot him?"

"They were but adding to the sum of sin; sin that he has pardoned, has washed away for ever in his blood."

At that point the conversation dropped, and days passed ere it was renewed. Don Juan was unusually silent; very tender to his son, making no complaint, but often weeping quietly. Carlos thought it best to leave God to deal with him directly, so he only prayed for him and with him, repeated precious Scripture words, and sometimes sang to him the psalms and hymns of the Church.

But one evening, to the affectionate "Good-night" always exchanged by the son and father with the sense that many more might not be left to them, Don Juan added, "Rejoice with me, my son; for I think that I have found again the thing that I lost—

'*El Dorado*
Yo he trovado.'"

XLIV.

One Prisoner Set Free.

"All was ended now, the hope and the fear, and the sorrow;
All the aching of heart, the restless unsatisfied longing,
All the dull deep pain, and constant anguish of patience."

LONGFELLOW.

HE winter rain was pouring down in a steady continuous torrent. It was long since a gleam of sunshine had come through the windows of the prison-room.

But Don Juan Alvarez did not miss the sunlight. For he lay on his pallet, weak and ill, and the only sight he greatly cared to look upon was the loving face that was ever beside him.

It is possible, by means of the embalmer's art, to enable buried forms to retain for ages a ghastly outward similitude to life. Tombs have been opened, and kings found therein clothed in their royal robes, stern and stately, the sceptre in their cold hands, and no trace of the grave and its corruption visible upon them. But no sooner did the breath of the upper air and the finger of light touch them than they crumbled away, silently and rapidly, and dust returned to dust again. Thus, buried in the chill dark tomb of his seclusion, Don Juan might have lived for years—if life it could be called—or, at least, he might have lingered on in the outward similitude of life.

But Carlos brought in light and air upon him. His mind and heart revived; and, just in proportion, his physical nature sank. It proved too weak to bear these powerful influences. He was dying.

Tender and thoughtful as a woman, Carlos, who himself knew so well all the bitterness of unpitied pain and sickness, ministered to his father's wants. But he did not request their gaolers to afford him any medical aid, though, had he done so, it would have been readily granted.

He had good reason for seeking no help from man. The daily penance was neglected now; the rosary lay untold; and never again would "Ave Maria Sanctissima" pass the lips of Don Juan Alvarez. Therefore it was that Carlos, after much thought and prayer, said quietly to him one day, "My father, are you afraid to lie here, in God's hands, and in his alone, and to take whatever he pleases to send us?"

"I am not afraid."

"Do you desire any help they can give, either for your soul or for your body?"

"No," said the Conde de Nuera, with something like the spirit of other days. "I would not confess to them; for Christ is my only priest now. And they should not anoint me while I retained my consciousness."

A look of resolution, strange to see, passed over the gentle face of Carlos. "It is well said, my father," he responded. "And, God helping me, I will let no man trouble you."

"My son," said Don Juan one evening, as Carlos sat beside him in the twilight, "I pray you, tell me a little more of those who learned to love the truth since I walked amongst men. For I would fain be able to recognise them when we meet in heaven."

Then Carlos told him, not indeed for the first time, but more fully than ever before, the story of the Reformed Church in Spain. Almost every name that he mentioned has come down to us surrounded by the mournful halo of martyr glory. With special reverential love, he told of Don Carlos de Seso, of Losada, of D'Arellano, and of the heroic Juliano Hernandez, who, as he believed, was still waiting for his crown. "For him," he said, "I pray even yet; for the others I can only thank God. Surely," he added, after a pause, "God will remember the land for which these, his faithful martyrs, prayed and toiled and suffered! Surely he will hear their voices, that cry under the altar, not for vengeance, but for forgiveness and mercy; and one day he will return and repent, and leave a blessing behind him!"

"I know not," said the dying man despondingly. "The Spains have had their offer of God's truth, and have rejected it. What is there that is said, somewhere in the Scriptures, about Noah, Daniel, and Job?"

Carlos repeated the solemn words, "'Though Noah, Daniel, and Job were in it, as I live, saith the Lord God, they shall deliver neither son nor daughter; they shall but deliver their own souls by their righteousness.'[1] Do you fear that such a terrible doom has gone forth over our land, my father? I dare to hope otherwise. For it is not the Spains that have rejected the truth. It is the Inquisition that is crushing it out."

"But the Spains must answer for its deeds, since they consent to them. They heed not. There are brave men enough, with weapons in their hands," said the soldier of former days, with a momentary return to old habits of thought and feeling.

"Yet God may give our land another trial," Carlos continued. "His truth is sometimes offered twice to individuals, why not to nations?"

"True; it was offered twice to me, praised be his name." After an interval of silence, he resumed, "My son always speaks of others, never of himself. Not yet have I learned how it was that you came to receive the Word of God so readily from Juliano."

Then in the dark, with his father's hand in his, Carlos told, for the first and last time, the true story of his life.

Before he had gone far, Don Juan started, half-raised himself, and exclaimed in surprise, "What, and you!—you too—once loved?"

---

[1] Ezekiel 14:14

"Ay, and bitter as the pain has been, I am glad now of all except the sin. I am glad that I have tasted earth's very best and sweetest; that I know how the wine is red and gives its colour in the cup of life he honours me to put aside for him." His voice was low and full of feeling as he said this. Presently he resumed. "But the sin, my father! Especially my treachery in heart to Juan; that rankled long and stung deeply. Juan, my brave, generous brother, who would have struck down any man who dared to hint that I could do, or think, aught dishonourable! He never knew it; and had he known it, he would have forgiven me; but I could not forgive myself. I do not think the self-scorn passed away until—that which happened after I had been nigh a year in prison. O my father, if God had not interposed to save me by withholding me from that crime, I shudder to think what my life might have been. I am persuaded I should have sunk lower, lower, and ever lower. Perhaps, even, I might have ended in the purple and fine linen, and the awful pomp and luxury of the oppressors and persecutors of the saints."

"Nay," said Don Juan, "that would never have been possible to thee, Carlos. But there is a question I have often longed to ask thee. Does Juan, my Juan Rodrigo, know and love the Word of God?"

He had asked that question before; but Carlos had contrived, with tact and gentleness, to evade the answer. Up to this hour he had not dared to tell his father the truth upon this important subject. Besides the terrible risk that in some moment of fear or forgetfulness the prior or his agents might draw an incautious word from the old man's lips, there was a haunting dread of listeners at key-holes, or secret apertures, quite natural in one who knew the customs of the Holy Office.

But now he bent down close to the dying man, and spoke to him in a long earnest whisper.

"Thank God," murmured Don Juan. "I would have no earthly wish unsatisfied now — if only you were safe. But still," he added, "it seemeth somewhat hard to me that Juan should have all, and you nothing."

"I *nothing*!" Carlos exclaimed; and had not the room been in darkness his father would have seen that his eye kindled, and his whole countenance lighted up. "My father, mine has been the best lot, even for earth. Were it to do again, I would not change the last two years for the deepest love, the brightest hope, the fairest joy life has to offer. For the Lord himself has been the portion of my cup, my inheritance in the land of the living."

After a silence, he continued, "Moreover, and beside all, I have thee, my father. Therefore to me it is a joy to think that my beloved brother has also something precious. How he loved her! But the strangest thing of all, as I ponder over it now, is the fulfilment of our childhood's dream. And in me, the weak one who deserved nothing, not in Juan the hero who deserved everything. It is the lame who has taken the prey. It is the weak and timid Carlos who has found our father."

"Weak—timid?" said Don Juan, with an incredulous smile. "I marvel who ever joined such words with the name of my heroic son. Carlos, have we any wine?"

"Abundance, my father," answered Carlos, who carefully treasured for his father's use all that was furnished for both of them. Having given him a little, he asked, "Do you feel pain to-night?"

"No—no pain. Only weary; always weary."

"I think my beloved father will soon be where the weary are at rest"—"and where the wicked cease from troubling," he added mentally, not aloud.

He would fain have dropped the conversation then, fearing to exhaust his father's strength. But the sick man's restlessness was soothed by his talk. Ere long he questioned, "Is it not near Christmas now?"

Well did Carlos know that it was; and keenly did he dread the return of the season which ought to bring "peace upon earth." For it would certainly bring the prisoners a visit; and almost certainly there would be the offer of special privileges to the penitent, perhaps sacramental consolation, perhaps permission to hear mass. He shuddered to think what a refusal to avail himself of these indulgences might entail. And once and again did he breathe the fervent prayer, that whatever came upon *him*, neither violence, insult, nor reproach might be allowed to touch his father.

Moreover, amongst the great festivities of the season, it was more than likely that a solemn Auto-da-fé might find place. But this was a secret inner thought, not often put into words, even to himself. Only, if it were God's will to call his father first!

"It is December," he said, in answer to Don Juan's question; "but I have lost account of the day. It may be perhaps the twelfth or fourteenth. Shall I recite the evening psalms for the twelfth, Te dicet hymnus'?"

As he did so, the old man fell asleep, which was what he desired. Half in the sleep of exhaustion, half in weary restlessness, the next day and the next night wore on. Once only did Don Juan speak connectedly.

"I think you will see my mother soon," said Carlos, as he bore to his lips wine mingled with water.

"True," breathed the dying man; "but I am not thinking of that now. Far better—I shall see Christ."

"My father, are you still in peace, resting on him?"

"In perfect peace."

And Carlos said no more. He was content; nay, he was exceeding glad. He who in all things will have the preeminence, had indeed taken his rightful place in the heart of the dying, when even the strong earthly love that was "twisted with the strings of life" had paled before the love of him.

And in the last watch of the night, when the day was breaking, he sent his angel to loose the captive's bonds. So gentle was the touch that freed him, that he who sat holding his hand in his, and watching his face as we watch the last conscious looks of our beloved, yet knew not the exact moment when the Deliverer came. Carlos never said, "He is going!" he only said, "He is gone!" And then he kissed the pale lips and closed the sightless eyes—in peace.

None ever thanked God for bringing back their beloved from the gates of the grave more fervently than Carlos thanked him that hour for so gently opening unto his those gates that 'no man can shut.' "My father, thy rest is won!" he said, as he gazed on the calm and noble countenance. "They can not touch thee now. Not all the malice of men or of fiends can give one pang. A moment since so fearfully in their power; now so completely beyond it! Thank God! thank God!"

The rain was over, and ere long the sun arose, in his royal robes of crimson and purple and gold—to the prisoner from the dungeon of the Triana an ever fresh wonder and joy. Yet not even that sight could win his eyes to-day from the deeper beauty of the still and solemn face before him. And as the soft crimson light fell on the pallid cheek and brow, the watcher murmured, with calm thankfulness,—"To him sun and daylight are as nothing, for he sees the glory of God."

XLV.

Triumphant.

> "For ever with the Lord!
> Amen! so let it be!"
> MONTGOMERY.

ARLOS was still sitting beside that couch, with scarcely more sense of time than if he had been already where time exists no longer, when the door of his cell was opened to admit two distinguished visitors. First came the prior; then another member of the Table of the Inquisition.

Carlos rose up from beside his dead, and said calmly, addressing the prior, "My father is free!"

"How? what is this?" cried Fray Ricardo, his brow contracting with surprise.

Carlos stood aside, allowing him to approach and look. With real concern in his stern countenance, he stooped for a few moments over the motionless form. Then he asked,—

"But why was I not summoned? Who was with him when he departed?"

"I,—his son," said Carlos.

"But who besides thee?" Then, in a higher key, and with

more hurried intonation,— "Who gave him the last rites of the Church?"

"He did not receive them, my lord, for he did not desire them. He said that Christ was his priest; that he would not confess; and that they should not anoint him while he retained consciousness."

The Dominican's face grew white with anger, even to the lips.

"Liar!" he cried, in a voice of thunder. "How darest thou tell me that he for whom I watched, and prayed, and toiled, after years and years of faithful penance, has gone down at last, unanointed and unassoiled, to hell with Luther and Calvin?"

"I tell thee that he has gone home in peace to his Father's house."

"Blasphemer! liar, like thy father the devil! But I understand all now. Thou, in thy hatred of the Faith, didst refuse to summon help—didst let his spirit pass without the aid and consolations of the Church. Murderer of his soul—thy father's soul! Not content even with that, thou canst stand there and slander his memory, bidding us believe that he died in heresy! But that, at least, is false—false as thine own accursed creed!"

"It is true; and you believe it," said Carlos, in calm, clear, quiet tones that contrasted strangely with the Dominican's outburst of unwonted rage.

And the prior did believe it—there was the sharpest sting. He knew perfectly well that the condemned heretic was incapable of falsehood: on a matter of fact he would have received his testimony more readily than that of the stately "Lord Inquisitor" now standing by his side. In the momentary pause that followed, that personage came forward and looked upon the face of the dead.

"If there be really any proof that he died in heresy," he said, "he ought to be proceeded against according to the laws of the Holy Office provided for such cases."

Carlos smiled—smiled in calm triumph.

"You cannot hurt him now," he said. "Look there, señor."

The King immortal, invisible, has set his own signet upon that brow, that the decree may not be reversed nor the purpose changed concerning him."

And the peace of the dead face seemed to have passed into the living face that had gazed on it so long. Carlos was as really beyond the power of his enemies as his father was that hour. They felt it; or at least one of them did. As for the other, his strong heart was torn with rage and sorrow: sorrow for the penitent, whom he truly loved, and whom he now believed, after all his prayers and efforts, a lost soul; rage against the obstinate heretic, whom he had sought to befriend, and who had repaid his kindness by snatching his convert from his grasp at the very gate of heaven, and plunging him into hell.

"I will *not* believe it," he reiterated, with pale lips, and eyes that gleamed beneath his cowl like coals of fire. Then, softening a little as he turned to the dead—"Would that those silent lips could utter, were it only one word, to say that death found thee true to the Catholic faith!—Not one word! So end the hopes of years. But at least thy betrayer shall be with thee amongst the dead to-morrow.— Heretic!" he said, turning fiercely to Carlos, "we are here to announce thy doom. I came, with a heart full of pity and relenting, to offer counsel and comfort, and such mercy as Holy Church still keeps for those who return to her bosom at the eleventh hour. But now, I despair of thee. Professed, impenitent, dogmatising heretic, go thine own way to everlasting fire!"

"To-morrow! Did you say to-morrow?" asked Carlos, standing motionless, as one lost in thought.

The other Inquisitor took up the word.

"It is true," he said. "To-morrow the Church offers to God the acceptable sacrifice of a solemn Act of Faith. And we come to announce to thee thy sentence, well merited and long delayed—to be relaxed to the secular arm as an obstinate heretic. But if even yet thou wilt repent, and, confessing and deploring thy sins, supplicate restoration to the bosom of the Church, she will so effectually intercede for thee with the civil magistrate that the doom of fire will be exchanged for the milder punishment of death by strangling."

Something like a faint smile played round the lips of Carlos; but he only repeated, "To-morrow!"

"Yes, my son," said the Inquisitor, promptly; for he was a man who knew his business well. He had come there to improve the occasion; and he meant to do it. "No doubt it seems to thee a sudden blow, and but a brief space left thee for preparation. But, at the best, our life here is only a span; 'Man that is born of a woman hath but a short time to live, and is full of misery.'"[1]

Carlos did not look as if he heard; he still stood lost in thought, his head sunk upon his breast. But in another moment he raised it suddenly.

"To-morrow I shall be with Christ in glory!" he exclaimed, with a countenance as radiant as if that glory were already reflected there.

Some faint feeling of awe and wonder touched the Inquisitor's heart, and silenced him for an instant. Then, recovering himself, and falling back for help upon wonted words of course, he said,—

"I entreat of you to think of your soul."

"I have thought of it long ago. I have given it into the safe keeping of Christ my Lord. Therefore I think no more of it; I only think of him."

"But have you no fear of the anguish—the doom of fire?"

"I have no fear," Carlos answered. And this was a great mystery, even to himself. "Christ's hand will either lift me over it or sustain me through it; which, I know not yet. And I am not careful; he will care."

"Men of noble lineage, such as you are—of high honour and stainless name, such as you *were*," said the Inquisitor—"ofttimes dread shame more than agony. You, who *were* called Alvarez de Meñaya, what think you of the infamy, the loathing of all men, the scorn and mockery of the lowest rabble—the zamarra, the carroza?"

"I shall joyfully go forth with Christ without the camp, bearing his reproach."

And stand at the stake beside a vile caitiff, a miserable muleteer, convicted of the same crimes?"

[1] From the Book of Common Prayer.

"A muleteer? Juliano Hernandez?" Carlos questioned eagerly.

"The same."

A softer light played over the features of Carlos. Then he should see that face once more—perhaps even grasp that hand! Truly God was giving him everything he desired of him. He said,—

"I am glad to stand, here to the last, at the side of that faithful soldier and servant of Christ. For when we go in there together, I dare not hope to be so highly honoured as to take a place beside him."

At this point the prior broke in. "Señor and my brother, your words are wasted. He is given over to the power of the evil one. Let us leave him." And drawing his mantle round him, he turned to go, without looking again towards Carlos.

But Carlos came forward. "Pardon me, my lord; I have a few words yet to say to you;" and, stretching out his hand to detain him, he unconsciously touched his arm with it.

The prior flung it off with a gesture of angry scorn. There was contamination in that touch. "I have heard too many words from your lips already," he said.

"To-morrow night my lips will be dust, my voice silent for ever. So you may well bear with me for a little while to-day."

"Speak then; but be brief."

"It gives me the last pang I think to know on earth, to part thus from you; for you have shown me true kindness. I owe you, not forgiveness as an enemy, but gratitude as a sincere though mistaken friend. I shall pray for you—"

"An impenitent heretic's prayers—"

"Will do my lord the prior no harm; and there may come a day when he will not be sorry he had them."

There was a short pause. "Have you anything else to say?" asked the prior rather more gently.

"Only one word, señor." He turned and looked at the dead. "I know you loved him well. You will deal gently with his dust, will you not? A grave is not much to ask for him. You will give it; I trust you."

The stern set face relaxed a little before that pleading look. "It is *you* who have sought to rob him of a grave," said the prior—"you who have defamed him of heresy. But your testimony is invalid; and, as I have said, I believe you not."

With this declaration of purely official disbelief, he left the room.

His colleague lingered a moment. "You plead for the senseless dust that can neither feel nor suffer," he said; "you can pity that. How is it you cannot pity yourself?"

"That which you destroy to-morrow is not myself. It is only my garment, my tent. Yet even over that Christ watches. He can raise it glorious from the ashes of the Quemadero as easily as from the church where the bones of my fathers sleep. For I am his, soul and body—the purchase of his blood. And why should it be a marvel in your eyes that I rejoice to give my life for him who gave his own for me?"

"God grant thee even yet to die in his grace!" answered the Inquisitor, somewhat moved. "I do not despair of thee. I will pray for thee, and visit thee again to-night." So saying, he hastened after the prior.

For a season Carlos sat motionless, his soul filled to over flowing with a calm, deep tide of awed and wondering joy. No room was there for any thought save one—"I shall see His face; I shall be with Him for ever." Over the Thing that lay between he could spring as joyously as a child might leap across a brook to reach his father's outstretched hand.

At length his eye fell, perhaps by accident, on the little writing-book which lay near. He drew it towards him, and having found out the place where the last entry was made, wrote rapidly beneath it,—

"To depart and to be with Christ is far better. My beloved father is gone to him in peace to-day. I too go in peace, though by a rougher path, to-morrow. Surely goodness and mercy have followed me all the days of my life, and I shall dwell in the house of the Lord for ever.[2]

[2] Reference to Psalm 23:6

"CARLOS ALVAREZ DE SANTILLANOS Y MEÑAYA."

And with a strange consciousness that he had now signed his name for the last time, he carefully affixed to it his own especial "rubrica," or sign-manual.

Then came one thought of earth—only one—the last. "God, in his great mercy, grant that my brother may be far away! I would not that he saw my face to-morrow. For the pain and the shame can be seen of all; while that which changes them to glory no man knoweth, save he that receiveth it. But, wherever thou art, God bless thee, my Ruy!" And drawing the book towards him again, he added, as if by a sudden impulse, to what he had already written, "God bless thee, my Ruy!"

Soon afterwards the Alguazils arrived to conduct him back to the Triana. Then, turning to his dead once more, he kissed the pale forehead, saying, "Farewell, for a little while. Thou didst never taste death; nor shall I. Instead of thee and me, Christ drank that cup."

And then, for the second time, the gate of the Triana opened to receive Don Carlos Alvarez. At sunrise next morning its gloomy portals were unlocked, and he, with others, passed forth from beneath their shadow. Not to return again to that dark prison, there to linger out the slow and solitary hours of grief and pain. His warfare was accomplished, his victory was won. Long before the sun had arisen again upon the weary blood-stained earth, a brighter sun arose for him who had done with earth. All his desire was granted, all his longings were fulfilled. He saw the face of Christ, and he was with Him for ever.

XLVI.

Is It Too Late?

"Death upon his face
Is rather shine than shade;
A tender shine by looks beloved made:
He seemeth dying in a quiet place."
E. B. BROWNING.

HE mountain-snow lay white around the old castle of Nuera; but within there was light and warmth. Joy and gladness were there also, "thanksgiving and the voice of melody;" for Doña Beatriz, graver and paler than of old, and with the brilliant lustre of her dark eyes subdued to a kind of dewy softness, was singing a cradle-song beside the cot where her first-born slept.

The babe had just been baptised by Fray Sebastian. With a pleading, wistful look had Dolores asked her lord, the day before, what name he wished his son to bear. But he only answered, "The heir of our house always bears the name of Juan." Another name was far dearer to memory; but not yet could he accustom his lips to utter it, or his ear to bear the sound.

Now he came slowly into the room, holding in his hand an unsealed letter. Doña Beatriz looked up. "He sleeps," she said.

"Then let him sleep on, señora mia."

"But will you not look? See, how pretty he is! How he smiles in his sleep! And those dear small hands—"

"Have their share in dragging me further than you wot of, my Beatriz."

Nay; what dost thou mean? Do not be grave and sad to-day—not to-day, Don Juan."

"My beloved, God knows I would not cloud thy brow with a single care if I could help it. Nor am I sad. Only we must think. Here is a letter from the Duke of Savoy (and very gracious and condescending too), inviting me to take my place once more in His Catholic Majesty's army."

"But you will not go? We are so happy together here."

"My Beatriz, I *dare* not go. I would have to fight"—(here he broke off, and cast a hasty glance round the room, from the habit of dreading listeners)—"I would have to fight against those whose cause is just the cause I hold dearest upon earth. I would have to deny my faith by the deeds of every day. But yet, how to refuse and not stand dishonoured in the eyes of the world, a traitor and a coward, I know not."

"No dishonour could ever touch thee, my brave and noble Juan."

Don Juan's brow relaxed a little. "But that men should even *think* it did, is what I could not bear," he said. "Besides"—and he drew nearer the cradle, and looked fondly down at the little sleeper—"it does not seem to me, my Beatriz, that I dare bring up this child God has given me to the bitter heritage of a slave."

"A slave!" repeated Doña Beatriz, almost with a cry. "Now, Don Juan; are you mad? You, of noblest lineage—you, Alvarez de Meñaya—to call your own first-born a slave!"

"I call any one a slave who dares not speak out what he thinks, and act out what he believes," returned Don Juan sadly.

"And what is it that you would do then?"

"I wish I knew! But the future is all dark to me. I see not a single step before me."

"Then, amigo mio, do not look before you. Let the future alone, and enjoy the present, as I do."

"Truly that baby face would charm many a care away," said Juan, with another fond glance at the sleeping child. "But a man *must* look before him, and a Christian man must ask what God would have him to do. Moreover, this letter of the duke demands an answer, Yea or Nay."

"Señor Don Juan, I desire to speak with your Excellency," said the voice of Dolores at the door.

"Come in, Dolores."

"Nay, señor, I want you here." This peremptory sharpness was very unlike the wonted manner of Dolores.

Don Juan came forth immediately. Dolores signed to him to shut the door. Then, not till then, she began,—"Señor Don Juan, two brethren of the Society of Jesus have come from Seville, and are now in the village."

"What then? Surely you do not fear that they suspect anything with regard to us?" asked Juan, in some alarm. "No; but they have brought tidings."

"You tremble, Dolores. You are ill. Speak—what is it?"

"They have brought tidings of a great Act of Faith, to be held at Seville, upon a day not yet fixed when they left the city, but towards the end of this month."

For a moment the two stood silent, gazing in each other's faces. Then Dolores said, in an eager breathless whisper, "You will go, señor?"

Juan shook his head. "What you are thinking of, Dolores, is a dream—a vain, wild dream. Long since, I doubt not, he rests with God."

"But if we had the proof of it, rest might come to us," said Dolores, large tears gathering slowly in her eyes.

"It is true," Juan mused; "they may wreak their vengeance on the dust."

"And for the assurance that would give that nothing more was left them, I, a poor woman, would joyfully walk barefoot from this to Seville and back again."

Juan hesitated no longer. "*I go*," he said. "Dolores, seek Fray Sebastian, and send him to me at once. Bid Jorge be ready with the horses to start to-morrow at daybreak. Meanwhile, I will prepare Doña Beatriz for my sudden departure."

Of that hurried winter journey, Don Juan was never afterwards heard to speak. No one of its incidents seemed to have made the slightest impression on his mind, or even to have been remembered by him.

But at last he drew near Seville. It was late in the evening, however, and he had told his attendant they should spend the night at a village eight or nine miles from their destination.

Suddenly Jorge cried out. "Look there, señor, the city is on fire."

Don Juan looked. A lurid crimson glow paled the stars in the southern sky. With a shudder he bowed his head, and veiled his face from the awful sight.

"That fire is *without the gate*," he said at last. "Pray for the souls that are passing in anguish now."

Noble, heroic souls! Probably Juliano Hernandez, possibly Fray Constantino, was amongst them. These were the only names that occurred to Don Juan's mind, or were breathed in his fervent, agitated prayer.

"Yonder is the posada, señor," said the attendant presently. "Nay, Jorge, we will ride on. There will be no sleepers in Seville to-night."

"But, señor," remonstrated the servant, "the horses are weary. We have travelled far to-day already."

"Let them rest afterwards," said Juan briefly. Motion, just then, was an absolute necessity to him. He could not have rested anywhere, within sight of that awful glare.

Two hours afterwards he drew the rein of his weary steed before the house of his cousin Doña Inez. He had no scruple in asking for admission in the middle of the night, as he knew that, under the circumstances, the household would not fail to be astir. His summons was speedily answered, and he was conducted to a hall opening on the patio.

Thither, after a brief interval, came Juanita, bearing a lamp in her hand, which she set down on the table. "My lady will see your Excellency presently," said the girl, with a shy, frightened air, which was very unlike her, but which Juan was too preoccupied to notice. "But she is much indisposed. My lord was obliged to accompany her home from the Act of Faith before it was half over."

Juan expressed the concern he felt, and desired that she would not incommode herself upon his account. Perhaps Don Garçia, if he had not yet retired to rest, would converse with him for a few moments.

"My lady said she must speak with you herself," answered Juanita, as she left the room.

After a considerable time Doña Inez appeared. In that southern climate, youth and beauty fade quickly; and yet Juan was by no means prepared for the changed, worn, haggard face that gazed on him now. There was no pomp of apparel to carry off the impression. Doña Inez wore a loose dark dressing-robe; and a hasty careless hand seemed to have untwined the usual ornaments from her black hair. Her eyes were like those of one who has wept for hours, and then only ceased for very weariness.

She stretched out both her hands to Juan—"O Don Juan, I never meant it! I never meant it!"

"Señora and my cousin, I have but just arrived here. I do not understand you," said Juan, rising to greet her. "Then you know not!—Horrible!"

She sank into a seat. Juan stood gazing at her eagerly, almost wildly. "Yes; I understand all now," he said at last. "I suspected it."

He saw in imagination a black chest, with a little lifeless dust within it; a rude shapeless figure, robed in the hideous zamarra, and bearing in large letters the venerated name, "Alvarez de Santillanos y Meñaya." While *she* saw a living face, that would never cease to haunt her memory until death shadowed all things.

"Let me speak," she gasped; "and I will try to be calm. I did not wish to go. It was the day of the last Auto, you remember, that my poor brother died, and altogether—But Don Garçia insisted. He said everybody would talk, and especially when the taint had touched our own house. Besides, Doña Juana de Bohorques, who died in prison, was to be publicly declared innocent, and her property restored to her heirs. Out of regard to the family, it was thought we ought to be present. O Don Juan, if I had but known! I would rather have put on a sanbenito myself than have gone there. God grant it did not hurt him!"

"How could it possibly hurt him, my tender-hearted cousin?"

"Hush! Let me go on now, while I can speak of it; or I shall never, never tell you. And I must. *He* would have wished—Well, we were seated in what they called good places; very near the condemned; in fact, the scaffold opposite was plain to us as you are to me now. But that last time, and Doña Maria's look, and Dr. Cristobal's, haunted me, so that I did not dare to raise my eyes to where they sat;—not until long after the mass had begun. And I knew besides there were so many women there—eight on that dreadful top bench, doomed to die. But at last a lady who sat near me bade me look at one of the relaxed, a little man, who was pointing upwards and making signs to his companions to encourage them. 'Do not look, señora,' said Don Garçia, quickly—but too late. O Don Juan, I saw his face!"

"His LIVING face? Not his living face?" cried Juan, with a shudder that convulsed his strong frame from head to foot. And the Name—the one awful Name that rises to all human lips in moments of supreme emotion—broke from his in a wail of anguish.

Doña Inez tried to speak; but in vain. Thoroughly broken down, she wept and sobbed aloud. But the sight of the rigid, tearless face before her checked her tears at last. She gained power to go on. "I saw him. Worn and pale, of course; yet not changed so greatly, after all. The same dear, kind, familiar face I had seen last in this room, when he caressed and played with my child. Not sad, not as though he suffered. Rather as though he had suffered long ago; but was beyond it all, even then. A still, patient, fearless look, eyes that saw everything; and yet nothing seemed to trouble him. I bore it until they were reading the sentences, and came to his. But when I saw the Alguazil strike him—the blow that relaxed to the secular arm—I could endure no more. I believe I cried aloud. But in fact I know not what I did. I know nothing more till Don Garçia and my brother Don Manuel were carrying me through the crowd."

"No word? Was there no word spoken?" asked Juan wildly. "*No*; but I heard some one near me say that he talked with that muleteer in the court of the Triana, and spoke words of comfort to a poor woman amongst the penitents, whom they called Maria Gonzalez."

All was told now. Maddened with rage and anguish, Juan rushed from the room, from the house; and, without being conscious of any settled purpose, in five minutes found himself far on his way to the Dominican convent adjoining the Triana.

His servant, who was still waiting at the gate, followed him to ask for orders, and with difficulty overtook him, and arrested his steps.

Juan sternly silenced his faltering, agitated question as to what was wrong with his lord. "Go to rest," he said, "and meet me in the morning by the great gate of San Isodro." Nothing was clear to him; but that he must shake off as soon as possible the dust of the wicked, cruel city from his feet. And San Isodro was the only trysting-place without its walls that happened at the moment to occur to his bewildered brain.

XLVII.

The Dominican Prior.

"Oh, deep is a wounded heart, and strong
A voice that cries against mighty wrong!
And full of death as a hot wind's blight,
Doth the ire of a crushed affection light."

HEMANS.

ELL the prior Don Juan Alvarez de Santillanos y Meñaya desires to speak with him, and that instantly," said Juan to the drowsy lay brother who at last answered his impatient summons, lantern in hand.

"My lord has but just retired to rest, and cannot now be disturbed," answered the attendant, looking with some curiosity, not to say surprise, at the visitor, who seemed to think three o'clock of a winter morning a proper and suitable hour to demand instant audience of a great man.

"I will wait," said Juan, walking into the court.

The attendant led him to a parlour; then, holding the door ajar, he said, "Let his Excellency pardon me, I did not hear distinctly his worship's honourable name."

"Don Juan Alvarez de Santillanos y Meñaya. The prior knows it—too well."

It was evident from his face that the poor lay brother knew it also. And so that night did every man, woman, and child in Seville. It had become a name of infamy.

With a hasty "Yes, yes, señor," the door was closed, and Juan was left alone.

What had brought him there? Did he mean to accuse the Dominican of his brother's murder, or did he only intend to reproach him—him who had once shown some pity to the captive—for not saving him from that horrible doom? He himself scarcely knew. He had been driven thither by a wild, unreasoning impulse, an instinct of passionate rage, prompting him to grasp at the only shadow of revenge that lay within his reach. If he could not execute God's awful judgments against the persecutors, at least he could denounce them. A poor substitute, but all that remained to him. Without it his heart must break.

Yet that unreasoning impulse had a kind of unconscious reason in it, since it led him to seek the presence of the Dominican prior, and not that of the far more guilty Munebrãga. For who would accuse a tiger, reproach a wolf? Words would be wasted upon such. For them there is no argument but the spear and the bullet. A man can only speak to men.

To do Fray Ricardo justice, he was so much of a man that sleep did not visit his eyes that night. When at length his attendants thought fit to inform him that Don Juan desired to see him, he was still kneeling, as he had knelt for hours, before the crucifix in his private oratory. "Saviour of the world, so much didst thou suffer," this was the key-note of his thoughts; "and shall I weakly pity thine enemies, or shrink from seeing them suffer what they have deserved at thy hands and those of thy holy Church?"

"Alvarez de Santillanos y Meñaya waits below!" Just then Don Fray Ricardo would rather have held his right hand in the fire than have gone forth to face one bearing that name. But, for that very reason, no sooner did he hear that Don Juan awaited him than he robed himself in his cowl and mantle, took a lamp in his hand (for it was still dark), and went down to meet the visitor. For that morning he was in the mood to welcome any form of self-torture that came in his way, and to find a strange but real relief in it.

"Peace be with thee, my son," was his grave but courteous salutation, as he entered the parlour. He looked upon Juan with mournful compassion, as the last of a race over which there hung a terrible doom.

"Let your peace be with murderers like yourselves, or with slaves like those that work your will; I fling it back to you in scorn," was the fierce reply.

The Dominican recoiled a step—only a step, for he was a brave man, and his face, pale with conflict and watching, grew a shade paler.

"Do you think I mean to harm you?" cried Juan in yet fiercer scorn. "Not a hair of your tonsured head. See there!" He unbuckled his sword, and threw it from him, and it fell with a clang on the floor.

"Young man, you would consult your own safety as well as your own honour by adopting a different tone," said the prior, not without dignity.

"My safety is little worth consulting. I am a bold, rough soldier, used to peril and violence. Would it were such, and such alone, that you menaced. But fiends that you are, would no one serve you for a victim save my young, gentle, unoffending brother; he who never harmed you nor any one? Would nothing satisfy your malice but to immure him in your hideous dungeons for two-and-thirty long slow months, in what suffering of mind and body God alone can tell; and then, at last, to bring him forth to that horrible death? I curse you! I curse you! Nay, that is nothing; who am I to curse? I invoke God's curse upon you! I give you up into God's hands this hour! When He maketh inquisition for blood—another inquisition than yours—I pray him to exact from you, murderers of the innocent, torturers of the just, every drop of blood, every tear, every pang of which he has been the witness, as he shall be the avenger."

At last the prior found a voice. Hitherto he had listened spell-bound, as one oppressed by nightmare, powerless to free himself from the hideous burden. "Man!" he cried, "you are raving; the Holy Office—"

"Is the arch-fiend's own contrivance, and its ministers his favourite servants," interrupted Juan, reckless in his rage, and defying all consequences.

"Blasphemy! This may not be borne," and Fray Ricardo stretched out his hand towards a bell that lay on the table.

But Juan's strong grasp prevented his touching it. He could not shake off that as easily as he had shaken off a pale thin hand two days before. "I shall speak forth my mind this once," he said. "After that, what you please.—Go on. Fill your cup full to the brim. Immure, plunder, burn, destroy. Pile up, high as heaven, your hecatomb of victims, offered to the God of love. At least there is one thing that may be said in your favour. In your cruelties there is a horrible impartiality. It can never be spoken of you that you have gone out into the highways and hedges, taken the blind and the lame, and made of them your burnt sacrifice. No. You go into the closest guarded homes; you take thence the gentlest, the tenderest, the fairest, the best, and of such you make your burnt-offering. And you—are your hearts human, or are they not? If they are, stifle them, crush them down into silence while you can; for a day will come when you can stifle them no longer. That will begin your punishment. You will feel remorse."

"Man, let me go!" interrupted the indignant yet half-frightened prior, struggling vainly to free himself from his grasp. "Cease your blasphemies. Men only feel remorse when they have sinned; and I serve God and the Church."

"Yet, servant of the Church (for God's servant I am not profane enough to call you), speak to me this once as man to man, and tell me, did a victim's pale face never haunt you, a victim's agonised cry never ring in your ears?"

For just an instant the prior winced, as one who feels a sharp, sudden pain, but determines to conceal it.

"There!" cried Juan—and at last he released his arm and flung it from him—"I read an answer in your look. You, at least, are capable of remorse."

"You are false there," the prior broke in. "Remorse is not for me."

"No? Then all the worse for you—infinitely the worse. Yet it may be. You may sleep and rise, and go to your rest again untroubled by an accusing conscience. You may sit down to eat and drink with the wail of your brother's anguish ringing in your ears, like Munebrãga, who sits feasting yonder in his marble hall, with the ashes yet hot on the Quemadero. Until you go down quick into hell, and the pit shuts her mouth upon you. Then, THEN shall you drink of the wine of the wrath of God, which is poured out without mixture into the cup of his indignation; and you shall be tormented with fire and brimstone in the presence of the holy angels, and in the presence of the Lamb."

"Thou art beside thyself;" cried the prior; "and I, scarce less mad than thou, to listen to thy ravings. Yet hear me a moment, Don Juan Alvarez. I have not merited these insane reproaches. To you and yours I have been more a friend than you wot of."

"Noble friendship! I thank you for it, as it deserves."

"You have given me, this hour, more than cause enough to order your instant arrest."

"You are welcome. It were shame indeed if I could not bear at your hands what my gentle brother bore."

The last of his race! The father dead in prison; the mother dead long ago (Fray Ricardo himself best knew why); the brother burned to ashes. "I think you have a wife, perhaps a child?" asked the prior hurriedly.

"A young wife, and an infant son," said Juan, softening a little at the thought.

"Wild as your words have been, I am yet willing, for their sakes, to show you forbearance. According to the lenity which ministers of the Holy Office—"

"Have learned from their father the devil," interrupted Juan, the flame of his wrath blazing up again. "After what the stars looked down on last night, dare to mock me with thy talk of lenity!"

"You are in love with destruction," said the prior. "But I have heard you long enough. Now hear me. You have been, ere this, under grave suspicion. Indeed, you would have been arrested, only that your brother endured the Question without revealing anything to your disadvantage. That saved you."

But here he stopped, struck with astonishment at the sudden change his words had wrought.

A man stabbed to the heart makes no outcry, he does not even moan or writhe. Nor did Juan. Mutely he sank on the nearest seat, all his rage and defiance gone now. A moment before he stood over the shrinking Inquisitor like a prophet of doom or an avenging angel; now he cowered crushed and silent, stricken to the soul. There was a long silence. Then he raised a changed, sad look to the prior's face. "He bore that for me," he said, "and I never knew it."

In the cold grey morning light, now filling the room, he looked utterly forlorn and broken. The prior could even afford to pity him. He questioned, mildly enough, "How was it you did not know it? Fray Sebastian Gomez, who visited him in prison, was well aware of the fact."

In Juan's present mood every faculty was stimulated to unnatural activity. This perhaps enabled him to divine a truth which in calmer moments might have escaped him. "My brother," he said, in a low tone of deep emotion, "my heroic, tender-hearted brother must have bidden him conceal it from me."

"It was strange," said the prior, and his thoughts ran back to other things which were strange also—to the uniform patience and gentleness of Carlos; to the fortitude with which, whilst acknowledging his own faith, he had steadily refused to compromise any one else; to the self-forgetfulness with which he had shielded his father's last hours from disturbance. Granted that the heretic was a wild beast, "made to be taken and destroyed," even the hunter may admire unblamed the grace and beauty of the creature who has just fallen beneath his relentless weapon. Something like a mist rose to the eyes of Fray Ricardo, taking him by surprise.

Still, the interests of the Faith were paramount with him. All that had been done had been well done; he would not, if he could, undo any part of it. But did his duty to the Faith and to Holy Church require that he should hunt the remaining brother to death, and thus "quench the coal that was left"? He hoped not; he thought not. And, although he would not have allowed it to himself, the words that followed were really a peace-offering to the shade of Carlos.

"Young man, I am willing, for my own part, to overlook the wild words you have uttered, regarding them as the outpourings of insanity, and making moreover due allowance for your natural fraternal sorrow. Still you must be aware that you have laid yourself open, and not for the first time, to grave suspicion of heresy. I should not only sin against my own conscience, but also expose myself to the penalties of a grievous irregularity, did I take no steps for the vindication of the Faith and your just and well-merited punishment. Therefore give ear to what I say. *This day week* I bring the matter before the Table of the Holy Office, of which I have the honour to be an unworthy member. And God grant you the grace of repentance, and his forgiveness."

Having said this, Fray Ricardo left the room. He disappears also from our pages, where he occupied a place as a type of the less numerous and less guilty class of persecutors—those who not only thought they were doing God service (Munebrãga may have thought that, but he was only willing to do God such service as cost him nothing), but who were honestly anxious to serve him to the best of their ability. His future is hidden from our sight. We cannot even undertake to say whether, when death drew near,—if the name of Alvarez de Meñaya occurred to him at all,—he reproached himself for his sternness to the brother whom he had consigned to the flames, or for his weakness to the brother to whom he had generously given a chance of life and liberty.

It is not usually the most guilty who hear the warning voice that denounces their crimes and threatens their doom. Such words as Don Juan spoke to Fray Ricardo could not, by any conceivable possibility, have been uttered in the presence of Gonzales de

Munebrãga.

Soon afterwards a lay brother, the same who had admitted Don Juan, entered the room and placed wine on the table before him. "My lord the prior bade me say your Excellency seemed exhausted, and should refresh yourself ere you depart," he explained.

Juan motioned it away. He could not trust himself to speak. But did Fray Ricardo imagine he would either eat bread or drink water beneath the roof that sheltered him?

Still the poor man lingered, standing before him with the air of one who had something to say which he did not exactly know how to bring out.

"You may tell your lord that I am going," said Juan, rising wearily, and with a look that certainly told of exhaustion.

"If it please your noble Excellency—" and the lay brother stopped and hesitated.

"Well?"

"Let his Excellency pardon me. Could his worship have the misfortune to be related, very distantly no doubt, to one of the heretics who—"

"Don Carlos Alvarez was my brother," said Juan proudly.

The poor lay brother drew nearer to him, and lowered his voice to a mysterious whisper. "Señor and your Excellency, he was here in prison for a long time. It was thought that my lord the prior had a kindness for him, and wished him better used than they use the criminals in the Santa Casa. It happened that the prisoner whose cell he shared died the day before his—*removal*. So that the cell was empty, and it fell to my lot to cleanse it. Whilst I was doing it I found this; I think it belonged to him."

He drew from beneath his serge gown a little book, and handed it to Juan, who seized it as a starving man might seize a piece of bread. Hastily taking out his purse, he flung it in exchange to the lay brother; and then, just as the matin bells began to ring, he buckled on his sword and went forth.

XLVIII.

San Isodro Once More.

"And if with milder anguish now I bear
To think of thee in thy forsaken rest;
If from my heart be lifted the despair,
The sharp remorse with healing influence pressed,
It is that Thou the sacrifice hast blessed,
And filled my spirit, in its inmost cell,
With a deep chastened sense that all at last is well."

HEMANS.

HE cloudless sky above him, the fresh morning air on his cheek, the dew-drops on his feet, Don Juan walked along. The river—his own bright Guadalquivir—glistened in the early sunshine; and soon his pathway led him amidst the grey ruins of old Italica, while among the brambles that half hid them, glittering lizards, startled by his footsteps, ran in and out. But he saw nothing, felt nothing, save the passionate pain that burned in his heart. During his interview with Fray Ricardo he had been, practically and for the time, what the prior called him, insane—mad with rage and hate. But now rage was dying out for the present, and giving place to anguish.

Is the worst pang earth has to give that of witnessing the sufferings of our beloved? Or is there yet one keener, more thrilling?

That they should suffer alone; no hand near to help, no voice to speak sympathy, no eye to look "ancient kindness" on their pain. That they should die—die in anguish —and still alone,—

> "With eyes turned away,
> And no last word to say."

Don Juan was now drinking that bitter cup to its very dregs. What the young brother, his one earthly tie, had been to him, need not here be told; and assuredly he could not have told it. He had been all his life a thing to protect and shield—as the strong protect the weak, as manhood shields womanhood and childhood. Had God but taken him with his own right hand, Juan would have thought it a light matter, a sorrow easily borne. But, instead, he stood afar off—he did not help; whilst men, cruel as fiends from the bottomless pit, did their worst, their very worst, upon him. And with refined self-torture he went through all the horrible details, as far as he knew or could guess them. Nor did he spare to stab his own heart with that keenest weapon of all—"It was *for me*; for me he endured the Question." The cry of his brother's anguish—anguish borne for him—seemed to sound in his ears and to haunt him: he felt that it would haunt him evermore.

Of course, there was a well of comfort near, which a child's hand might have pointed out to him: "All is over now; he suffers no longer—he is at rest." But who ever stoops to drink from that well in the parching thirst of the first hour of such a grief as his? In truth, all was over for Carlos; but all was not over for Juan. He had to pass through his dark hour as really as Carlos had passed through his.

Again the agony almost maddened him; again wild hatred and rage against his brother's torturers rose and surged like a flood within him. And with these were mingled thoughts, too nearly rebellious, of him whom that brother trusted so firmly and served so faithfully; as if he had used his servant hardly, and forsaken him in his hour of sorest need.

He shrank with horror from every wayfarer he chanced to meet, imagining that his eyes might have looked on his brother's suffering. But at last he came unawares upon the gate of San Isodro. Left unbarred by some accident, it yielded to his touch, and he entered the monastery grounds. At that very spot, three years ago, the brothers parted, on the day that Carlos avowed his change of faith. Yet not even that remembrance could bring a tear to the hot and angry eyes of Juan. But just then he happened to recollect the book he had received from the lay brother. He took it from its place of concealment, and eagerly began to examine it. It was almost filled with writing; but not, alas! from that beloved hand. So he flung it aside in bitter disappointment. Then becoming suddenly conscious of bodily weakness, he half sat down, half threw himself on the ground. His vigorous frame and his strong nerves saved him from swooning outright: he only lay sick and faint, the blue sky looking black above him, and a strange, indistinct sound, as of many voices, murmuring in his ears.

By-and-by he became conscious that some one was holding water to his lips, and trying, though with an awkward, trembling hand, to loose his doublet at the throat. He drank, shook off his weakness, and looked about him. A very old man, in a white tunic and brown mantle, was bending over him compassionately. In another moment he was on his feet; and having briefly thanked the aged monk for his kindness, he turned his face to the gate.

"Nay, my son," the old man interposed; "San Isodro is changed—changed! Still the sick and weary never left its gates unaided; and they shall not begin now—not now. I pray you come with me to the house, and refresh and rest yourself there."

Juan was not reckless enough to refuse what in truth he sorely needed. He entered the monastery under the guidance of poor old Fray Bernardo, who had been passed by, perhaps in scorn, by the persecutors: and so, after all, he had his wish — he should die and be buried in peace where he had passed his life from boyhood to extreme old age. Yet there was something sad in the thought that the storm that swept by had left untouched the poor, useless, half-withered tree, while it tore down the young and strong and noble oaks, the pride of the now desolated forest.

The few cowed and terrified monks who had been allowed to remain in the convent received Don Juan with great kindness. They set food and wine before him: food he could not touch, but wine he accepted with thankfulness. And they almost insisted on his endeavouring to take some rest; assuring him that when his servant and horses should arrive, they would see them properly cared for, until such time as he might be able to resume his journey.

His journey would not brook delay, as he knew full well. That his young wife might not be a widow and his babe an orphan, he "charged his soul to hold his body strengthened" for the work that both had to do. Back to Nuera for these dear ones as swiftly as the fleetest horses would bear him, then to Seville again, and on board the first ship he could meet with bound for any foreign port,—would the term of grace assigned him by the Inquisitor suffice for all this? Certainly not a moment should be lost.

"I will rest for an hour," he said. "But I pray you, my fathers, do me one kindness first. Is there a man here who witnessed—what was done yesterday?"

A young monk came forward. Juan led him into the cell which had been prepared for him to rest in, and leaning against its little window, with his face turned away, he murmured one agitated question. Three words comprised the answer,

"Calmly, silently, quickly."

Juan's breast heaved and his strong frame trembled. After a long interval he said, still without looking,—

"Now tell me of the others. Name him no more."

"No less than eight ladies died the martyr's death," said the monk, who cared not, before *this* auditor, to conceal his own sentiments. "One of them was Señora Maria Gomez; your Excellency probably knows her story. Her three daughters and her sister died with her. When their sentences were read, they embraced on the scaffold, and bade each other farewell with tears. Then they comforted each other with holy words about our Lord and his passion, and the home he was preparing for them above."

Here the young monk paused for a few moments; then went on, his voice still trembling: "There were, moreover, two Englishmen and a Frenchman, who all died bravely. Lastly, there was Juliano Hernandez."

"Ah! tell me of him."

"He died as he had lived. In the morning, when brought out into the court of the Triana, he cried aloud to his fellow-sufferers,—'Courage, comrades! Now must we show ourselves valiant soldiers of Jesus Christ. Let us bear faithful testimony to his truth before men, and in a few hours we shall receive the testimony of his approbation before angels, and triumph with him in heaven.' Though silenced, he continued throughout the day to encourage his companions by his gestures. On the Quemadero, he knelt down and kissed the stone upon which the stake was erected; then thrust his head among the faggots to show his willingness to suffer. But at the end, having raised his hands in prayer, one of the attendant priests—Dr. Rodriguez—mistook the attitude for a sign that he would recant, and made intercession with the Alguazils to give him a last opportunity of speaking. He confessed his faith in a few strong, brief words; and knowing the character of Rodriguez, told him he thought the same himself, but hid his true belief out of fear. The angry priest bade them light the pile at once. It was done; but the guards, with kind cruelty, thrust the martyr through with their lances, so that he passed, without much pain, into the presence of the Lord whom he served as few have been honoured to do."

"And—Fray Constantino?" Juan questioned.

"He was not, for God took him. They had only his dust to burn. They have sought to slander his memory, saying he raised his hand against his own life. But we knew the contrary. It has reached our ears—I dare not tell you how—that he died in the arms of one of our dear brethren from this place—poor young Fray Fernando, who closed his eyes in peace. It was from one of the dark underground cells of the Triana that he passed straight to the glory of God."[1]

"I thank you for your tidings," said Juan, slowly and faintly. "And now I pray of you to leave me."

After a considerable time, one of the monks softly opened the door of their visitor's cell. He sat on the pallet prepared for him, his head buried in his hands.

"Señor," said the monk, "your servant has arrived, and begs you to excuse his delay. It may be there are some instructions you wish him to receive."

Juan roused himself with an effort.

"Yes," he said; "and I thank you. Will you add to your kindness by bidding him immediately procure for us fresh horses, the best and fleetest that can be had?" He sought his purse; but, remembering in a moment what had become of it, drew a ring from his finger to supply its loss. It was the diamond ring that the Sieur de Ramenais had given him. A keen pang shot through his heart. "No, not that; I cannot part with it." He took two others instead—old family jewels. "Bid him bring these," he said, "to Isaac Ozorio, who dwells in La Juderia[2]—any man there will show him the house; take for them whatever he will give him, and therewith hire fresh horses—the best he can—from the posada where he rested, leaving our own in pledge. Let him also buy provisions for the way; for my business requires haste. I will explain all to you anon."

While the monk did the errand, Don Juan sat still, gazing at the diamond ring. Slowly there came back upon his memory the words spoken by Carlos on the day when the sharp facets cut his hand,

[1] At the Auto they produced his effigy, of the size of life, clad in his canon's robe, and with the arms stretched out in the gesture he had been wont to use in preaching; but it caused such a demonstration of feeling among the people, that they were obliged hastily to withdraw it. It was at this Auto that Maria Gonzalez was sentenced to receive two hundred lashes, and to be imprisoned for ten years, for the kindnesses she had shown the prisoners. An equally severe punishment was awarded to the under-gaoler Herrera for the offence of having allowed a mother and three daughters, who were imprisoned in separate cells, an interview of half an hour; while the many cruelties and peculations of the infamous Benevidio were only chastised by the loss of his situation and its advantages, and banishment from Seville.

[2] The Jewish quarter of Seville.

unfelt by him: "If he calls me to suffer for him, he may give me such blessed assurance of his love, that in the joy of it pain and fear will vanish."

Could it be possible he had done this? Oh, for some token, to relieve his breaking heart by the assurance that thus it had been! And yet, wherefore seek a sign? Was not the heroic courage, the calm patience, given to that young brother, once so frail and timid, as plain a token of the sunlight of God's peace and presence as is the bow in the cloud of the sun shining in the heavens? True; but not the less was his soul filled with passionate longing for one word—only one word—from the lips that were dust and ashes now. "If God would give me *that*," he moaned, "I think I could weep for him."

It occurred to him then that he might examine the book more carefully than he had done before. Don Juan, of late, had been no great reader, except of the Spanish Testament. Instead of glancing rapidly through the volume with a practised eye, he carefully began at the beginning and perused several pages with diligence, and with a kind of compelled and painful attention.

The writer of the diary with which the book seemed filled had not prefixed his name. Consequently Juan, who was without a clue to the authorship, saw in it merely the effusions of a penitent, with whose feelings he had but little sympathy. Still he reflected that if the writer had been his brother's fellow-prisoner, some mention of his brother would probably reward his persevering search. So he read on; but he was not greatly interested, until at length he came to one passage which ran thus:—

"Christ and Our Lady forgive me, if it be a sin. Ofttimes, even by prayer and fasting, I cannot prevent my thoughts from wandering to the past. Not to the life I lived, and the part I acted in the great world, for that is dead to me and I to it; but to the dear faces my eyes shall never see again. My Costanza!"—("Costanza!" thought Juan with a start, "that was my mother's name!")—"my wife! my babe! O God, in thy great mercy, still this hungering and thirsting of the heart!"

Immediately beneath this entry was another. "*May 21.* My Costanza, my beloved wife, is in heaven. It is more than a year ago, but they did not tell me till to-day. Does death only visit the free?"

Yet another entry caught the eye of Juan. "Burning heat to-day. It would be cool enough in the halls of Nuera, on the breezy slope of the Sierra Morena. What does my orphaned Juan Rodrigo there, I wonder?"

"Nuera! Sierra Morena! Juan Rodrigo!" reiterated the astonished reader. What did it all mean? He was stunned and bewildered, so that he had scarcely power left even to form a conjecture. At last it occurred to him to turn to the other end of the book, if perchance some name, affording a clue to the mystery, might be inscribed there.

And then he read, in another, well-known hand, a few calm words, breathing peace and joy, "quietness and assurance for ever."

He pressed the loved handwriting to his lips, to his heart. He sobbed over it and wept; blistering it with such burning tears as scarcely come from a strong man's eyes more than once in a lifetime. Then, flinging himself on his knees, he thanked God—God whom he had doubted, murmured against, almost blasphemed, and who yet had been true to his promise—true to his tried and suffering servant in the hour of need.

When he rose, he took up the book again, and read and reread those precious words. All but the first he thought he could comprehend. "My beloved father is gone to Him in peace." Would the preceding entries throw any light upon *that* saying?

Once more, with changed feelings and quickened perceptions, he turned back to the records of the penitent's long captivity. Slowly and gradually the secret they revealed unfolded itself before him. The history of the last nine months of his brother's life lay clearly traced; and the light it shed illumined another life also, longer, sadder, less glorious than his.

One entry, almost the last, and traced with a trembling hand, he read over and over, till his eyes grew too dim to see the words.

"He entreats of me to pray for my absent Juan, and to bless him. My son, my first-born, whose face I know not, but whom he has taught me to love, I do bless thee. All blessings rest upon thee—blessings of heaven above, blessings of the earth beneath, blessings of the deep that lieth under! But for *thee*, Carlos, what shall I say? I have no blessing fit for thee—no word of love deep and strong enough to join with that name of thine. Doth not he say, of whose tenderness thou tellest me ours is but the shadow, he will be *silent* in his love? But may he read my heart in its silence, and bless thee, and repay thee when thou comest to thy home, where already thy heart is."

It might have been two hours afterwards, when the same friendly monk who had narrated to Don Juan the circumstances of the Auto-da-fé, came to apprise him that his servant had fulfilled his errand, and was waiting with the horses.

Don Juan rose and met him. His face was sad; it would be a sad face always; but there was in it a look as of one who saw the end, and who knew that, however dark the way might be, the end was light everlasting. "Look here, my friend," he said, for no concealment was necessary there; truth could hurt no one. "See how wondrously God has dealt with me and mine. Here is the record of the life and death of my honoured father. For three-and-twenty years he lay in the Dominican monastery, a prisoner for Christ's sake. And to my heroic martyr brother God has given the honour and the joy of unravelling the mystery of his fate, and thus fulfilling our youthful dream. Carlos has found our father!"

He went forth into the hall, and bade the other monks a grateful farewell. Old Fray Bernardo embraced and blessed him with tears, moved by the likeness, now discerned for the first time, between the stately soldier and the noble and gentle youth, whose kindness to him, during his residence at the monastery three years before, he well remembered.

Then Don Juan set his face towards Nuera, with patient endurance, rather sad than stern, upon his brow, and in his heart "a grief as deep as life or thought," but no rebellion, and no despair. Something like resignation had come to him; already he could say, or at least try to say, "Thy will be done." And he foresaw, as in the distance, far off and faintly, a time when he might even be able to share in spirit the joy of the crowned and victorious one, to whom, in the dark prison, face to face with death, God had so wondrously given the desire of his heart, and not denied him the request of his lips.

XLIX.

Farewell.

"My country is there
Beyond the star pricked with the last peak of snow."
E. B. BROWNING.

BOUT a fortnight afterwards, a closely veiled lady, dressed in deep mourning, leaned over the side of a merchant vessel, and gazed into the sapphire depths of the Bay of Cadiz. A respectable elderly woman was standing near her, holding her pretty dark-eyed babe. They seemed to be under the protection of a Franciscan friar; and of a stately, handsome serving-man, whose bearing and appearance were rather out of keeping with his supposed rank. It was said amongst the crew that the lady was the widow of a rich Sevillian merchant, who during a residence in London some years before had married an Englishwoman. She was now going to join her kindred in the heretical country, and much compassion was expended on her, as she was said to be very Catholic and very pious. It was a signal proof of these dispositions that she ventured to bring with her, as private chaplain, the Franciscan friar, who, the sailors thought, would probably soon fall a martyr to his attachment to the Faith.

But a few illusions might have been dispelled, if the conversation of the party, when for a brief space they had the deck to themselves, could have been overheard.

"Dost thou mourn that the shores of our Spain are fading from us?" said the lady to the supposed servant.

"Not as I should once have done, my Beatriz; though it is still my fatherland, dearest and best of all lands to me. And you, my beloved?"

"Where thou art is my country, Don Juan. Besides," she added softly, "God is everywhere. And think what it will be to worship him in peace, none making us afraid."

"And you, my brave, true-hearted Dolores?" asked Don Juan.

"Señor Don Juan, my country is *there*, with those that I love best," said Dolores, with an upward glance of the large wistful eyes, which had yet, in their sorrowful depths, a look of peace unknown in past days. "What is Spain to me—Spain, that would not give to the noblest of them all a few feet of her earth for a grave?"

"Do not let us stain with one bitter thought our last look at those shores," said Don Juan, with the gentleness that was growing upon him of late. "Remember that they who denied a grave to our beloved, are powerless to rob us of one precious memory of him. His grave is in our hearts; his memorial is the faith which every one of us now standing here has learned from him."

"That is true," said Doña Beatriz. "I think that not all thy teaching, Don Juan, made me understand what 'precious faith' is, until I learned it by his death."

"He gave up all for Christ, freely and joyfully," Juan continued. "While I gave up nothing, save as it was wrenched from my unwilling hand. Therefore for him there is the abundant entrance, 'the crown of glory.' For me, at the best, 'Seekest thou great things for thyself, seek them not. But thy life will I give unto thee for a prey in all places whither thou goest.'"[1]

Fray Sebastian drew near at the moment, and happening to overhear the last words, he asked, "Have you any plan, señor, as to whither you will go?"

[1] Jeremiah 45:5

"I have no plan," Don Juan answered. "But I think God will guide us. I have indeed a dream," he added, after a pause, "which may, or may not, come true eventually. My thoughts often turn to that great New World, where, at least, there should be room for truth and liberty. It was our childhood's dream, to go forth to the New World and to find our father. And the lesser half of it, comparatively worthless as it is, may fitly fall to my lot to fulfil, another worthier than I having done the rest." His voice grew gentler, his whole countenance softened as he continued,—"That the prize was his, not mine, I rejoice. It is but an earnest of the nobler victory, the grander triumph, he enjoys now, amongst those who stand evermore before the King of kings—CALLED, CHOSEN, AND FAITHFUL."

Historical Note.

It may be asked by some thoughtful reader who has followed the narrative of the foregoing pages, How much is fact, how much fiction? As the writer's sole object is to reveal, to enforce, and to illustrate Truth, an answer to the question is gladly supplied. All is fact, except what concerns the personal history of the Brothers and their family. Whatever relates to the rise, progress, and downfall of the Protestant Church in Spain, is strictly historical. Especially may be mentioned the story of the two great Autos at Seville. But much of interest on the subject remains untold, as nothing was taken up but what would naturally amalgamate with the narrative; and it was not designed to supersede history, only to stimulate to its study. Except in the instance of a conversation with Juliano Hernandez, another with Don Carlos de Seso, and a few words required by the exigencies of the tale from Losada, the glorious martyr names have been left untouched by the hand of fiction. It was a sense of their sacredness which led the writer to choose for hero a character not historical, but typical and illustrative. But nothing is told of him which did not occur over and over again, if we except the act of mercy which is supposed to have shed a brightness over his last days. He is merely a given example, a specimen of the ordinary fate of such prisoners of the Inquisition as were enabled to remain faithful to the end; and, thank God, these were numerous. He is even a favourable specimen; for the conditions of art require that in a work of fiction a veil should be thrown over some of the worst horrors of persecution. Those who accuse Protestant writers of exaggeration in these matters, little know what they say. Easily could we show greater abominations than these; but we forbear.

As for the joy and triumph ascribed to the steadfast martyr at the close of his career, we have a thousand well-authenticated instances that such has been really given. These embrace all classes and ages, and all varieties of character, and range throughout all time, from the day that Stephen saw Christ sitting on the right hand of God, until the martyrs of Madagascar sang hymns in the fire, and "prayed as long as they had any life; and then they died, softly, gently."

It is not fiction, but truest truth, that he repays his faithful servants an hundred-fold, even in this life, for anything they do or suffer for his name's sake.

LAMPLIGHTER

Rare Collector Series

If you enjoyed *The Spanish Brothers,* you will treasure these featured selections.

Ishmael and Self-Raised E.D.E.N. Southworth - 1876

E.D.E.N. Southworth considers *Ishmael* to be her very best work, being founded on the life of one of the noblest of our countrymen who really lived, suffered, toiled, and triumphed in this land. Its inspirations of wisdom and goodness were drawn from the examples of heroic warriors and statesmen of the Revolution. Ishmael—born in the depths of poverty, misery, and humiliation and raised to the summit of fame—was *good* as well as great. His life is proof that there is no depth of human misery from which we may not, by virtue, energy, and perseverance, rise to earthly honors, and by God's grace, attain eternal glory.

The Hidden Hand Mrs. E.D.E.N. Southworth - 1859

Reader BEWARE—this is NOT your typical *Rare Collector* book! Strewn with mystery and suspense that never lets up, *The Hidden Hand* will keep you on the edge of your seat! There are not many books that make me laugh aloud (even when I'm alone!) Truly, laughter is like medicine, giving health to the bones! But please don't let the feisty, mischievous character of 17-year-old Capitola and the cantankerous personality of Old Hurricane derail you from seeing the gracious providence of an all-wise God.

Prisoners of the Sea Florence M. Kingsley - 1897

Amidst the tumult of life at sea, myriad adventures of piracy, capture, and escape stand in contrast to the heroic, steady determination of Huguenot heritage. The final chapter adds to the intensity as it meets us head-on with a bolt from the blue, making an unexpected, legendary disclosure!

To order a catalog, call us toll free at 1-888-246-7735, email us at mail@lamplighterpublishing.com, or visit our website at www.lamplighterpublishing.com.

ISBN 978-1-58474-134-3
52600 >
9 781584 741343